T0277809

Elle McNicoll

Some Like it Cold

W

WEDNESDAY BOOKS

NEW YORK

Published in the United States by Wednesday Books,
an imprint of St. Martin's Publishing Group

SOME LIKE IT COLD. Copyright © 2024 by Elle McNicoll. All rights reserved. Printed in the United States of America. For information, address St. Martin's Publishing Group, 120 Broadway, New York, NY 10271.

www.wednesdaybooks.com

The Library of Congress Cataloging-in-Publication Data is available upon request.

ISBN 978-1-250-33553-1 (trade paperback)
ISBN 978-1-250-33551-7 (hardcover)
ISBN 978-1-250-33552-4 (ebook)

Our books may be purchased in bulk for promotional, educational, or business use. Please contact your local bookseller or the Macmillan Corporate and Premium Sales Department at 1-800-221-7945, extension 5442, or by email at MacmillanSpecialMarkets@macmillan.com.

First U.S. Edition: 2024

10 9 8 7 6 5 4 3 2 1

Author's Note

This is a love story. It has an autistic heroine. I did not know I was allowed to read or write books like this when I was sixteen. I wish that I had. I'm making up for lost time now. Thank you.

Act One, Scene I:
Jasper

Coming home again brought on the snow.

Not a blizzard, just a firm, familiar fall.

The large roadside sign which read "Welcome to Lake Pristine" was as clean and as unmarred as the flakes that were beginning to form a blanket beneath it. It was not the kind of town to tolerate a dirty entrance greeting.

Jasper's hands tightened on the wheel of her old Jeep. She had never liked perfect, unblemished things.

Her hometown was full of them.

Lake Pristine was aptly named, perfect for hopeless romantics and people who were incapable of minding their own business. Affluent and picturesque, the town sat by the large, glassy lake with which it shared a name. It comprised of Main Street, the gazebo, the ballet studio, the maze (a sweet little tourist trap), the bookshop, the vintage boutique Trimmings, the town hall, the square, the market (where one could find doorstops carved into woodland creatures as easily as a pint of milk), the haberdashery, one bar and the Lancaster family's iconic cinema.

Unbeknownst to her, Jasper Montgomery's homecoming had been quite the topic of discussion in Lake Pristine recently. The news had traveled from Ester by the lemons in the market to Doreen as she swept the church steps. There had even been a mention in the local newsletter:

Our girl is coming home! Jasper Montgomery will be returning for a long winter holiday following her first eighteen months at university in the big city, studying psychology. Her family tell us she will move on to Law School after graduation. While we are all immensely proud of her for chasing academic acclaim, we wait for the day when she will return home permanently. Readers may remember our shared dismay at her absence last holiday season. We have all spent over a year pining for our Jasper and if you, like the staff of this paper, wish to welcome her back to Lake Pristine then please make your way to the Lakehouse on the first of the month for a homecoming party. Canapés at 7 p.m. sharp!

Lake Pristine's very own golden girl was returning home. Jasper who carried neighbors' grocery bags; Jasper who got up early to help set up for the town meetings; Jasper who told the little ones how to cross the main road safely; Jasper who read to the elderly; Jasper who volunteered to hold a clipboard during vaccination season or a blood drive; Jasper who would rake leaves, shovel snow and bring water to the dehydrated during the summer months.

Jasper who never said no.

Jasper loved the drive home. Her license was as new as her rickety-rackety Jeep was old and they made a nice couple. She blasted showtunes and allowed herself a moment in-between, where she was neither the student nor the hometown girl.

She drove the old car further into the main part of town and, as she reached the square, she could see almost everyone that she knew gathered by the old bandstand. No mind was being paid to the falling snow, because the townspeople were visibly ecstatic about something far more interesting than the cold weather.

"What the what?" Jasper muttered to herself, squinting at the strange scene before her. "What are they all doing?"

Christine, her older sister, was standing in fluffy snow boots, matching earmuffs and a faux-fur pink coat, holding court. Lake Pristine was a small pond and Christine was the biggest fish in it. As Jasper watched her sister smile out at the crowd of onlookers, she wondered for the most flickering of moments if this was a welcome party for her homecoming. Perhaps Christine had arranged a little gathering for her younger sister and invited most of the town.

Jasper quickly crushed that notion. Christine was always the celebration and Jasper was the one you called upon for help cleaning up. After seeing a little more of the world, Jasper had come to realize that in the waters of Lake Pristine, *she* would most likely be a sea urchin.

She slowed the Jeep to a crawl, squinting at the scene against the winter sunlight. Christine's long-term, long-suffering boyfriend Kevin was now parading around in the small square of stone before the steps of the bandstand, where Christine stood. People were applauding him and, as Jasper drew a little nearer, she understood why.

He was reaching into the pocket of his visibly fancy suit to draw out a small velvet box.

Jasper gasped, slamming her hand against the radio to stop Bernadette Peters from singing "Stay with Me." And, as Kevin sank onto one knee, both sisters were so engrossed, the younger lost all focus—

And crashed into a ditch at the side of the road.

Jasper swore loudly as the airbag deployed in a slowly humiliating fashion, and she was forced to kick open her door and stagger out onto the woodland path. Muddy, slushy water coated the bottom of her jeans and she could only smile weakly as the entire town stared at her in shock and sympathy.

Her future brother-in-law was still on one knee, the ring in his outstretched hand, gaping. Christine's mouth was open in surprise, but her eyes were quickly filling with thunder. Their friends and family were all gathered, clearly to bear witness to the proposal. One of the Lancaster boys was even filming it on an old camcorder.

Jasper locked eyes with him for the briefest of moments before her gaze shot down to her wet feet.

Arthur Lancaster.

Gruff, taciturn and judgmental. An old foe, in some respects.

Jasper and Arthur had both grown up in Lake Pristine and gone to high school together. She hardly wished to see him on a normal day in Lake Pristine, let alone when she was embarrassed and covered in snow and slush. His face was unreadable, just watching her with his typical cold intensity.

Jasper was known for being sweet and pleasant to everyone.

Everyone, that was, except Arthur Lancaster.

As Jasper took in all of the stunned faces of the crowd, his was the only one to give any hint of disdain.

Apparently the whole town had come out in all of its finery to witness its princess, Christine of Lake Pristine, and her marriage proposal.

And Jasper Montgomery, Lake Pristine's very own neurodivergent sheep, had just accidentally ruined it.

Act One, Scene II:
Arthur

Earlier that same day, before Jasper Montgomery's dramatic arrival, Arthur had found his father's old camera in his former office.

He had very few memories of Tayo Lancaster ever using it. His father had never been one for stillness or standing on the edge. He had always been in the middle of things, creating whirlwinds of joy and exuberance. A camera would have anchored him too much.

Arthur was not that way.

He saw so many sparks of his father still glowing in his older brother, Henry, and his younger sister, Grace. Both had inherited Tayo's zest and his love of other human beings. His generosity and his enthusiasm.

Arthur had inherited his camera, barely used.

"Will it work? I obviously need it to work." This question came from Marcus, Arthur's cousin and best friend.

"Seems to work," Arthur replied. "What's this all for, anyhow?"

Marcus dropped his phone onto the kitchen counter between the two of them and zoomed in on an open email. "The National Archives will award ten grand for the best short film about small-town life," he said, excitement lighting up his features. "Something to do with rural communities losing out on arts funding and access to film and cinema. They're looking for projects showcasing 'the ever unobserved' in small towns. Finally! Living in this circus will be good for something."

Arthur smirked in spite of himself. Lake Pristine was an affluent place, full of people who preferred the word "comfortable" to "rich." He and Marcus were from working families. They didn't summer anywhere, there was no second house. And the grand Lake Pristine Arthouse was not just Arthur's business, it was his home.

Earlier that year Arthur's mother had passed managerial responsibilities onto her two sons, as well as the care of their younger sister. Now she was in India with her new husband, finding herself and forgetting Lake Pristine.

And her dead first husband, Arthur thought bitterly.

They were both due back in a couple of days, but Arthur and Henry were used to taking care of Grace over the holidays, no matter what their mother was up to. Their sister loved being at the Arthouse. The cinema had been their father's pearl and he was alive still, living on in every inch of it. Arthur wanted to make all sorts of changes to the old cinema, he had vision for it, but whenever he voiced them, he felt guilt about altering his father's legacy.

"Help me make a film, nailing this place to the wall? The 'ever unobserved' of Lake Pristine?" Marcus asked, nudging his cousin's newly unearthed camera. Marcus was one of the Arthouse's part-time ushers.

Arthur eyed him. "Ten grand?" To Arthur, it was a transformative figure.

"Split two ways. You film, I edit."

"We don't even have a story. Plus," Arthur scrolled down to the submission date on the bottom of the email, which was highlighted with a red font, "it says entries must be in by January. That's no time at all."

"This loopy town *is* the story," Marcus insisted, snatching back his phone. He was clearly not about to let Arthur Lancaster influence him with pessimism.

Marcus's eyes were dancing; the idea of exacting some kind of revenge upon Lake Pristine was too much to resist. Arthur supposed it was understandable; his cousin had been mercilessly bullied at the high school and most of the elders disliked him because of his brief time spent as a graffiti artist when they were kids. Arthur had always rescued Marcus from his tormentors and now, at eighteen, the middle Lancaster sibling was still a deterrent to most aggressors, with his regular scowl and his six feet and four inches of height.

He was, in a word, unapproachable. He quite enjoyed being so.

"We can start today. This totally spontaneous proposal, that can be the opening scene," Marcus insisted.

"I'm not going to watch that," scoffed Arthur. He lifted his father's old camera and felt a quick, sharp nick of pain in his heart. He wished Tayo Lancaster himself was there to tell Arthur to go to the square and see what all the fuss was about.

But he wasn't. He wouldn't ever be again.

He quickly placed the camera back down on the table and as he did, he knocked over a pile of newspapers, bills and other items of paper that his older brother Henry had neglected to clean up. As he scraped them back into an ordered pile, he spotted the front page of the locally run, barely staffed town newsletter: *The Lake Pristine Courier*.

Marcus looked at what he was staring at and read out the headline. "'Golden Girl, Jasper Montgomery, to return home to Lake Pristine.' Huh. Slow news day, as ever."

Arthur said nothing. He simply stared down at the small photograph attached to the article. It was of her, during their senior year of high school. It was probably taken just before the last day of classes, the summer of the previous year. Before she packed everything into her parents' car and disappeared off to the city for her psychology degree. She was smiling warmly at whomever was behind the lens.

"I'll come for a bit, actually," Arthur said to Marcus, still looking down at the newsletter.

"Cool. We should head there soon, then."

"Should I take it to the square?" Arthur asked, lifting the camera up once more.

His siblings appeared in the doorway of the Lancaster family's dining room, both putting on scarves and hats for the new flurry of snow. Henry was the one who had informed them of Kevin's plans to propose to Christine Montgomery and Grace was the only one who actually cared to go.

"If you film it and do a decent job, you can charge Christine for the footage," Marcus pointed out, as the four of them made their way out of the back door.

Arthur familiarized himself with the camera as they all walked from the old, glamorous cinema to the center of Lake Pristine. Henry, who had never really cared for Marcus and his somewhat jarring sense of humor, walked ahead with Grace.

"I mean it," Marcus said to Arthur, picking the conversation back up with a cheerful intrusiveness. "Film it. Charge her. Heck, film the whole town and let's win ten grand."

Arthur stopped walking for a moment. He toed the newly fallen snow on the ground with his boot and rewound Marcus's words in his mind.

"A film? You really want to do this?"

"Yeah," Marcus said, gleefully. "I don't know. Something. We can just film and wait for a story to appear, or we can—"

"We're not going to miss out on a good view because you're both too slow," Henry called over his shoulder, his eyes landing briefly on Marcus and darkening a touch.

"Fine," Arthur called back, jogging to catch up to his siblings.

Many townsfolk were gathered around the square and the bandstand, which was now adorned with fairy lights in preparation for the upcoming winter carnival. The town became histrionic during the holiday season and always descended into camp levels of tweeness. People wore pastel colors and faux-fur earmuffs and said things like "hot-choccy." It was, in Arthur's opinion, unspeakably awful.

He looked down at the video camera he was still holding. His grip tightened and loosened upon it as he considered an epiphany.

Lake Pristine only seemed normal to the majority of its inhabitants because they had lived their lives in the pan while the water slowly grew hotter. They saw no strangeness in the town's obsession with order, soft colors and its regular campaigns to ban any alcohol besides that which could be used in eggnog.

Arthur had to acknowledge that it would be the perfect subject for a documentary. He could either expose the rigid oppressiveness of the place, or uncover something deeper and darker. A short film exploring the shades of gray in a town that wanted to be pale pink.

He had forgone university in order to stay and run his father's cinema and his dating life was a mausoleum. So, outside of work, he had the time.

As Christine Montgomery took to the steps of the town band-stand, feigning nonchalance, Arthur started to record. He silently allowed his father's old camera to drink in the scene. As Kevin stepped forward, people began to cheer and gasp. Arthur watched Henry's shoulders stiffen, but chose not to catch it on camera.

A wide shot captured the swarm of Lake Pristine residents, their curiosity and elation. Arthur panned across the crowd, bringing into focus the bubble they all lived inside.

Christine and Kevin had been Lake Pristine's golden pair for some time. They were well-suited. Kevin was mild-mannered and temperate. He remembered the names of people he had only met briefly. He asked about their families. He walked old ladies to their cars when it was icy. He was considerate and romantic, with a reputation for being a friend to just about everyone. Arthur had a lot of time for the man.

Christine would click her fingers at the waitress before demanding the food be taken back to the kitchen and prepared again.

Balance, Arthur thought. That was the only positive way to explain it.

Just as Kevin began to kneel, there was a shout and the sound of a collision. Arthur's eyes darted to Mrs. Lafferty, who had cried out. Then his gaze moved further, to the road leading in and out of town.

"Jasper!" Grace yelled in a mixture of delight and concern, her eyes sparking and her sweet face lighting up at the sight of the younger Montgomery sister. The one Arthur's age. The one who had been at college in the city for eighteen months without a single visit home. The one whose old, beat-up Jeep was now blasting showtunes and had a deployed airbag in the driver's seat, as it sat wedged in a ditch.

The sight alarmed Arthur. He was a safety obsessive in general, so when he saw Jasper exit the vehicle, he exhaled. She was shuffling out of said car and smiling tightly at her older sister, who looked highly unimpressed. Jasper, who hid behind Dior sunglasses. Jasper who had once been the town's greatest ballerina, which was why Grace adored her. Jasper who wore leopard-print ankle boots that made Christine hiss. Jasper who still carried an iPod. Jasper who had been popular in high school. Jasper, whose friends had tormented Arthur and Marcus in the cafeteria while she looked on, indifferent.

"So," Marcus said silkily, watching the scene unfold from Arthur's right side. "Jasper really is back."

There was a prodding nature to his tone that Arthur ignored.

Before Jasper could become the main focus of the gathering, Christine shooed her younger sister toward their parents and tried to get back into character. She fluffed her hair and pinched her cheeks and turned toward her kneeling boyfriend, who looked bewildered and distracted. However, he quickly snapped back to what he had been intending to do.

"Christine," he said, his voice easily heard among the silent onlookers. "Since the moment we met, I knew you were someone special."

Arthur let the camera stay close to the scene, which was intimate and public all at once.

"Christine, I've loved you since the night I asked you to turn your awful music down during a college party you were hosting and you threatened to have me thrown off the roof of the building."

Arthur watched Christine's beatific smile freeze while the crowd laughed receptively. Arthur focused the shot a little more and zoomed in on her expression. The clear duality of it all, the orchestrated trying to pass as spontaneous. It was fascinating to Arthur.

"Will you marry me?"

Despite Kevin's apparent deviation from the agreed line-reading, Christine loudly said "yes."

Arthur glanced over at Lake Pristine's newest arrival. Jasper looked dazed, as though this proposal was a surprise to her.

Every time Arthur saw Jasper Montgomery, he wanted to look for a long time without really understanding why. But he was always aware that her sister might appear a moment later to make a scene, so he did not.

Plus, he and Jasper had yelled at each other plenty of times, and he was the only person in town she seemed to dislike. Her popularity was a nettle to him. He was constantly being loaned out for errands, odd jobs and handywork in town, but the minute someone saw Jasper, they would gently push him to one side in order to converse with her instead.

"I'm so glad she's back," Grace said dreamily. "I heard a rumor she was casting *The Nutcracker* this year, for her mum."

"Oh, yeah?" Arthur said testily. "What other rumors have you heard, bean?"

"Well, one of the ballet girls said that, before she left in the summer, she had this, not like a *fight*, but, like, a strongly worded discussion with her mum in the ballet studio."

Arthur looked at his sister, hoping he would remember to cut their conversation out of the background of any footage. "About what?"

"Maybe something to do with college?"

That wouldn't have shocked Arthur. Jasper had always been a

darling in the art classroom at Lake Pristine High School and she had designed a lot of the musical theater club's sets and costumes. He had been surprised when her graduation destination revealed a degree in psychology. The Montgomerys were famously quite strict. They were a beloved family in the community, but the girls had always been held to curfews and regulations.

Perhaps that was why Christine, now twenty-three, was so wild.

As he watched the town instantly forget the dramatic entrance of the youngest princess, too preoccupied with celebrating and congratulating the elder, Arthur slowly lowered the camera.

Jasper was back.

She glanced over at him for the most fleeting of moments and then away again. He was used to that. He had never been within her notice. She had floated above him in school and there was nothing for them to be friendly about. He had probably snapped at her one too many times, and she had remained loyal to her terrible friends.

Still. She was conspicuous in Lake Pristine. The little town that nobody ever left.

Arthur raised the camera and directed it toward his older brother.

"So," he said gruffly, his breath visible in the crisp air. "What do *you* think about Lake Pristine? And what don't you love? Be as candid as you like because we're making a documentary."

Act One, Scene III:
The House by the Lake

Jasper stood awkwardly on the edge of the town square as Christine and Kevin were enveloped by well-wishers and excited town members. Her parents, of course, joined them.

She wanted to speak to her family. It had been months since they had last said goodbye, over a year of secrecy at university and lying to them on the telephone. She wanted to celebrate her surprising new development with them—her decision to end her degree after eighteen months. She wanted to cross the square and tell her parents and Christine everything, because the truth was starting to feel like poison and it just needed to come out.

Yet the family picture looked so complete without her. It always did.

"Jasper!"

A Lake Pristine elder, and one of the *Courier* volunteers, smacked a loud and loving kiss on Jasper's left cheek.

"Nice to see you again, Mrs. Calloway," Jasper said warmly.

"Oh, we've *missed* you," gasped the older woman. "Please say you'll be done with your studies soon. I haven't seen you in two years!"

"Only eighteen months, Mrs. Calloway," Jasper corrected gently.

"But you're moving back permanently after graduation? Your parents said as much," Mrs. Calloway said firmly, as if this was already decided and agreed upon among the wider community.

In a way, it probably was. Teenagers who left Lake Pristine for their studies always returned. They graduated, they came home, they started working for their parents or friends of their parents, they got married, they had children and then they started volunteering for the newsletter or the council after retirement. That was the way of things.

That was the path Christine was on. It was the path they wanted for Jasper.

"You'll move back, of course," Mrs. Calloway prompted when Jasper did not answer.

Jasper slid her hand into her denim pocket. A small but significant scrap of paper was tucked away inside and touching the strip made her feel easier.

"It's lovely to be home," was all she said.

She glanced back at her car and inwardly cursed her own clumsiness. It had taken her seven attempts to get her license and she had never had anything close to an accident since finally passing her test.

She returned to the Jeep, glad to see that there was no long-lasting damage: the only injury was her pride, bruised by the humiliating return to her tiny, talkative hometown.

"Hey, you."

Her father's voice surprised her. She peered over the roof of the Jeep and smiled sheepishly at him. "Sorry about pulling the focus, Dad."

He pulled her under his arm and she gave him a sideways hug as he steered her toward the crowd of people. "Don't apologize, we'll all find it funny one day."

"Someday." She didn't believe Christine would ever see the humorous side of it, but she kept that to herself.

"Yes, a long time from now."

Her father obviously knew what she was thinking.

Jasper grimaced. "Okay. Why didn't you tell me this proposal thing was happening? I would have come back earlier."

"No, no, none of that. Besides, this was all very unplanned."

Jasper snorted. "Sure."

"We're throwing you a homecoming party at the Lakehouse tonight, so if you need to conserve your small talk, I would suggest heading home now."

Jasper's heart lurched at the prospect of having a party in her honor. For all of her childhood, her parents had thrown parties like they were socialites. But none had ever been for Jasper.

She held onto her good spirits as she unpacked back at the Lakehouse. Her room was untouched. Vintage film posters still adorned the walls. There was even a little powder left on one of her puffs on the vanity. The bed was made and she collapsed onto it, allowing herself to forget about her secrets. College, the course from hell and the overly pushy welfare team. It was almost good to be home again, if she could just pretend that none of that had happened.

She noticed a stack of unread copies of *Architectural Digest* by the door, neatly placed there by her father, no doubt. Her chest tightened at the sight. Design. Creativity. Beautiful interiors and artistic expression, it all felt so far away from Lake Pristine, her science degree and her family's expectations.

When she heard clattering voices, shoes being kicked off and the front door slamming, Jasper obediently left her room and moved downstairs. Her family all glanced up at her as she appeared on the stairs.

"Nice fucking entrance," Christine spat, finally free of spectators and able to wear her usual look of disappointment.

"Christine," Andrea chided her eldest, but her eyes were irate as she glared at her youngest. "Language."

"I didn't mean to crash my car during your public proposal, Christine," Jasper said flatly, her tone as dry as a piece of sandpaper. "Sorry."

"She's not sorry," whined Christine before her father interjected.

"We've got most of the town due here in an hour, team," he said briskly. "I suggest we start prepping canapés. Unless you want me to serve them my famous cheese sculptures."

"Let's not expose anyone to that travesty," Andrea said glibly, removing her coat and leaving it in the entryway, along with all traces of the almost-argument.

Christine and Jasper were alone by the front door.

"Congratulations," Jasper whispered.

Christine's scowl softened into a grateful, fragile expression. "Thanks."

An uncomfortable silence shrouded the two sisters.

"I'm so happy for you," Jasper said.

Christine could obviously sense the genuine joy in her younger sister for she smiled demurely and murmured another thank you.

"You know what I can be like," she told Jasper softly. "I'm going to be worse over the next while."

"Got it," Jasper noted, her voice gentle. "Weddings are stressful. I hear you."

"I might be meaner than I intend to be."

"I know."

"And things may come out, not how I mean to say them."

Jasper shrugged, still smiling. "No one gets that more than I do."

"This morning, I told Kevin I'd call the police on him because he scolded me for putting the toast knife back in the butter," Christine admitted, staring at her younger sister in vulnerable disbelief.

Jasper knew Christine's ways. When she was stressed, when she felt backed into a corner, she became a Hyde. She would experience rages and outbursts and have very little memory of them once they were finished. While she was their mother's favorite, Christine still bore the burden of being the eldest daughter.

"It's okay, he obviously forgives you," Jasper said soothingly. "He just asked you to marry him."

"It's exciting but . . . it's a lot."

"Chris," Jasper spoke softly, as though Christine were a wild horse she was trying to calm. "It's fine. It's good. You're not going to be yourself while you're planning. I get it."

Christine nodded, seemingly satisfied. Her disclaimers were spoken with firmness, but Jasper could sense the helplessness beneath them.

"Can I see the ring?" she asked brightly, changing the subject and forcing herself to look overly enthusiastic.

Being autistic often meant that Jasper's expressions were misread. She was sometimes called "stand-offish" when she was shy. "Judgmental" when she was daydreaming. When she was feeling positive or passionate, it never seemed to come across to other people the way Jasper wanted it to.

So while her fervent expressions and exaggerated tone of voice felt insincere and cartoonish to Jasper, it seemed to satisfy other people.

"It's being resized," Christine replied, only just managing to conceal her irritation at that fact.

"Well, that's a good thing," Jasper persevered. "Nothing worse than when something . . . doesn't fit."

Christine sniffed, looking her younger sister up and down casually. "Mm."

They did not speak another word to each other until the guests started to arrive.

"Arthur, look!"

Arthur Lancaster's little sister pointed ahead of them. A short line of people were already queuing to get into the Montgomery party. As they ascended the gravel path to the Lakehouse, it became clear that this was not going to be a small or quiet gathering.

It was the first time they had been invited to one of the Montgomery parties and Grace was struggling to contain her excitement. Their parents had often gone to previous evenings at the Lakehouse, but this was a ceremonial moment for both Arthur and Grace.

"Do I look all right?" murmured Grace.

Arthur looked at his sister. At thirteen, she didn't smile in pictures anymore because of her braces. She would obsessively cover up her one blemish on her chin with make-up. She flitted from one social media platform to the next, trying on different versions of herself. Not seeming to realize that they all came together to make up one of the best people he had ever known.

"You're going to be the most beautiful person in there," he told her, trying to keep her calm.

"After Jasper," Grace said dreamily.

Arthur looked away quickly and did not respond.

As they approached the front entrance, he could see Christine greeting guests with her best friend Rebecca and Rebecca's younger sister, Saffron. The latter had been in his year at school, he vaguely remembered her. He saw her around town occasionally. She was friendly with Odette, Jasper's best friend from childhood, and Odette's terrible boyfriend, Craig.

"Oh," Christine's smile tightened as she noticed them. "Hello."

"Hello," Arthur said, peering into the house which was now teeming with guests. "Thank you for inviting us."

"I didn't, my father did," she replied bluntly, looking behind them for someone more interesting to talk to.

"Hey, Arthur!"

Saffron was beaming at him and leaning a little too close.

He nodded in greeting and gently steered Grace forward, into the party.

"That girl likes you, Art," Grace told him when they were a safe distance away.

"Yeah, even I got that hint," he said conspiratorially, poking her between her shoulder blades, making her laugh.

He glanced around the spacious home they were now standing in. Varnished floors, expensive lighting and the back half of the house looking out through large windows and sliding doors onto the vast Lake Pristine.

He regarded the walls—and then he saw it.

A photograph of her.

Most of the black-and-white portrait photographs on the wall were professionally taken shots of Christine. But there was one of Jasper. She was taking a bow, following one of her ballet performances. Her legs were positioned in a way that looked so uncomfortable and yet so natural, and her eyes were lowered as she accepted applause. Her face so serious.

"Her last *Swan Lake*."

He swung around to see Odette sitting on the stairs, pointing at the photograph.

"Oh," he said, a little stupidly. "Cool. I was just thinking how sore that position must be."

Odette had been in the popular group at school with Jasper. She, like Jasper, was friendly with most, but unlike Jasper, she had a darker side. She had been going out with Craig, one of Marcus's worst bullies, for a few years.

"All ballet is sore," laughed Odette. She looked to Grace. "Hey, kid. Haven't seen you in the shop for a while." Odette's family ran Trimmings, the vintage clothing store.

Grace grinned and looked away, shyly. "I'm saving up my money."

Arthur didn't know a whole lot about her and Jasper's relationship, but he did know Odette had not lived up to her dancer's name. While her mother had desperately tried to get her into Andrea Montgomery's dance company, six-year-old Odette had staunchly refused. Arthur had always liked her, despite her sharper side.

He had been so used to seeing the two of them together, when they were all in school. Jasper and Odette would laugh their way around town, arms linked and sides glued together. The two of them had started the first LGBTQIA+ club at the Lake Pristine High School, opening with sessions about bi visibility, and then they petitioned to have the sexist kissing booth charity event retired.

Arthur wondered how their friendship was coping now that Jasper was away.

As the party got underway, Arthur kept one eye on Grace. He also threw the occasional surreptitious glance about the place for one specific person. However, even though Christine and her fiancé Kevin were already preparing to make a speech, there was no sight of said person.

Christine tapped a tiny golden fork against her champagne glass with a clanging intensity. It silenced the conversations happening all about the house with great efficiency.

"Thank you all for coming," she crowed, her eyes scanning the room. "And thanks to those of you who came out this afternoon. Apologies for the somewhat catastrophic arrival of my younger sister."

Laughter warmed the room.

Arthur folded his arms and threw glowered looks toward anyone who chuckled a little too loudly.

"I'm confused," Odette murmured. "I thought this was a home-coming party for Jasper."

Arthur shrugged one shoulder. "Guess it's Christine's party now."

"Kevin and I are so excited about our wedding, especially as it's going to be shared with our new friends, as well as all of our old ones," Christine went on.

"She talks like a politician," Odette whispered.

Arthur had to agree. But in a strange way, that was almost what Christine and Jasper Montgomery had always been—unofficial representatives of the town.

"Hey, if Christine's terrible music taste gets too much for either of you, some of the cool kids are chilling out in Jasper's room," Odette told Arthur and Grace.

Arthur spotted Saffron looking for him, while Christine's speech continued in the background. "That sounds like a good deal."

"Then come this way!" Odette hopped to her feet and gestured for the two of them to follow her up the wide staircase to the next level of the house.

She led them to a bedroom that was almost as large as the foyer of the cinema. There was a queen-sized bed with an ottoman, bookshelves stuffed with colorful titles, plus more piles teetering all around the floor, magazines too. By the doorway, there was a dressing table adorned with perfume bottles and cosmetics and a distressed old mirror. Clothes hung everywhere. He could see tissues with lipstick stains discarded in the wastepaper basket.

It felt intimate.

Odette and Grace jumped onto the enormous bed and Arthur's sister shrieked with delight at the sheer size of it. He felt a pang of both guilt and bitterness at the fact that neither he nor his brother could afford to give their sister this kind of room. They were one of the newer families to Lake Pristine and Arthur had never truly forgiven the town for the whispers and the looks that he and Henry had experienced before Grace was born, and before his father had ingratiated himself to the community.

Arthur noticed more pictures on Jasper's walls, of her and her fellow dancers backstage. These were not posed or formal in any way. All smiling in full color.

"Where are the rest of the cool kids?" he asked. For a moment, he wondered if Ross, Adam and Craig (the dreadful boys from Jasper's clique in school) were about to come flying out of the en suite bathroom.

"Here!" Odette announced, bending over and fishing under the bed. When she popped up again, she was holding a bright-eyed and very heavy British Blue cat.

"Oh, so cute!" squealed Grace.

"This is Chum," Odette told them, kissing the cat on its head. It blinked very slowly.

She bundled the animal into Grace's arms.

"What's up with the film camera you had earlier today?" Odette then asked Arthur.

"He's making a documentary about Lake Pristine," Grace answered for her brother.

"Really?" Odette said.

"Yeah, sort of," Arthur replied.

"Can I be in it?"

"Everyone's going to be in it," Grace assured Odette, while stroking the loudly purring cat. "The whole town."

"I'm kind of hoping to capture the real side of the Montgomery family, you know."

"Art," Grace admonished gently. It was a conversation the three Lancaster siblings had quite regularly. They would vent about Christine's behavior and then Grace would marvel at how composed and gentle Jasper seemed in comparison. Arthur never found Christine's antics as amusing as his family did.

"No, it's true," he said, shoving his hands into his pockets. At six foot four, Arthur felt too tall and clumsy for the room. He did not want to bump into anything. He glanced at one of Jasper's pictures and squinted. He knew, though he was not sure how, that there was more to her than the sweet, accommodating girl who did whatever her family, and the town, wanted. It frustrated him to see her constantly hiding behind a demure mask. Just once, Arthur wanted to see who she was beneath all of the people-pleasing. "I like Mr. Montgomery a lot, I really do. He was always good to Dad. But Mrs. Montgomery and Christine really want us all to act like this is their town and we're all just lucky to live in it. And the wedding is going to make them worse!"

"People love a wedding," Odette said fairly. "So what if Christine is a bit of a nightmare? Kevin's nice enough."

Images of Christine snubbing Grace flashed through his mind.

Mrs. Montgomery ignoring his mother at town functions.

Jasper.

Just Jasper, breezing through school with the adoration of everybody.

Marcus being shunned by the town for a few childish mistakes, while Christine's behavior was constantly overlooked and excused.

"But why is it such an event? A public proposal? A New Year's Eve wedding ceremony, with the whole town expected to go?" Arthur laughed scornfully. "Everything Christine Montgomery does is always such an event. Never mind that she's a complete pill to anyone she feels is socially irrelevant to her. Which is almost everyone. If you can't help her get what she wants, she can't even be decent to you. Did she manage to say hello to Grace when we arrived this evening? No, she did not. Even though my sister is in every class at that dance school she helps her Mum run. Went to every show Christine was ever in. Has looked up to her for years. And not even a glance."

"I know," Odette said softly, reaching over to squeeze Grace on the arm. "She can be rude."

Feelings he couldn't identify welled up inside Arthur as he looked around at the beautiful pictures on the walls.

"And we're all supposed to just act like that's fine. And be grateful. She's a brat and a bore, and her family being rich doesn't excuse it. I hope this film manages to capture just how much terror she inflicts on people around here. Who cares if we win the prize money, as long as we can do that, I'll be happy! Christine Montgomery, and Jasper as well, they're spoiled rich girls and not as interesting as people want to pretend."

He could smell the perfume before he had finished speaking. Hers, with its notes of orange.

Jasper stood in the doorway of her bedroom, holding an ice bucket with some pink lemonade and a few flutes. She was staring right at him, green eyes boring into his hazel ones. It was the closest he had been to her in a long time. She must have come up the stairs so silently, her dancer's feet moving gently on the upstairs carpet.

Arthur sniffed. "Hey, Princess."

She glowered at him. "Grumble."

The nicknames they had thrown at each other during backstage arguments, many years before. He had barked at her to stay out of his way while he was helping the stage manager and she had openly resented his grumpy exterior. They had argued in English lessons, fighting over what the text really meant. He had once, foolishly, stupidly, lashed out and called her *Princess* when she tried to break up a fight he was having with one of her male schoolfriends. He could still remember the surprise and hurt on her face. Then her features had hardened and they had never been civil since.

Jasper moved into the room, passing him without another word, and she placed the bucket and glasses down onto her little dressing-table stool.

"Here," she said, smiling shakily at Grace and Odette. "Thought you might be thirsty."

At the sight of his mistress, Chum mewled and wriggled free of Grace. He butted his head against Jasper's wrist as she handed over the glass flutes.

"Grumpy as ever, I see," Jasper said, eyeing Arthur from her spot on the end of the bed. "Congrats, the party has barely started, and you're already pulling us apart. Didn't even wait for the glass clearing to begin."

"What happened to it being your homecoming?" Arthur fired back, his glower mirroring hers. "All about Christine, as usual. And, also, as usual, you're not going to say anything about it."

"Are you calling me a pushover?"

"No, I'm—"

"Oh, God," cried Odette, exchanging a look with Arthur's sister. "Stop. We're out of school, you don't have to do this. Let the feud go."

"There's no feud," Jasper replied, her gaze still fixed upon Arthur. "I've just given up trying to be nice to him. It's a true Sisyphean task."

"Greek myths, cool, I thought you were doing psychology at that fancy university?" Arthur retorted.

"Stop!" barked Odette, desperately trying not to laugh, but Jasper leaped back up to her feet in one fluid movement, ignoring her best friend's weak attempts at intervention.

"What's the alternative, Lancaster? Stay here forever?"

"It's good enough for your sister, in fact, it's good enough for all of us. Why not you?"

"Jasper's not going anywhere," Odette interrupted, reaching over to squeeze her friend's hand. "She's studying and then moving home."

Arthur arched an eyebrow at the youngest Montgomery girl. "That true, Princess?"

Jasper almost said it. She almost let the truth slip out like a hasty insult. She had no intentions of going back to that course and the university her parents were paying for. Every class, every lecture and every horrible lonely moment of college had felt sour to Jasper as she remembered her parents wanted it more than she did. But that was not the worst of it.

She was done. She was dropping out. And here, she had good-byes planned. She had things to do—a whole list of things—before the town became something picturesque in the rear-view mirror.

"What's up with them?" Grace whispered to Odette, who laughed once again.

"They've been like this since forever," Odette answered. "Now, don't you or your brother get upset when I say this, but I think he's always disapproved of me and Jasper."

Arthur bristled. "That's not true."

"Oh, come on, Art," Odette said, her voice teasing and reprimanding him in the same breath. "You have. You didn't like how we were in school, who we went around with, that's fine. Water under the bridge? Give Jasper a break?"

"Oh, don't negotiate with him on my account, babe," Jasper said loftily. "Why are you even here, Arthur? If Christine is such a monster and I'm such a pushover, please don't feel like you have to stay here and endure us. The spoiled little rich girls will be fine without you here, lording it over all of us."

"That's not what I meant and you know it."

"I don't know you, not at all, and I don't want to."

Jasper spat out the words and they lingered for a moment.

Grace's eyebrows shot up into her hair and Odette let out a low whistle. Chum made a grumbling sound, displeased with all of the raised voices.

"Jasper . . ." Arthur spoke through gritted teeth. "I'm sorry. I didn't mean—"

"Look, he was being a bit harsh, but he's not entirely wrong," Odette said gingerly, scratching Chum on his side and smiling up at her unsmiling friend. "Christine is—"

"My sister," Jasper said quietly. "Family."

An unbearable silence fell upon the whole room. Until Chum meowed so pathetically that Grace and Odette burst into laughter. Even Jasper's lips twitched.

"Nice to see you back home again," Odette spoke softly to Jasper, who begrudgingly handed Arthur a glass of lemonade before laying down on her bed and closing her eyes. "I'm . . . I'm sorry I didn't drive in to the city to visit you. Things got busy here with the shop, and I—"

"Don't apologize, I understand," Jasper said softly, and it sounded genuine.

"It really is good to have you back," Odette repeated.

"So nice to be back," Jasper said evenly. She opened her eyes to look at Odette and the two girls stared at each other for a long moment.

Arthur could see the last eighteen months hanging between them, things that neither were ready to say. He suddenly felt as though he and Grace were being intrusive.

Jasper's black cocktail dress must have looked comfortable to

Chum, because he lumbered over to her and promptly curled up on her stomach. Her elegant hands fell to rest upon his blue fur. Arthur noticed that her black tights were covered in little silver gems and her nails were painted like a rainbow.

"Hey, you." Jasper nudged Arthur's sister with her toe. "You auditioning for *The Nutcracker*?"

Grace blushed as red as Jasper's lipstick. "I'm not sure."

"Oh, you've got to. I'm helping Mum with it this year, and I want a Clara with some personality for once."

Grace lit up at Jasper's words and it gave Arthur a joyful ache to see it.

"You were a wonderful Clara," his sister murmured. "Everyone says so."

"Nah," Jasper exhaled, eyes closed and face serene. "My form was never quite right."

Arthur saw a look flash across Odette's face and he knew that she was wondering the same thing that he was: who had told Jasper that and how many times had she heard it?

While Odette and Grace chatted about ballet classes, Arthur looked around the room again. He took in the film posters. Lots of black-and-white classics and cult favorites. Everything from *It's a Wonderful Life* to *Little Shop of Horrors*.

Not a ballet film among them.

"Psst. Art."

He glanced back to the bed. Odette was pointing to Jasper. She was fast asleep. Completely still and silent, with the cat nestled on her abdomen. Odette got to her feet and tiptoed from the room, pulling Grace along with her. She flipped the light switch and gestured for Arthur to follow. He obeyed until they reached the landing.

"The ice bucket," Odette whispered.

"I'll get it," he replied.

He slipped back into the room, moving as quietly as possible until he reached the silver pail. Just as he began to lift it—

"Don't talk about my sister like that again."

The words were so quiet. Sleepy.

He took a good long look at Jasper. Even in the dark, he could make out her green eyes, latched onto his and incredibly serious.

"I'm sorry," he said genuinely. "She was rude to Grace, is all."

Her face softened. "Then I'll talk to her."

He picked up the bucket and made to leave. Then stopped. He didn't know when he would be near Jasper Montgomery again.

"Are you back for good?" he asked.

She took a long pause before saying, "I'm back for now."

He did not tell her that he had wondered about her life in the city. What classes she had decided to take, what her new friends were like. He had definitely let his mind wander into questioning how many guys had asked her out.

"I hope you . . ." His words died and he felt a flush of embarrassment. He didn't finish his thought.

She was asleep, regardless.

She wouldn't have heard him anyway.

Act One, Scene IV:
Jasper's List

Jasper woke to more snow and the lake frozen over. The water looked like frosted glass and the woodland surrounding the edges of the lake was crystallized, gleaming when the cold moonlight hit the winter stones and trees. It was vast and wide, and if someone were to stand on the opposite side of the lake, they would seem as small and as insignificant as the forgotten autumn leaves.

A small beach by the Lakehouse was the perfect spot for a blanket, a hot drink and a book: Jasper could see it all from her window, a view she had sorely missed the year before when she had spent the holidays alone in her dorm room.

She had changed so much, but the bedroom-window view was as frozen as the water.

It was dark, and Christine's affirmations were still playing on repeat, the ones she put on for her REM cycle. Her family were all good sleepers.

Jasper was not.

She crept downstairs and slipped her father's gardening shoes on and grabbed a coat from the closet by the door. She savored the crunch of the snow as she made her way around the house and down the small mound toward the shimmering lake of ice.

Jasper had always been a devoted disciple of "the rules." When you were born with a cloudy understanding of why certain rules existed, you soon moved from confusion and questioning to the sad realization that you would lose all of your neurotypical connections if you did not automatically obey.

So, Jasper had become an expert on the rules. She had studied them and been dutiful to them.

One of "the rules" was to never walk on ice. It was a sensible, comprehensible one.

Jasper did hesitate before placing her foot on the frozen water. But she stepped forward nevertheless.

In a world that was always loud and hard and insistent, there was something cooling and calming about the silence of the lake. The openness of it. It was made to glide upon and it was more permanent than anything in Jasper's life.

It was like a long, frosty runway. The woods surrounded it like disapproving onlookers while it lay completely at peace with itself.

Jasper's grandfather had always enjoyed telling her that there was a mermaid living at the bottom of the lake. In winter, she would be trapped beneath the ice and would have to wait for spring and warmth to let her breathe the air again.

"Things to do before leaving this town forever . . ." Jasper said, the words only for her and the lake. She took another step forward. "Number one: skate on Lake Pristine."

Her mother had sent her to ice-skating lessons when she was young. Saturdays had been ballet class from nine until noon, then ten minutes for a green lunch. Then an hour of tap. Then two hours of ice skating (her mother claiming that it would help with the dancing) and then finally an hour of elocution or the child psychiatrist.

Jasper would fall into bed on Saturday nights, from age six to sixteen, with no knowledge of who she was. Only knowing that she was tired.

Still. She had always wanted to skate on Lake Pristine, not on the artificial rink two miles out of town.

"Skate on the lake," she repeated for her own benefit.

She slipped one foot out of her father's shoes and pressed it down, hissing at the cold but savoring the sensation.

"Number two: find a better boyfriend, girlfriend or partner for Odette," she said, mentally composing her list and adding little check boxes. "Note: Imperative."

She glanced back up at the Lakehouse. The only light on was the small bedside lamp from her bedroom. It was the only glow visible in the vast clearing, besides the half-hidden moon and the stars.

"Three," Jasper went on, removing the other shoe. She flexed her toes with their teal polish against the frosted glass of the water. "Cast and direct an amazing *Nutcracker*."

There were other small, easily achievable items on the list: cupcakes at Vivi's, a frolic in the Christmas maze, buying some trinket from the Winter Market.

"Seven. Tell Mum and Dad I've dropped out of the expensive university that they're currently paying for, the one they said I had to attend if I wanted to remain welcome in their house, and I'm going to design school instead."

Jasper was surprised at herself as the words escaped. They were the ones she had been hiding from for the last few months. She instinctively glanced up at the house in a moment of fear, afraid that someone might have overheard. It felt forbidden. A privileged childhood was just that: a great privilege. But sometimes it felt like a down payment on lifelong subservience.

Jasper knew she would have to go it alone. She was prepared. But saying the words aloud made that lonely, aching fact feel like a bruise.

"Eight. Get into design school," she added quietly. "That would help with seven."

She scribbled it onto the palm of her hand as she walked across the shore of the lake. Once home she wrote up an official piece of paper, her goodbye tasks all written down and numbered.

1. Skate on Lake Pristine
2. Find Odette a better boyfriend/girlfriend/partner— anybody but vile Craig
3. Make Mum proud with an amazing *Nutcracker* performance
4. Eat cupcakes at Vivi's
5. Visit the Christmas Maze
6. Buy an ornament from the Heywoods at the Winter Market
7. Tell family I'm leaving Lake Pristine (and college) for design school
8. Get into design school
9. Help Christine have the most beautiful wedding
10. Catch the late-night shows at the Arthouse
11. ~~Try to be civil with Arthur Lancaster~~
12. Enjoy Christine's bachelorette party
13. Do something brave

Once done, the list felt sealed with a silent promise. She'd crossed out number eleven, because she didn't want to delude herself with the impossible. Lake Pristine was soon to become a stranger to Jasper—a place she would only visit and no longer live in. Her family would not take her defection well, very few people would. She would be completely independent, in every sense of the word. She would have no safety net, no town behind her with a pot of tea or a piece of pie. She would be a lone traveler.

It was not her ideal scenario.

If only she could stay and study design *and* be herself in Lake Pristine, a town she had always loved. But Lake Pristine needed her to be something she was not.

And her family would never relent.

The list made this conclusion all the more final.

This was goodbye.

"Welcome home, Jasper! It's been an age!"

Jasper smiled wearily up at Frank Carstairs, owner of Lake Pristine's only pub. The whole family was there for lunch and her sister and parents were too hungover for good manners. Jasper was, as usual, their spokesperson.

"Still do your pancakes with halloumi?"

"Sure do," Frank beamed down at her.

"The rest of us will need a minute," their mother said crisply.

Frank took that as it was intended and left them all alone to read the menus.

"You missed all of the speeches last night," Christine told her sister, snippily.

"Technically—" Jasper glanced over at the doorway and flinched as she noticed Arthur Lancaster, his cousin Marcus and their video camera walking through the entranceway—"it was my home-coming party. That's what you said."

Christine looked straight to their mother.

"Jasper." Andrea spoke sharply, taking her cue from Christine. "A wedding is a big affair. A huge family responsibility. The next month is going to be about Christine and Kevin, and that's just a fact. Let's not be selfish."

"Yes," said Jasper, slipping on her sunglasses. "Let's not."

She did not mention the hurt of it. The unfairness of it. It felt pointless and petty. Her sister's wedding was more important than Jasper coming home for a month over Christmas. Of course that was true. Besides, they didn't even know about her list and her plans. It would be read as a betrayal and, more importantly, it would detract from Christine's day and that was genuinely the last thing Jasper wanted or intended.

December, like the rest of the year, was going to be about Christine.

"Oh, Jasper, by the way." Christine reached over and grabbed her sister's wrist. "Saffron really likes that Lancaster boy. The grumpy one."

"And?"

"Well, he was in your room last night!"

"Was he?" their father demanded, startled.

Yes, he was, thought Jasper. But she said nothing. One did not actually need to say much in conversations with Christine. In fact, it was wise to give her as little ammunition as possible.

"Saff wants him to take her out and, honestly, while he is good-looking, he's super crabby and sullen, so he should be grateful."

"I'm sure he would love hearing that from me," Jasper said dryly, sipping her juice and keeping one eye on Marcus and the man in question, who were setting up in the corner. "*Please call this girl, Arthur, and remember that you should be glad for the opportunity.*"

"Fine, don't say it like that. But tell him Saff is free Friday at eight and she likes the cupcakes at Vivi's."

Vivi's Bakery. Everyone liked it there. Yet the image of Arthur Lancaster hunched over one of their tiny tables while eating equally tiny baked goods seemed comical to Jasper.

"If I see him, Chris, I'll tell him."

Christine frowned. "He's right over there!"

"Yes," Jasper whispered, frowning in return at her sister's volume. "With a camera and a mic and another person. I'm not your messenger, I'll tell him when it's appropriate." She always did what Christine asked, out of devotion and because of her natural desire to have an easier life, but wedding-Christine was already proving to be laborious.

"I thought you two hated each other," their father said casually.

"They do," Christine said quickly. "I used to have to separate them during technical rehearsals. He'd be helping backstage, Jasper would be dancing and I'd go to check something in the front of house only to come back and find them yelling at each other."

"Hate is a strong word," their mother chimed in.

"There's a picture in Jasper's yearbook of the two of them," their father said, turning to his wife with a knowing smile. "They looked ready to murder each other in front of witnesses."

"Debate club," Jasper confirmed. "Yeah, that was a bad afternoon; we didn't know they were taking senior class pictures. Which is exactly why I don't want to go over there now."

"You don't hate anyone," their father said, quietly, talking as though this was a subject he had often thought about on his own. "I've never seen you angry or short with anyone in this town. Except him."

"Well, he's very unapproachable," Christine remarked. "Jasper's nice to everyone; if he doesn't like her, he's the problem."

Jasper stared at her older sister in astonishment. A compliment from Christine was almost as rare as a word of encouragement from their mother.

"What did the two of you fall out about?" their mother asked silkily.

Jasper shrugged. "We never really fell in. We weren't friends. He hung around with a pretty tight little group; they didn't seem to like outsiders. I think I made a joke once and he called me a name and then we just . . . never got on."

Princess. She remembered the name. The bitterness in it.

"Is his sister in my class?" their mother asked absent-mindedly.

"Yeah," Christine said, smirking. "The one who has one leg shorter than the other."

The look Jasper gave her stopped the smirk. Of course, Christine's goodness was only ever a small scrap of blue sky during a rainstorm. She would always have to make up for any decency with a healthy dose of something dreadful. "Christine. Fuck off with that nonsense. Don't say that."

Jasper looked over, making sure that Arthur Lancaster had not overheard her sister's casual nastiness. She was used to it being directed toward her, but there was something deeply unpleasant about it being hurled at someone like Grace.

"Jasper," their mother sighed, as if in pain. "Language, please."

"What about Christine's language?" challenged Jasper.

"Enough," Christine said, rolling her eyes. "Don't be oversensitive. She does!"

"You're being ableist."

"Jasper," their mother spoke breezily now, taking a long drag of her Bloody Mary. "No one likes a preacher, especially when it is not a Sunday."

Jasper looked to her father, but he was studying the menu. Jasper wished he would sometimes step over and be fully on her side. Andrea and Christine were a united front at all times, but Howard Montgomery liked to stand in the middle of the road.

"Back to the subject of the wedding," Christine said pointedly. "Jasper, you can come to the bachelorette party—it's going to be soon."

"Well, what date's the wedding?"

"New Year's Eve."

Jasper almost dropped her drink. "Christine!"

"What? Everyone's going to be partying anyway, they might as well party in a nice marquee with Kevin and me. Also, I want you to talk to the wedding planner about the design of the room. Your taste is better than hers. Same for the bachelorette night as well."

Jasper almost cracked a smile. "Fine. Winter solstice party it is."

"Oh, no, Jasper, nothing themed," gasped their mother, missing the sarcasm completely.

"Who are your bridesmaids?" Jasper asked.

"Rebecca, Charlotte and Anna."

Her old school friends, of course.

Jasper frowned. "Is that it?"

"Yep."

Jasper's eyebrows shot up into her hairline. She wasn't even a bridesmaid at her own sister's wedding.

"Family should always be in the bridal party," their father said softly, still keeping his gaze glued to the laminated menu. "It's traditional."

"It's my wedding," Christine snipped. "And Jasper's too busty."

Silence. Even their mother's eyes widened at that. Their father's face fought with an almost angry expression—it was a rare and amazing sight.

"They're going to be wearing halters," Christine insisted indignantly, though her voice was a little less assured. "I want people looking at me and Kevin, not wondering if Jasper's going to fall out."

"You've made your point," Jasper said curtly, getting to her feet and pulling on her jacket. "I'll call your girlfriends."

"Again, don't be so sensitive!" Christine called after her as she left. "You're not in the city anymore, you're back in Lake Pristine! Also, you're only eighteen. We're all twenty-three, it's about consistency and patterns! I thought you of all people would appreciate that!"

Jasper turned, ready to shout something back, but stopped herself just as quickly.

The cameras were on. Marcus had nudged Arthur and the latter had reluctantly raised the lens to take in the room. Jasper had to quickly slap on the mask, turn pain into breeziness and make for the door with a casual everyday flippancy that she did not feel.

Jasper took a walk around Lake Pristine, from Main Street to the town square. She greeted familiar faces and smiled politely when people commented on her "long absence." Now, she was home for the season of holiday parties. She wasn't sure if she could keep the list and her escape plan a secret from so many watchful eyes.

But refusing to attend the gatherings would mark a blemish on her almost impeccable record, so retreating was not an option.

Lake Pristine would never change.

She had felt from a very young age that her family needed her to be perfect. Like Lake Pristine in winter.

She remembered being diagnosed. Her constant visits to different doctors because her mother wanted a second opinion. Jasper couldn't understand why no one would talk to her about it. She liked it. She liked knowing why she was the way she was, it was a relief. A welcome key to her own mind. She could not stand how her family treated it like a negative. She returned home from the appointment and ran, ran to Odette's house. Mrs. Cunningham had made them pork dumplings and told her she was just right.

Whenever her family, or the world outside, failed—Lake Pristine was always there. It was familiar and reliable. It just wasn't made for someone like her. Somehow, being told that the world would consider her imperfect had been enough to make her a servant to the art of *seeming* perfect.

"Jazz!"

She resented the breaking of her reverie. "Not now, Chris."

Christine wrapped herself up in her faux-fur jacket and jogged over to her younger sister. She wore fluffy boots to match and people darted out of her way as she crossed the square.

"Hey," she said, catching up to Jasper. "What's wrong?"

"You're being mean, Chris," Jasper said flatly.

"It's like I said," Christine sighed. "I'm . . . I'm not myself right now. Or I'm a bad version. You'll get it when you get married."

"I'm never getting married," Jasper said tonelessly, avoiding her sister's gaze.

"Well," Christine studied her younger sister. "Not until you've got your big career, no."

"I know you're under a lot of pressure," Jasper allowed. "But some things just aren't acceptable. You can't dish out a premature apology and hope that it covers all the things you do and say."

"Jasper," Christine was exasperated, but Jasper could spot a flush of embarrassment. "It's not as easy for me as it is for you."

Jasper frowned. "What?"

"Life."

Jasper shook her head very slightly. "Christine . . . let's not—"

"Yeah, I know, your diagnosis. I get some things are harder for you. But you're everyone's favorite. Everyone adores you. This wedding is the best thing I've ever done, it's the proudest Mum has ever been of me—hey, don't roll your eyes at me, I hate when you do that."

"I'm not rolling my eyes, I'm taking a break from eye contact," whispered Jasper, pinching the bridge of her nose and exhaling slowly. "It's part of that whole diagnosis thing you so easily glossed over."

"You're the perfect brainy one, and I'm the flake," Christine said, as though Jasper had not even spoken, let alone revealed something personal.

"Chrissy," Jasper chose her words with great consideration. "Mum is proud of you no matter what. She dotes on you."

"I was never smart like you," Christine said, as if divulging a great, shameful secret. "I never wanted to work. I don't want to work! Does that make me a bad person, Jazzie? I can't think of anything worse than going to work. I want to enjoy my life. I want to live it with Kevin in a house full of kids and I don't want a boss or an employer."

"You're privileged, Chrissy," Jasper reminded her. "This is your choice, and you're lucky you get to make it. Most people have no choice but to work and lots of people get married without safety nets."

"Jasper, I get it," Christine said. "But they'll never be as proud of a wedding as they will be of you in your cap and gown."

It was the worst thing she could have said. Jasper felt anxiety in her stomach like wasps being let out of a shaken-up jar. The reminder of what she was walking away from, what she was taking away from her parents, it was unbearably painful for Jasper. It panicked her.

But it was too late. She had officially interrupted her studies in the Psychology department. She had made the call before driving home to Lake Pristine. Right now, only she and her supervisor knew. Her time there was done. All she needed to do now was break the news to her parents.

"And look," Christine went on, oblivious to Jasper's internal disquiet. "I know you wanted to go and study interior design somewhere, but Mum and Dad said they were paying for the other course and you had to go to that one—"

"I didn't have to. I could have walked away," Jasper murmured bitterly.

"—But guess what? When Kevin and I move into the new house, I want you to do all of the interiors!"

Jasper stared at her older sister. "Me?"

"Yes. You did such a good job with Dad's office last spring. I want you to do our whole house."

"Are you seriously telling me that if I had gone to design school, I would be coming home to my first assignment? And I would be able to charge you? But because I've been schlepping at a psychology degree, I now have to do it for *free*?"

There was a moment of silence and then both sisters burst out laughing.

"Oh, God," Jasper covered her face with both hands while Christine kept going. "Fine. I'll do it."

"As a wedding present."

"Uh-huh, sure."

"Good old Jasper, you never say no. Kevin says thank you, too."

"Of course he does."

Christine's laughter subsided and she reached for her sister's hands. "Love you. I just need to give Mum the perfect wedding and then everything will get easier."

Jasper did not correct her. She could reassure Christine by promising to do something so destructive her parents would never bother about any of Christine's flaws again.

Instead she said softly: "Ever wonder what it would be like to have a less controlling family?"

"They're controlling because they care," Christine replied, towing the line perfectly. "You'll appreciate it someday."

Jasper said nothing more. She let Christine squeeze her arm one last time before she watched her older sister scamper back to the pub. Jasper looked up at the December sky. She stood en pointe for a split second.

The brief elevation, despite the small shot of pain, was euphoric.

"Good old Jasper," she sighed. "Never says no."

She let her feet drop back down onto the earth and then glanced around the town square, only to notice some old schoolmates, kids from the year below, sat over by the bowling alley.

They were staring at her, a couple of them even whispering behind their hands.

The five of them stopped talking as she neared them. Their open stares felt, to Jasper, like a sunburn.

"Is . . . is that—"

"Yeah, it's me," Jasper said loudly, causing Mia Henderson to squeak and stop talking.

They all avoided her eyes as she walked by. She stopped after a couple of seconds and threw her voice back to them.

"Any of you seen Odette Cunningham?"

"The Asian girl?" Mia giggled to the boy next to her.

Jasper whistled sharply, causing Mia to start and look back in her direction. "I'm talking to you. Is she at her mum's shop?"

One of the boys threw her a bone. "I saw her with Craig and some other girl." She could tell by his earnest expression that he knew her father somehow. People who knew Howard Montgomery knew never to cross his daughters. Jasper would normally never be this abrupt, but she felt untethered. "Over by the cinema."

He pointed to the building behind her but she did not need him to. The Arthouse was her favorite place in town.

She gave him a curt nod of thanks and briefly locked eyes with a girl she didn't recognize who was sitting with the other whispering kids.

She spotted her best friend in the window, surrounded by new acquaintances of hers, strangers to Jasper. The girl next to Odette was strikingly pale, with fiercely drawn-on eyebrows and dark brown lipstick. Jasper didn't recognize her.

Jasper was ready to scarper and head back to the Lakehouse when someone gently touched her on the elbow.

It was the unknown girl from the group by the bowling alley.

"You're new, too?" she asked, without any preamble. "I'm Hera. It's a weird name, I know. My dad teaches Classics in the city. God, I'm so relieved it's not just me. I had no idea until we moved here how *small* this town is. I'm—"

"I'm not new here."

Jasper said the words while taking in the bright-eyed, fast-talking new visitor. Hera. Jasper liked the name, though the smiling person before her did not quickly conjure up a likeness to the fearsome wife of Zeus.

Hera's smile faded and she looked rightfully confused. "You're not new?"

"No. I mean, I'm from Lake Pristine. My sister's the one getting married."

Realization spread across Hera's face. "You're *Jasper* Montgomery?"

Jasper knew rumors and whispers about her would have circulated. "Yeah. I've been at college in the city, but I went to school with most of this lot." She gestured liberally to the chattering people behind the two of them, and then her best friend and the other girl in the window of the Arthouse. "I've been gone for a while. And being gone for a while, in Lake Pristine, is the equivalent of going missing."

Sometimes it even felt like coming back from the dead.

University had been hard. It had been so hard. Maybe going straight into a degree one had no heart for, after years of masking at a competitive small-town high school, was bound to be difficult. Jasper had struggled with all of it. Yes, she was smart. Academic. "A pleasure to teach," according to most. But the social aspects and the constant overstimulation had turned her into something of a recluse. The more she had retreated from the world, the more ashamed she had felt. And the harder it had been to go home.

Jasper held out her hand and gave Hera her undivided attention. "My name is Jasper. I turn nineteen next month and my sister is getting married. You're invited to whatever introverted get-together I decide to throw after recovering from said sister's wedding. Nice to meet you, Hera. And, for what it's worth, I love Greek mythology."

She caught the flash of relief and appreciation in the other girl's brown eyes. She could see an easiness in her as she realized that Jasper was nothing like the group she had just left. "Nice to meet you, too."

Jasper continued to stare through the Arthouse window, at her friend who had yet to notice her. She could feel Hera regarding her as she watched Odette.

"If you don't mind me asking," Hera broached a change of subject carefully, "why are you standing out here and not going in?"

"Well," Jasper spoke, not looking away from the window, "I think I went from being a best friend to somebody she sort of just . . . knows."

Hera's silence gave away her confusion, but Jasper's gaze remained glued to the window. She wanted nothing more than to burst through the doors and hug her oldest friend, but she was surrounded by new people. It made Jasper feel like a guest actor, walking in on a regular ensemble cast.

Jasper had been juggling many plates of late and it would be fair to say that she had dropped the friendship one. Not on purpose, certainly, but down it had fallen nonetheless. It was possibly chipped and cracked from the drop.

She had called Odette as often as possible while she had been away. At first, they had gossiped and laughed and replayed old inside jokes, enjoying the worn and cozy feel of them. Shared experiences from their time in high school often felt like familiar old sweaters that could keep them warm.

But Jasper had been too afraid to get seriously vulnerable over the phone. She had her secrets and now, as she glimpsed Odette's laughter with other people, she acknowledged that her best friend obviously did, too.

She knew saying all of this aloud, and to a total stranger, would make her sound ridiculous. She couldn't even pinpoint a certain event or catalyst to prove that something was wrong. Somehow that made it easy for her anxiety demon to whisper that she was stupid.

Jasper stared at her best friend's profile, the first true love of her life, and wondered how she could get her regular slot back again without ruffling feathers. Friendship groups in Lake Pristine were fragile, she knew that after years of watching Christine.

"Are Mia and that lot your friends?" she asked Hera, casually.

"No," Hera said quickly. "It's just . . . this isn't an easy town to move into. Everyone knows everything about each other and I feel like I'll never catch up."

"Are you at the high school?"

"No, I work in the alley. I give out the bowling shoes."

This made Jasper release a fond laugh. "Cool."

"It's not, but it pays better than some of the more glamorous jobs in town."

"I'm saving money," Jasper said, and as she uttered the words, she felt her breath catch in surprise. It was one of her many secrets— she had not even told Odette.

"Where do you work?"

"At my mum's dance studio. But I'm looking for something else. If the alley is hiring, I can hold the bowling shoes while you spray that stuff in them?"

Now Hera laughed. "If anything comes up, I'll find you."

"Come inside with me," Jasper said brightly, pulling open the door to the Arthouse. "You'll like Odette, if you haven't met her already. She's the best. Plus, it's December. The holiday party invites will start going out soon, and they're a great way to meet the town."

Jasper did not wait to see if Hera was following her as she entered the luxurious cinema. As she walked into the lobby, she watched as Odette and this other girl Jasper did not know linked arms and headed toward one of the screens, deep in conversation. Neither of them noticed Jasper's arrival and she did nothing to alert them. Her whole plan had been to find her friend and now that she was staring at Odette with someone else, she found she could not move or speak.

"Jazz? Jasper!"

Craig. He was Odette's on/off boyfriend of many years and Jasper could only hope that he was not the boy she knew when they had all gone to school together.

She greeted him with lukewarm acknowledgment.

"Royalty, right here with us commoners," Craig said with a hard laugh. "Where's my hug?"

"Ew," murmured Hera.

"No, thanks," Jasper said glibly. "Craig, this is Hera."

Craig mumbled a greeting and threw her a nod.

"Are you going into screen two?"

Craig, Hera and Jasper all turned at the sound of the fourth voice.

Arthur Lancaster was looking Craig up and down with an impressive amount of aloof disdain. This was his small fleck of the town after all and he was clearly protective. He was wearing a thick shearling coat and a camera bag, both of which he removed as he moved behind the box office counter, ready to clock in for his shift. Jasper should have known that running into him would be inevitable. While she had left for university at seventeen, Arthur had spurned higher learning and taken over his father's business instead. This was both his business and his home. If she wanted to take in a film, his presence was almost always a guarantee.

Jasper had gentle and fond memories of Mr. Lancaster, Arthur's late father. He had loved the romance of cinema in a fashion that made Jasper less self-conscious of her own deep obsession with her favorite films. Mr. Lancaster would cheerfully shout *Some Like It Hot* quotes at Jasper in town, and she would happily finish the scene with her best Marilyn voice. Then they would laugh and wave and he would be gone. The town was duller without him in it.

The Arthouse was his legacy, proud and regal and standing tall in the middle of the town. Jasper thought of it as a kind of temple. She stole a quick look at the man's tall and intimidating middle son and she wondered if he felt the same.

"Dude!" Craig's face split into a wide smile, but, as ever, his little gray eyes did not match the rest of his expression. "How are you, man? Haven't seen you in days, you've been hiding behind that old camera."

"I'm fine," Arthur said lifelessly. His eyes landed on Hera and he nodded, politely. "Welcome to the Lake Pristine Arthouse."

"Thanks," she replied, brightly. "I didn't catch your name."

"Arthur," he said. His eyes flashed briefly to Jasper. "Arthur Lancaster, my family run this place."

"Oh, it looks so cool," Hera said excitedly, glancing up at the high ceiling. "You hiring?"

"No," he said with a bluntness that Jasper had beaten out of herself. Frankness was dangerous for any girl, let alone an autistic girl. People could close ranks very quickly over the smallest infraction.

Arthur obviously heard how it sounded and so he quickly added, "But if that changes, I'll let you know."

"Only, Jasper is looking for a job."

Jasper bristled slightly as Arthur's gaze flashed to hers at Hera's words. "You are?"

Jasper shrugged. "I'm going to try the cafe, the maze and then if neither of them are hiring, I'll start busking."

The maze was one of Lake Pristine's most famous attractions and they were always in need of new employees to rescue tourists who had become lost inside the vast puzzle.

"Aren't you going back to university?" Arthur asked, his gaze now quite intense.

"Of course," lied Jasper. "But college doesn't start back until late January. I've got weeks and weeks."

"Ballet studio not paying?"

She glowered at him. "That covers rent."

His face morphed into an expression of genuine shock. "Your parents make you pay to stay at your own family home?"

Jasper felt the cold, wet trickle of embarrassment. Her family were wealthy, but rich families stayed that way by being stern and possessive of their coins. Jasper didn't mind working for her mother, and letting that small salary go toward the house, but when Arthur Lancaster looked at her as if it were the most revolting thing he had ever heard, her defensiveness scraped against her heart like a thistle.

"They pay for school," she said, in a tone that was very close to blunt. "I owe them, I'm very privileged."

"Speaking of owing people, Jazz," Craig said, jauntily reaching into his backpack. "My parents are throwing their holiday party tomorrow night—"

Jasper threw a look to Hera, one that communicated a "what did I say?" attitude which made the other girl smile.

"—and you've missed so many good parties while you've been away at that fancy college. Here!"

Jasper hesitantly reached out to take the crumpled flyer he was offering her. "Uh . . . I—"

"You owe us, Jasper. You owe the town," Craig said jokingly, but with an undercurrent of gravity.

Arthur made a noise of distaste while Jasper gestured to Hera.

"You should come too," she told the other girl.

"I'd love to! I'm not working at the alley tomorrow night."

"Well," Craig's seemingly sunny attitude died a little as he finally took her in, "it's invite only, sorry."

Jasper casually and calmly handed her invitation over to Hera. She made herself meet Craig's eyes with gentle reproach in her own. "She's new to Lake Pristine. Inviting her is the polite thing to do."

Craig regarded her for a moment and then his face broke into a tight smile. "That's Jasper. Too nice for her own good."

"For real," Hera said, missing Craig's biting tone. "Jasper, you're one of the only people who's been nice to me since we moved here."

"Your screening is about to start," Arthur interjected, speaking to Craig.

Craig made a popping sound with his mouth. "Back to the old ball and chain."

Jasper arched an eyebrow at that. "Craig."

"Just kidding, cutie. I'll tell Odette you're coming tomorrow. And you," he said, finally acknowledging Hera with a modicum of warmth. "But not you." He pointed to Arthur, who shrugged.

"I'll be there."

Craig spluttered in surprise. "Nah, when I invited you and Marcus last week, you said you'd rather—"

"I'm going, it's not a big deal," Arthur bit out.

"What's changed?"

"Your film is starting."

"You said holiday parties were only good for spreading winter colds—"

"Your. Film. Is. Starting."

Craig looked longingly at the exit, clearly pondering if he had enough time for one last cigarette before joining Odette and the other girl in the cinema screen. "Cool beans. Guess I'll catch you all tomorrow night."

He decided to spurn the nicotine hit and sauntered off toward the smaller of the two screens.

"Are you guys joining them in the show or . . ."

Arthur's words trailed off and Jasper shook her head. "I'm not. Wanted to grab Odette but she's . . . busy."

Jasper always felt odd in groups, both before and after her diagnosis. She preferred people who would overshare instead of commenting on the weather. She liked deep, devoted conversations with complete strangers in the corner of the party. She was great at those. She was a listener. An advice guru, if asked. But when it came to shining in front of a group of people who were uninterested in baring their souls, Jasper always faltered. Small talk was the dragon she could never take down.

She began to back out of the cinema, giving Hera a nod of farewell.

She didn't know where to go. If she went home, she would be chastised. If she went elsewhere in town, she would be guilted.

She never quite knew where she fit.

She barely heard Arthur call after her, asking if she was feeling all right.

"I'm fine," she called back.

She couldn't imagine why he cared.

Act One, Scene V:
First Day of Production

"Arthur!"

Arthur entered the Lake Pristine library, completely exhausted after a late-night stocktake at the Arthouse, followed by an early-morning shift. He had officially embarked upon his mission to start making a documentary about the town. He had mapped out a schedule. He had bought a new hard drive and some additional equipment. He had spent the entire day filming the comings and goings of the Arthouse, as well as interviewing Mrs. Heywood and Mrs. Lafferty about their thoughts on the town (all positive) as well as their forty-year friendship (mostly positive).

Arthur was exhausted and there was still no angle in sight. No hook, no subject matter. Everyone spoke well of the town, all of their memories seemed to be sweet and mundane, and the most controversial thing he had unearthed was the fact that Lake Pristine had attempted a beautiful baby competition one summer and two of the mothers had ended up throwing grass at each other.

If Arthur wanted to make a gripping, unflinching documentary, he was going to have to unearth some real dirt or find something truly awful. Working in a cinema had taught him a lot about people's curiosities and most only seemed to want to watch things that were awful.

"Hey, Marc."

Marcus and their mutual friend, Danny, waved him over to their table.

"You look like shit," Danny said sympathetically. He was short and always cheerful.

Arthur gave him a nod of greeting and shrugged. "I've been filming."

"How was it?" Marcus asked brashly, his face expectant.

"Bad."

"A good kind of bad?"

"No, a boring kind of bad. There is nothing to report on in this town. Nothing sinister. Nothing weird. Nothing dramatic."

"Arthur and I are going to make an 'it could never happen here' documentary about Lake Pristine," Marcus told Danny, conspiratorially. "Only, people are good at the façade around here."

"Nuh-uh," Danny said loftily, shoving Marcus. "This is a nice place! Why can't you make a film about how nice it is?"

"Because no one would watch it," the cousins said in chorus.

"I reckon we could get a lot of footage at Craig's family's holiday party tonight," Marcus added. "Everyone will be there."

"I thought you weren't going," Danny said accusingly to Arthur.

"Plans changed, I am now," Arthur replied. "And, yeah, we can see how chatty people feel after Craig gets his dad's liquor cabinet open."

At that moment, the doors of the library burst open and a small group of women entered. Two held back from their group's leader, looking slightly embarrassed, but the apex predator at the front walked with purpose and decided confidence.

"Christine of Lake Pristine," muttered Danny, bitterness creeping into his voice. "There's your 'not nice' right there."

Marcus and Arthur exchanged glances and both had the same thought at the same moment. He could see it reflected in his cousin's face. Arthur slowly unzipped his backpack and drew out his father's old camera, pointing it at the unfolding scene.

Christine moved to the front desk of the library and smacked the little attention bell as if she had been waiting for forty minutes rather than less than forty seconds.

Arthur focused the lens, grateful that they were close enough to capture sound.

Mrs. Holden emerged from the office of the library, smiling nervously at Christine. She approached with the caution of a zookeeper entering the lion cage without a tranquilizer gun. "Can I help you with something, Miss Montgomery?"

"How much would it take to rent this venue for New Year's Eve?" demanded Christine, without any preamble.

"Oh," Mrs. Holden said in surprise, clearing her throat and dusting invisible lint away from her cardigan. "For the wedding? Oh, I'm not sure—"

"And when will you be able to get rid of all the books?"

Christine's second question caused Marcus and Danny to turn their faces to the back of the library, their shoulders shaking in painful, silent laughter. Arthur steadfastly filmed. He kept the lens on the scene, the camera now the fourth member of their group.

"I don't think we'll be able to move the books out, Christine," Mrs. Holden said gently. She spoke to the bride-to-be with such compassion, rather than the affront and disbelief Christine deserved for such a remark.

"It smells in here, Chrissy," one of the bridesmaids said nervously.

"Yes," Christine agreed, eyeing the grand columns of the room before sneering at the shelves against the wall. "Too much of books."

"Again," Mrs. Holden said, with only a modicum of steel in her tone this time, "I can't remove the books."

Arthur had captured every word on camera and it was clear to him now. Their documentary would not be about the humdrum of a small, would-be tourist-trap town. Instead it would focus on the privileged, spoiled princess at the heart of its social scene.

The queen bee who ruled the hive with fear.

His attention was quickly diverted from his epiphany by the automatic doors of the library opening to reveal the younger Montgomery sister. She was carrying two large hardback books and seemed as surprised to see Christine in the library as Mrs. Holden was to see Jasper.

"Hey," Jasper addressed her sister, who gave her the most cursory of glances.

"Jasper, you're home!" cried the librarian, joyous delight and relief flooding her ruddy face.

"Just for the holidays," Jasper said warmly, still eyeing up her sibling. "Here. I found these under my bed. I'm very remorseful and prepared to pay more than a year of late fees."

Mrs. Holden laughed so heartily, it caused Christine to scowl and flounce out of the building, her dutiful bridesmaids fluttering behind her. Jasper said something under her breath and Mrs. Holden smiled in agreement.

Arthur leaned a little closer, adjusting the camera.

"I can't believe she's back," Danny whispered, as he and Marcus realized who Arthur was staring at. "Why would she want to come back here? Is she here for good? I thought she got into some fancy university in the city."

"Her sister's getting married," Marcus reminded him. "Family affair and all that. They'll want her close to home. My mum said it's in a few weeks and they're rushing all of the planning."

Arthur was not really listening. Jasper was unpinning her long hair, all while fishing out some money for her late fees. Mrs. Holden seemed reluctant, so the young woman had to physically force the money into the older woman's hands. She was objectively beautiful, but even more so when she laughed. It was rare; he had only seen it happen once or twice.

"It's not been the same without you, Jasper," Mrs. Holden said wistfully. "You hurry and get that degree and then come home for good. This town's no good without you."

"Oh, that's kind," Jasper said, and Arthur thought he heard a slight undertone of panic. "But I'm sure no one's even noticed I'm gone."

It was clearly meant to be a flippant remark, a modest redirection, but it hardened Mrs. Holden's resolve and caused the older woman to grip onto Jasper with quiet intensity. "No, it's true. The other kids, so many of them followed your example. And you were always so helpful. Without you here . . ." She shook her head, as if the thought was too unbearable. "You'll move back to Lake Pristine once your studies are done? Your poor father can't take you being away forever."

Arthur tasted bitterness under his tongue. The guilt. He knew it well, no one employed it better than the elders of Lake Pristine.

"I'm not leaving Lake Pristine, Mrs. Holden," Jasper said weakly. "I'll see you on New Year's Eve, yes? For Christine's wedding?"

Arthur and his friends watched the girl and the camera captured everything.

"Weird," Danny muttered, caring not a bit if he was heard on film.

"The family must be stressed with all of that planning," was all Arthur could think to say.

"Trust her sister to have a New Year's Eve wedding," Marcus added. "It's not like the guests might have plans of their own."

"Ah, it's New Year's," Danny said, ever the reasonable one. Always the devil's well-mannered advocate. "People want to dance, drink champagne and kiss. I don't think they will mind a few speeches and vows thrown in somewhere before all of that."

"She's so odd," Marcus remarked, a tinge of something deeply unpleasant in his voice. "Jasper, I mean. It's so uncanny valley, you know? When you talk to her? It's like you're not talking to a normal person."

"When have you ever spoken to her?" Arthur challenged quietly. "She hasn't been here for eighteen months and you were never friends in school, despite your best efforts."

"Keeping tabs?" Danny jibed, while Marcus blanched at the reference to his social-climbing attempts in high school.

Arthur rolled his eyes and paused the camera. "Marc?"

"Art?"

"Are you still down to edit this thing? Whatever it turns out to be?"

Marcus leaned across the small library table, his eyes flickering over Arthur's head to Jasper Montgomery for the briefest moment. "One thousand percent. Let's start with that party tonight."

As Jasper pretended that she could not hear the murmuring of Arthur Lancaster and his friends, she once again questioned her decision to return to town at all. She had a few weeks to stage a junior ballet performance and then her family expected her to return to university. Everybody did.

She started a new chapter of the novel she was reading and glanced at the clock on the wall. She had a virtual interview for the Davenport School of Design—the arts course she wanted to be accepted into—and she was too afraid to take it at the house.

She was frighteningly early. That was one of her unbreakable habits. She would always arrive twenty minutes early for most things, thirty for the theater and hours before necessary when catching a flight. She couldn't help it. Lateness was something she found terrifying.

Which was why her entrance back into Lake Pristine had been so horrific. If Christine had given her a time, or perhaps mentioned that she had intended to get up on the bandstand and make a speech, then Jasper could have avoided everyone looking at her.

As well as driving the car into a ditch.

She heard Marcus and his friend Danny leave the library, talking loudly about a Dungeons and Dragons campaign. Arthur remained behind and Jasper was stoically ignoring the boy who had insulted her sister only a few nights before. Without looking, she could feel him pulling up a chair near her and dropping his camera bag onto the desk.

"What are you reading?" he asked, his voice deep.

"A very smutty book," she replied, without looking away from the chapter she had been scanning. When he was too shocked to respond, she regarded him coolly. "Sorry if that makes your low opinion of me even lower."

"You're mad at me?"

"Still," she corrected. "I'm *still* mad at you."

"For what I said about Christine."

"Yes," she replied. "And I intend to continue being mad."

"I wouldn't have said it if I had known—"

"I wouldn't bother finishing that sentence, it's not going

to change anything. Saying it behind our backs doesn't make it kinder."

Jasper put an earbud in one ear. She almost dropped her book when Arthur leaned over and took the bud out.

"I'm sorry. I apologize. I shouldn't have opened my mouth about Queen Christine of Lake Pristine."

There was an insufferable dryness about him as he said it.

Jasper slammed her book down on the table and glared at him. "Some apology."

"What? Sorry if I find your sister a tad ridiculous. That doesn't reflect on you."

"Yes, it does. You're insulting a member of my family and therefore me."

"Nope. Henry and Grace are both lactose intolerant, that doesn't stop me eating ice cream. I think I said something stupid about you, too, but you're not mad about that, are you? Just about me insulting Christine."

"Ice cream. Aren't you sweet enough already?" Jasper said with as much sardonic contempt as she could muster. "Why come over to our house if you can't stand us? I think it's kind of bad manners to slink around someone's private home, eating their food, then bitching about them."

"I was not bitching. I was—"

"All right, loudly complaining. Nice example for Grace, by the way."

"Grace thinks the world of your sister and she treats her like dirt."

"I know," Jasper said with a sigh. "I've spoken to her about it. She's under so much pressure, but it's not right. I don't condone any of that."

"Then why stand up for her?"

"Because she's my *sister*. You wouldn't understand because your siblings are lovely, but one is still required to defend family members, even when they're acting like a troll."

"Grace thinks the world of you, too, but you don't treat her like a burden. Maybe you should ask Christine to do the same."

"I just told you, I've said to Chris to be nicer to Grace, that's not—"

"I meant to *you*. She should be nicer to you."

Jasper's mouth was a dainty o, as she had nothing to say to that. She could feel color rushing to her neck, so she quickly busied herself with her book once more.

"You're contemptible, Grumble," she eventually muttered, turning a page with enough ferocity to bring on a papercut.

"You're in denial, Princess," Arthur countered. He reached into his bag and hauled out a tiny first-aid kit. "And I should have been nicer about you, too. Shouldn't have said what I said."

Jasper stared in surprise at the little green box, wondering what on earth he was doing. He withdrew a plaster and handed it to her. She frowned but accepted. She wrapped her cut in the little beige plaster and thanked him under her breath.

"I am genuinely sorry," he finally said, too quietly for anyone else in the room to hear.

Jasper gave up on reading and searched for a makeshift bookmark. She settled on her Lake Pristine list, scrawled in her horrific handwriting on a piece of scrap paper. In her eagerness to grab it, she caused a wave of air to blow it from the table, and it landed delicately on the blue carpet of the library floor. Jasper made a dive for it, but Arthur had already scooped it up. He frowned upon realizing that there was something written on it.

"A list?"

Jasper grabbed it out of his hands and shoved it in between the novel's pages. "No."

"It was."

"Well, so what if it was?"

"What's it for?"

Jasper was never sure, afterward, what made her tell the truth in that moment. "The things I'm going to do before I leave this place for good."

The words hung in the air between the two almost-strangers. Two teenagers from the same small town, one its golden girl and the other a grieving, grumpy cinema manager. Jasper could not understand why she had felt the need to reveal it. Maybe she needed to feel if it was true.

"You're . . ." Arthur spoke haltingly and Jasper found it even more painful than usual to make eye contact, "you're leaving for good?"

Jasper suddenly felt a sense of panic. Lake Pristine was too small a town for this kind of rumor, it would spread around the place like a bad smell. "No, I mean . . . it's just some stuff I want to do before going back to the city. Before I go back to school."

He did not seem mollified by this, so Jasper nodded toward his camera bag.

"Are you filming something?"

She watched his face filter through a number of expressions before settling upon indifference. "Uh, kind of. It's just something

Marcus and I are talking about. A short film for a competition about small towns."

"That's . . . cool."

He seemed surprised by that. "Would you be in it?"

Jasper blinked at him, grateful that the matter of her list had been put aside but feeling a little exposed by his question. "In your film?"

"We're trying to get interviews with lots of different townspeople. To get a clear picture." He shrugged, seemingly blasé. "Would be good to hear your thoughts."

She looked down at the table in front of her. Splayed before her were her computer, her book and her tote bag—one she had been given by a sympathetic bookseller in the city, after they had realized she was in their store most evenings because she didn't have any friends.

"I have to take a call in here," she said, opening up her laptop. "But I can maybe do afterward? Give me an hour."

Arthur nodded, still seeming nonchalant. "By the bandstand?"

"Sure. But won't it be too dark?"

"Not with those ridiculous twinkle lights."

Jasper had to acknowledge that he was right.

They mumbled cordial goodbyes and she watched him leave the library, his shoulders hunched and his walk stiff. Arthur Lancaster was a staple of Lake Pristine, whether he wanted to be or not. While Jasper knew his gruff exterior made him unapproachable, she also knew that those who knew him always had good things to say. The senior citizens of Lake Pristine adored him. He seemed to be the first on call when a fence needed mending or a cistern was misbehaving.

He was like the late Mr. Lancaster in that fashion, she supposed.

The virtual call she was waiting for suddenly linked up and an unfamiliar but friendly face appeared on Jasper's laptop screen.

"Hi, is that Jasper?" the middle-aged woman with brilliant reading glasses and fabulous white hair asked chirpily.

"Yes." Jasper smiled as widely as she could. While she struggled with processing the audio on a virtual call, she liked being able to monitor what her facial expressions were doing. "Thank you for seeing me."

"Not at all," replied the stranger, who Jasper knew to be Marcia Davenport, the dean of the Davenport School of Design. "Are you at home at the moment?"

"Uh, no," Jasper said quickly. "I'm in my local library, in my hometown. Lake Pristine."

"Ah, I know it! My husband and I love visiting the winter fair there. You're in the library, okay. I'm used to seeing prospective students in their bedrooms with their pets, so this is a nice change."

Jasper hesitated before responding, wondering if it would come across as conceited, but then chose to be brave. "I actually helped redesign the interior after its renovation, three years ago. I thought . . . maybe I could show you?"

The dean smiled, real warmth entering her face this time. "I'd love that."

Act One, Scene VI:
Trapeze Artist

Arthur met up with Marcus by the bandstand and hoped that his short answers to his cousin's questions wouldn't give away his nervousness. They had quickly agreed over text to set up for this specific interview and Arthur was trying to hide his desire to find something special. Marcus kept making knowing remarks about the subject of the interview, but Arthur barely noticed those either. He was in the mode of a perfectionist—trying to ensure that everything was exactly as it should be.

"I take it you didn't go to this much effort for your other interviews," Marcus said dryly.

Arthur rolled his eyes. "It's dark, I'm just making sure the shot won't deteriorate."

"Listen to your weird camera talk. Jasper's not very chatty, is she?" Marcus said, as if he didn't know. Arthur mentally resented the fact that Marcus was merely speaking to make noise. "Will she even give us any material?"

"Shut up," Arthur said calmly. He could see Jasper walking down Main Street, slowly and deliberately, with her tote bag over her shoulder. She knew they were watching her, but she made no effort to speed up in order to reach them.

She was always unpredictable. A different person to everyone. Not that she was deceitful—but everyone knew a different Jasper. Everyone had handfuls of her. As if she was a trapeze artist who had lightly reached out her arm and brushed your fingers with hers while you sat in the stands, watching her perform. But as soon as you tried to grab hold of her, the trapeze would swing back. And she would be gone.

She released a small smile upon finally reaching the bandstand, but she was looking directly at Marcus.

"Thanks for doing this," he said jovially and she nodded with a demure smile.

"Yeah, thanks." Arthur ignored the flicker in his ribcage. He wanted her to look at him. Not Marcus.

"Tell me where you want me," she said brightly, her eyes quickly flashing to Arthur and Marcus before landing on the camera.

"Yeah, Art," Marcus murmured, "tell her."

"Just over here," Arthur said, bumping Marcus out of the way with his shoulder so he could show her the spot they had set up. "Okay to clip this somewhere?" He handed her a microphone pack.

"Sure," she said. She attached it with the expertise of someone who had performed onstage plenty of times. "All good?"

She shifted her position and looked down at her knees. Arthur clenched and unclenched his fists and then sat just behind the camera on its tripod.

"We're rolling," he said. "Can you just state your name for the tape? As a slate."

"Jasper Montgomery," she said quietly.

"Arthur's just going to ask you some questions about the town," Marcus said from Arthur's side. "Don't answer if you don't want to. Just be aware that any uncomfortable silences will be kept in during the edit."

"Marcus," Arthur said sharply. "Fuck off or sit down."

The camera caught Jasper's surprised reaction to that statement. Marcus was also, noticeably, chagrined.

"How long have you lived in Lake Pristine?" Arthur asked, his voice huskier than he meant it to be.

"My whole life," Jasper replied, her eyes wide. She was not staring into the lens like the other townspeople Arthur had interviewed. He did not need to instruct her about on-camera particulars. It was as if she was constantly in performance mode. "I was born in my parents' bedroom," she went on.

"Really?"

"Yeah," she flushed slightly while she spoke. "I came a couple of weeks early and I was very quick. By the time my dad had started the car, I was out. He likes to joke about how I'm terrified of being late. I'm always early."

Arthur smiled and Marcus made an audible sound of appreciation. Arthur's smile faded and he cast his cousin a look of reproach, jerking his head toward the camera. Marcus mimed zipping his mouth shut, but not without his own look of irritation.

"What's Lake Pristine like, for you?"

Jasper considered the question. It was unendingly complicated, as Arthur Lancaster well knew.

"I love this town," she answered.

"But you defected?"

Jasper froze. She could feel her eyes narrowing before she could censor her reaction. "Sorry?"

"Wrong word," Arthur added hastily. "I mean, you left. You . . . you—"

"I went to college in the city."

Arthur pressed. "You left town completely. No return visits. No living at home, like most other kids. Why?"

Jasper felt her heart quicken. She felt her palms dampen.

"I wasn't fitting in," she finally chose to say. She hoped it would be enough.

"Ah," Marcus suddenly said, as if this was a eureka moment for him. He tapped his own temple. "Because of the, uh—"

"That's not something you're up to par on, Marcus," Jasper said. She rarely got short with people. Hardly ever with friends and never with strangers. Yet there was something about people prodding her about being neurodivergent.

Because that was what Jasper was. Neurodivergent. A word a kindly psychiatrist had given her, one week after handing out a diagnosis on a piece of paper, something Jasper had not known girls could even be.

"Neurodivergent is difficult to spell, but it will let you keep a little privacy about your disability," the woman had said. "If you don't want everyone knowing the particulars."

"She won't need it," her mother had said, "as she won't be telling anyone she's autistic. She has it mild, she can hide it, no one will know the difference."

"There's no mild or spicy with autism, Mrs. Montgomery. It's a spectrum, not a binary. Perhaps—"

The conversation echoed in Jasper's memory.

Her mother was terrified of labels. Jasper felt liberated by them.

However, people like Marcus often heard a label and, despite the fact that they had woken up that morning without having thought about said label for one moment in their life, they suddenly imagined themselves to be experts with insightful things to say.

"I just think it's interesting," Marcus said, holding his hands up and grinning. "People like that . . . don't often look like you, do they?"

"Neurodivergence, autism, ADHD, none of it has a *look*," said Jasper. "Okay? Crap like that is what keeps people from getting a diagnosis. I might be the only girl in town who has it on paper, but trust and believe, there are people going about their business knowing something inside them is waiting to be understood. And nonsense like that, stupid statements like 'you don't look like' or 'you can't tell,' that is stopping them from getting there."

An astonished silence met her monologue. Jasper was amazed, herself. It was the most she had said since crashing the Jeep.

"He's a dick," Arthur said firmly.

Jasper glanced at him and there was something about the empathy in his face that made her feel panicked. Something that made her feel a little too exposed.

"Is that what you want for your film?" she asked softly. "A reaction from the weird sister? Poke the neurodivergent one until you get some good shots?"

"Not at all," Marcus said, getting to his feet and reaching across to squeeze her elbow. Jasper saw Arthur's eyes follow the movement and darken in distaste, enough for her to feel even more mortified. He thought so little of her, he didn't even want his friend to touch her.

"Arthur Lancaster, you have been a grump since the day I met you. I don't know why I even agreed to this."

Now Arthur rose to his feet, defensive. Neither seemed to care that the camera was still rolling. "Steady on—"

"I love Lake Pristine, but the thing that drove me out, and the thing that has made coming back so difficult, is the fact that nobody here minds their business," Jasper decreed. "They don't want to help, they just want to stare."

"I agree," Arthur said coolly.

"Yes, I'm sure," Jasper retorted. "You've always stood on the side, glowering at everybody. Too good to take part in town activities, too good for the parties, too good for the festivals. But, like I said, I love this town. I'm going to soak up every minute that I'm here."

"For the last time?"

She drew back at that, glaring at him. Arthur winced.

"You've always been there," she eventually said. "In the wings, judging."

"I'm not judging you, Princess. I just wonder how much you can love a town if you're so keen to leave it."

"Of course I love it, I just don't . . . love me in it."

It was an epiphany, of sorts. Jasper loved Lake Pristine, but things were missing in her life. Things a beautiful town couldn't quite fill.

Yet there was something invigorating about fighting with Arthur Lancaster. She had returned from college with every intention of being cordial to the entire town. It was not a disguise, her politeness and her congeniality, but rather an armor. But Arthur Lancaster always made her want to climb out of it and pick up a sword instead.

"I'm helping you and your film out, Grumble," she said, pointing a finger at him. "Or are we done?"

"How do you feel about Christine's wedding?" he parried.

She softened her expression. "I'm so thrilled and excited."

"Liar."

"Excuse me?"

"You may be thrilled and excited for her marriage, but one month to execute a wedding? You must all be—"

"We are all delighted. Besides, I'm not really involved in the planning."

It was Marcus's turn to intercept. "You're not a bridesmaid?"

His gentle tone of surprise was enough to make Jasper's sadness over this matter resurface, but, as ever, she kept it buried. "No. She wasn't sure if I would be in town or not. And it's a small bridal party."

"Always defending her," murmured Arthur.

"The one thing," Jasper said pointedly, staring down Arthur Lancaster while she spoke, "that I would change about Lake Pristine is the fact that we all sort of know each other. Or at least, we think we do. So, some boy who was a stagehand at one of your mother's ballet productions thinks that he knows everything about your family. For example."

Her lips almost curled into a smile at the end of her little speech and Arthur nearly mirrored the expression.

Jasper pushed her long hair over her shoulders and made her way to the steps of the bandstand, untangling herself from the microphone pack. "Good luck with your film," she said blandly, handing back the device to Marcus. "Sorry if none of that was usable."

She set off in the direction of the Lakehouse. Just before joining the woodland path, she turned and called back.

"Arthur?"

He turned his head quickly. "Yeah?"

"Call Saffron Billingham."

He squinted at her and then shook himself, as if trying to dislodge the words. "Huh?"

"Saffron. You should call her. Maybe a date will get some of the grumpiness out of you."

Marcus said something Jasper was unable to hear, but whatever it was, Arthur pinched him for it. She made her way home without looking back.

Act One, Scene VII:
Ice Cream Man

"How was town today, lovely?"

Jasper smiled at her father from across the dinner table. There was the slightest tinge of worry in his kind brown eyes, so she plastered on her brightest expression and said, "It was great. Really glad to be back."

Relief spread across his gently lined face and it broke Jasper's heart. It would kill him to hear that she was dropping out of college. It would break him to hear she was planning to leave Lake Pristine for good.

"Kept your room exactly as it should be," he went on to say.

"You resisted the urge to turn it into a gym," teased Jasper.

"That room will always be yours," he said, subtly refusing to allow the conversation to move to jesting. "When you graduate, you're moving right back in. Save money on rent; city rates are extortionate."

Jasper felt a pang of guilt and knew not to take the conversation any further. She was good at masking, not something anyone should boast about, but it was a sad fact and her father was an observant man. Their house, the Lakehouse, sat by the water and the trees—completely separate to the rest of the town: isolated, peaceful. The furthest thing from student accommodation in the city. The rent would be lower, her room would be larger, and the environment would be wonderfully familiar.

But she couldn't stay. Not when things could never be on her own terms.

Jasper picked up her fork and started to eat the chilli con carne that her father had prepared.

Her mother was getting out the large wedding diary that she had been constructing since the proposal, clearly oblivious to the conversation Jasper and her father had been having.

The two sisters eyed the heavy thing with apprehension. Even Christine was intimidated at the sight of it.

"We have to get serious with planning if we're having a New Year's Eve wedding—we have mere weeks until crunch time," their mother said firmly. Jasper found it amusing, and telling, that her mother always said "we" in regards to her eldest daughter's wedding. "Now, invitations are the first hurdle. I'm opening my whole rolodex. Who do we *not* want there?"

"I want everyone to be invited," Christine said. It sounded like a generous statement, so Jasper waited for the true reason behind it. "Cast a wide net. I want my worst enemies to see how expensive everything is and how happy Kevin and I are."

There it was.

"Menu?" their mother asked, unfazed.

"Chicken or fish," Christine answered with a shrug.

"No vegetarian option?" Jasper pressed gently.

"Salad on the side, then," Christine retorted, with an eye roll.

"You just worry about showing up and telling people 'anywhere but the first two rows,'" her mother said to Jasper, giving her a look of discernment. "Leave the rest to Christine and me."

"Fine," Jasper said, taking a big bite of chilli and then lifting her almost empty plate. "I'm going to the Hobsons' holiday party."

"Say hello to Catherine for me," her mother said, dismissing her with a queenly wave.

Craig's family home was a six-bedroom property on the other side of the lake. It was one of a handful of large houses closer to the main hub of the town. Detached and important, these houses belonged to some of the oldest families in the area. Craig's was lit up like the rest of Lake Pristine, in pale white twinkle lights, and it was already bustling with people when Jasper arrived.

She went straight to greet Craig's parents, handing them a bottle of wine from her father's collection—something they gratefully remarked upon. Apparently no one else had thought to bring a gift.

"Young people in the den, grown-ups in the living room," Catherine, Craig's mother, said dutifully. "But come say goodbye before you leave, Jasper, I always love seeing you."

Jasper nodded and then moved into the den. She noted Marcus and Arthur Lancaster over by the Christmas tree, the former filming a slow pan of the large room with the camera. Jasper retreated into the hall, avoiding the shot and preparing herself for the busy noise of the room.

"Jasper?"

The voice was Hera's and she looked both thrilled and terrified in equal measure. Jasper watched the other girl carefully avoid bumping into one of Catherine's modern sculptures. The whole house was a mixture of different design impulses and it made Jasper want to haul out paint colors and give Catherine advice. In a house so large, Jasper envisioned tasteful wallpaper with just the smallest touch of golden foil. Matching upholstery and smooth, varnished floors instead of once-white carpet.

"Come sit with me," was all she said to Hera, gesturing toward a tired old sofa in the den.

"Thanks again for actually being nice to me," Hera said hurriedly as they settled on the cushions. Her eyes took in the fragmented make-up of the den; all the teenagers sequestered into their own corners with their own groups. "This town can sometimes feel . . ."

"Like a secret society?"

"Oh, my God, yes."

"Yeah. It's even a bit cult-like. It must be weird for new arrivals."

"People expected me to know their shoes sizes at the bowling alley."

"Yup," Jasper said with suppressed laughter in her voice. "That checks out."

"That guy with the camera, who's he?"

Jasper glanced over at Marcus and Arthur. The former was still filming the general atmosphere, while the latter was glued to the wall and looking as though he wanted to be anywhere else.

"Marcus Lancaster, Arthur's cousin. You met Arthur at the cinema. The handsome one. I'm happy to reintroduce you to him."

The handsome one. The words had somehow slipped out. What a horrible surprise.

"No, it's okay, I guess we'll bump into each other at the alley. And as for handsome, I only like girls."

Jasper made a mental note and smiled. "Got it."

"And he's filming something?"

"A documentary short on Lake Pristine."

"Why, is there a dark underbelly?"

Jasper did laugh at that. "Not that I know of. I've lived here my whole life. Well. Until recently. Not sure they've developed a seedy secret since I've been gone."

"Everyone talked about you like you were dead."

Jasper turned to stare at her in shock and Hera backtracked at once.

"Sorry! That came out all wrong. I just meant, they all speak about you with such reverence. It feels a bit like meeting a famous person."

Jasper regarded Hera a little more closely. "Are you . . . No. Sorry. Never mind."

Hera smiled a small but knowing smile. "Am I like you?"

Jasper felt the urge to be defensive, but she shoved it down. "Um. Well—"

"I'm ADHD," Hera interjected matter-of-factly. "I clocked you earlier and thought . . . Well. I just get a feeling sometimes."

"Autistic," Jasper supplied, surprised by her own openness. "I don't . . . I don't talk about it much."

"No, I get that," Hera answered softly. "This town is beautiful. It's like something from a glossy magazine, and the people are superficially friendly, but . . . I don't know if it's the best place to be outnumbered in."

"Small towns never are," Jasper said with a shrug, "but, if I'm being really honest, I've spent the last eighteen months in a dorm in the city and it wasn't any more empathetic or knowledgeable there."

"Suffer in silence approach?"

"Well, that," Jasper allowed, "but also, inspiration porn or nothing."

"Ah. The worst."

"Yep."

There was a fluidity to their conversation, a shorthand. They spoke in a dialect that most others never touched.

"Sorry to hear that."

"I mean, that's why I'm pretty private," Jasper said. "I like being ND. But it sometimes feels like you've been shoved onstage in front of thousands of people. There's a huge orchestra there and a pianist, and your job is to turn the pages of their music. Only you don't read music. And no one is going to tell you how to do it. So, you have to guess. And if you get it wrong? The whole orchestra will get thrown off and blame you for it."

"That's—" Hera gave Jasper an appraising look—"accurate."

"And when you try to explain that to a counselor, who is being paid to look after students' welfare, when you try to tell them about overstimulation, routine disruption, masking, all that stuff—they just tell you that everyone has trouble fitting in some of the time."

"Gah," Hera sighed. "I hate the belittling."

"So, you shut up. You get on with it. And . . . and you hate it. The hiding and the pretending. It makes you forget who you are."

Jasper was surprised at her own oversharing. She could feel Hera watching her. It made her pull her hair in front of her face and avoid eye contact.

"Do you have anyone here you can talk to about this?"

Jasper gestured to the garden, which the two of them could see through the window next to the den sofa. Odette and Craig were standing a little distance from the house. Odette's arms were crossed and she was glaring at the ground, while Craig gesticulated. It was clearly not an amorous moment for the couple. "My best friend has bigger problems right now," Jasper said quietly.

Hera inspected the scene. "She's so pretty."

"Odette? Yeah. And she's wasted on Craig, he's a loser who may never grow out of it."

"Isn't this his house?"

"Yes, and it's the only interesting thing about him. Just wish the décor was better. This room is so great, but Catherine loves her dull white walls."

"You're an interior designer then?"

Hera said it teasingly but Jasper didn't smile. "No, I'm . . . No."

Sensing the other girl's sudden change, Hera got to her feet and moved toward the speaker system. "Fancy some dancing? I've heard you're the best in Lake Pristine."

"Not to this terrible playlist," snorted Jasper.

Hera smirked and started scrolling on the device linked to the speakers. "Who's your poison?"

"Tom Waits. We're meant to be together, he just doesn't know it yet."

"Song?"

"Ice Cream Man."

Hera laughed and pressed play.

Arthur watched as his cousin did yet another slow pan of the room.

"I think you've got enough B-roll," he said flatly.

"Well, I don't want some drama to kick off and for us to miss it," Marcus replied. "I only got a bit of Odette and Craig before they took it outside."

"I should get back to the cinema," Arthur said, more to himself than to Marcus. "I made Henry change a lot of our upcoming program, so I should really be there to check the—"

"What do you think they're talking about?"

Arthur stalled, like a car. "Who?"

Marcus nodded toward the other side of the den. Arthur knew who he was referring to without having to look, but look he did. Jasper Montgomery was sitting next to the new girl, Hera, and they were having a conversation that seemed almost intimate.

"They seem very friendly," Marcus said icily.

Arthur said nothing. Instead he watched as Hera moved to the speakers, changing the music. A mindless, thumping headache of a song was suddenly replaced by nostalgic piano playing. Jasper clapped in delight and leaped to her feet. As the bluesy song kicked into its chorus, Arthur and Marcus watched the rest of the room take notice of the two girls while they danced. Hera was a little jerky and self-conscious, taking her cues from Jasper.

Arthur had seen Jasper Montgomery dance many times before. Her ballet performances were always so regimented and honed to perfection. But now, as a gravelly-voiced man sang over Craig's sound system, she danced with complete surrender. Her long hair fell across her face and she moved with the natural gift that dancers were born with, the connection to the music driving every muscle.

Sophie, a girl Arthur had seen a few times with Odette, was suddenly at his right side, as the rest of the room slowly started to join in with the dancing, despite their unfamiliarity with the song.

"She's so annoying," she said under her breath, almost too quietly for Arthur to hear. "Who knew a ballerina's music taste could be so trashy. Weirdo."

As he watched Jasper spin Hera around, letting the whole room see that she accepted this girl as a friend and therefore they should too, Arthur thought of many words to describe Jasper, but annoying was not one of them. Infuriating. Superior. Spoiled. Smart. Gorgeous—

He shook himself away from the wall and turned to Marcus, speaking lowly. "I'm going to call Grace, check she's okay."

Marcus gave him a contemplative look but did not reply. He also did not turn off the camera, which was focused on the dancing pair.

Act One, Scene VIII:
Omar Sharif

Jasper left the party without getting a moment with Odette. She didn't want to go home, so she walked down the woodland path toward the shimmering lights of the town and thought about her list. The heart of Lake Pristine was the town center, a nucleus that drew everyone in. It was surrounded by trees and the forest, with houses positioned throughout the woodland. If people wanted to leave their homes to reach the lights and the noise, they had to first walk the quiet paths.

Every building in town was glimmering, adorned with winter finery. Tourists were queuing to enter the maze and the gazebo was wrapped in twinkle lights. Vendors were still manning their stalls as the evening light began to dim. The air was crisp but not chilled and Jasper smiled at every person she passed by.

"We're so excited for Christine and Kevin," one of the vendors said and Jasper chose to smile graciously and nod.

"Thank you," she said warmly. "On behalf of the family, we appreciate it."

"Jasper?"

She started suddenly at the sound of her name, but it was only Saffron. She and Jasper knew each other, of course, as neighbors of the town. Saffron's older sister, Rebecca, was also very close with Christine and one of her bridesmaids. But Saffron, if Jasper was being honest, had always been one of the meaner girls at school.

"Hey, Saff," Jasper said. "How's things?"

"Fine," Saffron replied curtly, her eyes dancing in a fashion that told Jasper she was not interested in small talk, which Jasper did not really mind at all.

"Listen, I told Art Lancaster to call you."

She half expected Saffron to play coy, but she beamed with satisfaction. "Good! I tried catching him at Christine's engagement party, but he's slippery. What did he say when you told him?"

"Oh," Jasper wondered if she should lie. "He, um . . . He was getting ready to shoot some footage for that film he's making, so he got distracted, but I told him."

She should have gone with the lie, she realized, as Saffron exhaled in frustration at this answer.

"As long as you didn't make me sound desperate," she said.

"Of course not," Jasper promised. "I think it's cool you made a move. It's modern."

"Yeah, yeah. Is Christine at the house?"

"Yes, I left them a while ago, but she's probably still planning with Mum."

"I've just come from the cinema, but Arthur wasn't there. But if you're sure that you told him?"

"I was there," Jasper teased very gently. "I definitely told him."

Saffron's words sparked in Jasper a sudden desire to visit the Arthouse. It was on her list, after all. If Arthur was still at Craig's party, she could take in a film without worrying about another argument with him.

The Arthouse was the only building in Lake Pristine that was lit up all year round, not just for the holidays.

People were leaving an earlier showing as Jasper arrived. She made her way to the box office and smiled when she noticed that it was Henry Lancaster manning the desk.

"Hello, young lady!" he shouted, making her laugh.

"Hey, you."

Jasper usually got into a panic if she saw someone unexpectedly. But Henry always made things so easy for people.

"You're too late for the cash cow everyone's just seen," he said cheerfully. "And, uh, I heard about earlier. Marcus is a dick and Arthur always gets so weird when you're around."

Jasper hardly heard him, as she looked up at the display of film posters behind his head.

The Arthouse's Classic Film Festival.

There were so many of her favorites, it was almost as though she had designed the line-up herself.

She threw her money on the counter. "I'm here for Barbra, Lancaster."

Something unnameable crossed his face. "Oh, really? *Funny Girl*?"

"That's right."

"You might be the only one in there."

"Even better."

"Gotta get some stale popcorn on the house."

Jasper laughed again and accepted his offer.

He punched her ticket and led her to the smaller of the two screens. It was intimate and beautiful. Old, soft lights. Red velvet. She was instantly relaxed.

Henry was right, she was the only customer. She loved it. As the film began, she sank into her seat and silently celebrated the wonder of it. She loved shutting herself away from the world for a few hours. No checking her phone. No speaking. Just falling into the story that was being told. It pleased her as much as reading. They balanced each other out well.

Jasper liked repeated patterns. It's why she enjoyed performing onstage. Knowing, for the most part, what to expect. Which step came next, which musical phrase was about to happen. It was the same as watching an old film that she loved. The steps were predictable, but the feelings could be entirely new and surprising. She could watch an old scene that she knew all of the words to, perform a routine that she could do in her sleep, and yet still be confronted with fresh waves of emotion.

It was a blissful couple of hours.

When it was over, she left an empty cinema for an almost empty foyer. The ushers had gone home and she was the last customer in the building. Henry was cashing up in the box office, smiling when he saw her.

"Thanks, Henry," she called to him. "That was heaven."

"Don't thank *me*," he responded, waving to her as she left. She didn't fully understand his meaning, but it was late and she was too tired to engage.

Jasper pushed against the heavy theater doors and as she went to step into the biting December night, she crashed into something tall and sturdy.

Hands grabbed her elbows to steady her.

"Sorry." Arthur Lancaster's deep voice murmured the apology as they maneuvered around each other.

"Are you driving home, Jazz?" Henry called over, innocently.

Jasper glanced back at him and leaned against the heavy door, using all of her weight to keep it open. "It's been a hot second since I crashed into the ditch, but I *am* still allowed to drive. But I'm going to walk home."

Henry stopped grinning, moving toward the door to peer out at the dark square. "No way, it's pitch black."

"I'll be fine."

"No, no. Art, walk her home."

Both Arthur and Jasper grimaced at that suggestion.

"I'm fine, Henry," she insisted. "The most dangerous things in this town are the beavers."

"He's not going to take 'no' for an answer," Arthur said soberly, turning to step out onto the street. "Let's go."

Jasper winced. But it was dark. Dark and silent, the whole town winding down to sleep. So, she relented.

As the two of them walked along Main Street, she could stand the dead air no longer.

"Have you called Saffron?"

He did not answer, deflecting her question with one of his own. "Were you the only one watching that film tonight?"

"Yes, and it was fabulous," she reported, without any embarrassment. "I love going to the cinema alone. Plus, you can't miss *Funny Girl.*"

"Never seen it."

She let her mouth fall open in over-animated shock.

He laughed. "Sorry. Is it good?"

"It's brilliant beyond brilliant. Barbra in a leopard coat. With the hair and the jokes! But, most of all . . . Omar Sharif."

He threw her a sideways glance, almost smiling. "Omar Sharif?"

"There's just something indescribable about him," she said dreamily. "He's so perfect. I've been in love with him since the age of five."

She felt him look at her again. "Why?"

"I couldn't tell you. It's not just that he's handsome. He is, obviously. But it's the way he looked at her. Like he wasn't just attracted to her, but that he also really *liked* her. He truly drank all of her in. Saw all the great pieces she hadn't even let herself find yet. And he did all that with a look."

She was surprised by her own words and horrified at the honesty of them.

"Sorry," she mumbled. "Oversharing."

"No, it's . . . it's okay. We want people to leave the Arthouse feeling . . . whatever that was."

His expression was gentle—*charmed*.

She snorted. "That's generous of you, thanks." They were almost at the Lakehouse. "Everyone will be asleep, I think," Jasper said softly, getting her key out.

"Why aren't you?"

She looked up at him. He was watching her intently. She realized that she did not have her sunglasses to hide behind, so she dropped her gaze quickly.

"I don't sleep well. Not at the moment."

She found her key and was about to slide it into the door, smiling as she heard the tinkle of Chum's bell and the sound of his paws as they thundered down the hall. She stopped for a moment.

"Thank Henry for me."

"Sure thing," Arthur said. "What for?"

"For showing that movie. For Omar Sharif."

The front door of the house was suddenly jerked open and Christine appeared, in a fluffy robe and a face mask. It was camp and comical, enough to make Jasper bark out a laugh.

"Where the hell have you been?" cried her older sister. "You just took off and turned your phone off."

Jasper was taken aback. It was unlike Christine to be worried about her. "I went to catch a film."

Christine's brow was furrowed in annoyance. "I had samples to choose from and you *know* I need your eye on stuff like that."

Jasper flushed in realization, and Arthur released a low whistle from the bottom of the steps. Christine suddenly noticed him and her scowl deepened.

"Can we help you?" she snapped at him. "This is private property."

"He's been nice and walked me home, Chris," Jasper chastised softly. "Let's go inside."

"My friend's little sister fancies you, but quite honestly? I think she can do better," Christine said to Arthur with remarkable dislike, as if Jasper hadn't spoken.

"Chris," Jasper said tartly. "Let me in, I'm tired and I have *Nutcracker* auditions tomorrow."

"Nuh-uh. You have wedding business to do before you slink off upstairs."

Arthur chuffed out a derisive noise at Christine's words and looked down at the frost beneath his feet. "Scrub the floors, Cinderelly."

"What?" snapped Christine. "What was that?"

"Don't order your sister around like a servant," Arthur snapped back.

"Or what?"

"Stop it, both of you," Jasper exclaimed. "Christine, go and put your samples on the dining table. I'll deal with it."

Christine was glowering heavily, but she relented. She threw one final look of loathing toward Arthur before returning inside.

Jasper shook her head and flexed her hands, trying to dispel some of the tension in them. Her warm glow from the film and a few hours of escape were quickly dimming.

She turned to Arthur and said curtly: "I'm going to ask you once again to keep your opinions about my sister to yourself."

Act One, Scene IX: White Swan

Arthur turned to go, stomping down the garden path. Then came the sound of her feet storming after him.

"So, what? You can be polite and normal and nice for a fifteen-minute walk and then time's up? You're all out of charm?"

"Yep, that's me all dried up, I'm afraid."

"I know she's brusque—"

"Brusque?" He stopped walking so suddenly, Jasper almost crashed into his torso. "She's a fascist."

"Here was me actually starting to think you were decent company," Jasper said, turning back to the house.

"Don't worry," Arthur called after her. "Christine can still use the Arthouse for her bachelorette night. We got that email, by the way! We'd be too afraid to refuse. I hope it surpasses her enormously high standards. Maybe Henry and I can install a photobooth or some other tacky add-on?"

"Bite me."

Arthur fought a smile as he watched her slam her way into the house. He was alone by the lake for mere seconds before the door was wrenched open once more and Jasper reappeared on the steps.

"I'm not like this!" she yelled over to him and it made the smile even harder to suppress. "Okay? I've never told anyone to bite me in my life. I'm not like this, Lancaster!"

"You are with me!"

"I would like to formally request that we conduct our business with Henry, if we do end up using the Arthouse for any of the wedding events. And I LOVE a photobooth!"

"You don't have to use fancy words now, Princess, it's just us two. No professor from your degree here to grade you."

He felt an immediate pinch of anxiety, wondering if he had taken the sparring too far and landed a serious blow. But she took his words rather merrily and shouted something obscene over to him. His smile almost broke into a deep laugh, until they both noticed an upstairs light switch on inside of the house. Jasper's face fell and she was gone.

Arthur waited for a moment, wondering if she would return. He stood for five long minutes and then watched the same light turn off again. He was about to leave when Jasper's own bedroom lamp was lit. She appeared in her window and looked over at him, which prompted him to nod once before turning to leave.

He walked back to the Arthouse and it was pleasant to be the only one on Lake Pristine's streets. It was a beautiful ghost town. As strange as it probably sounded, he could pretend that his father was walking beside him. They did not need to speak.

When he reached the cinema, Henry was sitting at the bar, drinking soda from a bottle. He was alert, clearly waiting for Arthur to return. He took a long swig from the green bottle and regarded his younger brother with a knowing glint.

"That better be paid for," Arthur chided him, locking the door. "Or written up on the wastage sheet."

Henry took another long gulp, never breaking eye contact. "How was the walk to the Lakehouse, Art?"

"Shut up."

"Why that film? I kept asking myself why on earth you picked that film. Why, out of the blue, does Arthur want us to host a 'classic movie' festival with a bunch of old films? Now I can see why."

Arthur grabbed a bottle for himself and cracked it open, using the edge of the bar to pop off the lid. "Drop it."

Henry smirked, but then his face fell. "Dad always loved her."

Arthur gripped the cold bottle and wiped away some condensation. "Yeah."

"Because she always called him 'sir.'"

"She has good manners. Usually."

There was the ghost of a smile as he remembered her moonlight profanity.

"Yeah, unlike her sister. Who is having her hen party here, by the way."

"I know. In the ballroom."

"You can handle that one, little brother."

"Not sure they'll like that," Arthur replied.

"Hey, Art?"

"Mm?"

"You should have some fun. You've given everything to this place since Dad went. Chaperoned Grace all around town. Not sure what you'll do with your free time now that she's at school and in ballet class all of the time."

Arthur downed the last of his drink and chucked the bottle into the recycling bin, enjoying the crash. He watched the great plastic thing, wondering if it would fall. "I'm fine."

It did not. It teetered and steadied.

"I . . ." Henry's voice was faint as Arthur made to head next door, to their family annex. "I don't think you are, Art."

"Turn off the lights and bolt the doors," Arthur called over his shoulder.

"Call that Saffron girl."

The words followed Arthur into his room. He crashed into bed and punched a dent into his pillow, before settling his head on it. Saffron had messaged him online, giving him her number. He had put off calling her because he never wanted to lead anyone on and he just did not see her in that light. He had maintained polite conversations with her during their schooldays, but she had never said a thing that lingered in his memory.

However, he could be wrong about people, and a date was not a commitment. It didn't even have to be dinner.

He kicked off his shoes and slid his phone out of his pocket.

His father had always said that doing things over and over again and expecting different results wasn't just a symptom of madness, it was also a sign that you were boring. So, Arthur pulled up the message and copied the phone number, getting ready to dial.

She likes me, he told himself. *She's interested.* They could fall in love or they could just be friends. Either was a gain.

He needed to stop wasting time on things that did not have a chance of ever coming true.

He knew he needed to stop. But his finger could not press the call button.

It's late, he told himself. Not a gentlemanly look.

He would call in the morning.

It was only Grace at the breakfast table when he came through the next morning. She was up, dressed and scrolling over her cereal. Arthur inwardly noted that she seemed so collected these days.

"Morning, bean."

"Morning, Art," she said cheerfully. "You slept late."

"I was up late."

"Walking Jasper Montgomery home?"

He frowned, glancing over at her. She was grinning back at him, her spoon hovering over her bowl, dripping milk.

"Eat your breakfast."

She laughed her laugh that sounded like their father. Arthur winced and poured some coffee into a chipped mug.

"*Nutcracker* auditions this evening," Grace said after a comfortable silence.

"Yeah?" Arthur regarded her, carefully. "You're going, right?"

"Technically, we all have to audition. If we want to be in the company."

"But you want to be the lead, right?"

"No," she said sharply. "Hilly is going to be Clara. For sure. I just want, like, a small part. As something. I mean, I just want to get into the company. It's a tough few weeks of rehearsal, but I've always wanted to do it."

Arthur sipped his coffee, still watching her. "Okay."

He fully intended to launch into a monologue about why she needed to believe in herself and how proud their father would have been, pleased to see her trying new things, when he heard loud, clattering voices coming from the cinema foyer.

"Back in a bit," he told Grace, jumping up, grabbing his work lanyard and heading for the cinema. As he arrived in the entrance lobby, he instantly regretted it.

Christine, Jasper and the rest of the bridal party were standing in the middle of the room, taking it all in. Saffron was there with her sister.

"Dust," Christine announced imperiously. "I feel like I can smell dust."

"Well," Henry was already there, his eyes resentful and his tone sarcastic. "It is an old building."

"Can it be deep-cleaned before the party?"

"Come and have a look at the ballroom, Christine," Jasper said, directing the other women toward the room they were hoping to hire. Her tone was calming, polished after a lifetime of dealing with her sister.

Henry led them through to the ballroom, but Saffron lingered behind. She had seemingly joined her older sister—the maid of honor—on this bridesmaid outing. Arthur swallowed. Suddenly last night's compromise did not seem like such a healthy idea. Every nerve was yelling for him to run.

"Good morning, Saff," he said gruffly, nodding in her direction.

"Now it is," she replied.

"How've you been? How's your mum's fence?"

He had visited their home a few weeks prior, fixing the old thing and giving it a fresh coat of paint. Saffron's mother had arthritis and it was just the two of them now that her older sister was out of the house, so Arthur had offered to take on the job.

"It's good," she said, sidling closer. "Thought about breaking the whole thing so that you could come over again."

He instinctively took a step back, casting a glance toward the open ballroom doors. Jasper was smiling at something Henry was saying to her. Her dark brown hair was piled high on top of her head and her face looked fresh. Arthur caught himself wondering about how much sleep she'd had. Her face was glowing.

"Saff," he said her name and every bit of it was uncomfortable. Unnatural. But being outside of his comfort zone should feel like this, he supposed. Maybe the desperate need to escape was just him leaving the circle of familiarity he had drawn around himself. Perhaps it was supposed to feel this awful. This anxiety-inducing. "I was wondering if you wanted to grab a coffee sometime?"

She clucked her tongue and then barked out a laugh. "Uh, yeah. Obviously."

His eyes wandered back to the ballroom. Jasper was scribing notes while Christine dictated. She was concentrating hard, getting down every word that her sister uttered.

She was completely oblivious to Arthur.

"Cool," he told Saffron, still watching the younger Montgomery sister. "Well, I'll text you."

And he would, even if it felt unnatural. The town was starting to mark him, like a piece of clothing that itched and felt too tight. And if the definition of madness was in fact doing the same thing over and over again, while expecting different results: Arthur knew he needed to start making different choices.

"Are we cool?"

Jasper almost shouted the words at Odette as she entered Trimmings, the Cunningham family's business.

Odette glanced up from her usual spot by the counter and stared at her old friend in surprise. She pulled her earbuds out and smiled, but it was a guarded expression. One that was full of civility rather than warmth. "Of course."

"I'm sorry I hardly spoke to you at the party. I was—"

"Exhausted, I could tell."

"I was going to grab you at the Arthouse the other day but you went into the screening with . . . Anyway. Thought I'd come by to see you."

They stood in an awkward silence before Jasper edged a little further into the shop.

"I think Christine and her bridesmaids will be coming by sometime soon, to do their fittings."

"I can't believe you're not a bridesmaid, Jazz."

"It's one less thing to worry about, to be honest."

"How's planning going? The wedding is in less than a month."

"It's fine," Jasper fibbed. "Mum is in her element. Everyone is working overtime and the family are calling in all the favors. I take it you got your save-the-date?"

"Yes, it's pinned to my fridge."

Her wry tone made both of them smirk.

"She'll be better when it's all over," Jasper added softly. "She gets so anxious about things being perfect, and making Mum happy, she forgets how to behave."

"Look," Odette shrugged and pushed herself away from the counter, pretending to busy herself with some of the vintage dresses hanging by the window. "Christine has never been easy to handle, but these last few days have been off the scale. And then this film thing. This documentary Arthur and Marcus are doing. They're capturing all kinds of things—"

"I thought it might make her behave better," Jasper admitted. "That was my hope, anyway. When I heard they were cracking a camera out, all over town."

"Nope. Same old Christine."

Jasper glanced around the shop, remembering the days they had spent in it as children. Her in a tutu, Odette in an oversized Nirvana T-shirt and Converse.

"So, how are things with Craig?" she asked Odette.

Odette snorted and made an obnoxious noise, like a game-show buzzer. "Next question, please."

"All right," Jasper said. "How are things with Craig?"

Odette threw her head back and started imitating a car alarm, which resulted in both of them giggling.

"Just tell me if it's off or on," Jasper finally gasped, clutching her side and nudging her friend lightly with her foot.

"It's on," Odette said, relenting. "But he's on probation."

"Why?"

"I'm eighty percent sure he's texting other girls."

"Yikes," Jasper said, all humor vanishing. "Babe? That's not okay."

"It is if it's just friendly and not sexual," Odette replied, shrugging.

"Did he tell you that?"

"Look, no one ends up with the person they're going out with at eighteen," Odette said, clearly telling herself this, not just Jasper. "I'm pretty sure Ma is getting ready to hand me the shop soon, and that's way more amazing than some boy."

"Amen," Jasper cried. "That's so exciting."

"Dad is still so set on me getting a degree."

"Okay, but you've wanted Trimmings since you could work a sewing machine."

"I have."

"You could do both?" Jasper pointed out, gently. "Get a degree or a diploma and have the shop waiting for you."

"Along with lots of student loans? Degrees aren't for everyone, Jazz, I'm going to be fine."

"I want you to be more than fine."

Something passed over Odette's face and it was a new expression. Jasper had once believed that she knew how to read Odette completely; that there was nothing mysterious about her oldest companion. No secrecy or illusion. A friendship that had once felt like a steady bridge now seemed like a narrow path with mist concealing what lay in the distance.

"What about you?"

Jasper blinked. "What about me?"

"Your degree," Odette said quietly. "You've not mentioned it since coming home. Not once. How's it going?"

"Fine," lied Jasper.

Odette was silent for a moment, still inspecting one of the gowns. Then, "It's so good to have you home, Jazz. Even if it's just for a bit. It's not the same here without you. I'm sorry, again. For not visiting. I only just got my license, and the bus never comes, and when it does, it takes forever. It's like they don't want us to escape this place!"

Jasper thought about making a flippant joke, one that would reference Lake Pristine's stubborn refusal to ever change in the slightest. However, she decided against it. "I'm sorry, too. For staying away. I will come back occasionally, though. While I'm studying."

She neglected to include a single grain of the real truth.

"Yeah, you'll come back over the holidays and we'll walk around the market and pretend like everything can pick up from where it was."

"It can for me," Jasper said, quietly. "I could go ten years without seeing you and nothing would change."

"You're loyal like that," Odette said, her tone both admonishing and admiring. "It's why I feel so guilty."

"About what?"

"About Craig and Sophie."

Jasper supposed that Sophie was the pale girl with the brown lipstick, the one Odette had been at the Arthouse with, two days before. "Why guilty?"

"I see them more than I see you! All the things we used to do together, I now do with them."

"I'm not mad at you for that," Jasper said, aghast. "Why would I be? You can't mope around town by yourself because I'm gone."

Odette finally turned to look at her friend and she shook her head while smiling. "You're always so good, Jazz. You always say the reasonable thing. You're allowed to be mad at me for kind of ghosting you for new people. You're allowed to say mean things. You're allowed to have, like, an emotional reaction."

"Odette." Jasper's voice was surprised and a little reproachful.

"It just hurts, you know. Every time I'll have to watch you drive off to the city after New Year is done. Every January, knowing it'll be months until you come back. Maybe even another eighteen. You're at university now, once Christine is married, you'll go back to that and who knows when you'll blow back into town." She looked surprised at her own candor and then threw her arms up. "See? This is what happens when I'm around you. I just get real honest."

Jasper nudged her jokingly. "It's the neurodivergence rubbing off on you."

"For sure."

"Leaving your hometown is normal," Jasper pointed out carefully, choosing not to tell her friend, her very dear friend, that university was actually a sore and secretive subject. Choosing not to reveal the horrid parties, the nasty dates and the snide professors. The rigid, infantilizing system that brought back the worst memories from school.

She kept all of that folded and rolled away inside of herself like a piece of parchment. The hard, painful things were scrawled across the page, but it was neatly tucked away where no one could read it.

"Guess I just really miss you," Odette said ruefully, with a weak smile. "Even when you're right in front of me. It's the weirdest thing."

Jasper smiled too. She wanted to tell Odette that the reason she always said the "reasonable thing" was because crossing an invisible, undefined but absolutely one hundred percent *there* social line with neurotypicals would always result in ostracization and exile. Every time. When she was overworked or stressed, her ability to predict social cues fell away and every interaction had the potential to feel as if she was walking on a landmine. She lacked the instinctive navigational ease that Odette possessed. Christine, too, when she chose to use it. So, Jasper's habits and her need to please were entrenched because of those fears and anxieties.

These days, everyone said they were accepting of neurodivergence. In theory. But Jasper knew better. She knew that if the social lines were ever crossed, if the complex and unwritten rules were ever broken, she would be cast out. She had worn the golden girl mask for so long and sometimes it was too frightening to imagine removing it. It splintered her face, it made her eyes tired, it dulled the taste of life, but it was easier to be accepted as a watered-down version of yourself than rejected for who you really were.

Being an autistic young woman came with so many sacrifices to the altar of "normal," just to purchase some peace.

Odette would understand. Odette always had.

But Jasper didn't feel like voicing these feelings. She was quite happy in her denial.

"I'm sorry," she offered up instead, unsure what she was apologizing for. Perhaps for leaving. For being secretive about why she was planning to go for good. For the hidden list of goodbyes. For having the audacity to even come back at all. For her communication skills, which often seemed to fail her when she needed them the most.

I'm sinking and I don't know how to call for help, Jasper thought. The words circled in her mind but did not dare come out of her mouth.

Odette was about to say something when the shop door opened, its little bell tinkling.

Sophie, Odette's new friend, entered and scowled as her eyes landed upon Jasper.

Jasper pushed away her feelings and smiled. "Hey. Nice to meet you, finally. I'm Jasper."

"Yeah," Sophie said. She dragged her eyes up and down Jasper's form. "I know."

"Small town," Jasper offered gingerly, still smiling. She took in the other girl's outfit with desperate speed, frantically looking for something to compliment. "I like your shoes—"

"Pardon?" Sophie interrupted, pulling a bud from her ear with exaggerated nonchalance before releasing an irritated sigh.

"Nice shoes," Jasper said, a little more loudly.

The other girl shrugged one shoulder and turned to Odette. "You ready to go?"

"Yep, lemme just grab my keys," Odette replied. As she did, she smiled warmly at Jasper. "Come with us."

"Uh, no," Sophie said sharply.

Jasper had to laugh softly at her reaction, while Odette threw the other girl a look of disbelief. "What? Jasper can come."

"It's a campaign," Sophie replied stiffly. She glanced swiftly at Jasper. "It would take too long to explain it to you. Sorry."

She did not sound sorry in the slightest, but Jasper nodded, regardless.

"Dungeons and Dragons," Odette told Jasper. "We've been meeting once a fortnight with Marcus and Danny whatshisname." She turned to address the other girl. "Jasper can come and hang out, Soph."

"That's okay," Jasper said quickly. "Sounds really fun, though. Have a good time."

"Yeah, sorry," Sophie said, still unapologetic by anybody's standards. "It's just . . . you don't strike me as a D&D female. You're more . . . girly."

"I've never played," acknowledged Jasper, still determined to be friendly and civil. Even though Sophie's use of the word "female" made her want to be violently ill. "But I'm sure lots of girly girls play."

There was only the tiniest hint of frost in her voice as she said the words.

"Nah," Sophie insisted, opting for another slow look up and

down. "It's not pink or glittery or anything to do with fashion so . . ."

Jasper raised her eyebrows, almost imperceptibly. She could be what this girl wanted her to be. Easily. The vapid mean girl with big breasts and long hair. She liked bright colors and fashion and things that sparkled. Therefore she couldn't possibly be intellectual or deep. She could play the role for Sophie, if the notion took her fancy.

But "I see," was all she said.

"I want you to come," Odette announced, as the three of them left the shop and Odette locked the door. "Please."

"It's all good, I have to get back to the house," Jasper said. "Can we have milkshakes soon, though?"

"A thousand percent."

"Oh?" Sophie said, with an impatient sigh. "We're already late."

"I'll call you," Odette called back to Jasper, as she slid into the passenger seat of Sophie's car. "Promise!"

"Can't wait," Jasper said, waving as the car drove off.

Odette was right, she thought. Watching your best friend drive away, when there was already distance between you both, really did feel horrendous.

Act One, Scene X:
At the Barre

Jasper was a little sweaty as she let all the girls into the ballet studio. It was situated at the end of Main Street, a small, windowless room with a tiny porch right on the edge of the town. Heavily mirrored inside, and somehow never warm despite all of the exercise that went on within, it was Andrea Montgomery's joy, with Christine being her pride.

And Jasper being the one to actually run the rehearsal.

She had just spent the last fifteen minutes trying to get Arthur and his little film crew settled into a corner where they could not be seen in any of the mirrors, but would also have a wide shot of the entire floor. They had ambushed her on her way into work, asking if the ballet studio could be part of the documentary, and she had told them that, as long as all of the dancers were all right with it, she could allow it. A part of her had hoped the kids would refuse them entry, but the company had all heartily consented via the group chat, excited by the prospect.

"Thanks, Jasper," Arthur whispered as she fixed her required microphone and checked that her bun was still intact.

"It's fine," she said briskly, swinging open the door. "Come in, Nutcracker hopefuls."

Nutcracker auditions: a brutal affair. Friends became enemies, toes would bleed and there were usually a few snotty tears. It was probably a positive thing that Jasper was overseeing them this year instead of Christine. Her older sister enjoyed the tears a little too much. Jasper did not believe in punishing people into being talented. She thought great performances either came from gentle coaxing or just leaving gifted people well enough alone.

"Warm up at the barre, please," she told the swarm of ballerinas, as they buzzed into the room and quickly took notice of the film crew tucked into one corner. "Ignore the boys, they're here for some B-roll."

She caught Arthur's eye and quickly looked away again. She hadn't had any expectation of seeing him when she'd donned her black leotard and pale pink rehearsal skirt. It felt as though they were fourteen again, she the lead ballerina, he helping backstage.

But even when they had been yelling at each other, she couldn't help remembering that there had been something about his eyes when he was animated that made her catch her breath. Even while they had been screaming themselves hoarse, she always noticed those eyes.

"All right, girls," she said, pulling herself back into the room. "Like I said, just ignore the cameras. Concentrate on your conditioning."

Hilly and Eve, certainly the two most confident dancers, positioned themselves in the prime position to be filmed. The others filed into their places accordingly. Only Grace Lancaster took a moment to find her spot, eyes on the floor and shoulders stiff.

Jasper knew her mother would not arrive until they were well into the auditions; she had not the patience for warming up.

Their rehearsal pianist started to play and Jasper watched the dancers as they prepped.

"Lovely feet, Eve," she said, projecting her voice over the music. "Open the shoulders, Dasha. Thank you. Now demi-plié. Good."

Grace glanced over at Jasper, her face nervous and her shoulders still too stiff. Jasper did an overexaggerated mime of taking a breath and Grace smiled, accepting the silent reminder. She relaxed into the movements a little more.

"Looking lovely, everyone," Jasper called as they neared the end of the barre work. "Thank you for showing up and keeping focused."

Andrea Montgomery arrived as soon as they moved to the floor. She was wearing her rehearsal skirt and carrying her cane. *Nutcracker* auditions meant business and she was here in full ballet mistress mode.

"Are we Clara today?" Andrea asked, addressing Jasper and surveying the room.

"Clara and Sugar Plum Fairy," Jasper confirmed, handing her the clipboard with everyone's names and numbers. "Want me to start?"

"No, I have it."

"Of course." Jasper complied, moving back a little so that her mother could attend to the girls.

"This December's *The Nutcracker*," Andrea said slowly, and with salient solemnity, "has to be the best we've ever done. I can have only the best. Okay? I can't have any weak links this season, not if these lovely boys are going to film parts of it and let the whole world see. I can have only the most committed, the most serious and the most brilliant company this year."

Eve and Hilly exchanged knowing looks and Grace checked to see if her feet were still in first position.

"So—" Andrea hit the floor with her cane—"let us begin."

The girls were put through their paces, Andrea going full Balanchine on some of them, which made Jasper wince. While Hilly and Eve were clearly the best, technically, Jasper could not keep her eyes from Grace. Although the young girl's movements were not as regimented and precise as the other two, there was so much passion in her performance. Her entire body told a story. Jasper found herself caring less about the technique while she fell in love with her enthusiasm and emotion. Jasper watched her move across the studio floor, enraptured. The character was alive in Grace. She was wearing a leotard, tights and some very tattered shoes, but she might as well have been dressed in the costume. She was perfect.

There were red faces and damp bangs when it was all over. Andrea revealed nothing, her expression blank. Jasper could see the girls all trying to gauge her mother's thoughts, hands on hips and torsos bent over as they caught their breath.

"Call-backs for Clara and Sugar Plum Fairy tomorrow," Andrea finally barked, sliding a written list of names to Jasper.

She examined it, rolling her eyes as she felt the camera zooming in behind her to get a shot. Eve. Hilly. Piper. Bryce. Jasper felt something steely inside of her. Something defiant.

"We have the boys all cast, besides the prince, so they will be present tomorrow too," Andrea informed the girls, while they retrieved their jackets and sipped on some water. "Jasper will now read the names of the girls we'll be seeing again. The rest of you can wait to hear if you've made company or not."

"And remember," Jasper added, "there is no shame in being in the company without a principal role. In fact, we need some of the strongest dancers for that because they always have to take on multiple parts as well as swing duties."

The girls all nodded, their eyes fixed upon the paper Jasper was holding.

"Tomorrow, we will be calling back—"

"Before anything else," Marcus spoke up all of a sudden, sounding apologetic, "we would love to film the call-backs, but this space is a little small. We would want to get in among the dancers, not just wide shots."

Andrea's face froze. Jasper almost smirked. No one interrupted Andrea Montgomery's dance classes. But the camera was on, and Jasper could see that very fact crossing her mother's mind.

"What about the ballroom in the Arthouse?" Arthur said. Jasper noted the speed of his suggestion. "It's got the right kind of floor and it is massive. We can film all we want and we'll have plenty of room."

"What about Bertie?" Andrea retorted, gesturing to their rehearsal pianist.

"I'll bring my keyboard," he said, shrugging.

"Yeah, and we have a sound system," Arthur added.

"Well, fine," Andrea said, gripping her cane and pursing her lips. "Now who are we calling back, Jasper?"

Jasper paused for a moment. Then: "We're calling back Eve, Hilly, Piper, Bryce . . . and Grace." She crumpled up the paper and fixed Andrea with a look that said *we will talk about it later*.

Jasper felt perfectly at home with her decision, especially when she saw Grace light up the whole room upon hearing her name. That kind of joy, that love for the art, that would never be the wrong decision.

Once the girls had filed out, Marcus approached her. "Was Grace's name on the list, Jasper?"

"Yes," she said crisply. "It was on *my* list."

The words made her think of the crumpled paper in her possession, her own personal list, the one marked and marred by her many planned ends and goodbyes.

"She's only just got enough technique for the party scene," Andrea said flatly. "She's not a principal dancer."

Arthur loudly cleared his throat and Jasper noticed that the camera was still rolling. She looked into the lens for a fleeting moment and then pulled her eyes away quickly. She hadn't given much thought to the short film or what it would end up looking like, but she was not sure if she wanted her mother to be any part of it. Andrea Montgomery was someone who deeply valued reputation, without understanding how vexing she could be to the average person.

"Not a principal dancer *yet*," Jasper said loudly, eyeing her mother carefully. "But she has better storytelling skills than any of the others. And that's what people really pay to see."

"They pay to see excellence. You know that better than anyone."

Jasper stifled a flinch. "I'm calling her back."

Andrea's eyes narrowed, but she still refused to unleash her true opinions while the two boys were there.

But once they had locked up the studio, she descended upon her daughter.

Jasper could see Arthur Lancaster lingering on the road, watching her. She felt hideously raw, as if he could see all of her family's indoor parts. The pieces that families are supposed to keep behind closed doors and away from prying eyes.

"Jasper, it's cruel to give the child false hope."

"It's a ballet performance, Mum. It's not that deep."

Andrea glared at her. It was as though Jasper had said something blasphemous. "It is *The Nutcracker*."

"And it will be excellent. All of those other girls will be at call-backs, too. All of your favorites. I just really want to see her work with a prince, that's all. And you told me I had to take an active part in rehearsals this season. Well, that's what I'm doing."

As they made their way into town, Andrea Montgomery whistled at the young man a few yards ahead of them. His hunched shoulders stiffened even more and he turned at the noise.

"What is that film you're making then, Mr. Lancaster?"

Jasper felt shy as they walked with Arthur into town, her mother making conversation to be polite. A rarity.

"It's my dad's old camera," Arthur said, the gruffness in his tone settled at a comfortable seven rather than its usual ten. "It's a documentary about Lake Pristine. The National Archives are holding a contest for films about small towns. I'm just dabbling."

"Well, make sure you get plenty of content about our *Nutcracker*."

"I will, ma'am."

"Because I don't know how to do any of that social media rubbish, so some proper footage would be good for marketing purposes."

"I'll try my best."

"Your father's camera you said?"

"Yes, Mrs. Montgomery."

Andrea paused and then spoke with a softer tone. "We all miss him."

Jasper's eyes flashed to Arthur's. He was already looking at her. Eye contact felt too intimate for her.

She broke the connection.

They had reached the town and Jasper smiled at all of the stalls set up for the winter fair. It had started as a German market but now contained a plethora of vendors selling all kinds of things, from food to jewelry to tarot cards. She stopped at Mrs. Heywood's. The older woman had a large display of pine cones, which had little pieces of ribbon attached to them.

"Want one?" she asked Jasper, eyes wide with excitement at a potential customer.

"What's the gimmick?" Jasper replied, humoring her.

"You write your beloved's name on it and I'll hang it somewhere in town for them to find."

"What a waste of money," her mother murmured, pulling the fur collar of her coat tightly around her long and slender neck. Arthur made a quiet noise of agreement.

"I'll take one," Jasper said brightly, ignoring them both. Arthur moved away to talk to Mr. Friars, who was selling roasted chestnuts.

"Excellent," fizzed Mrs. Heywood. "And the name?"

"Well, I don't have a beloved," Jasper admitted, laughingly. "Can I put my best friend?"

She could feel her mother watching her in disapproval.

"Of course," Mrs. Heywood obliged. "Odette, it is." She didn't even need to ask.

Jasper handed her the money and wished her a good evening, the woman's cheery demeanor making Jasper smile all the wider.

These were the moments that made her love Lake Pristine. When she didn't feel the heavy weight of her family's expectations, the town was a place of warmth and kindness, a place a person could put down roots in, where they could learn how to grow.

If only her family could be happy for her change of direction in life, perhaps Lake Pristine could have stayed her home. A part of her longed for the possibility.

"This place really does turn into a social experiment when the cold comes in," her mother said drearily as they headed for home.

But it wasn't a possibility.

"Nah," Jasper said softly, allowing herself a small rebellion. "I like it."

Act One, Scene XI:
At the Bar

Arthur was meeting Saffron at Junior's, the only bar in Lake Pristine. He knew it was probably not every girl's dream to meet with a date who was still thinking about the ballerina he had been filming earlier.

Luckily the bar was busy and noisy enough to distract him as he arrived.

Arthur was just telling himself that this whole ordeal was a good idea and that he was going to enjoy himself, when he spotted Saffron already in a booth with Marcus.

"Arthur!"

He was forced to make his way over. The bar had been the backdrop for a few memories in his life. His father used to sneak him in with Henry when his older brother was just shy of eighteen. He once had to come and rescue his mother from a really bad date, before she met Brian. Then, when she and Brian had become official, they had thrown their engagement party there.

His father's wake had been there, too.

He was about to greet Saffron and tell his best friend to disappear when she said, "Marcus said he would pay our tab if we let him film us, so I've agreed."

Marcus gave him that same apologetic grimace that he had been sporting during their earlier session at the ballet studio. It was starting to wear thin.

"I don't think so," Arthur said icily, glaring at his cousin.

"Come on," Marcus poked. "I think viewers want to see our director within the story we're telling."

"I don't."

"Too late," Saffron said. "Sit down."

Arthur hesitated and wondered if it would be too awful for him to just leave. In the end, he settled inside the booth, casting Marcus a look of loathing but dutifully handing over his camera for his cousin to wield. He hated public scenes. He wanted to capture them, not star in them. But something told him not to press the matter.

Saffron ordered some of the most expensive things on the menu and Arthur did not stop her. If he was going to document this whole thing, Marcus was free to pay through the nose for the pleasure. Arthur ordered a non-alcoholic beer—some fancy craft brewery concoction, with a ridiculous name: Dumb Blonde.

"What took you so long to ask me out then?" Saffron demanded, snatching her glass out of the waiter's outstretched hand and looking at Arthur expectantly. He was startled. The waiter gave him a look of disbelief at the grabbing they had both just witnessed and Arthur wondered if the behavior was a misguided attempt at flirtation.

"Thanks," he told the waiter dutifully, as he gave Arthur his own drink. "Um . . ." He was so aware of the camera and the microphone. He realized with a sinking feeling that this was what he had been putting other townspeople through of late.

"Was it seeing me at the Lakehouse?" she prodded.

The Lakehouse. The party.

When she wore the black dress and fell asleep with a cat on her lap.

Her.

That her.

This was a different her. A her that actually liked him.

Arthur shook his head and blinked. "Well, actually my brother thought it would be a good idea for me to go on a date." He knew instantly by her reaction that it was a mistake so he rushed to clarify. "I mean, I wanted to. I did. I'm not so great at this, but Henry encouraged me. So, I did."

She nodded, barely satisfied.

He asked her about her job. She said she hated it. He asked after her family and she complained about her mother earning less money and needing more care. Arthur felt a little at sea, unsure of a safe topic of conversation.

"How is Christine's wedding coming along? Has your sister said anything?" he finally managed to ask, knowing that it would at least be relevant to the documentary—as Christine and her wedding were its backdrop.

Saffron laughed, knowingly. "Have you got your invitation?"

"I have, actually," he smiled. "I'm shocked to have been asked."

The invitations had arrived that morning. One for all three of the Lancaster children, and one for their mother and Brian. Henry had made a joke about Jasper forcing Christine to invite all of them and Arthur had scowled. The invites were cream cards embossed with rose gold. They smelled of lavender.

Arthur had spotted many townspeople sporting them boastfully earlier that afternoon, as if they had been invited to some exclusive coronation rather than a local girl's wedding.

"Well, the whole town will be there. Chrissy does love a lavish affair."

"Looks like she's going to get it," Arthur allowed.

"We're meant to be having the hen night at your cinema."

"Yes, the ballroom is booked. I'll do my best to give you all a good night."

Arthur realized how that sounded and he winced. Marcus snorted, but Saffron was too busy clicking her fingers for the waiter to take another drink order from her. She had not heard him.

The night carried on. Arthur just chose to ask Saffron lots of questions about herself and she was more than happy to answer each one with a full monologue. He could tell by her occasional flurry and wink for the camera that there was a lot of performance going on, but he didn't mind. It suited her and seemed to make her happy.

"Can you believe Jasper is back in town?" Arthur asked the question without thinking.

Saffron smarted slightly. "Can I believe it?"

"I mean," Arthur was not sure how to articulate his thoughts, "time kind of works differently here. It feels like she's been gone forever. Instead of a year and a half."

"Well," Saffron shrugged, her demeanor suddenly quite distant. "Her sister's getting married. That's probably why she's here for a longer spell. I thought she'd be back last Christmas, but no. My sister said Christine was secretly heartbroken, but you know her. Never in public."

"Yeah. Do you remember school with her? With Jasper?"

"Not really," Saffron said snippily. "It was a long time ago."

Arthur had memories. Arthur remembered how much the teachers had loved her. He remembered her laughter in the art classroom as she washed everyone's wet paintbrushes. Her brilliant set designs for the school musicals.

"She's always so well-dressed," he remarked pensively. "Like, even in casual clothes, she's always been stylish."

He was not aware that Saffron and Marcus were watching him in disbelief.

"I always thought she hung out with a shitty group of people," Marcus piped up. "Ross, Adam, those guys were all assholes."

"They were my friends, too," Saffron said sharply, throwing Marcus a look of disgust.

"But Jasper was always nice enough, I suppose," Marcus continued. He looked at Arthur. "I know you and her have been at odds for years, but I always thought she was okay."

"At odds?" Saffron asked. Her voice was hungry for gossip.

"I was a bit gruff with her during our younger years," Arthur admitted, trying not to reveal his very real regret. "She's so famous for being lovely to everyone in Lake Pristine. Except me. I ruined that for myself."

"Why do you care?"

Saffron's question disarmed Arthur. He suddenly looked at her, disturbed to see how irritated she was. "I . . . I don't—"

"Like, why would you care if Jasper Montgomery liked you or not?" she repeated, folding her arms and leaning across the booth with a piercing gaze.

"I don't care."

The words fell flat and lifeless upon the small table between the three of them while the camera whirred in the background.

"I don't care," Arthur eventually repeated, hoping that the second chorus of his dismally unconvincing theme song would be catchier. He was so aware of the camera lens bearing down on him now, he felt pressured to continue and so he just began to speak rapidly. "I obviously don't see myself why she's such a golden girl around these parts. And I think she needs to stand up to her family more!"

"Well, because she's helped out every old person in this town," Marcus suggested. "Or because she was always so great with your dad, especially when he started getting ill. Oh, and she founded that loneliness and good mental health walk at the community center—"

"All right," barked Arthur. "I know, I know."

Silence fell and he suddenly realized that Marcus now possessed footage of them arguing about Jasper, with Arthur very much on the offensive and Marcus on the defensive.

"Everyone always wants to talk about Jasper," Saffron finally said quietly, pushing her hair out of her eyes and looking despondent.

Arthur shook himself and cleared his throat. "Do you want another drink?"

After a third round, Marcus started asking questions again.

"Saff, what is it you like about Arthur?"

"Dear God," Arthur growled, leaning away from the table and scowling.

Saffron laughed. Hard. "Oh, I like lots of things about Arthur. I like that he's six five."

"Four," Arthur corrected under his breath.

"He has big hands," she said, taking a considerable swig of her drink and eyeing the camera lens like it was a third person. "And . . .

I don't know. He always has this strong and silent thing going on. Broody. Sexy. I like it."

Arthur wanted the seat beneath him to splinter apart so that he could fall through it and become so bedeviled with cuts from the wood, he would be able to escape. He looked across the bar, which had become busier as the night had grown darker and colder.

"What do you like about Saffron, Arthur?"

Arthur opened his mouth and tried to formulate some kind of reply, but the words parted ways with him. Odette and Jasper had just walked through the front entrance. They were both dressed up, hair and make-up done. Jasper was wearing leather pants and a sequin top and Arthur found himself staring at her exposed upper back. It was a night out for the two of them. Or they were meeting someone? That thought needled at Arthur.

"Art?"

Arthur watched Steve, the bartender, greet the two of them with great enthusiasm. Jasper said something that made the man throw his head back and laugh loudly. Then she playfully pinched his cheek.

Suddenly Arthur wanted to be somewhere else. Anywhere else.

"I like that Saff knows what she wants," he eventually said, answering his friend's question with quiet finality. "I respect that. I like people who are direct. She knows who she is. She's not a people pleaser."

He could feel their confusion as he continued to watch Jasper. So, he pulled his gaze back to the table.

"This was really nice," he said stiffly. "But I think I need to head back to the cinema. Got some inventory to do. Thank you for a lovely evening, Saff."

He rose to his feet, pulling on his father's tattered old coat.

"Are we doing this again?" Saffron asked. "Without your little chaperone here?"

"Yes," he blurted out. "Sure. Fine."

He really did need the cold air on his face. The bar suddenly felt too crowded. He would have to walk by Jasper and Odette to get out, but they were so into their conversation, he was sure that they would not notice him. His hand reached for the door when—

"Arthur Lancaster!"

He stopped. Turned on his heel. Offered a tight smile to Odette, who had called out.

Jasper looked beautiful. In the dim light, her top was casting little sparks all around the room, little flecks of brightness.

Arthur didn't know what it was about her. He didn't know what it had been, when he had stood in that backstage wing, watching her put on a show for everyone. Making her feet bleed and her muscles ache just so a few hundred people could feel some joy.

It was so much easier when she was not around, when she was in the city.

Sometimes, when he was hungry or tired, he would go into a new kind of being. Too tired to even notice it anymore. Too hungry to think about eating.

That's what it felt like when Jasper was away.

He had always rolled his eyes at his mother. Before Brian, she would go out with man after man. Arthur could never for the life of him work out what she saw in any of them. He thought relationships were just things people did when they got bored. He had never believed in needing other people for completion. That was not healthy.

But he was now starting to see that some people could feel like keys to doors inside you that had never been unlocked before.

"Grace did really well at auditions today."

His little sister's name pulled him back into the room. Jasper was talking to him. Just being polite. Her face expectant.

"Thank you," he said. And he meant it. "She'll be so pleased you said so."

"She's sweet," Odette said, thumping her fist against his arm. "Want a drink?"

He glanced back at Marcus and Saffron. "I better not. Just left my date alone with my new film partner."

"Oh, you called Saff," Jasper said, sounding delighted. It made Arthur feel wretched, how positive she was about it. "Good for you."

"Yeah," Odette said sardonically, tilting her head to the side and eyeing him. "Good for you, Arthur. Just how painful was it?"

Jasper bumped her in admonishment. "You can't talk, look at Craig."

Arthur felt color on his neck. He muttered something about getting back to the Arthouse, the same dull excuse he had given his cousin and Saffron, and then he ducked out of the bar.

Winter was fully settled in Lake Pristine, the wind frosty as it hit him in the face.

"Arthur?"

It was as if her voice had some invisible chord to his spine, making him stop in his tracks at any given moment.

"Yup?"

Her sequins did not shine in the darkness of the evening, but she did. She just always did, somehow.

"Are you going to film the call-backs tomorrow? Henry said it was all right for us to film in the Arthouse ballroom, like you suggested."

The large function room at his family's cinema. "Oh. Sure. Yeah, we can film."

"I know you're not making a documentary on small-town ballet companies," Jasper went on, smiling sheepishly. "But maybe it will provide some good B-roll?"

Arthur wasn't sure what sort of story he was telling anymore, or of his role in it.

Since his father had died, Arthur knew he had much more than a chip on his shoulder. It was easier to deal with this slightly kooky town if he didn't take it too seriously. He could cover up negative feelings by fixing someone's fence or oiling their door. Then, they didn't see the caution tape and the barbed wire that he had encased himself in. He felt so effortlessly at ease and so comfortable behind the armor he'd made, of eye rolls and flippant remarks. Maybe this film was his way of lashing out. Maybe he wanted to hold a mirror up to all of the town, one that was not—for once—adorned with twinkle lights and mistletoe.

But Jasper Montgomery was a rich girl who picked up the tab and gave away her cash. She would always check to see if the person on their own at the party was having a good time. She would let elderly men tell her all about their youth, and when she focused her entire attention on them while they did, you would come to realize you had never seen someone truly listen before. She would instantly pretend to make friends with the girl at the bar who was being pestered by a drunken letch. Then, two minutes later, they actually *were* friends. She was popular for exactly the right reasons.

She was beautiful.

And she saw his little sister. Saw her vulnerability and her bravery and her grief. She did not pity Grace. She did not avoid her. Instead, she gave her a call-back to a ballet Grace had been obsessing over for months. Arthur wondered if she even knew what that would mean to his sister.

He wanted to say all of this. But he just—"Yeah, that would be good."—could not do it.

She smiled. "Great. We start at six."

And then she was gone. And he would walk home alone.

He watched through the window as Jasper ordered a cup of tea. She giggled as the bartender rolled his eyes at the request, then thanked him profusely when he obliged her.

Arthur could not stay here, in this tiny town, and keep feeling like this. Grief was bad enough. Unrequited whatever this was, it was too much.

Act One, Scene XII:
Land of Sweets

The following day, Jasper arrived at Trimmings to find Christine and her bridesmaids already arguing. Odette was sitting with her legs tucked under herself on the cash desk, head in her hands.

"I thought it would be more of a salmon," Rebecca said on an exhale, holding up her dress and wincing. "Chris, you said salmon."

"The website said salmon," Christine hissed, putting her hair up with the speed of the veteran ballerina that she truly was. "Don't start complaining about the color when we need to check the fit."

"Never fear," Jasper said calmly. "I can alter anything that's too tight or too loose, that's why I'm here."

Charlotte and Anna both beamed at her. Jasper liked them both, they were far too sensible to be friends with Christine, but there they were.

Jasper put her little seamstress toolbox next to Odette on the counter and hopped up to watch the fashion show. Odette was notably the superior modiste out of the pair, but she had only agreed to accommodate the fitting, not assist with it. She knew Christine's antics too well and her temper was not as even as Jasper's.

"So nice of Jazz to offer up alterations when she's not even allowed to be a bridesmaid," Odette said tartly. "Really generous of her."

"Get changed," Christine told her friends, ignoring Odette completely. "And tuck in your bra straps, I need to see the full effect."

As the bridesmaids moved to obey, the shop bell tinkled—signaling the arrival of Saffron. Jasper offered her a warm smile—one that was not returned.

"I'm here to get my sister. We're picking up Dad from the airport," Saffron told Odette when the latter looked bemused by her entrance.

"This may take longer than she first anticipated," Odette told Saffron.

The strapless dresses were made with pretty chiffon but they were definitely not salmon. They were blood orange. Jasper could sense that this appointment might take up the whole afternoon, so she quietly reminded Christine that she had call-backs to conduct at six.

"Hilly as Clara, Eva as Sugar Plum," Christine said, irritably. "Done. Easy."

Jasper pushed her hair out of her eyes and shrugged. "I don't see that yet."

Christine fixed her with a look of derision but said nothing more. They knew not to get into ballet matters, which were also family matters, in front of company.

Christine's friends sauntered back in from the dressing rooms. Anna's dress was too tight, Rebecca looked fine, but Charlotte needed hers brought in a little. Jasper picked up her measuring tape and got straight to work.

"So, Saff," Rebecca addressed her younger sister and jostled her dress, trying to get more comfortable. "How was your hot date with Mr. Gruff?"

Jasper's hands fumbled a little as she gathered up her clips. It *had* been a while since she had done any alterations.

"Well, I don't think he was overly keen on the camera filming the entire thing," replied Saffron, smiling a secret smile.

"Isn't it his film?" Odette asked, frowning.

"Yes, but it was Marcus shooting. Arthur didn't seem that happy about it."

"Embarrassed to be seen with you?" taunted Christine.

Saffron scoffed. "Hardly."

"He's really good-looking, but I don't know if there's a lot going on in his head," Christine added, settling on the floor and scrolling through her phone.

"Look who's talking," muttered Odette.

"Also, he's been hung up on someone else for ages."

Christine said the words almost inaudibly, but they were loud enough for Jasper to glance across at her older sister. Christine did not look up from her scrolling but her thumb did pause on the screen for a millisecond. Jasper waited to see if her sister would expand on the statement, but no one else had heard, it seemed.

"He's just got something sexy about him," Saffron went on, oblivious. Jasper was measuring Charlotte's bust while the other girl spoke, wishing she were invisible. "He was pretty hostile to Marcus and I kind of got, I don't know, I kind of got protective vibes from him, you know? Like he really wanted to get me alone but was too polite to say anything."

Anna, Charlotte and Rebecca all made noises of supportive delight. Christine did not look up. Jasper stared at her sister. Christine was the one who had told Jasper to arrange this strange little courtship. She was the one who had told Jasper to give Arthur the message.

"He seemed pretty eager to escape the bar when we arrived,"

Odette said jauntily. Jasper threw her friend a look that told her to behave, but it only made the mischief in Odette's face strengthen. "Couldn't stop him from running out the door."

Jasper sensed Charlotte tensing up at the sudden awkward silence while she was measuring, so she quickly changed the subject.

"Should we get Char a sash or something, Chris?" she queried. "Something to accentuate her lovely figure?"

Christine looked up and gave Charlotte the once-over. "No."

Anna offered Jasper a small eye roll, one that said, "What is she like?" and Jasper smiled back. She moved to Charlotte's waist.

"Are you seeing him again?" asked Rebecca, picking up the conversation once more.

"Oh, for sure." Saffron responded with cool certainty. "Without the cameras this time."

Jasper recited some measurements to Odette, who noted them down.

"How's college, Jazz?"

Jasper glanced up at Anna, who had asked the question. "Oh, fine. Early days, you know."

Lies. Massive lies.

The lies were so easy. But then she had always been good at hiding.

No one had the slightest suspicion of just how close to drowning she really was. There were moments when she thought her dad and Odette might just have an inkling. But then they would blink and it would pass. They thought, *Not Jasper. She would never. She's our good girl. She clears her plate, she gives up her seat on the train and she would absolutely never lie to us about something this important.*

In the silent hours, when the insomnia was a haunting, taunting, unwanted intruder, Jasper wanted to scream. She had no one to touch. Her friend was behind thick glass, her family had never tolerated dips in mental health. Jasper had taken to sitting down in the shower. She wanted to stay in love with Lake Pristine but the harder she hid, the more difficult that was.

There was another late-night film that night at the Arthouse and she intended to be there. Alone with the escapism. In denial about the yawning night.

The appointment did not overrun, mostly thanks to Odette. She was a strict timekeeper and had little tolerance for Christine's protagonist syndrome. Jasper kissed her friend goodbye, bid farewell to Christine and her bridesmaids and then dashed off toward the Arthouse for the call-backs. She was wearing a vintage denim jacket over her full-body black leotard and a pale pink skirt. She wrestled her hair into a bun as she entered the lobby.

Arthur Lancaster was there with Marcus, both of them fussing over their camera setup.

"Sorry. I'm here," Jasper puffed, striding into the foyer. "Can we prep?"

Bertie poked his head around the door and waved. His keyboard was already in position and his sheet music was out.

Marcus was pleased with the location, gushing about how much room they would have. They all moved into the vast, beautiful room and Jasper automatically straightened her spine. She slipped off her jacket and dumped it into a corner, sliding to the floor to put her shoes on. Arthur leaned against the wall by the door and watched her.

"If you're trying to make me nervous, it won't work," she informed him, not looking up from her task.

"Are those the ones that hurt?" he said in return, his deep voice echoing slightly in the massive room.

"No," she chuckled. "I'm a long time out of pointe shoes."

"Do you dance at college?"

It was an innocent question. The college had plenty of dance clubs and societies. But Jasper had not been able to find the courage to join one. She had gone to one meeting and realized she was a coward. Everyone else knew each other. They had inside jokes and nicknames. They had done absolutely nothing to her that would give her any reason to feel unwelcome or unwanted.

And yet she had.

She did not love dance enough to be brave in that place.

"No, I don't really dance anymore," she said matter-of-factly.

She could feel him watching her as she rose to her feet and stretched her ankles. It was odd, she had once been completely at ease in front of hundreds of people. Being onstage had been the safest place in the world. But being in front of a handful of people had always made her feel so exposed.

Being in front of disapproving, taciturn Arthur Lancaster always felt like being caught out. Or X-rayed.

She watched him surreptitiously while warming up and stretching. He was good-looking. Objectively. Christine would never have said it if it weren't empirically so. Dark hair, dark eyes. Tall. He was nothing like the boys that her mother had made her partner with while dancing in her own ballet days. He made her feel short, standing next to him. That was certainly a new feeling.

If he smiled, really smiled, he would probably be dazzling. She was certainly not in the habit of telling people to smile, particularly as she despised it when men would yell the command at her while she was walking in the street and minding her own business. But she would like to see Arthur's smile.

His hands were big, she noticed. She had a sudden vision of them on her ribs.

It was enough of an image to make her shake her head roughly, revolted at her own ridiculousness.

She smiled in relief as some of the girls appeared in the doorway. She could hear some of the boys' voices behind them.

"Start warming up," she ordered.

Grace Lancaster materialized. Curls tightly scraped into a bun and rehearsal clothes on, shoes too. She slipped into the room and cracked a wide, delighted smile when she saw her brother standing next to Bertie.

Arthur Lancaster's entire demeanor softened as he gave his little sister a discreet wave.

Jasper glanced away, touched.

"I want to run some of the party scene," she told the whole group once everyone had arrived and warmed up. "I'll be looking at your acting as much as your technique."

The scene was supposed to be a holiday party and while Hilly and Eve had perfect technique, their facial expressions were stiff and unyielding. Grace, meanwhile, threw her whole body into the scene and played an excitable Clara so brilliantly, Jasper caught herself smiling.

"Your count was off during that last bit, by the way," Hilly said to Grace when they all took a break. "Just letting you know."

Grace lifted her water bottle to her lips, looking downcast.

"Hilly," Jasper said sharply. "Why are you looking at what Grace is doing when you should be focusing on your own audition?"

Hilly flushed red and flounced over to her dance bag to get a drink.

"While we're breaking, let me just say this, everyone," Jasper said, addressing the whole room. "The leads in this show will have way more than choreography to think about. You'll be leading the company. I don't need people who are going to throw a strop or sigh or roll their eyes. I don't need people who will put down their castmates. I need people who will lift everyone around them up. That's what it takes to lead a company. So, think on that."

The room was completely silent, only the sound of Jasper's feet as she walked back to stand by the piano. She could feel the camera on her, but it was nowhere near as intense as Arthur Lancaster's eyes on her face.

"Grace and Vic, can I see you two do the scene, please?"

Grace as Clara and Vic as the young prince were quite charming. They worked well together. But Jasper could sense Grace's shyness at having to play opposite a boy.

"Really good, guys. Vic, can you make sure you extend all the way to the tips of the fingers? Carry that movement through the whole arm. And Grace, a quick note on Clara."

Grace nodded enthusiastically, eyes wide.

Jasper took a moment, lifting up the prop they were using as the nutcracker toy in the opening act. "So, Clara is surrounded by lots of other people her age on this night. They all think this nutcracker is ugly. They mock her for liking it. But she doesn't care about that. She sees his true nature."

Jasper looked down at the wooden toy. It was the same one she herself had held when she had danced the role, years before.

"It's not that she sees potential," she said quietly. "Or some imagined version of him. She sees him. All his nobility, all of his intelligence. His real heart. She sees it all."

As she gripped the prop, she felt a pang for all of the waste. All of the somedays that somehow turned into maybes. The beauty of a ballet that melted away into nothingness, the farther that she fled from Lake Pristine.

"It's the promise of other people," she said softly. "The possibility that you don't have to be on your own anymore. Clara's independent. She's intelligent. She's all of the things girls are told to be. But she also wants a friend. She wants a companion. Someone to break apart the loneliness."

She stared down at the old prop, a familiar friend in a strange, bygone way. Silly. It was silly.

"There are so many people at this party," she added. "But she can't be herself around any of them."

"This is a lot," murmured Vic, frowning slightly. It shook Jasper out of her reverie and she threw both dancers a wry smile.

"So, dance that," she said, offhandedly. Breaking the strange tension that had gathered about them like a fog. "Dance all of the things Clara is thinking and feeling, as well as the steps. You can do it, I know it."

She stepped back to let them perform the scene. She could feel her smile become a beam as Grace fully embraced the changes and relaxed more into the demonstration, moving lightly and precisely, but also really acting the part. Her dancing allowed Jasper to envision the luscious set, the candlelight and the tapers. The snow falling outside.

Grace's leg swept up into the air like a child throwing a handful of snow up over their head. She became her name. She extended her arms in a way Jasper almost envied. She was so open and so vulnerable, showing love and a need to be loved in every turn and every glance. It brought a lump into Jasper's throat. A touch of shame here. A flickering of a question there. She was humbled by Grace's talent and her ability to reveal her heart.

The best kind of dancing told a person a thousand stories and made you wish for just one more. Grace gave Jasper that. It was sensational.

She was Jasper's Clara.

Act One, Scene XIII:
Jack Lemmon

Arthur was clearing away the dinner plates and trying not to smile too hard. Grace was completely crackling with adrenaline and joyous energy. She had described every single moment of the call-back in minute detail, and Arthur had given up on trying to remind her that he had, in fact, been there. That he had captured it on film. That he had promised their overexcited mother a copy of said footage over the phone mere moments after the call-back was finished.

"Art." Grace took a moment to stop gushing and shook her head in wonder. "Jasper's just so *nice*. You know?"

"Yes, bean," he concurred. "I know. But you're not giving your-self enough credit. You're really good."

She blushed but did not fight the smile. "Thanks, Art. But she was better. I mean, you know that! You were backstage all those times she danced. She's just the best. And she could be a total bitch if she wanted, but she's not. She never is! She's the best." She was beaming at him in determination, almost challenging him to deny it.

"You're the best, kid."

"Arthur!"

The use of his whole name shocked him a tad. "Grace?"

"Say it! Say she's the best. You know she is, you think she is, too, Art. Come on!"

Arthur blinked and stumbled on his words. "Am I being bugged here? Is there a microphone under this table?"

Grace smiled at his teasing but she grew serious. "Art. I mean it."

"She's great, bean. She was a great dancer and now she's a great leader. When she goes back to school and leaves us all again, don't miss her too much, 'kay?"

Grace floated off to her bedroom, while Arthur scrubbed the dinner plates, and he felt as though a weight had been lifted. Whatever the cast list eventually said, Grace's confidence had not been this healthy since before their dad had passed away. Arthur felt a natural high from seeing her so changed.

He was wiping down the table when the door burst open and Henry marched in, beelining for the fridge.

"Closed?" Arthur asked, glancing out of the door that connected their house to the cinema.

"Nope, Agnes is closing," Henry said.

Arthur knew that he should leave it. Work/life balance and all that. But Agnes, lovely as she was, never remembered to cash up properly.

"Art, are you serious?" Henry called after his brother in disbelief, as Arthur grabbed his lanyard and headed into the cinema.

Agnes was sweeping when he reached the concession stand.

"Agnes, I can close if you want to get home," he told her. She was his mother's age and he did try to avoid giving her later shifts. She didn't even live in Lake Pristine.

"Oh, Arthur, I appreciate it," she said brightly. "Thank you."

"Is anyone in?" he asked, jerking his head toward the two screen doors.

"Just one in screen two," she replied, already heading for the small staffroom. "Some girl watching the old black-and-white film on her own."

"That was tonight?"

Agnes nodded.

Arthur pushed his hair back out of his face, silently cursing himself for letting it get longer than his usual short, back and sides. There had been other things on his mind.

He checked the running time. It had twenty minutes left. So, he quickly cashed up. Recorded wastage. Busied himself in the lobby and locked up every door possible, besides the front. He walked off nervous energy on the red carpeted floor, glancing from twinkling crystal lights to the darkness outside.

He was somewhat stupidly organizing the popcorn boxes when the doors finally opened and she exited the screen. He stared openly, feeling ridiculous.

She finally looked over at him and he cleared his throat. "Good film?"

She smiled, a little sadly. "Very good. Ever seen it?"

"No. Is it actually about an apartment or is it just called that?"

"It's actually about an apartment."

"Oh."

He turned his back, feeling like an idiot. He was giving her ample time to run out of the building and away from the emotionally illiterate cinema manager. But when he turned around, she was still there.

"Thank you for giving my sister the time of day."

She looked up, surprised. "Of course."

"Not everyone does. She . . ." He battled with how to phrase it. "She's the best person I know. But she's easy to pick on. According to some people."

He waited for her to feign confusion, but instead, she nodded sagely.

"I had that a lot too."

He almost sputtered. Then he fixed her with a look of reproach. "No."

"Yes."

"Sorry, no. Nobody bullies Jasper Montgomery. No one would dare."

"They absolutely did," she said, glaring at him. But with a little humor in her eyes. "Maybe not here, not in Lake Pristine. But at college, yes. Maybe because they could just read that Kick Me sign that was sort of faded on my forehead. Or maybe it's some kind of scent they can pick up on."

"You sure it wasn't because you were a terror?"

"Well," she grinned but glanced down at her hands, suddenly a little fragile. "Maybe. I don't know. I've never tried being a terror. I think being neurodivergent was enough for some of them."

In an instant, Arthur felt like a complete ass. He had not thought for a moment how getting singled out for being different might make some people smell blood. He couldn't imagine anyone disliking Jasper, but he had been reminded that he did not actually know her life. He didn't know what that diagnosis meant for her. What kind of nonsense people had given her because of it.

"There's still this idea that only boys can really be neuro-divergent," she went on, more to herself than to Arthur. "You know? Like, if you're a girl and you're neurologically different, then the margins just get even narrower. So, you step outside them and accept it might get ugly."

He could only stare at her.

"Sorry!" She looked horrified all of a sudden. "I don't know why I said all of that."

Arthur imagined that she had needed to say that to someone for a few years. He wanted to say something profound or reassuring in return.

"Just be glad I'm not filming right now," he replied, gingerly.

She smiled wanly. "You'll just use your security footage, will you?"

He inhaled with a slight laugh. "No, you're good."

"Oversharing," she said apologetically, splaying her hands. "It's a trait I'm trying to keep a lid on. Sorry."

She was heading for the exit and it felt as though a really great song was beginning to fade out, and he just wanted to listen a little longer.

"Yikes."

She staggered back inside and, as Arthur automatically stepped forward, he could see why. The skies had opened and snow was striking down on Lake Pristine. Not the usual gentle kind that fell softly in the December afternoons, or the kind that had welcomed her home after being gone for so long. This was aggressive.

"Do you have an umbrella?"

Her eyes were wide and she was not wearing a coat.

"I'll drive you."

"Oh, no," she protested strongly, but he had already retrieved his keys.

He did not have time to be embarrassed about how messy his old car was as he opened the passenger door for her. He climbed into the driver's seat and it only took a few tries for him to start the ancient thing. As they set off, Arthur hastily tried to turn the heating on.

"It's really okay," she said amiably. "It's not that cold."

But she was hugging herself and pressing back against the seat really hard.

Arthur pressed down on the pedal and yanked the handbrake. He punched and pummeled the old heating system until some warmth started to fill the car.

He was a little out of breath by the time this display was over. When he turned to glance at Jasper, she was laughing.

"Sorry," she snorted. "That was quite the show."

He smiled reluctantly and pulled away.

"So, is that Omar Sharif in the film you just saw?"

She pulled her long hair out of its messy updo and he was hit with a wave of orange scents for a moment. "No. Jack Lemmon."

"Is he better or worse?"

"I don't compare my men."

The car stalled very briefly and Arthur grabbed the wheel. "Oh."

"Let me tell you why Jack is so great," she said sunnily. "He's a nice guy. But, you know, not a Nice Guy."

Arthur stole another quick glance. "Is there a difference?"

"Oh, yes. The latter are only nice to girls in order to get with them. The former are genuinely good people."

"And Jack is genuinely good?"

"Yes. It radiates out of him."

"That sounds painful."

She smiled. "He's just such a good guy, and he puts himself through so much discomfort and ridicule. He doesn't stand up for himself enough. And you're watching him up there on the screen and you're pulling your hair out and screaming at him to tell everyone to go to hell. And he just won't."

"That also sounds . . . painful."

"Hey, it's your cinema. If you don't care for soppy old films, why are you running them?"

Arthur paused. Feeling a little numb. "It wasn't my idea. Dad mentioned doing it once. Long ago."

Silence fell, allowing just the groaning of the car to be audible. Then, "Sorry. I can't imagine how much you must miss him."

Arthur blinked fiercely and shrugged one shoulder. "Well. Yeah."

The trees flashed by them as they drove along the lonely road between the lake and the town. One bus stop. One road sign. One bench just by the side of the dirt for people to sit and watch the exits and entrances of the town.

"He had incredible taste in films," Jasper added softly. "I can't watch *Some Like It Hot* without thinking of him. That's another Jack Lemmon film. I'm going to be patronizing your cinema until Christine's wedding, I think."

"How's all that going?"

"Uh," she laughed dryly. "It's going."

"Fair enough."

When they reached the Lakehouse, Arthur parked and turned off the engine. But Jasper did not move to get out of the vehicle. They sat still for a moment in the quiet.

"I miss seeing your dad out and about in Lake Pristine."

When people talked about Arthur's father, it was not painful. It was more like the first breath after a deep plunge. He often wondered if some people were afraid to speak of Mr. Lancaster for exactly that reason. They did not know what it felt like.

"Yeah, I miss that, too."

Her eyes were shining as she spoke. "He got into town craft fair stuff, which is my favorite thing about this weird old place. The other day, when they were selling those pine cones? Telling people to write their favorite person's name on it? I thought, Mr. Lancaster would have loved this. He'd have bought hundreds. Put them all over town."

Arthur experienced a tight pang, because she was exactly right.

"He would have given the film some great material, too," he said, for some levity.

It worked, she beamed. "Yeah."

They sat together for another moment without speaking. His grief and her compassion side by side in an old car.

"Thanks for the ride," she finally said, opening the car door and nodding politely. "Saved me from hypothermia."

She was about to shut the car door when he asked, "You bought one, didn't you?"

She smiled graciously but looked bemused. "Bought one what?"

"A pine cone."

"Oh. Yeah!"

The unspoken question lingered for a second too long.

"I put Odette's name on it."

Arthur felt a strange relief and then something unidentifiable. "Of course."

"She's my rock, you know. If it weren't for her . . ."

He arched an eyebrow. "What?"

"Well." She laughed again, but it was a little hollow. When she continued to speak, it was with a breath of sadness. "Without her, I could walk right out of this town and never come back. And nobody would really notice. Or care."

Arthur stared at her, stupefied. It was not crass self-pity. She really believed what she had just uttered. He wondered if she was so unable to see all of the love people had for her. Perhaps she thought it was all superficial.

Before he could tell her just how ludicrously mistaken she was, she waved and jogged up the path to her front door.

Act One, Scene XIV:
Miscast

The Montgomery family were sitting in the breakfast room eating muesli and bickering when Jasper finally arrived downstairs with the casting list.

"Hilly?" Andrea asked, taking a sip of her flat white and checking her gold watch.

"No," Jasper said, raising her chin a little defiantly. "Grace Lancaster."

Christine peered up from her tablet, jaw slackened and eyes wide in horror. "Are you serious?"

Jasper shrugged. "She gave the best audition."

"Nah, no way," Christine sneered. "She's not got the right look."

"Shut up," Jasper said, quietly. "You've got to stop. She's perfect for the part and I didn't ask your opinion."

"Girls." Their mother held up her hands, her long fingers tightly posed together like a panpipe. "Casting isn't about who we like best, it's about who did the best."

"Right," Jasper said sternly. "And Grace did the best. She took direction and can do the steps. So, she's Clara."

"Hilly's mum is going to murder you," Christine said blankly, going back to her socials. "You know that, Jazz? Amanda is going to make a whole scene."

"I can take it," Jasper replied, with as much nonchalance as she could muster. "Maybe Arthur can film it for the documentary."

"Oh, Jasper," their mother snapped. "Don't be smart with us."

"Hilly is Sugar Plum Fairy; it's a perfectly good part," Jasper said. "I wouldn't cast Grace as Clara if I didn't think she could do it. I know she can. So, it is what it is. You asked me to do this, I'm doing it."

"All right," their mother said. "If you're sure."

"I am."

"Okay, fine, whatever," Christine muttered. "God. Just don't let Hilly's mother give you a black eye. You have to look nice for pictures this weekend."

Christine's bachelorette party. Jasper felt relieved that the night was finally on the horizon; it felt like the halfway point before the wedding.

"The ballroom is booked for eight on Saturday," Christine reminded her sister.

Jasper put the cast list into her bag, ready to head out. However, just as she began walking to the front door, her father nudged her into the living room.

"Everything okay, Jazz?"

Jasper could not make eye contact, just in case he saw. She sometimes felt as though her secrets were hidden in the corner of her irises. If anyone looked too closely into her eyes, they would spot them. If anyone in this family could figure out what was going on with her, it would be her father. While he didn't ask many questions about college or Odette, he could definitely sense that something was off.

"Everything's fine," Jasper fibbed smoothly. "I'm just a bit burned out from school. Plus, you know, Christine's wedding. I'm awake at night, praying that everything goes without a wrong napkin or badly ironed tablecloth."

The joke managed to strike the right chord. He thought she was just worked up over Christine's demands. Nothing deeper. Good.

"The Lancaster girl is a nice choice," he added conspiratorially. "Well done."

Jasper felt her expression grow a little sheepish. "Thanks, Dad. I may need security when Amanda finds out her daughter isn't the lead this year, but thanks."

"Keep your phone charged when you and Christine go out on Saturday," he said gently.

"Dad." Jasper put her own gentleness into the reproachful tone. "It's a classy, low-key evening. I'll be fine."

"Okay, okay." He glanced back toward the breakfast room, where Christine was loudly speaking to Kevin over the phone. "I just know you and your sister socialize on different levels."

Jasper sighed. No one in the family had ever been able to talk about it. Her diagnosis. They had spent years demanding to know why she was different, why she found certain things overwhelming and overstimulating. Why she did not enjoy their massive parties as much as Christine. Why she could smell things they could not, see details that were beyond their notice. They had wasted years wondering what spell had been cast upon their youngest.

But, of course, there was no spell. It was just her. Her brain, the way it was made. And after a doctor had confirmed that, it was never spoken of again.

No one will feel sorry for you. No one will cut you a break. You can't let that label be an excuse.

Jasper's mother had never liked the answer to the question she had, at one time, asked every night before sleeping. *What am I?* But Jasper did. She liked the answer a great deal. It was a map. A key.

An explanation that opened up parts of her and alleviated so much confusion and guilt and fear.

"Phone will be charged," was all that she said to her father, though. Even if Odette was always her first contact in a crisis. "Never fear."

He bobbed his head, satisfied.

The rest of the day went quickly. Jasper ate noodles with Odette and her surly friend Sophie and Odette's useless boyfriend. Then she left for the studio. She crossed through a gaggle of young dancers, all pretending that they were not about to pounce upon the list that she was holding. She moved to the board and pinned up the sheet of paper, feeling every one of them tensing behind her.

She kept her face blank, giving no emotion away.

Jasper stepped away and gave a barely imperceptible nod.

They all flooded toward it.

Jasper heard gasps, she heard murmurs. She rotated to watch. Grace was standing at the back of the huddle. Last to know. Jasper watched them part to let her through. Not everyone looked happy for her.

Jasper witnessed the exact moment when Grace spotted her name: her whole body reacted to it.

"Time to stretch," Jasper called firmly, nodding to the rehearsal pianist.

Grace was light, completely without gravity as Jasper led the class. One by one, the cast went out into the cloakroom to do their talking head interview with Arthur and Marcus. Hilly was outside for fifteen minutes longer than everyone else and returned to the room red-faced and blotchy.

When the class was over, the dancers fetched their belongings and the film crew packed up. Hilly, tearstains still marking her face, slunk over to Jasper.

"This isn't fair," she blubbed, in a shaking, broken voice. "Jasper, it's not right."

"Hilly," Jasper spoke with empathy but also a stern undertone of authority, "it's absolutely the right decision and it's mine. I understand you're disappointed, but you've still got an excellent part."

"She's not Clara," sobbed the ballerina. "She doesn't look right for the part. She's not . . ." She searched for the word that she wanted and then let out a shuddering sigh before settling on, "Blonde."

"Another word," Jasper said firmly, "and you won't be in this company at all. Okay, Hill? I mean it. Another word."

She could see shock in the young girl's eyes and she knew why. Jasper was always the easy-going one out of the Montgomery women. She was the one who gave them extra water breaks and never made sly or cutting comments about their appearances. She was warm and funny and gentle with them. This side of Jasper was a stranger to her—but Jasper did not feel guilty at letting it finally be seen.

She dismissed Hilly and was getting changed, when she spotted Grace hovering by the door.

Jasper straightened up and nodded sagely at her. "You earned it."

That released something in the younger girl. She bleated a mumble of gratitude and quickly wiped her eyes. "I won't let you down."

"I know you won't," Jasper said. She knew it was obnoxious to think such a thing at eighteen, but Grace reminded Jasper of herself at thirteen. Only a handful of years between them, but it felt like so many more.

Grace scampered out and Jasper was left alone in the studio. She looked down at her ballet flats next to her kitten heels. She wanted to turn her phone off and dance alone for a few moments. But she put on the heels. A little lipstick. She slammed the locker shut and bolted up the studio, leaving it in darkness.

She consulted her list. So far, she had only completed three items on it.

1. Skate on Lake Pristine
2. Find Odette a better boyfriend/girlfriend/partner—anybody but vile Craig
3. Make Mum proud with an amazing *Nutcracker* performance
4. Eat cupcakes at Vivi's—COMPLETED
5. Visit the Christmas Maze
6. Buy an ornament from the Heywoods at the Winter Market—COMPLETED
7. Tell family I'm leaving Lake Pristine (and college) for design school
8. Get into design school
9. Help Christine have the most beautiful wedding
10. Catch the late-night shows at the Arthouse—COMPLETED
11. ~~Try to be civil with Arthur Lancaster~~
12. Enjoy Christine's bachelorette party
13. Do something brave

An amazing *Nutcracker* performance felt closer than ever and refusing to cast Hilly could possibly be classed as "doing something brave." Her interview with the design school had gone extremely well. Even self-critical Jasper knew that to be true. She could complete the list by New Year's Eve.

Arthur slapped himself lightly in the face, trying to stay engaged. He was sitting in front of a monitor in his cousin's room, pretending that he was as interested in editing film as capturing it.

"You should just let me do the edit," Marcus finally said, noting his creative partner's deep boredom. "I find this way less tedious than the filming bit."

"The filming bit is the only interesting part," Arthur objected. "This is the bit that makes me question why I'm even doing this."

Marcus whistled and let out a derisive laugh. He paused the footage they had been reviewing. The film froze on a shot of Jasper Montgomery, watching the ballet auditions. Marcus chuckled and pointed at the screen. "You're doing it to unveil the weird hierarchy in this town. Which includes her family."

"That's not true." Arthur snapped the words. He instantly wished he could take back his tone. "That's not it," he clarified, a little more civilly. "I'm still trying to figure out the throughline."

"Spoiled princesses run nice wannabe-tourist town with fear," Marcus said, as if it were the most obvious thing in the world.

"Jasper scares you?" contested Arthur. "The girl you were spouting compliments about in front of Saffron?"

"Well, no, Jasper doesn't scare me," acknowledged Marcus. "But her sister does."

"Agree with you there," said Arthur. "And we've got plenty of footage of Christine monstering around town."

Whenever Arthur was filming quiet shots of the town, footage for transitionary scenes and B-roll, Christine would usually appear. She seemed to be ubiquitous. Many a peaceful shot had been impacted by Christine's arrival. She would be yelling about a florist or invitations or table settings, while her bridesmaids scurried behind her.

"There are fifty reality television shows dedicated to women who get stressed during the planning and execution of a wedding," Arthur pointed out. "We don't need to add to that."

"There are a million documentaries on small towns," retorted Marcus with a shrug. "What's different about this one?"

Arthur's eyes unconsciously flashed to the paused image on the screen.

"Aha," snorted Marcus. "Got it."

"You've got nothing," said Arthur, getting to his feet. "Focus on the wedding stuff if you want to be super derivative, but I don't think we should bother meeting again for an edit until we have something more worthwhile."

"Whatever you say," murmured Marcus, watching his cousin leave.

Act One, Scene XV:
Carried

Arthur was in a foul mood as he arrived at the Arthouse.

"Everything okay?" Henry asked, watching his younger brother slam into the cinema.

"Fine," snarled Arthur, as he made for their apartment.

He entered the kitchen to find Grace dancing around to music and looking utterly resplendent.

"Good day?" he asked, his mood instantly shifting into something lighter and more pleasant.

"Art!" Grace shouted over the music, tears welling in her eyes. "She cast me!"

Arthur blinked. "What?"

"Jasper cast me as Clara! I'm going to be the lead in *The Nutcracker*!"

It took Arthur five whole seconds to fully process what his little sister had said. Then his own voice was shouting over the music. He scooped Grace up and they both screamed with delight and danced around the room. So loud and boisterous were their screams, Henry came pummeling into the room, looking afraid and ready for a fight.

"What's wrong?" he demanded.

"Nothing!" sobbed Grace. "I got the lead, Jasper made me Clara!"

Henry's expression became one of complete jubilation and he instantly joined the celebrations. The two brothers hoisted their sister up and the three siblings danced around in their tiny kitchen, hoarsening their voices with delight.

"You have to phone Mum and tell her," Henry said, when they finally stopped to draw breath. "She'll be over the moon for you."

Grace nodded. "Already have. She was. I just wish . . ."

Both older brothers reached out to squeeze her arm. Nothing was said, but they all understood.

Henry had to return to work and Grace rushed to her room, claiming that she needed to start preparing for the role right away. Tchaikovsky was soon blasting from her bedroom door. It left Arthur alone in the kitchen.

Jasper had given her the role, Grace had said. It had been the youngest Montgomery sister's call.

He had to thank her.

Upon arriving at the house, Arthur stopped. The family were out on the veranda, all swaddled in heavy winter coats beneath a patio heater. There was no sign of Jasper, but her Jeep was parked neatly in its spot. Arthur retreated, suddenly feeling ridiculous. She hadn't done this for him. She'd done this because Grace deserved it.

He was about to return to town when Mr. Montgomery spoke.

"Arthur?"

"Evening, sir," Arthur called up. "Sorry, was just leaving."

"We've enjoyed seeing you and Marcus filming around town," the man said, hearing none of Arthur's attempts to leave. "Will you screen the film before sending it out?"

"Definitely," promised Arthur.

"Are you here for my sister?" Christine asked, and there was something he couldn't name in her voice. She was not being rude or making fun, or even trying to make him feel small. None of her usual tricks. She almost sounded worried.

"I wanted to thank her for casting Grace," he said honestly.

Mrs. Montgomery sniffed, but something softened in her face. "She danced very well."

"It was the right call," Mr. Montgomery added gently. "We'll pass that message along, Arthur. I think she's doing some course-work up in her room."

"Aren't you dating my best friend's younger sister?" Christine suddenly asked.

"I went on one date with Saffron," Arthur replied, blinking rapidly in surprise.

"Hm," Christine said, watching him intently.

"Can you just tell Jasper thank you from me," he said through gritted teeth.

"If I remember," Christine said, glibly.

He was thoroughly dismissed. He turned to leave and cursed himself for even going there in the first place.

It was Saturday and the night of Christine's party. Jasper reached the ballroom at the Arthouse early in order to set up, armed with as many candles as she could manage without making it a fire hazard. Jasper had designed individual boxes for the bride and her bridesmaids, each one filled with tailored memories. Photographs, trinkets and mementos. There was a disposable camera in each box and a small album with empty pages, waiting to be filled with pictures not yet taken. She knew Christine hated anything that resembled bunting, so the décor was tasteful while still playful. She was proud of her accomplishment. She had made the room beautiful, not only in accordance with her own tastes, but with Christine's. The kind of room she had heard her sister hope for. She hoped that their time apart would be bridged by the room, and wiped clean by the love and attention she had given it.

She set Christine's playlist up and checked the sound. Everything was ready to go as Henry arrived to prepare the bar, so Jasper fired off a text to Charlotte, asking if they were on their way. Jasper knew that the other girl had probably stopped by the Lakehouse to get ready with Christine.

"Now, if you've hired an exotic dancer to swing by, I need to know. For fire safety purposes," Henry teased, as the two of them dimmed the lights and started the music.

"I haven't booked one, but I can't vouch for the bridesmaids," Jasper shouted over the first song.

She was joking with him, but both of them were highly aware that the girls should have arrived by now. Jasper decided to call Christine, stepping out of the ballroom and into the foyer, covering her other ear with her palm.

Christine did not answer the first time, but picked up on Jasper's second attempt.

"Chris, are you on your way?" Jasper asked, wincing at the minor tinnitus she was experiencing and the headache which had arrived early in the day and was lingering still.

She could hear loud music on the other end of the line, and then Christine bellowed, "Change of plan!"

Jasper went cold.

She could see Henry adding ice into the buckets that were storing the champagne. Champagne that had already been paid for. She had sudden recollections of Christine making them miss flights as a family because she liked prolonging her time in Duty Free. Jasper had the same headache then. She could feel it ramping up now. "What?"

"We'll swing by and pick you up! We're going to Stone."

Jasper knew what she should say. Christine was speaking to Jasper like she was an assistant. As if it was Christine's money, and not Jasper's, that had been spent getting the whole room set up, exactly as Christine had commanded her to. "Christine—"

"We'll be there in six. Rebecca got us on the list, Jazz. She's got Saff with her so you won't be the only baby here. I had to, Jazz, Rebecca and Saff got us in, their mum knows the owner—you won't get carded."

It was a ridiculous remark to make. Christine had never felt obliged to anyone in her life.

"Christine." Jasper hated herself for sounding so afraid. "A club . . . I don't think—"

"A club will be fine, you're eighteen now, Jasper. Right! We're in the limo. See you in a bit, wait outside for us."

"It's not about age, Chris, I can't—"

The line went dead and Jasper's heart rate quickened. She could feel Henry approaching and asking if she was all right, but all she could do was stare at the phone in her grip. As if willing it to ring again, with Christine on the other end of the line saying that she was only joking.

"Henry, I'm so sorry," Jasper finally said, completely mortified. She despised herself even more for the quiver in her voice as she spoke. "Christine's changed the plans; she wants to go to a club. Rebecca and Saff have got everyone on a VIP list or something."

"Okay," Henry said slowly, looking as dazed as Jasper felt. "Are they pre-drinking here and then going out?"

Jasper had decorated the room into beauty, but Henry had been the one to clean and polish it. They had both given up so much time for Christine.

"Um." Jasper stared at the room so she didn't have to meet his gaze. "No, I think they want to go straight there."

She could see the disgust before he managed to conceal it.

"Look, I'm going to tell her to go without me," she bargained quickly. "And I'll stay behind here and clean all this up. I'm so sorry, Henry."

She still could not bear to look at him. She was too ashamed on Christine's behalf. She was saved from more apologies when the sound of the car pulling up outside of the main entrance could be heard.

Jasper stalked toward it, ready to haul Christine out by the elbow so that she could frogmarch her to stand before Henry and apologize.

The door swung open and her sister, who seemed rather merry, beckoned Jasper closer. "Get in."

"No, you get out. You need to apologize to Henry, Christine," Jasper snapped. "This is disrespectful and insulting."

"Boo!" jeered Saffron from inside the limo.

Jasper almost scowled at her. She was not one to judge others for having few friends, but why Saffron only had her older sister and her older sister's friends to be with on a Saturday night, Jasper did not know. Then again, she, admittedly, had very little in her own life, so she could not throw stones at Saffron's glass house.

"Where did you get this car?" Jasper demanded, slapping Christine's hand away as she attempted to pull her younger sister inside the open door.

"We booked it," Christine replied, snorting at the question with annoyance. She grabbed Jasper's wrist and tugged. "Come on."

"No, I'm staying to clean up, Chris. This isn't right."

"Hey," Christine became suddenly very serious and stared intensely at her sister. "You promised to be there for me during all of this. No matter what. I need you to come tonight."

Jasper softened for the briefest moment before Christine added, "Someone has to take the pictures. Get. In."

Jasper clambered inside, throwing one last look of devastated mortification toward Henry. She slammed the door behind her, eyes quickly scanning the limo for any further signs of substance abuse. Christine seemed animated, but it could just be down to a few gin and tonics.

"This club only plays songs that came out while the Rolling Stones were a band," Christine told Jasper, with a strange amount of pride for someone who could not name a single Rolling Stones song if her life depended on it.

Jasper was squashed between her sister and the door. This was her first time in a limousine and she was not enjoying it, especially when Rebecca lit a cigarette.

Jasper stared intently at her sister and squeezed her arm, trying to get Christine to focus on her. "Christine, this behavior isn't okay."

"Shut up, Jazz, God," Saffron barked. "This is her night."

You were not even invited. Why aren't you on another date with Arthur Lancaster? The jealous thought pierced Jasper's tongue, but she managed to avoid spitting it out.

Jasper bit her tongue. Literally. So, she had a throbbing tongue, a piercing headache and every nerve in her body was crying out for some silence and some stillness. She was shaking by the time they all reached the club.

There was a line of people waiting to get in and, as they approached the doorman, Jasper allowed herself a moment of desperate hope. Maybe Rebecca was all talk and they were, in fact, not on the list. They would have to wait, which meant Christine would get bored and they would end up heading back to the Arthouse after all.

But their names were there. Even Jasper's.

They were permitted to enter the building, Jasper and Saffron both getting stamps on the palms of their hands to let the bartenders know they were under twenty-one. Jasper followed the others down a dark stairwell with music pounding and it felt as though the sound was inside her skull. Each throb of the bass hit Jasper like a bullet. She could not explain it to them. They were all allistic. She could not make them feel what she was feeling; she could not make them understand.

The lights became more frantic and irregular. Too much darkness and then blasts of brightness. The music was in her blood. Too many bodies pressed up against her. Dampness and aroma all too much.

She watched Christine and her friends head for the booths, but Jasper could not make her legs follow them. She could not force herself to push through the gyrating bodies. She stumbled into a corridor, where people were waiting to use the bathroom. A woman was crying, another seemingly passed out. Jasper bent down to check her pulse and make sure she was all right, her hands violently tremoring, but the other girl waved her away like she was a bluebottle. Jasper fell against the wall and slid down onto the carpet.

She dropped her phone three times before her hands were able to grip it and dial. It was like trying to grab a falling object underwater.

"Hey," she rasped out when the other line connected. "I . . . need . . . help."

Arthur dropped a still-delighted Grace at their mother's house for the night. She had recently returned from India with a notebook full of new recipes so it took a few grunts and one firm "No" before she stopped trying to get him inside for a late dinner. He parked the car outside the Arthouse and was about to go inside when he spotted Marcus.

"I should follow you around for a bit?" his friend called out gingerly. "For B-roll?"

"I'm going inside, checking on the employees and then going to bed," Arthur shouted back. "Riveting stuff." But his tone said, "Do what you want" and Marcus did.

He filmed him from behind as Arthur walked through the entranceway. He must have captured the stiffening of Arthur's shoulders and the sudden stop he came to upon seeing that the doors to the ballroom were wide open. Henry was inside, cleaning up with an air of deep resignation.

Arthur forgot that Marcus and the camera were even there, as he walked toward his brother and threw his hand against the doorframe. "What happened?"

Henry offered up a sullen look. "Christine Montgomery happened."

It painted a quick picture. No opened bottles, candles blown out and the music off. They had not spent a moment in this room for the party, and after Arthur's brother had spent ages getting it prepared.

"Where are they now?" Arthur asked.

"Don't know," Henry said, his voice weary and jaded. "Jasper was helping me set up and then Christine called saying they were going somewhere else. Then they all rolled up in a limo and pulled Jazz inside. She was pretty mortified."

Arthur pinched the back of his neck. He had started helping Henry clean, while Marcus unhelpfully filmed them, when they were interrupted by the crashing sound of the front doors bursting open. All three young men turned to see Odette Cunningham running toward them. Her hair was wet and she was wearing a coat over what looked like pajamas.

"Arthur." She exclaimed his name like a dart hitting its target. "Can you drive me into the city? Now?"

There was enough urgency laced into her voice as well as the panic in her posture—it was all Arthur needed to see before he nodded and took out his keys.

"What's the matter?" Marcus asked, jogging alongside the two of them as they marched out to Arthur's car, camera still rolling.

"None of your business," Odette barked at him, getting into the passenger seat and slamming the door in his inquisitive face.

"Where are we going?" Arthur probed, disorientated, blasting the heat and getting his lights on.

"Stone. It's a club on Market Street."

It was a thirty-minute drive to get to the city, so Arthur pressed his foot down, hard. "What's wrong?"

Odette wiped her face and shook her wet hair. "I was with Craig, we were drinking, back at my place. So, I can't drive."

"Fine," Arthur acknowledged. "But what's the problem?"

She looked as worried as he was starting to feel. "Jasper called me. From the club. She's having a shutdown."

Arthur pressed the accelerator a little harder. "Okay."

"She can't take clubs," Odette breathed, sounding close to tears. "She's not made for them. They're too overstimulating. And Christine knew that." She made a fist and, for a moment, she looked frighteningly angry. "Christine *knew* that."

"Is she safe?" Arthur demanded.

"I don't know," she snapped. "Sorry. Sorry, but I don't know. She called me asking for help and every time I've tried calling her back, she hasn't answered."

Arthur swore quietly.

"Yeah. I know. Do you know how bad it has to be for *Jasper* to ask for help? She could be on fire and she wouldn't bother anyone for a bit of water. So, this is bad. Really bad."

Arthur's knuckles were as tight as a vice on the steering wheel.

"I don't even know why they're at a club," Odette added, falling back against the seat with a thump.

"Christine changed her mind about her party," Arthur muttered, pulling sharply around a corner and slowing down briefly for a speed camera. "She got hold of a limo and they all went into town."

Odette made a noise of disgust.

"Try calling Jasper again," Arthur insisted.

Odette was already dialing. She put the phone on speaker and they sat together in tense silence while it rang. When it went unanswered, they both released frustrated breaths.

"Do you have Christine's number?" Arthur asked, after a pause.

"No," Odette sighed. "Which is probably a good thing. I have nothing nice to say to her right now."

They fell into silence for most of the drive, until reaching the city. Odette directed him to the club and, upon arriving, he parked like an absolute menace. They both slammed out of the car and dashed toward the entrance. People were waiting to get in and they were happy to voice their displeasure with Arthur and Odette for pushing to the front, but neither of them cared. Odette argued with the doorman, while Arthur jumped the velvet rope and flew down the stairwell, barely touching the steps.

He winced at the atmosphere in the basement club. Humid and crowded, with the faint scent of male body odor and cheap perfume. He could barely see, but he heard Odette arrive behind him.

"Where would she be?" Arthur yelled over the terrible music.

They moved into the main club area, where the dance floor was packed, and then he spotted them. Christine and her friends, over in one of the booths. Saffron was standing up and posing with a bottle of champagne that she was not even legally allowed to drink while their camera flashes lit her up, but there was no sign of Jasper.

Odette and Arthur shouldered their way through the pulsing crowd toward them.

Saffron spotted Arthur before the others could and her face went from confusion to excitement. "Hey!" she slurred, reaching out. "You came."

Arthur did not bother to point out that the idea he had ever been invited was a complete joke.

"Where's Jasper?" he thundered over the bass, which was loud enough to shake the building.

Her gaze tightened and she stared at him. "What? Are you serious?"

Odette got right up in Christine's face and looked as though she could smack the camera out of her hands. "Where is your sister, Christine?"

Christine glanced about her, as if expecting to see Jasper sitting there on the leather with the rest of them. Arthur thought there was almost a hint of worry in her demeanor, but maybe that was a generous assessment.

"She must be in the bathroom," Christine finally managed, her eyes briefly scanning the dance floor. She avoided looking at him or Odette.

Arthur set off toward a door on the other side of the floor that people kept stumbling in and out of. He could hear Odette raising her voice as he moved, but he did not stay to find out what was being said.

It was a long stretch of corridor with toilet doors dotted up and down the wall. Arthur pushed against two eager people itching to get back onto the dance floor—and then he spotted her. She was sitting slumped against the wall. Her eyes were closed and, if he did not know better, he would have thought she was high.

Worry and relief hit him in equal measure.

For a moment, he was frozen, and then Arthur moved toward her, kneeling down and carefully shielding her from the doorway that was producing all of the noise and chaos. "Jasper?"

Her eyes flickered open and, while they were slightly dazed, exhausted recognition flashed in them. Recognition and bemusement.

"My car's outside," he said calmly. Half on the pavement, half on the road, but he left that part out. He was hoping to bring her out and find the car without a clamp on the wheel. "Wait here while I get Odette, then we'll get you out."

Her eyes widened, but she did not speak.

Arthur jumped up and sprinted back to the doorway, nodding as he noticed Odette shoving her way through bodies. He waved her over and relief flashed across her face.

"She's here," he shouted as she passed through drunken dancers like a boat pushing through stiff reeds.

"Excellent," she puffed as she reached the corridor. They turned to retrieve Jasper and both started as they simultaneously spotted a lascivious man leaning down and whispering something into her ear. Jasper flinched away from him, her face pinched.

Arthur had moved before Odette had even opened her mouth to bark at the guy. He threw the stranger up against the greasy wall with his forearm against the man's clavicle.

"What the fuck?" the interloper squawked.

"Walk out of this building right now," Arthur said quietly. "Don't look at anyone while you do it."

"You—"

"Do it or I'll drag you out. Get gone."

He released him and the man sloped off, muttering curses as he went.

Arthur moved back to Jasper, who was letting Odette help her to her feet.

"Here." He handed Odette his car keys. "Go start the car and warm it up. I've got her."

Odette nodded and darted off, forging a path for the two of them.

"This is so embarrassing," Jasper croaked. "D-didn't want to make a fuss."

She made to take a step, but her ankle gave away, her legs still too unsteady. Without any preamble, Arthur swept her up. One arm under her shoulders, the other under her legs. He turned sideways to carry her through the door.

"Sorry, it's going to be loud," he grumbled, apologetically.

Her head was against his neck. She did not answer.

He made a beeline for the other door, knowing that he just needed to get them through it and up the stairs and then they would be out of the sensory nightmare. The club was making him grit his teeth and clench his jaw, so he could only imagine how awful she must be feeling. He had to consciously tell himself to release.

He got them out onto the street, exhaling in relief as the cool air hit his face, caressing the parts that the club had dug its nails into.

"Car's just here, Jasper," he said gently.

"Arthur?"

It was not the voice he wanted to hear.

He turned to see Christine and Saffron. The latter looking at him with uncertainty, the former at Jasper with worry. Saffron had said his name with surprise and trepidation. Christine looked pale with concern.

Good, Arthur thought. Christine should be worried.

"Jazzie?" Christine said fearfully, her voice very small. "Jasper?"

"Why," Saffron looked off balance, like she was trying to seem sober, "why are you carrying her like that?"

"Why are you even here?" he railed at her. "Because your sister is?"

"Yeah, same as her," Saffron said weepily, pointing at Jasper. "You gonna yell at her, too?"

"It's her sister's party!" Arthur snapped. "She didn't want to be here, she's here because of her fucking stupid sense of selflessness. And her big sister should have been looking out for her!"

Arthur did not have time to deal with either Saffron or Christine. He strode to the car, which was, mercifully, still parked on the curb. Odette opened the back door and he slid Jasper inside. Odette followed, sitting next to her friend and getting her situated. Putting her seat belt on for her.

Arthur closed the door and leaped into the front. He was about to take off when he locked eyes with Christine. For a moment, he caught her looking completely ashamed—perhaps even devastated. Then, when she saw he was watching her, her face hardened. Any chance of empathy was quickly washed away after just one moment in her own head. For whatever voice resided in there, it was not one of conscience or responsibility. It was one full of excuses. Of "I never do anything wrong. And if I did something, it's not my fault."

Arthur looked away, coldly. He did not spare a glance at Saffron.

He waited until they were out of the city and back on the country roads to Lake Pristine before finally speaking.

"How's she doing?"

"Best get her home and into bed," Odette replied weakly. "Get some water in her. She'll have a headache oncoming, if not already."

Arthur cleared his throat. "You've seen this before."

It was not a question.

"A couple of times," she said forlornly. "Once, long ago, during school. She's . . . well, it's hard to explain."

"She's on a different level," he said, unhelpfully. "I mean, she feels things differently, right? Like, more? Stronger, louder."

"Faster, better," murmured Jasper and Odette and Arthur laughed, despite themselves.

"I think this has pushed me over the edge," Odette said coolly. "I'm going to finally murder Christine."

"Why is Arthur here?" Jasper asked huskily. "Were you two on a date?"

Arthur snorted.

"*I* was on a date," Odette said pointedly, stroking Jasper's ear. "With Craig. I'd been drinking wine at home when you called, so Arthur had to be my designated driver."

There was a pause while Jasper absorbed this information. Then, almost inaudibly, "Sorry."

"Nope," Odette said swiftly. "No sorry. Friends come when they're called."

"You're family," Jasper whispered.

"I know," Odette said, almost as if she was in pain. She kissed the top of Jasper's head. "I know."

There was subtext that Arthur had no shorthand for within the car. Something deeper was going on, some past conversation haunting the two of them. It felt as if Jasper wanted to admit defeat. Like Odette wanted to say she told Jasper so. Her university can't have been far from the club, as they were in the city center. He wondered if she had needed help like this before but been completely alone.

But it was not Arthur's business, he told himself. He just had to drive to Lake Pristine.

Act One, Scene XVI:
Rouge

Now that Jasper was safely out of the club, the humiliation she felt was strong enough to finish her off. The rational and logical part of her brain knew that there was no shame in what had happened. Her sensory needs meant nightclubs were not really made for her. That was not a crime.

Logically, she knew that.

Emotionally, she felt incredibly fragile and on show.

Calling Odette had been an absolute last resort. Not because she did not trust her, or expect that she would help. Rather because she knew that she would. She knew she would drop everything, do anything.

Now, the shame and embarrassment were taking the painful places of the flashing lights and loud noises of the club.

And Arthur.

Arthur Lancaster was here.

That made the whole thing so much worse.

They reached the Lakehouse. Jasper tried to shut the car door, but it did not slam fully closed; she wasn't able to execute enough strength. Her mind and her words were coming back to her, but her body was slow and sluggish, sensory overload and a neurodivergent shutdown weighing her down like wet clothes in cold air.

She stubbornly tried to hold up her head as she made her way toward the front door that Odette was quietly opening. She had to grab hold of something and it turned out to be Arthur Lancaster's elbow. He steadied her, his face impassive.

"Thanks," she said, staring at the gravel path beneath her unstable feet.

He did not let go. He guided her into the house and helped her up the stairs.

When they reached Jasper's room, Odette was already there, turning on her fairy lights and little candles. Jasper's best friend burrowed under the bed and hauled out the weighted blanket she had given Jasper three Decembers ago.

Odette was relentless in her attentiveness. Tucking Jasper in. Opening the window just wide enough to let in a little cool air. Sourcing a hot-water bottle. Dragging the heavy gray blanket so that it covered Jasper completely.

"I'm filling this up and getting you some drinking water," Odette finally said, when she was satisfied with Jasper's care. "Keep her company, Lancaster."

Jasper finally allowed herself a look at him, pushing her hair out of her face. The room was dimly lit and warm. He was pressed against her bedroom wall, next to the vanity, as if he was trying to stay as far away from her as possible. She decided that she couldn't blame him. She felt tremendously exposed.

"I didn't know it could be that hard for you," Arthur murmured. "I mean, Grace gets anxious about stuff, but my knowledge of . . ."

"Being ND?"

"Yeah. I don't— I didn't . . . It's not how I imagined. Like, as a non, uh, ND person."

"Neurotypical."

"Right. I've never really thought about how sounds and lights and stuff can be . . . you know . . . You were always so great on stage. I guess I just didn't realize."

His discomfort with the topic was endearing, but Jasper did not wish to discuss the matter.

"Thank you for getting me out of there," she managed. She was too chagrined to let herself dwell on the fact that he had physically carried her, bridal style, out of the club. She did not want to remember how the club had wrapped itself around her throat and squeezed. How every organ in her body had objected to its assault.

But they did not object to being carried out by Arthur Lancaster.

Which was interesting.

"How are you feeling?" Arthur asked gruffly.

"Much better."

He glanced down at the vanity and moved one perfume bottle away from the edge. Then his hand landed on a small glass box of deep crimson powder.

"I got that in Paris," she told him. "With an ex-girlfriend, Katie. She wants to be a burlesque dancer." She sat up a little and felt a small spark of power. The harmless, playful kind. "It's nipple rouge," she informed him.

His hand slipped and he almost knocked the red powder from the dresser. He quickly righted it and Jasper laughed, not unkindly.

He smiled, a real smile. "It is not," he said throatily.

"No, but it could be. She swore by it. Said I should get some to wear onstage as a blush." She could feel her own smile falter a little. "But I never have. That trip to Paris was a while ago and I haven't been on a stage since."

He touched one finger to the case of rouge. Pressed it gently, saying nothing. Then looked around at all the posters and photographs on the wall.

"There he is," he said at last.

She did not need to look. "Omar Sharif."

They laughed. It felt, to Jasper, so bizarre. An inside joke. Something shared. With *Arthur Lancaster*.

Odette reappeared, carrying a hot-water bottle and a chilled glass. Her eyes darted between the two of them, sensing the embers of something. She raised an eyebrow in amusement but did not comment. She slid the hot-water bottle under Jasper's feet and handed her the glass. Jasper downed the water in two gulps.

"Get back to your date," she said to Odette. Her voice was breathless from the water. "Don't worry about me."

"We've rescheduled, it's fine," Odette said, batting away like cigarette smoke Jasper's attempts at distancing. "Shut up and feel better."

Jasper snorted.

Odette sat on the edge of the bed and they both turned to look at Arthur.

"I'd better head back to Henry," he said quickly.

"Oh, God," Jasper sat up, looking embarrassed. "Please, Arthur, tell him I'm sorry. Really sorry."

"It's okay," he said reassuringly. Generously. "He knows, it's honestly fine."

"It's not," Jasper insisted. "It's not fine. He's not Christine's staff. And even if he were, this wouldn't be acceptable. I'm going to apologize in person tomorrow, Arthur, but please—"

"If Christine wants to apologize, she can," Arthur said firmly. "You have nothing to be sorry for. Henry knows that."

He was staring at her. Intensely. Jasper stared back, ready to fight this point.

Odette glanced between the two of them again and made a smug sound. It caused Jasper to look down at her hands, which were still shaking a little.

"I'll head off now," Arthur finally murmured.

"Thank you for coming to the rescue," Odette said warmly, getting into bed next to Jasper and yelping when she realized that Chum, the cat, was hidden under the duvet. She laughed and moved him onto Jasper's lap.

By the time Jasper looked over once more, Arthur had vanished.

She didn't know why that made her feel disappointed.

"She knew what would happen to you," Odette said stiffly. "She knows what happens to you when you get overloaded."

"Let's not talk about Christine," Jasper said. "Tell me about your date with Craig."

"Not the world's worst boyfriend anymore," Odette insisted, but her whole neck was flushed.

"Not anymore?" Jasper teased, poking her friend in the ribs.

"Not yet," Odette corrected, but she was grinning.

Jasper was glad to be laughing, and she teemed with love for her best friend as the post-shutdown exhaustion hit.

For the first time in weeks, she slept well.

Jasper woke to the sound of the coffee machine. She could hear her mother and father laughing downstairs. Odette was next to her, still dead to the world and laying on her front, with Chum stretched happily across her back.

Jasper got up and moved into her en suite, brushing her teeth and hair with measured strokes and scrubbing at her face with a soft flannel, trying to rub away the night gone by. Pulling on some casual clothes, she mentally prepared for what she was going to say upon joining the rest of the family at the breakfast table.

She was going to confront Christine. She was going to do it in front of her parents.

Jasper braced herself as she descended the stairs. She was ready for sulking, for a bad temper, for Christine to be resentful and bitter about the night before. She was ready for her mother to be her sister's trusty lieutenant and for a lecture to be forthcoming.

But when she reached the breakfast room, which was flooded in sunlight, she wavered.

Both of her parents and Christine were sitting in their usual spots, as expected. Her mother was sipping a flat white and her father was reading his paper. Christine was drinking a cold glass of water with two cucumber slices in it.

"You've slept late," her mother remarked pointedly, her eyes drifting toward the direction of her youngest daughter, silently admonishing Jasper while warning her to behave all in one movement.

Jasper sat stiffly at the table. She poured some water, sans cucumber slices, and took a massive drink.

"So, how was last night?" her father asked.

"Awesome," Christine said swiftly. Her hair was piled up and hidden beneath a silk turban and her pale lilac eye cream was visible beneath her lower lashes. "I had such a lovely night, Rebecca and the girls did such a wonderful job."

"I thought Jasper was in charge of last night," her father said.

"Well, Rebecca is maid of honor and she got us into this really great club at the last minute," Christine barreled on before Jasper could even draw breath. "We all had a great time."

"What was your favorite part of the evening, Jasper?" their father pushed.

Jasper took her time with her water before selecting a slice of toast. She buttered it. She took a bite. She considered getting up and making some scrambled eggs.

"I saw a really handsome guy," she finally said.

Her mother's head jerked up in surprise. Her father coughed uncomfortably and loudly faffed with his paper. Christine watched her sister, stonily. Daring her to say more.

Jasper bit off another loud crunch of her toast and smiled serenely. "Practically carried me out of the place."

"What's got into you?" her mother said, eyeing Jasper as though her daughter's body had been taken over by someone else.

Jasper proceeded to say nothing more for the remainder of the meal. She waited until Odette was gone before she returned to her room, a cheerful goodbye written in lipstick on her mirror. She kicked the vanity stool over in a rare show of temper and then instantly righted it again.

A soft knock on the door made her jump, before she called out, "What is it?"

"It's Mum. Can I come in?"

Andrea Montgomery never knocked—but she did enter without waiting for an answer to her question. Jasper watched her warily, alert for whatever criticism was about to be unleashed. Jasper could feel herself starting to disassociate, past experience readying her for an escalation. Her mother was a true artist when it came to ballet, but she had a volatile temper to go with her love of control.

"Christine is under a lot of stress." She stated the words calmly to Jasper, who did not visibly react. "There is nothing like a wedding to give you silver hair," she went on, touching her dyed blonde hair with a flicker of self-consciousness. An outsider might hear the words, and her perfectly reasonable tone, and deduce that they were coded words of comfort. Jasper knew better. She knew when a scold was on its way. "You have to give your sister more leeway."

Jasper closed her eyes and exhaled. "I am, Mum."

"She is going to say things, and do things, that she does not mean because of the pressure that she's under."

Jasper had always been their father's favorite, and Christine had always been their mother's. It had seemed fair once.

"I thought we didn't let labels define or excuse us in this family," Jasper said quietly, a tinge of bitterness entering her voice. "Why does the word 'bride' excuse Christine's behavior? I seem to remember a label I received a few years ago being used as a reminder that I should never step a foot out of line."

She found enough courage to meet her mother's glare. Andrea's nostrils flared very subtly and Jasper wondered if she would snap, but she just said, "A good ballerina never steps a foot out of line."

"Well," Jasper's eyes flitted to the pictures on her wall, the ones of her dancing days, "I'm not a ballerina anymore, so . . ."

"Jasper. You will always be a dancer. I don't know if this is your teenage angst talking, but you will always be a ballerina, my girl."

Jasper was nettled by the words, enough to make her move to a different corner of the room. She busied herself with some folded clothes from her laundry pile. "It's not the same anymore."

"Are you dancing at college? I know your degree will take up time, but some of the societies—"

"I'm not dancing at college," Jasper said bluntly.

She could feel the words that she needed to say waiting in the wings. Awaiting a cue to go on.

I'm not going back.

Jasper wasn't brave enough to say them aloud, let alone in front of an audience.

Arthur was still waiting for Christine to offer his brother an apology. Henry was far more exonerating; he brushed the whole thing away when Arthur mentioned it. Arthur was far less forgiving. If he were to be honest with himself, he was furious about so much more than Henry's time being wasted and an empty ballroom at the Arthouse. He was angry when he remembered Jasper crumpled on the floor, against the nasty wallpaper. He did not know a thing about her reality, but even he knew that forcing someone with her sensory needs into that environment was disgraceful.

"If it were anyone else, they would have refused. But not Jasper."

Arthur was doing something that he knew he should not. He was answering Marcus's questions about the night before. On camera. Miked up.

"Why not Jasper?" Marcus prodded. He was all set up while Arthur was checking receipts. An usher was watching the entire conversation.

Arthur continued to log things in the book and then check again, slamming each receipt down with as much restraint as he was capable of at that moment.

"Because Jasper—" he crossed out something in the book with

a ferocity that the camera could not possibly miss—"Jasper puts every single human being on earth before herself."

Marcus leaned closer, about to encourage him to continue, but Arthur needed no such reinforcement.

"If Jasper's sister wanted her to run into a burning building, she would. Hell, if some person she met on the street asked her to, she would."

Arthur meant it as the highest compliment, but his tone came across as gruff and aggressive.

"Look, I don't know her that well," he insisted, for clarity. "But this is a small town, we all knows bits and pieces of each other. And if there's one thing I know about Jasper Montgomery, it's that she just does whatever is easiest for other people."

It sounded far harsher than he meant it to.

"Are you—" Marcus crossed his arms and danced from one foot to the other—"are you . . . sweet on her?"

It was such an old-fashioned expression, it made Arthur laugh and think of Jasper's old movies. He continued to stare down at the receipts and take his time crossing off dates.

"I just think she needs to stand up to her family," he finally settled on.

"Small towns," Marcus said, gesturing around. "They're goldmines. They're full of secrets. And that family? They're about to bubble over. I can tell. We just need to be patient."

Arthur dumped the receipts back into the open till and shoved it closed, never taking his eyes from his old friend. "Don't try to make a fool of her."

He didn't care if they were filming or not.

"If you mean Jasper, she's far too controlled for that," Marcus said, sounding a little resentful of the fact. "But her sister? She's a ticking timebomb."

Arthur opened his mouth to reply, but someone walked through the doors of the Arthouse and it shut him up at once.

She was right on time for the Jimmy Stewart film.

Jasper spotted the back of Marcus's head. Her eyes widened in horror at the notion of being on camera when she was out to unwind, and so Arthur made a subtle nod toward the cinema screen. She raised her eyebrows as if to say, "Are you sure?" and he lowered his chin. *Yes. Go in.*

She did. Unspotted by Marcus and the camera lens who were fixed on Arthur.

Arthur's phone buzzed. Another missed call from Saffron. He was not exactly ignoring her; he always let calls go to voicemail during his working hours. However, he would not go as far as to say that he was desperate to hear from her after last night's performance. She was not Christine, but she had been more than happy to go along with the others. If *she* had been passed out in the corridor, or coming down from a bad high, Jasper would have sat right there next to her. Arthur knew it.

Arthur had once gone out with a girl called May. They had been in the same geography class. They had broken up amicably when her family had moved away. It was the best kind of first serious relationship because she was kind and polite and got on with his family, and they had been really good friends who clumsily discovered each other a few times when the house had been empty. Now she was going out with a football player in her new town and they both seemed really happy together. Arthur realized that, while it might be perfectly healthy for him to be pleased for May and her new partner, it was not the most romantic idea. He should probably be pining.

"Art, there's something you're looking for in this place," she had said. *"I don't know how you're going to find it; you must know every square inch by now and you'll have turned over every stone. But whatever it is, it's here. And it's not me."*

She had been right.

Arthur was protective of May. He liked making her laugh. He missed her as a friend. She could not have been more different from Saffron. He could not quite picture he and Saffron ever being friends, to be frank, but he was still willing to tolerate it. To see if there was someone in her, someone better than the person he had seen at the club.

Because it was lonely.

It was lonely in Lake Pristine without his father, and with his mother leading her life elsewhere.

It was lonely now that Grace liked going to dance classes and hiding in her room.

Lonely with Henry always working, or out with a different girl.

Lonely to walk the same familiar streets by himself.

He looked back at the door to the cinema screen.

It was lonely, knowing what it was you were pining for but understanding that the whole thing was fruitless.

Act Two, Scene I:
Career Moves

Jasper was picking up a shift at Pete's cafe, to make a little extra money. Most of her salary went on fabrics for the ballet company, and so when Pete had loudly complained about needing extra help when she and Odette had been there having milkshakes, she had stepped up at once, right there and then.

As she quite literally got to work, with promise of payment in cash, she thought about dating. It was a great place to bring a date.

There were guys she had gone out with during her recent term at college. When she was scared of going to sleep, she would let some sneak back to her dorm with her. They all adored her mask, the smooth and protected version of herself she wore for the world. She could feel it. They loved being able to project their imaginary girl onto her. The rare occasions when she was honest about who she was, they always looked so dismayed.

She did not want to feel like that again. She did not want to be reminded of the noise and the lies and the fakery that was woven into people's prejudices.

So, when she seemed to automatically let her guard down with Arthur Lancaster, that was a surprise.

Everything felt so different with him. The night at Stone, being carried out of hell, it had changed everything.

Maybe he liked her. Maybe, she let herself wonder, he liked her as Jack Lemmon had liked Shirley MacLaine. Maybe they were entwined in a story like the movies she loved so much, and she was just missing the parts of the bigger picture that made it make sense.

She halted her imagination from going there. She refused to think about how hard a worker he was, how good a brother, how sad he seemed whenever his father was mentioned and yet how endearingly relieved he became when she shared loving stories of Mr. Lancaster. But still, Jasper would rather die than admit that she had been thinking about Arthur Lancaster more than just about anyone of late.

He would slip into her thoughts while she was sitting up repairing a tutu. And when they had walked from the Arthouse to the Lakehouse, there was a kind of electricity that scared Jasper as much as it thrilled her. She felt out of control and less able to hide.

"If you have any questions or problems, Jazz, just shout," Pete said, handing her a till key and squeezing her on the shoulder. She had undergone one quick training session and was now looking forward to earning her tips. She smiled and nodded at him before moving behind the counter.

Every envelope of cash and every tip was going into the box under her bed. A fund to get out of Lake Pristine and go to design school, once Christine was married. She knew her mother would rage like an inferno when she finally told them she wasn't going back to the university they were paying for, so she would need her own savings, loans and financial aid. She welcomed it. Her privilege was not something she was scared to look at in the eye, but she no longer wanted the conditions that came with it.

It was a nice first shift with a steady flow of people. Jasper enjoyed making drinks and doing the necessary mental arithmetic—a repetitive task that she found soothing. She kept herself busy and occasionally dropped a lime and soda off for Odette, who was manning her booth in an attempt to be encouraging.

As she neared the end of her shift, Jasper began to feel truly confident in the new role.

And then a couple came in.

Pete had dimmed the lights to make the cafe a cosier atmosphere, with a roaring fire in the stone fireplace.

The couple moved into the booth behind Odette. They were clearly on a date.

Jasper picked up two menus from the pile and a jug of water and made her way to the table, a little dazed. She dropped the jug unsteadily onto the wooden table and laid the laminated menus down.

"Hi," she said, her voice forcefully breezy. "Can I start you with drinks?"

Arthur Lancaster and Saffron looked up at her in astonishment. Saffron's face broke into an amused expression while Arthur looked utterly taken aback.

"Jasper," Saffron laughed, while she glanced around the cafe. "Is this a gag?"

"Nope," Jasper said through a grimace. "Need extra cash. Got an expensive wedding guest dress to pay for."

It was a silly joke, and not really like her at all, but Saffron laughed nonetheless.

Jasper couldn't look at Arthur, she was suddenly aware of exactly how she had felt days before when they had been together. How she had let herself become soft for the briefest of moments.

Because he had carried her out of a nightmare. Everything was shifted on its axis after that. He was not so much of a stranger now. She knew what it felt like to be crushed up against him. For ten shining minutes, she had known what it felt like to be his sole focus.

She had never wondered about that before, but now it was hard for her to think about anything else.

She was suddenly embarrassed by her earlier wonderings. Of course he didn't like her. At least, not in any sense that moved beyond banal acquaintanceship. He tolerated her and walked her home from the old movies at the arthouse merely out of moral obligation, she told herself. He was a good person and his behavior reflected that. It would be naïve and presumptuous to think that any attentiveness he showed her reflected something deeper.

He clearly liked Saffron. He was on a *romantic* date. With Saffron. They were right in front of her, together. Arthur had not asked Jasper out, not once. He had never shown any kind of desire for that. It humbled the strange new feelings that were familiarizing themselves with her heart.

"I'm going to look at the mocktail list," Saffron announced, jolting Jasper back into the moment. "I'll need a minute."

"There isn't a mocktail list, Saffron, this is a tearoom," Jasper said dully.

"Well," huffed Saffron. "I'll still need a minute."

Jasper was thrilled to give it to her. "Okay."

She moved behind the counter and opened up a tab for their table on the system, her hands shaking a little. She flicked them, stimming ever so slightly—her whole body humming. Desperate to move, desperate to flit.

"Jasper?"

She had heard his deep voice plenty of times before, but this was the first time it had done something unfamiliar to her. She did not want to face it. She clutched her hands together to stop them from tremoring and spun to face him, putting on her social mask and smiling pleasantly.

"Hey."

He was looking at her just a little too closely. He was alone at the counter and his hair looked great and she knew he would smell fantastic. She suddenly wondered what it would be like to press her face into his neck and she pinched her own wrist to banish the image.

This was *so* inconvenient.

"You okay?"

Am I? Jasper asked herself. A shutdown during her sister's party. Lying to her entire family and her best friend. Having absolutely no idea how to start making her life work for her own happiness instead of against her. There were so many things wrong with Jasper Montgomery.

Eighteen felt so much harder than seventeen. She had thought growing up and coming of age was just something you rushed to, and once you crossed the finish line, everything would fall into place and make sense at last. Instead, all structure and certainty had fallen away like the net beneath a trapeze artist and the choice seemed to be hold onto the bar for dear life and keep swinging, or fall to the hard ground.

Eighteen felt like being lied to and letting everyone else down all in one breath.

"I'm fine," was all she was able to say.

I'm about to crack, she thought. *Can't you see it, Arthur?* She wasn't so sure the pieces would stick together as well this time around. She was not certain they would stick at all. She had spent her whole life dancing around shutdowns by pretending and pleasing and pressing her back to the wall. It was getting harder to pull off now.

"You weren't at last night's screening," he said, and it might have been her imagination, but there was a small note of accusation in his voice.

Some Like It Hot. It was her favorite.

"Two jobs now," was all she said. "*The Nutcracker* and now this."

"Grace is loving it."

"Good," she said, and she meant it. "She's doing really well."

She snatched up a cloth and started to wipe specks of coffee from the varnished bar. She avoided his eyes.

Jasper liked Arthur. Maybe she always had. She liked his loyalty. His occasional charisma. His code of conduct, something he never wavered from. His inability to conceal his distaste for certain things, and certain people. His handsome face and gentle eyes. His dimples. His love for his family.

Now she spent more time than she cared to admit wishing they could be friends—or something more than friends. These new realizations were proving incredibly jarring.

"Are you ready to order?" she finally said, when there was nothing left for her to clean.

Now Arthur just looked disarmingly handsome and concerned.

Jasper glanced across at Odette and spotted her staring at the two of them with a quizzical expression. Maybe Jasper looked as caught in a lie as she felt.

He placed an order and she took great relief in punching it into the till. When she was done, she found that he was still at the coffee bar.

"All good," she said with feigned cheer. "I'll bring everything to your table."

"Jasper, what's wrong?"

What a question, Jasper thought with just the slightest shade of bitterness. *That I process things differently and cannot always identify what I'm feeling. It's a lot, I know that much. Filling me up like water in a ship-wrecked boat. I can take in the details of all that I see, of the people that I'm with, but looking inside of myself always feels forbidden. I've made me a stranger to myself, because I'm playing parts for other people. Wearing a mask in a neurotypical world erodes the person underneath. Did you know that?*

"I'm fine, Arthur," she breathed. "Please."

Just let me do this in peace, she silently begged. *Let me fall apart over whatever hidden thing I'm dealing with here and go back to Saffron.*

Saffron who treated her like dirt when no one was looking, and sometimes when they were. Who posted long essays online about how important female friendship was, only to then talk about girls behind their backs.

Arthur interrupted her internal monologue by reaching out to grab her hand. It was like a static shock. He ran the pad of his thumb across her palm, as if he was passing a secret code to her.

Then he was gone.

Jasper went to the back room, pretending to look for till receipts.

"I think I like him," she said, frantically and under her breath to no one at all. She was alone with crates and boxes and delivery notices. "God. I think I really like him."

Arthur moved stiffly back to the booth Saffron had chosen for the two of them. The whole reason he had brought Saffron here was to firmly and resolutely tell her that they were only meant to be friends. Nothing more. But she had cleverly avoided every single one of his attempts to initiate a serious conversation. He had chosen the tearoom to end things, completely oblivious to Jasper's new job. Her presence was making it very hard to concentrate on Saffron.

When Saffron finally took a sip of cranberry juice, he tried to steer the discussion toward what he wanted to say but she held her finger up.

He hesitated.

"I know what you're going to say," she said once the juice had gone down.

"You do?"

"Yes. You gave me the silent treatment after everything that went down at Stone."

Arthur shook his head. "No, I just didn't—"

"It's fine, I get it. But I do think it's a bit toxic to judge a girl for having a wild night. If we were guys, no one would bat an eye."

Arthur wasn't following. If she were a guy and had facilitated Jasper's shutdown and abandoned her, he would still be furious. Also, he had *not* been giving her the silent treatment. He had been too busy trying to bump into Jasper.

Which was why this whole thing needed addressing. If Saffron was counting on some kind of relationship, it was not fair.

"Sorry if I've been distant," he said softly. "I wasn't meaning to be."

The apology transformed her. She beamed. Satisfied. "That's okay. I forgive you."

"The thing is, Saff, I think you're a great girl and I've really enjoyed getting to know you a bit better. But I don't want you to think—"

"What?"

He stopped, startled. "Um. I was just going to say—"

"Are you serious?" she asked the question with a bright smile on her face but piercingly sharp and angry blue eyes. "Tell me you're not serious."

Arthur paused. "Saff, I just want to be upfront with you. I don't want to give the wrong impression."

"Yes, taking a girl out on dates gives a very precise impression."

"I know, that's why I want to say this before things carry on. I like you, I think you're great, but I just don't—"

"*You* called *me!*"

He refrained from pointing out that it had taken a little pestering before he had considered doing so, and that the inclination had certainly not been an organic one.

"I'm sorry. I thought it would be better to bow out now."

"Don't have such a haughty tone about it," she snapped back. "Acting like I'm so fragile and like I'll burst into tears. We went on a couple of severely average dates. I'm not in love with you."

Arthur nodded, relieved. "Good. Glad you see it that way, too."

To his chagrin, her face morphed into hurt and anger. He had obviously said the wrong thing.

"What I meant was—"

"As if I would actually consider you for a boyfriend anyway," Saffron interjected loudly, her cheeks starting to get a little pink. "You're surly, you're a loner. You work too much at that creepy old cinema. Your little sister's a freak—"

"Hey," Arthur snapped, all niceties gone. "Don't you dare."

"The whole town is sorry your dad died, don't get me wrong, but your mum taking off to live it up with her new boyfriend while you and your brother man the Arthouse? It's too much drama for me. I'm sorry, I'm not taking in strays from broken homes."

Arthur forced himself to swallow. "You're upset. That's okay. It's valid—"

"I'm not upset, I'm relieved," she snarled, getting to her feet and grabbing her clutch. "Now I don't have to let you down gently."

"Sure," said Arthur quietly. "Whatever you like."

"Do not bother calling me again," she said, before making to storm out of the cafe. Just as she reached the exit, she spun back around and pointed her clutch at him as though it were a loaded gun. "You have made a huge mistake, Arthur Lancaster."

"Slightly conflicting narratives going on there, Saff," Odette Cunningham said from her own secluded booth. As soon as the remark left her lips, she threw Arthur a look and took a long sip of her lime and soda.

"Mind your own business," hissed Saffron. She was halfway out of the building before she turned around to throw another loud remark back to Arthur. "Oh, and by the by, Lancaster? She's never going to see you like that."

Arthur's fist tightened around the paper napkin he had been fiddling with and he threw Saffron a thunderous glare. "I don't know what you mean."

"You do," she said, her voice quivering. "The whole town sees it. You are aching for her. It's so transparent. And you're kidding yourself."

She slammed out of the building, the door swinging in her wake.

The whole cafe had heard. Arthur could feel shame and embarrassment creeping up his back. He looked at Odette, only to find her pretending that she could not see him. In fact, most of the other people in the room were doing the same. Staring at their menus and acting as though he was completely invisible.

Only Jasper was looking at him, when she emerged from the kitchen, oblivious to the whole scene. But he was too abashed to look back.

Act Two, Scene II:
Girl Code

Jasper came downstairs after another terrible night of sleep and handed Christine a piece of paper.

"These are the 'regretfully declines,'" she said quietly. "Not many at all. It's going to be a full house."

Christine stared at the paper for a moment and Jasper turned to leave, grabbing an apple from the fruit bowl as she did so.

"Thanks, Jazz."

Jasper froze. She turned to look at her older sister, who was sitting at the breakfast table in her robe, silk turban and freshly painted nails. "What?"

"Thank you. This is so helpful. You're doing me a big favor."

Jasper could have cried, she was so shocked. "Any time, bub."

"Kevin says thank you as well. He actually said we owe you our first child."

Jasper laughed at that. "No, thanks, but the offer is nice."

"Hey, I'm going to get my actual wedding dress in town at the weekend. Do you want to come?"

Jasper nodded. "Of course. Do you need me to take pictures?"

"No, I just want you to be there."

"Oh."

"Cool. I'll text you where and when."

"All right."

Jasper walked to her car in a daze. She didn't know what had prompted Christine to have this miraculous change in behavior, and she was not going to count on it being permanent, but it felt lovely.

She confirmed details with the venue on speaker phone as she drove out of Lake Pristine and into the city, heading to pick up more tulle. Mere seconds after hanging up, her phone rang again. She pressed "answer," smiling at the caller identification.

"Hey," she said.

"Hey, stranger," said the affable voice, belonging to her sister's fiancé. "Long time since we last spoke, still remember the sound of my voice?"

"The weirdest thing just happened to me, Kev," she said, laughter in her voice as she concentrated on the road. "Christine thanked me for helping you guys out."

"About time."

"You put her up to it?"

"No, not even. I did lecture her about what a lifesaver you've been, though."

"Ah, it's nothing."

"No, really, Jazz," his voice grew serious. "You've been a superstar. Putting up with her when she's stressed. All while that rotten camera is filming you."

"Happy to do it, Kev, I swear."

"Please go out and have some fun tonight, Jasper. It's Friday, you deserve it. You working?"

"Nope."

"Ballet?"

"No, that was last night."

"Then treat yourself. Block Christine's number for the night and do something for you."

Jasper grinned. "I'll think about it. Your tux appointment is on Monday at three."

"Take a day off! You're meant to help, not arrange every last detail!"

She giggled before hanging up the phone. She was truly happy about Kevin becoming her brother in-law; she really did like the strange man who had decided to spend the rest of his life with Christine.

As Jasper reached the long, stretching, isolated path connecting Lake Pristine to the city, her eyes landed on something happening just ahead. A bus leaving the city and heading for the smaller surrounding towns had dropped a couple of people off at the stop a little further along. It was a bus stop which had caused a lot of controversy in Lake Pristine, as it was a good twenty-minute walk from town and the bus tore through their boundaries without stopping again—meaning one either embarked on the uphill climb to Lake Pristine or hung around for a lift.

But that was not what Jasper was worrying over. As the bus drove away, she spotted a familiar figure.

Grace Lancaster. Huddled into herself, looking as if she wanted to disappear. Two other girls and a man with a baseball cap pulled low stood behind her, having also alighted the bus. Jasper recognized the girls, Hilly and Eve. They were clearly laughing a little too loudly, their eyes pinned to Grace's stiff shoulders. Arthur's younger sister stepped aside to let them pass, scrolling frantically on her mobile.

Jasper parked the car on the side of the woodland road and turned off the engine. She kept both hands on the wheel and leaned forward, watching as the two girls threw another pointed look at Grace before shrieking in laughter again.

Then the man following the three of them said something which ended the laughter, all while wearing a troubling grin. Jasper had no idea who he was, which was something that never happened in Lake Pristine. And his behavior was causing her alarm.

Another remark thrown toward the girls, one that made them look even more uncomfortable, and that was enough for Jasper. She leaped out of the Jeep, slamming the door behind her. All of the girls glanced over and relief entered their faces at the sight of their company leader, none more thankful than Grace.

"Are you lost, sir?" Jasper asked loudly.

The man turned, his licentious expression freezing as he took in the new arrival. He quickly recovered, giving her a slow and deliberate perusal.

"What a town," he said.

"Get in the Jeep, girls," Jasper said coolly.

The thirteen-year-olds did not need to wait for a second command. They jogged to the car and let themselves inside, Grace in the front and the other two in the back.

The man sauntered toward Jasper.

"I have a golf club in the trunk of my car," Jasper said silkily. "So, that's just about close enough, thanks."

Doubt flickered in the man's dull gray eyes. "No, you haven't."

Jasper smiled sweetly and moved to her Jeep. She jauntily popped the trunk and reached inside to draw out a long, slim silver club. She swung it around gaily as she re-joined the man on the side of the road.

"Yes, I have. It's my daddy's old driver, actually. Really tough, this old thing. Now, my motor skills aren't great, I'm not quite the champion golfer he is—retired judge, you know—but I can still whack anything that gets in my way. Hard."

The man stared in horror. "You wouldn't."

Jasper's eyes were cold, but her smile was wide. "It would be my pleasure."

"What?" snapped the man. "It's illegal to look at girls now? Talk to them?"

"You've got no business looking at or talking to underage girls. I'd recommend you turn around and head back to Balary Port or catch another bus back into the city. Before I start swinging this thing."

The man looked about ready to spit, but he turned and sloped away, throwing daggers at her as he did. Jasper waited without moving until he was out of sight and then returned to the Jeep.

She needed all three of the girls to know that she would always do this for them. And that they needed to do it for one another. It was so easy to buy into silly competitions as a girl. Jasper knew this better than anyone. But she had pulled herself out of that societal brainwashing and she needed to set an example for her young dancers.

She let herself into the driver's seat and turned to face them. "You all right?"

"Fine," Eve said cheerfully. "We were on the top deck, we didn't know he was there until we got off. He was creepy, though. Said some gross things."

"I was on the lower deck," Grace said softly. "He was talking to me for most of the ride home."

Jasper reached across to squeeze the girl's arm. "You okay?"

Grace nodded and shrugged. "Yeah. He didn't touch me."

Jasper shook her head, wishing that she had clubbed the man over the head. "I'll drive you all back into Lake Pristine."

"Arthur's coming to get me," Grace said quickly. "He'll have already left."

"Ah, okay," Jasper said, recalibrating. "We'll wait for him then."

"We can head in on foot," Hilly said frankly. "Thanks for almost kicking his ass, Jasper."

"Now hold on a moment," Jasper said, as they both opened their passenger doors. "A quick word: what are you two going to do next time you see a fellow company member looking upset?"

Both of them had the decency to look chastised.

"We'll step in," Eve finally said.

Jasper held the silence for a moment before nodding in dismissal. They left and set off for town, while Grace fidgeted. Jasper looked down at the golf club in her lap and almost laughed. The whole thing seemed absurd, now that the adrenaline was wearing off.

"He's lucky your brother didn't catch him," she said, trying to make Grace laugh.

It worked. The girl grinned and some of the tension in her dissipated. "Yeah. Though you looked pretty scary."

"I can be very scary, Grace," Jasper said, and that made Grace laugh even more. "What? I can! You don't grow up as Christine Montgomery's little sister and come out without self-defense skills."

"You've had to fight Christine off with a golf club?"

"Not yet, but wait until she finds out that I can't actually arrange for painted gold peacocks to walk down the aisle with her."

The mention of the wedding made Grace ignite with delight. "I got my invitation, it's pinned up in my room. I'm so excited."

Jasper smiled warmly at her. "Good. I'm glad, Grace."

She opened her car door and gave a little wave with her father's golf club. She moved to the trunk of the car to put it back, when Arthur Lancaster's car abruptly pulled up. He parked shambolically and leaped out.

"Grace, you all right?" he asked, peering into Jasper's open car door.

"Fine, Art," she said, frowning. "How did you know something was wrong?"

"Well, you kept telling me to hurry up." He glanced over at Jasper, who was closing the trunk. "Everything okay then?"

Grace nodded fervently, but Jasper regarded the two siblings thoughtfully.

"I think Grace needs a bit of real fun," she told Arthur.

He was visibly surprised by her words. "Oh?"

"Yeah," Jasper said confidently, grinning. "Want to go bowling?"

Grace's entire face lit up in delight. She turned to Arthur and raised an eyebrow in question.

"You come, too, Art," Grace said, slapping Jasper's dashboard in excitement. "We haven't done anything fun in forever."

Jasper glanced a little shyly at Arthur's stern expression. "I'll have her home at a reasonable hour. If you don't want to join us."

Arthur was the one raising his eyebrows now. "I'll come. As long as you're both okay with being absolutely smoked."

Jasper released a startled laugh. The giddiness of having a crush, then having him near her, was like scissors cutting away all of the unnecessary strings that were restraining her. "Oh, yeah?" She turned to Grace. "Want to team up against him?"

Grace put on her seat belt extra emphatically in reply.

"Welcome to the Lake Pristine Lanes!" Hera cried as the three of them walked into the bowling alley. Grace rushed to the counter and started slipping out of her shoes.

"Can we have lane five for three games?" asked Jasper, smiling at Hera and then using a pleading tone as she added, "And is there any way I can veto the shoes?"

"Bowling policy, Princess," Arthur said understatedly. "Take 'em off."

"Sorry, Jazz," Hera said, shrugging. "He's right."

Jasper sighed but relented, bending down to remove her Mary-Janes. She handed them over with an exaggerated pout, which made Grace laugh. She was clearly itching to play, grabbing the bowling shoes from Hera with ferocious speed. Jasper and Arthur took theirs, though it took a little while for Hera to find size twelves for the latter's feet.

They all sat on the bench by the counter while they put on their bowling shoes. Jasper kept up her efforts to make Grace laugh, openly grimacing as she put her feet into the shoes.

"Gross! They're still warm," she joked, making Grace shriek with delight. She could even feel Arthur smiling, though she wasn't looking at him. He was next to her on the bench and he leaned a little nearer, his shoulder pressing against hers.

"Apparently a lot of alleys are doing away with the bowling shoes now," Hera called over to them. "They're not really necessary anymore, they were always a part of the sporting aspect. Which not many people do now."

"Then why are my feet in them?" Jasper barked, making everyone snort.

"You're stalling, Princess," Arthur said quietly. "You know I'm going to win."

Jasper clucked her tongue and nudged Grace. "Come on. Let's go and wipe the floor with him."

The three of them moved to their waiting lane and punched their names into the machine. Jasper wrote Grumble for Arthur and he retaliated. Grace rolled her eyes but smiled at the two of them, choosing her first bowling ball.

"Start us off strong, Gracie," Arthur said as his sister lined up her shot.

She knocked down a very respectable seven pins, smiling sheepishly as Jasper and Arthur applauded.

"There's no way to walk back from bowling and look cool," Grace muttered.

"Well, let's see," Jasper said, picking up her ball of choice and stepping up to the lane. She bowled her first shot and screamed in frustration as it only knocked down one pin.

"That was dreadful," Grace said cheerfully.

"I want a redo," Jasper said, turning to call over to Hera. "Hey, Hera? Can I have those barrier things on the side?"

"The ones for children?" Hera replied tartly.

"Yes," spluttered Jasper indignantly. "Don't say it like that, I need all the help I can get!"

"Don't give them to her, Hera," Arthur shouted, causing Grace to turn red with laughter and Jasper to gape at him in outrage.

"Why is everyone ganging up on me?" she said, her voice deliberately whiny, but her eyes sparkling with amusement.

She watched Arthur get to his feet and move over to her.

"Want some instruction?" he asked furtively.

Jasper was shocked at her physical reaction to his closeness. She looked up at him and shrugged one shoulder. "Maybe."

The rest of the alley seemed to vanish as he smirked down at her and gestured for her to turn around and face the pins again. All nine of them stared back at her, but she could not focus on them. She was too aware of the tall figure behind her, pressing close and smelling amazing.

"I think I should see your attempt first, before I let you tell me what to do," she said irreverently.

"I'm very good. Trust me," he replied, his voice a low rumble that made her feel like a ribbon was running up and down her spine. "Breathe in and throw on the released breath."

"You are so full of—"

"It's true."

She laughed nervously. Then obeyed.

The ball slid into the gutter and then into the darkened corner at the end of the lane. Grace's laughter was high and loud and Jasper released a cry of annoyance and turned to lightly smack Arthur on the shoulder.

"I trusted you! That was sabotage."

He grinned down at her, one of the rare but dazzling Arthur Lancaster smiles, and it made her dizzy. She was mortified to find that she almost swayed into him. She felt his hand on her waist as he steadied her and it was only the piercing sound of Hera wolf-whistling from the front desk that made her leap away, remembering that they were there to cheer up Grace after a creep had made her uncomfortable.

She was *not* there to flirt with Arthur Lancaster.

Even if it felt really good.

She went to sit down next to Grace while Arthur took his turn. The two of them loudly booed him, but it didn't work. He knocked down every pin, then made Jasper read out the scoreboard in celebration and she shoved him playfully.

"Dad brought him here a lot when he used to try skipping school," Grace told Jasper. "That's why he's really good."

Jasper's smile faded just a touch. "I didn't know that."

"This whole town is full of memories of Dad," Grace said, matter-of-factly. "Hard to avoid it."

Arthur won the first game, but Grace was determined to trounce him during their second. Jasper's shots improved a little and she grew more confident, turning to smile smugly at Arthur every time she managed to score a split or spare. As the game progressed, he bought her cold drinks and plied Grace with food.

Jasper couldn't remember the last time that she had enjoyed herself like this. Every time she laughed, took a drink or brushed against Arthur, she felt all of her worries disintegrating into giggles and the sound of a bowling ball hitting pins.

"You're getting better, Princess."

It took Jasper a moment to realize that Arthur was referring to her game and not something else. "Thanks, Grumble. Still think you're going to win?"

"I know it, sugar."

She choked out a laugh and made to grab his bowling ball. He held it up high, out of her reach. She glanced around for an exact twin and then spotted the men in the next lane playing. Waiting to be used by their console was a bright pink bowling ball.

"Aw, I want that one," Jasper said sadly.

Arthur followed her gaze and he chuckled as he laid eyes on it. "You want that one?"

"Yeah, why are ours all green and boring while they get that one?"

"It's the only one in the whole alley," Grace said, conspiratorially. "The one pink ball."

Jasper was about to line up her shot when Arthur made his way over to the group next to them.

"Hey," he said to the guys, who looked up at him with surprise and suspicion. "Can our girl have the pink one?"

Jasper suddenly had visions of the men vehemently defending the hot pink bowling ball and a fight starting, but they seemed unbothered.

"What's he wanting?" asked the man taking his shot.

"His girlfriend wants the pink one," another said, making to hand the ball over.

"She's not his girlfriend," Grace said quietly and knowingly, smirking at her brother's back.

Jasper's cheeks went as pink as the bowling ball which Arthur was now offering to her. She took it with a reserved smile and they stared at one another for a moment.

"Thank you," she finally said.

"You're welcome. It reminds me of you."

She looked down at the sparkling orb in her hands. "Because it's silly?"

"No. Because every other one in here is dull, lackluster, uninspiring. Then there's this one. Standing out. Impossible to miss."

The world flickered for a moment, like an old piece of film catching and slowing down. Jasper breathed in the words and it was suddenly her Lake Pristine again. The one she loved.

She hurriedly backed up and took her shot. To her astonishment, her little pink bowling ball earned her a strike. Arthur let out a long whistle and Grace clapped her hands while cheering. Jasper was stunned into silence for a millisecond and then she, too, shrieked in delight, completely bewildered but delighted by her turn.

"I did it!" she cried out.

"See," Arthur said, while readying for his own turn. "When you're yourself, things go well."

She stopped and stared at him. "What?"

He shook his head lightly. "Nothing. My turn."

Jasper lingered as he made to start his go. "Want some advice? I just scored a really good strike, so I'm kind of a bowling guru now."

His mouth twitched, but he continued to stare at the pins. He lined up his shot. Just as he was about to release his breath and the ball all at once, Jasper gently blew in his ear. He shuddered and the ball scuppered into the gutter of the lane.

Grace leaped to her feet and cackled at her brother's complete misfire. Arthur was too stunned to speak and Jasper was covering her mouth with the palm of her hand, trying not to laugh too loudly.

"That's it," Arthur said under his breath, fighting a smile. "You've gone too far, Princess!"

He bent down and threw her over his shoulder, causing her to screech and squeal with laughter. She yelped apologies through snorts of laughter, but he loudly spoke over her, drowning out her attempts.

"Just typical, cheating us peasants out of our winnings. Disgraceful."

"I'm sorry," gasped Jasper, tears of mirth forming in her eyes as she desperately reached back to stop her skirt from riding up. "Put me down, I'm sorry!"

He jiggled her instead, causing all three of them to laugh. He spun around and she suddenly felt his whole body go taut. His laughter stopped abruptly and he gently lowered her back to the ground. Jasper straightened up, wondering if she had done something wrong. She glanced at his face and then followed the direction of his gaze.

Saffron and Rebecca were standing by the shoe counter, drinking large slushy drinks. They both looked disgusted.

"So, you're here with her," Saffron said stiffly. "And *you*," she glared at Jasper. "Christine's wedding is like, ten days away, and you're playing silly games here. With him."

Rebecca also looked disapproving of the whole thing and it was enough to wake Jasper up from the pink, fluffy dream she had been playing in all evening.

"You're right," she said, feeling duly reprimanded. "I should get back to the Lakehouse."

She ducked out of the lane, giving Grace a quick kiss on the cheek. She passed her sister's bridesmaid and jogged toward the exit.

"The shoes, freak," Saffron called after her coldly.

Jasper winced and stopped dead. The arcade and alley were loud and busy, but the word seemed to shut everything down. It echoed and hung in the air.

Jasper kicked the shoes off and scooped them up. She dashed over to Hera, blushing, refusing to look back at any of them. Hera smiled apologetically at Jasper, returning her Mary-Janes.

"You two looked so right together," Hera said, almost inaudibly. "And you're not a freak. No more than me. Fuck 'em."

"It's just silliness," Jasper replied. "Don't know what I was thinking."

And with that she put on her real shoes, the ones she had put on that morning before knowing anything about pink bowling balls and how fun and gorgeous Arthur Lancaster could be.

Act Two, Scene III:
Frost

If Rebecca had told on Jasper to her sister, detailing her evening of fun and frivolity, Christine did not give it away. She did not mention it at breakfast the following day and Jasper took this as a sign to put the evening out of her mind and get back to her multitude of family responsibilities.

Later that day, she was enjoying the official opening of the Lake Pristine Winter Market so much, she didn't keep a weather eye out. A whole corner of the town had been transformed into a space for tons of little stalls. In the summer, it was the book festival. In the autumn, it was the fair. Now, in December, it was the market with hot foods, warm drinks, sweets, trinkets, presents and stocking fillers.

Jasper took in the colors and the smells. One minute she was admiring the topaz rings that were on display in one of the stalls, the next she was staring into the lens of a camera while Marcus thrust a boom mike toward her.

"Can we walk and talk?" he asked.

"Um," Jasper smiled apologetically at the stall owner. "I suppose."

Arthur walked up behind his best friend and scowled upon realizing that the camera was rolling. "Sorry, Jasper," he said, his voice gruff. The boy from the day before was gone. Serious, cold, shutdown Arthur was present again.

"It's fine," Jasper said. "But I don't think I'm a subject that's going to win you that contest."

She let them attach a microphone to the waistband of her jeans and they walked casually through the market. People found it difficult to behave naturally around the camera, many of them darting out of its viewpoint as the group shuffled along.

"How is the wedding coming along?" Marcus asked innocuously.

"Nicely," Jasper said, and it was not untrue. "Kevin and the best man had some really great fittings. The RSVPs are back. The marquee is hired, the menu is decided. I don't know why people get so stressed about weddings."

The last statement was uttered with the deepest shade of sarcasm. Jasper had almost pulled her hair out when some of Kevin's extended family had called in a rage, furious that their invitations had never arrived. Jasper had assured them that this was a case of invites being lost in the mail. In actual fact, Christine had deliberately excluded them from the list. Kevin offered to handle it, but Jasper had taken the hit, posting out fresh invitations for the offended parties and refiguring the seating plan. Then calling the venue. Then ringing up the family members to note down their menu choices, all while they hurled abuse at her over the phone.

However. Those were private matters.

"How is the filming going?" Jasper asked.

Marcus looked perturbed at being asked this question on camera, thereby breaking the fourth wall and making the footage briefly unusable.

"It's going well," Arthur said. "I think we'll have a very rough cut to preview for people, before we film the wedding."

Jasper's eyebrows shot up. "Oh, really?"

"Yeah, hope so."

"You know where you could screen some of it?"

Arthur grinned. "The thought had occurred to me. It's all just a heap of footage right now."

"I'm going to edit the first cut," Marcus said, nudging his friend. Jasper could tell that this was a conversation they had already had a few times. "Art can do his director's cut later."

Before Jasper could respond, a loud and excited shriek caused them to start. Jasper turned toward the sound of the cry and felt a pang of something strange. Odette was the one who had yelped. She was walking with Craig and Sophie, moving together with them like an amoeba, and heading for the maze.

Odette and Craig appeared to be in one of their more positive moods. Odette had been panicked the other day, calling Jasper and venting down the phone to her. She had been completely convinced that Craig was seeing another girl and Jasper had not been much help when it came to comforting her. She knew that the done thing was to assure Odette that she was imagining things.

The neurotypical custom always seemed to be gaslighting. Jasper was not very adept at that. She was better at curbing her personal instinct to be blunt, but when it came to falsely reassuring her friend about Craig, Jasper was not dextrous with her white lies.

Perhaps that was why Odette had not called to invite her to their outing.

Jasper felt the sick and familiar feeling of being left out and she hated it. She would rather have toothache than feel this way. She knew the camera was on her face, capturing her reaction to her best friend and the gaggle of other people as they headed into one of Lake Pristine's biggest attractions. It was the perfect winter day for it.

Twinkling lights were dotted around the town and the air was crisp and it felt as if snow was on the way again. The maze loomed large in the busy town square and crowds were wearing their colorful winterwear. It all looked straight out of a holiday card. The sun was bright and cold, and although a busker stood under the gazebo playing beautiful music, Jasper could only hear the blood pounding in her ears.

She was not welcome.

"How does that make you feel, Jasper?" Marcus asked softly.

"Hey," Arthur said, chastising his friend.

Her real feelings were none of their business, Jasper thought bitterly. They were being filmed, potentially for all to see, so she saw no reason to articulate them. She felt exposed, and she had to marvel at how quickly the feelings had come on. She wanted to take her phone out and check for messages, to see whether she really had been invited.

They disappeared as a group through the entrance of the maze. The entrance and exit were side by side, and there were attendants on hand in case anyone actually ended up lost inside the vast green puzzle.

"Let's discuss something else then," Marcus said, offering an olive branch. "How are the *Nutcracker* rehearsals going?"

Jasper allowed herself to be warmed by fondness for the ballet. "They're great. Grace Lancaster is a dream."

It was true. Grace made Jasper remember what it was that she loved about dance and ballet. She took direction, she was sweet to work with and she was committed to the part in a way that made Jasper emotional.

"I can't wait for people to see it," she said.

"When is the show?"

"Christmas Eve. Days away."

"Jasper, I must say, you've got college, a part-time job . . ."

"Yes?"

"You're directing and prepping your mother's junior company for this short run of one of the most famous ballets ever staged. Then, on top of all that, there's your sister's wedding. Where you are not even a bridesmaid."

Jasper prickled at his words and stared at the maze exit, watching as people excitedly ran out of it, delighted to have bested the challenge. "Is there a question in there?"

"How do you do it?"

Jasper couldn't really answer that question, not that she intended to. Her busy schedule suited her just fine. It allowed her to fight the insomnia with sheer exhaustion and kept the anxious and intrusive thoughts at bay. She was about to say something flippant when the words were stolen from her by the sight of something she knew was instantly wrong.

Craig staggered back out of the maze, laughing obnoxiously and bumping into one of the attendants without an apology. He reached back to help a companion exit the maze as well, all while wearing a knowing look. An intimate look. He did not know that Jasper and a film crew were witnessing this.

They watched him help Sophie step out onto the square. She laughed, pushing her fringe out of her eyes and looking up into Craig's face with something like adoration. Jasper felt ill. It was a snapshot. It was just body language.

But she knew. She just knew.

The way she knew when someone was about to give bad news

or tell her someone had passed away. The energy in the air, it was palpable. Easier to understand than words. Jasper had been told at a young age that she was not good at reading people, and yes, that was true. When people were being dishonest with their words or body language, when they were saying the polite thing instead of the true thing, that was when she had difficulty reading people.

When they were finally being truthful, she had no issue. And Craig and Sophie, unaware that their little moment was public, were being very truthful.

"Don't put that in the film," she told Marcus and Arthur, her eyes still fixed on the couple as they grew closer to each other. "I'm begging you."

Marcus whistled. "Can't promise that, Jasper. I mean, I— Hey!"

Jasper shoved the camera out of her way and grabbed the boy by the lapels. She did not look to see what Arthur thought of her behavior, it didn't matter. Her friend was not going to be embarrassed. "Listen to me," she said softy. "I don't care what waivers you've got people to sign, no one signed up to be humiliated. If you hurt my friend, if you embarrass her, I swear, your film will have a very dramatic and tragic ending."

"Jasper, we won't."

She finally turned to look at Arthur. "I mean it, Lancaster. Don't put this in."

"We won't," he said gently.

Jasper released his cousin.

Marcus looked horrified for a moment, but then his face morphed into delight. "Oh, Jasper, I knew this was in you. It's fantastic!"

"What's the matter with you?" she said, backing away from him. "You've gotten meaner, Marcus Lancaster. You used to be nice."

The remark disarmed him for a split second, but he quickly recovered. "We're all grown up now, Jasper. I don't have to be nice anymore. I don't have to worry about what you and your popular friends want anymore. School is over."

But in Lake Pristine, high school was never truly over. It was one of Jasper's reasons for wanting to leave.

"Marcus, don't put it in," she repeated. "Me, Odette, we've done nothing to you. If you're mad at Craig and his friends and the old days, this won't hurt *him*. Just us."

"He won't put it in," Arthur maintained, looking at his cousin, dismayed, as if this behavior was both surprising and disappointing to him.

Jasper dashed away, heading for the entrance to the maze. Craig and Sophie had scurried off to the market stalls, completely oblivious. Jasper ran into the maze, cursing its genuine level of difficulty. She called Odette's name as she wound her way through the passages.

"Follow your right hand," she told herself. "That's what they always say."

She made choices when forks in the path appeared and, on occasion, she turned back to retrace her steps. She called her friend's name, getting more and more agitated.

"Jasper?"

"Oh!" Jasper called. "I'm trying to get to you, don't move."

"I'm next to the topiary of the dinosaur," Odette called back.

"That doesn't help me," Jasper muttered.

She moved through the green and earthy corridors before finally finding Odette. She exhaled in relief at the sight of her friend and then suddenly remembered what it was she was coming to report.

"I've been stuck for a while," Odette said merrily. Then she noticed the look on Jasper's face. "What's wrong? Also, what are you doing here? I thought you'd be swamped with Christine and ballet stuff!"

Jasper did not believe in keeping secrets from friends, but in that very moment she was hit with all of the doubt that she had seen other people express in the same situation. She had always rolled her eyes when people said ignorance was bliss and it was better to let sleeping dogs lie, all of the clichés. Now that her dearest friend was looking at her in worry, the truth just seemed cruel.

But Jasper would want to know.

"It might be nothing," she prefaced, moving closer to her friend.

Odette's face fell instantly. "Craig. It's Craig, isn't it?"

Jasper felt a tremble in her voice as she said, "How much do you know?"

"Fuck," Odette gasped, pressing back against the ridiculous dinosaur made of the hedge. "Nothing. It's just a gut feeling. Why, what do *you* know?"

"I saw him leave the maze with Sophie. They looked . . . close."

Odette frowned. "But . . . did anything happen?"

"Well," Jasper wildly thought about how to word what she had seen. "No. But . . . there was just a vibe. Just a really intimate—"

"Jasper," Odette said, her tone hardening. "I'm . . . I'm not throwing away my relationship because of a *vibe*."

"You didn't see them. I did."

"Do you even know what you saw? I mean . . . did you—"

"Don't do that," Jasper said, almost inaudibly. "Don't. Odette, no. I understood what I saw. I did. I'm not misreading this, it was—"

"I have to find him," Odette said, stumbling forward and heading for one of the other connecting paths within the maze.

"Odette!" Jasper called after her friend, following her footsteps through the intricate web. "Since when did we do this? We don't talk to each other like this, especially not when a guy is involved."

"He's my guy, Jasper, and he's been there for me while you were off in the city with your posh college friends."

It hurt. But Jasper knew it was just the anxiety talking. She wanted to shout back that she didn't have any posh college friends. Odette had been her only friend, even in high school. Adam, Ross and Craig were just three rancid boys that Jasper had tolerated because it meant being with her best friend. She was not going to be shut out now. "Odette, I might be wrong—"

"Exactly. So why are we even having this conversation? Enough! I'm done discussing something that potentially did not even happen."

"I shouldn't have said 'vibe,'" Jasper said, frustrated. "But I don't know how else to explain what I saw."

"If you want to talk about vibes," Odette remarked, stopping to look at her friend with a heavy degree of judgment. "Why do you never talk about who you're 'vibing' with?"

Jasper stared. "What?"

"Come on. Let's talk about *vibes*, Jasper. You never mention it, but you surely don't think I'm stupid enough not to see it."

"Odette—"

"You two were always skulking around each other in school, always glaring at each other, and I thought it was weird. You're nice to everyone, he never gives anyone the time of day and yet there the two of you always were. Eyeing each other up. I thought it was just a strong rivalry, but I guess I was stupid. But you won't even tell me about it."

"I don't—"

"Nevermind," her friend said rashly. "I won't pry. It hurts that you don't confide in me about it, but maybe you just don't want to admit it yourself. You can be in denial. That's fine."

"This month was meant to be about you and me getting time together before things change forever," Jasper said weakly. "Not some guy who doesn't treat you right."

"Let's not talk about people who don't treat us right, Jasper. Don't be a hypocrite."

"What the hell is that supposed to mean?"

"*I* was the one you called when you were almost passed out in that club! Not your sister, your big sister, who was only a few feet away."

"I know that," said Jasper, as if in pain. "Because I trust you more than anyone."

"Just not enough to tell me what's actually going on with you. And what do you mean? 'Before things change forever,' what's that supposed to mean? What is going on with you, Jasper?"

Jasper shook her head and spoke with a crack in her voice. "Nothing's going on with me, I'm just busy."

"Yeah, busy being in denial. You never talk about college. That's never up for discussion. And you never talk about you and him."

"I know you're upset and worried about Craig," Jasper said slowly, turning over scripts in her mind, trying to find the right words, "but we don't do this. We never do this. I'm on your side. Always. And I'm not making this up, just because I don't like Craig.

I *don't* like him, he's not good enough for you, so what? But I saw what I saw. And I would want you to tell me, if the tables were turned."

Odette paused, her back to Jasper. She was breathing heavily, clearly fighting a bit of panic. "Thing is, Jasper," she finally said. "The tables would never be turned. Because you don't open yourself up to a single person. You've never been in a relationship for more than a summer, because in order for that to work, in order to actually fall in love, you need to be vulnerable. And you'll never do that for anyone. So. It is what it is. It's why you'll always be alone."

There was only the sound of the maze leaves moving in the December wind.

Jasper covered her mouth with her hand as her friend tore away. Jasper held everything inside, waiting for the sound of Odette's rustling and rummaging to dissipate. Then she sank to the ground and curled up, huddling up against the green hedge. She tried to withhold the tears, but it just made her body jerk and shake with the suppression. So she let a few drops fall down. She wiped at them, but they kept coming.

She felt like a flightless bird that could only watch the rest of the flock soar. A couple of them had difficulty mastering the ascension, but they made it eventually. They joined the V in the sky and flew away, while she gazed up from the ground.

She had always told herself that she did not need the flight.

But she wanted it. More than anything.

She dug out her list with shaking hands. A tear landed on the thin, wrinkled paper. She ran her thumb over number two and felt a choking sob in her throat. She added COMPLETED to number five and then folded it away once more.

1. Skate on Lake Pristine
2. Find Odette a better boyfriend/girlfriend/partner—anybody but vile Craig
3. Make Mum proud with an amazing *Nutcracker* performance
4. Cupcakes at Vivi's—COMPLETED
5. Christmas Maze—COMPLETED
6. Buy an ornament from the Heywoods at the Winter Market—COMPLETED
7. Tell family I'm leaving Lake Pristine (and college) for design school
8. Get into design school
9. Help Christine have the most beautiful wedding
10. Catch the late night shows at the Arthouse—COMPLETED
11. ~~Try to be civil with Arthur Lancaster~~
12. ~~Enjoy Christine's bachelorette party~~
13. Do something brave

Act Two, Scene IV:
Surprise

Jasper stood in front of her dancers after an exhausting rehearsal. The kind of rehearsal where every dancer seemed to have forgotten their motivation, their blocking and their choreography. Jasper was exasperated and tired. She rubbed her eyes and tried to smile.

"So, today was tough," she acknowledged. "I appreciate that. Not the best dress rehearsal. You need to be taking notes during your water breaks at rehearsal and you still need to come to dance class for body conditioning, even if you're not a principal."

She fixed some of the company with a pointed look.

"But," she allowed, "we will get there. Maybe this was a painful turning of a corner. But I know you know your blocking. It's about telling the story now. Okay?"

Everyone nodded enthusiastically. Jasper tapped her foot once, dismissing them. They rushed to their lockers and bags while Jasper moved over to the piano.

"Thanks, Bertie," she told the pianist, wincing as she bent to rub her left foot.

"Old injury?" he asked softly.

"Something like that," she replied.

Grace Lancaster advanced toward the two of them with reservation. Jasper gave her a small smile, one that said it was safe for her to approach. Grace looked relieved.

"Henry and I are throwing Arthur a surprise birthday party," she told Jasper.

"That's fun," Jasper said warmly.

Grace hesitated and then said, "Will you come?"

Jasper blinked in bemusement. She thought back to Arthur at the alley when Saffron had arrived. He had become gruff and firm, not the fun and alive person she had glimpsed when they were bowling. "I'm not sure your brother will want me there, Grace."

Grace opened her mouth to rebut that, but then closed it again, clearly thinking better of it. "I would love you to come."

"When is it?"

"Tonight. Arthouse at nine o'clock."

Jasper spluttered out a laugh. "In two hours?"

"Yeah," Grace said with a grin. "I know after rehearsal, you limp home and get in the bath and then read. You don't have any plans."

Jasper turned to the pianist. "Can you believe the way she speaks to me, Bertie?"

He laughed. "You need to have some fun, Miss Montgomery. No doubt about that."

"I'm quite happy being Lake Pristine's mysterious spinster in the making, thank you," Jasper said stoutly, nudging Bertie until he laughed again. She turned to Grace and her smile faded a little. "Thanks, Grace. But I have wedding prep to do. And I don't really feel like being around people."

Grace looked so crestfallen, Jasper had to fight her people-pleasing urge.

"Well. If you change your mind."

Jasper smiled weakly and nodded. "I know where to find you."

She slung an arm around the young dancer and walked her out of the studio, toward the changing room. "You're very persistent. See you at final dress before curtain up."

When she was back at the Lakehouse, Jasper went up to her room and dragged a ribbon around for Chum. He was delighted with the game and when he lovingly licked her palm with his sandpaper tongue, she felt a stab of guilt. He still loved her without any strings, despite being without her for eighteen months.

"Love you," she whispered sadly. "Love you, sweet boy."

People always joked about cats feeling no love, but Jasper knew the truth. Their kind of love was hard to earn but the biggest reward. A forever kind of thing.

Love is still love, even if it doesn't look like everyone else.

She showered and took her time with some fancy skincare products that her mother had left on her ottoman. She hauled out the hairdryer and shaved her legs.

A quiet knock on the door made her jump, but she called out, "Come in?"

She was expecting her father, so it was quite the shock when Christine meekly entered the bedroom.

"You okay?" Jasper asked without wavering. "What's wrong?"

"Nothing," Christine rebuffed, moving to sit next to Jasper on the bed. "Does something have to be wrong for me to come and see you?"

Jasper did not reply, but Christine held up her hand.

"Don't answer that, I know. I know."

Jasper looked down at her soft, cream-covered hands. She massaged the lotion into her palms and sighed. "You've been stressed, Chris."

"And you've been an angel. As usual." There was only a tiny speck of resentment in her words.

"You only get one wedding," Jasper said.

"Oh, you are so naïve."

Jasper laughed. "Nah, you and Kevin are forever. It's obvious."

Christine smiled faintly. "I hope so. He's far too good for me."

Jasper smirked. "You said you hated him when you first met."

Christine barked out a small laugh. "Well, I did. He stormed into one of our dorm parties and yelled at me to turn the music down. He was studying and we had, in his words, 'abused our fresher privileges.'"

Jasper snorted. "And you calmly and politely apologized and offered to turn down the music."

"No . . . not exactly."

"Well," Jasper was beaming, "he knew who he was marrying from the jump then."

"Precisely. He can't claim otherwise."

The two sisters rocked with laughter for a moment, Jasper basking in Christine's good mood.

"I heard rumors of a party at the Arthouse," Christine finally said, when their laughter had subsided. "Are you going?"

"Of course not," Jasper said, gesturing to the tie-dye hoodie and silk shorts she was wearing. "I'm in for the night."

"Yeah, but with a fresh face and fresh hair," argued Christine.

"Fresh bedding, too. I'm having one of those nice, undisturbed twelve-hour sleeps. Thank you very much."

Christine laced their fingers together. "Come on, Jazz. Have some fun."

"Why do people never believe that quiet time to myself after being around people all week is fun for me?"

Christine looked down at their hands and squeezed. "Something's keeping you away."

Jasper was surprised. "Maybe."

"What?"

"Well," Jasper sniffed and shifted her position, feeling unprotected. "Odette will probably be there. With her horrible boyfriend."

"And?"

"And we had a massive fight. In the maze. And we never fight."

"No," Christine agreed, looking surprised. "You don't. What was it about?"

"I saw Craig, her boyfriend, with her other friend Sophie. The girl she basically replaced me with. They looked . . . intimate."

"He's cheating?"

"I don't know," Jasper said, doubting herself. "It looked . . . off."

"Then it probably was."

Jasper felt quietly validated by Christine's assessment. "Odette did not see it that way."

"Of course not. She knows she and that loser are toxic. She knows she should dump him, but sometimes saying you have someone who loves you is worth being miserable."

"Look at you," marveled Jasper. "Very perceptive, Chris."

"Plus the bad news came from you," Christine went on.

"What does that mean?"

Christine smiled and pushed a long, not quite yet dry strand of hair out of Jasper's face. "You . . . are the golden girl. You are the princess. The angel. You are the one who just seems to be stronger and better and more sensible than all of us mere mortals here in Lake Pristine. It's oppressive, sometimes. It can make people want to lash out."

Jasper inhaled wearily and shook her hair so that it fell over her face once more. "That's not true."

"Yes, it is," whispered Christine. "It's one thing to be potentially heartbroken or humiliated. That's bad enough. But to be heartbroken and humiliated in front of the great Jasper Montgomery?" She gently tapped Jasper on the nose. "That would be unbearable."

Jasper could only gape at her sister. "Is that really what you all believe? That I think I'm better than all of you?"

"No," Christine allowed. "You don't think it. You don't think anything close to it. But we all know it. And that's what makes it even harder to swallow."

She turned Jasper so that they were both looking into the vanity mirror opposite the bed. Christine fluffed Jasper's hair and played with some of the dark brown tendrils.

"I'm giving you permission to be someone else tonight," she said firmly. "Forget the weird rules you always put on yourself, forget the good-girl persona."

"I don't have a persona—"

"It's not an act, you've just molded into it. So, tonight, unmold. Be the version of you that those stupid child psychiatrists said no one would like."

"Christine," Jasper admonished quietly. "Come on . . ."

"I mean it. And wear a choker! The best kind of bad girls always wear a choker!"

Christine hurried from the room and returned with a small

trunk of accessories and three dresses, which she unceremoni-
ously dumped onto the bedspread. Jasper leaped up, examining the
gowns.

"I say red or black," Christine said authoritatively. "You always
wear sunny, daytime colors. Time for something sensual."

"You said it yourself," Jasper pointed out. "I'm too busty."

If Jasper had not known better, she could have sworn a flicker
of shame crossed Christine's face.

"Most people would kill for your bust. So tonight: flaunt it."

"Oh, come on. People will get the wrong idea."

"What wrong idea? Who gives a flying, festering turd what
other people think? You get dressed for you! No one else. If people
want to tell themselves stories about you, let them. You spend so
much time worrying about people projecting onto you, you've become a blank canvas. Not tonight. Time for a statement."

Jasper's fingers brushed one dress with red satin. "It'll be too
tight on me."

"Only where it counts. Come on. I'll zip you in, by hook or by
crook. Put it on."

Arthur was dropping off some things at the dump; rubbish that
Henry had promised to take care of earlier in the week. He was in
a tetchy mood as he parked up outside the Arthouse afterward. He
locked the car and frowned. The cinema lights were all out.

Even if the last show had finished, it was still a little early for
that. He unlocked the front door and stepped inside—

Fifty people leaped out at him, some wearing party hats, and
they all screamed, "Surprise!" Arthur blinked rapidly and stared at
them all.

"Happy birthday, Arthur!" Grace chirruped, pushing to the front of the crowd and beaming up at him. "Are you surprised?"

"Well, obviously," Odette Cunningham said and there were murmurs of laughter.

Arthur took an unsteady step forward. "This is . . . this—"

"Crank up the music!" someone yelled to Henry, who was set up at the back. He saluted the person and music began to blast through the speakers.

The foyer had been transformed into a mingling space, and the ballroom doors were open. Everyone pushed into the second space, chattering and excited. Arthur continued to stand, glowering, and trying to work out why anyone who knew him would think this was a good plan.

"Are you surprised?" Grace repeated, hurrying up to him.

He nodded, dazedly, while looking at each face in the crowd. His mother and Brian were at the back, sharing a carafe of wine. Henry's friends were there. Marcus and Danny were gesturing for him to come over. Saffron was nursing a cranberry juice and pretending not to notice him. Odette and Craig were leaning against the counter and talking, while Sophie watched on.

He continued to search.

"She's not here, Art," Grace said softly.

He jerked his attention back to his little sister. "Sorry?"

Grace smiled wanly. "I invited her, but she couldn't make it."

Arthur's face clouded with determination. He was not going to disappoint Grace by being disappointed himself. "No idea what you're talking about, bean. But you got me. I'm surprised. So, when you and Henry ordered me off to the dump?"

"A cunning ruse."

"Very cunning. Well done. I was well and truly deceived."

He kissed the top of her head and then made the rounds, greeting people and pretending to be delighted by the surprise. He reached Marcus and Danny, who both slapped him on the back in greeting.

"How sweet is Grace for this?" Marcus said, his face splitting into a wide and warm grin. Arthur was happy to be with his old friend without his father's camera. It had changed Marcus, the filmmaking. Now, he felt relieved to see the old, familiar smile.

"Very," Arthur acknowledged, smiling tightly. "I'll put up with it for her sake."

He glanced over at the counter, his brow furrowing as he noticed the tension between Craig and Odette. They appeared to be having a heated discussion.

"It's just nice to have a town event without the two princesses," Danny said heartily, tapping his drinking glass against Marc's.

"Oof," Marcus said, a laugh in his voice. "Spoke too soon."

Arthur followed the direction of his friend's gaze and his heart picked up speed. By the entrance to the Arthouse stood the two sisters, the doors sliding closed behind them. Most people did not notice them arrive, nor did the two sisters seem to seek a grand entrance. They moved casually into the room, Christine going straight to Saffron and Rebecca, and Jasper opening her arms so that Grace could run into them.

Jasper wore red. Her hair looked different. Sleeker. Her lips and cheeks painted rouge. He thought of the pot in her room, the Parisian powder, and it felt like an intimate secret.

Arthur was frozen in place once more. His reaction was physical. Seeing her always made the rest of the world slip away, but it was more urgent now. It was embarrassing, really.

He moved to the middle of the room, as if in a trance. He could hear his friends speaking, but the words were as unimportant to him as the lyrics of the terrible song Henry was playing. He reached the two of them, Jasper and his sister, and they both looked up at him expectantly. Jasper had a flash of shyness before she steeled her resolve and raised both eyebrows at him.

"Hey, Princess."

"Hey, Grumble."

He smirked and she fought a smile. Grace glanced between the two of them, grinning.

"Doesn't Jasper look great, Art?"

"Yes," Arthur said dryly. "She does."

Jasper's eyes flared with warmth and she looked him up and down. "Happy birthday."

"Thank you. It was . . . a surprise."

"When's your birthday, Jasper?" Grace asked innocently.

Jasper's eyes dropped to the youngest Lancaster. "January."

Grace frowned. "You won't celebrate?"

"No, my last birthday was spent in bed with some great black-and-white movies and a huge bowl of popcorn. I'll do the same for the next."

Arthur bent down to whisper in his sister's ear. "Why don't you check on Mum and Brian?"

Grace looked reluctant, but she stole away, heading for their mother and stepfather. The two of them were left looking at one another, while bodies danced around them and Henry put on another song.

"Do you dance with amateurs like me?"

He surprised himself by saying it and Jasper looked taken aback.

She was about to respond when Odette appeared by their side. She gave Arthur a quick greeting and then turned to Jasper.

"Can we talk?"

Jasper's eyes widened and Arthur was surprised to see nervousness in her demeanor.

"Yes," she told Odette.

She gave Arthur a regretful smile. He kept his face as neutral as possible. He gave a feeble little wave, as she and her friend moved away to a more secluded part of the room.

There was a tap on Arthur's shoulder.

"Don't bite my head off, but can we have a birthday interview? For the birthday boy's very own documentary film?"

Arthur threw Marcus a glum look but shrugged his shoulders in defeat. "Fine."

There was a little snug in the farthest corner of the cinema lobby. Henry's music was pounding in the ballroom and Arthur did not resent being granted a small moment of respite from his brother's questionable music taste and the feelings that were becoming harder and harder to push away. He sat across from the camera and let his directorial partner attach a microphone to him.

"How are you feeling about this party?" asked Marcus. "If you can look at me when you answer and not the camera lens?"

"I know how this works," Arthur grumbled. "And I am . . . surprised."

Marcus laughed. "Do you enjoy your birthday?"

Arthur was ready to fire off another flippant, monosyllabic retort, but he decided on the truth instead. "I preferred birthdays when my dad was around."

Marcus nodded emphatically. Arthur would normally try to veer away from topics that could be milked for content, but he was feeling open. He was happy to see everyone he cared about gathered in the same room, but . . . grief made him mad more than anything else. It angered him. The unfairness of it.

"What do you think your father would say to you, if he were here today?" Marcus asked.

"I think he would tell me to shut up and ask a pretty girl out," Arthur said honestly.

"Which pretty girl?"

Arthur rolled his eyes and forced himself not to turn around and look back at the crowd of people.

He suddenly had a memory from school. A few weeks into January, after he had worked backstage at Andrea Montgomery's *The Nutcracker*, he had been in the school cafeteria. He had spotted May, Marcus and Danny eating lunch by the large windows and they had waved him over. While crossing the room, Ross and Adam had backed into him, almost knocking him to the ground. He had scowled at them and muttered something rude, and the next thing he knew, he was face down on the ground. He had fought back, releasing every bit of angst until the teachers had to pull the three boys apart.

He remembered Jasper's face. She and Odette had been making their way over to the "popular" table, carrying their lunch trays. He remembered her shock. He remembered his embarrassment.

And he remembered how he had allowed his insecurity to turn Jasper into an enemy.

His father would never have stood for Arthur's bad temper.

"My dad really loved his life. I wish I could be more like that," he finally said. "I want to love my life. I want to love everything in it. I love my family, but, right now, I'm just going through the motions. I don't love this town, I don't love my work. Mostly because I don't have full control over the business and what I want to do with it. But one day, I will. And, one day, I won't have to drag myself out of bed. I'll get up, ready to do a job that I love—the way I want to do it."

"With someone?"

Arthur flinched. "What?"

"Well, this is a film revolving around a romantic little town and a wedding. We've interviewed a lot of the people living here, plenty of them want to see you happy."

"I'm fine on my own." He was curt, irritated at the thought of being whispered about.

"We've heard conflicting accounts."

Arthur glared. "From whom?"

Marcus's eyes glinted. "That's a cut." He waited until the camera was no longer rolling and then turned back to Arthur. "Speaking of all this, I wanted to run something by you."

"Oh, yes?"

"I've been fiddling with the edit, I think I have enough of a cut for a screening. Shall we do it here? At the Arthouse? A film by Lake Pristine's very own Arthur Lancaster!"

Arthur, who was so proud of his father's cinema, felt a spark of gratification at the idea. "Let's do it."

Act Two, Scene V:
Real

Jasper allowed Odette to lead her to a small dark corner and she coughed awkwardly as the two of them settled, aware of how uncomfortable the air felt between them.

"So," Jasper said guardedly, "what's up?"

Odette was finding it difficult to meet her friend's gaze. "Um. So, I talked to Craig."

While the words were casually spoken, and Odette was looking at her with calm civility, there was a catch in the air. Jasper's inability to read her friend's mind felt like an attack. While no person could ever truly understand what another was thinking, Jasper always struggled with predicting other people's behaviors or thought processes.

"He says you really misunderstood what happened at the maze."

Jasper felt as if she had swallowed a stone. "What?"

Odette was determined, but her voice shook just a touch. "He said when he left the maze, Sophie was still inside. He said he waited for a bit, to see if anyone else was coming out, then went to the market. Sophie got there five minutes before I did and they were just getting hot dogs when I saw them. So . . ."

Jasper gave Odette her hardest stare. "So, that's it? His word against mine."

"It's totally possible you misunderstood—"

"I did not misunderstand and I did not hallucinate. He was not there by himself, O. I did not lose my faculties and imagine Sophie there."

"I know it's been hard to see me close with someone else," Odette said. "I appreciate that. But Sophie wouldn't do that to me. Same way you wouldn't do that to me."

"Odette." Jasper stared at the girl she had loved for so long. Her closest friend, the person she had saved and been saved by too many times to remember. "I'll ask you once. Are you saying that I lied to you?"

"No," Odette said, ardently. "I just think you got the wrong—"

"Goodbye," Jasper said quietly, rising to her feet and walking away.

"Jasper? Jasper!"

She could hear Odette calling after her, but for the first time in her life, for the first time in their friendship, Jasper did not look back.

She moved to the counter in the lobby and poured herself a large, slushy drink. Christine was still talking to a very tearful-looking Saffron and Arthur was dancing with Grace. Jasper had to smile at the adoration on the young girl's face. Arthur was relaxed enough, he almost seemed approachable—flickers of the guy she had gone bowling with now visible in his face.

"Mind giving us a quick fifteen?" asked a voice.

Jasper sighed. "Sure, Marcus. But this might be the last time."

"Better make it count, then. Me, I mean. I had better make it count."

Jasper sat in the empty seat, opposite the camera, and tried to find an unused bottle inside of her for her feelings. She imagined shoving her emotions into the bottle and casting it out to sea. "Shoot."

"How's the evening going for you, Jasper?"

Jasper screwed the lid of her invisible bottle on tight. "Nice."

"What's nice about it?"

"I thought it was very sweet of Grace to surprise her older brother."

"Have you wished Arthur a happy birthday?"

"Yes."

"Not very talkative tonight?"

She shrugged one shoulder. "I'm feeling peaceful."

An erroneous statement. She did not feel anything close to peace, but she knew that the surface would not betray her. She was like a swan. Smooth and calm on the water, feet going like mad beneath. She smiled serenely at Marcus, almost revelling in the knowledge that her feelings were hidden away from prying eyes. It was one thing to feel betrayed by your best friend. But to have the world access those feelings, that was too much for Jasper.

"Well, come on," Marcus said. "You're a hopeless romantic, Jasper. You come here to watch old movies. Talk about that!"

"I love a love story," Jasper accepted. "But it's fiction. I enjoy love stories; my mother and sister enjoy shows about murder. My father loves golf and gardening programs. We all have our niches."

"What do you get from love stories?"

"Probably the same thing my mum and sister get from murder shows," Jasper said glibly. "The ending is usually the same. A happy ever after. The detective always catches the killer; someone always says 'I love you, too.' It gives you some order in a world full of cynical chaos. In the real world, real murderers get away with the crime, two times out of three, and most relationships don't make it."

"Ah, so you're a cynic who misses being an optimist."

"No," Jasper said. "I just like seeing people be good to each other."

She surprised herself with the words. They were true. It was why she could never watch people getting their throats slit or their bodies cut up. She liked softness. She liked gentle things. She liked to see them earned.

In a world with war and famine and too many horrors to even confront, two humans embracing always seemed like a miracle.

"Not that you ever see people like me in love stories," she added, loftily. "Patronizing dating shows that infantilize us? Yes. Feel-good Oscar-bait films where we die and teach the allistic character a powerful lesson? Sure. Actual love stories? Not so much."

The small speech seemed to silence Marcus and Jasper felt a flicker of triumph.

"Anything else?" she prompted.

"A lot of people in this town love you," Marcus stated.

Jasper nodded. "Yes. It's felt."

"Your friends are all dating. But not you?"

She felt the piercing gaze of the camera and wondered if this strange moment of film would make the final edit. If it did, she did not want it to capture something candid. She did not want to be vulnerable about this topic, or anything really. Her inner resources would not let that part of her go, they would not let her be hurt.

So, she was flippant. "No one's asked me."

"Ah, come on now."

"No, it's true," she said lightly. "I must give off very unapproachable vibes or no one in town has any interest."

She slapped her knees and rose to her feet, handing back her microphone with a wry smile.

"I hope you found your story," she told Marcus unemotionally. "I'm not sure you and Arthur are on the same page creatively. But I hope you got what you're looking for."

"Oh, I definitely did," he said softly, watching her slip back into the crowd of people. "Thanks, Jasper."

Jasper had to fight the urge to find her best friend again. Instead, she slipped out of the cinema, firing off an explanatory text to Christine, and then began walking home. The air felt ready for snow and there were still townspeople milling around Main Street, peering at the Christmas market stalls. One vendor was telling a young woman that she looked beautiful wearing moonstone, which made her throw her head back and laugh before reaching for her purse. A father was buying his son a small snow globe.

Jasper walked through the crisp air and watched her visible breath fill the dark in front of her. She loved the feeling of the cold.

"You always slip away from parties without saying goodbye."

She stopped walking at the sound of his voice. "Yes. I really recommend it."

She turned. Arthur Lancaster had his hands in his pockets and was braced against the chill.

"Aren't you freezing?" he asked, his eyes running up and down her dress.

"Nah," she said. "The shoes are so tight, it heats up the rest of the body."

"They do look painful."

"They've got nothing on pointe shoes."

He reached her. "Hold on a second."

He started lightly jogging toward his car.

"I want to walk!" she called, when he opened the door and gestured for her to get in.

"Are you mad? It's freezing!"

"I like it."

He looked torn but finally decided to close the car door. He moved instead to his back seat, grabbing a shearling coat. He jogged over to where Jasper was slowly walking and held it out for her.

"Here," he said. "Put this on."

He opened up the coat for her and she slipped her arms inside before shrugging it on. It dwarfed her, but she felt instantly warmer. "Thanks."

"No problem."

"Are you being gentlemanly or do you just disapprove of my dress?"

He choked on a laugh and she smiled.

Some of Lake Pristine's residents were walking through Main Street, admiring the new winter decorations. Jasper was suddenly aware of how many couples there were. Young parents who were taking their kids to the stalls on Main Street for the very first time, looking tired but happy. People on dates, sharing a mulled wine. Elderly pairs who were so familiar they looked almost part of the scenery. And around them all, the stall vendors who made ordinary things meaningful and pretty. It was a hot dinner of a town.

It was a gorgeous place to live.

"Evening, Jasper," Ester said as she passed the two of them with her dog. "Happy birthday, Arthur, son."

"Hello, Ester," they both replied in chorus. They were walking as if trying to prolong the journey.

"So, what's with the running out on parties early?" Arthur finally asked.

"I hate goodbyes. You know, public ones. In front of everyone. I usually get overstimulated and need to leave things early and I really hate drawing attention to the fact. I'd rather just sneak away."

"But you know," he said, "when you sneak off, people do notice after a while. And worry something's happened to you."

"That's where Christine comes in," Jasper said craftily. "I text to tell her that I'm leaving early and she does damage control."

"Smart."

"You know, in the city, you can sneak away from a party after twenty minutes and nobody gives a rat's ass. But in Lake Pristine? Where your every move is watched? Blasphemy."

"Well, it's like I've always said. You are the princess."

Jasper's smile died. "Don't say that," she whispered.

He glanced at her. "But it's true?"

"You're the only one who has ever called me that. And don't think that I don't remember how nastily you used to say it."

Arthur was taken aback. "When?"

"Backstage. All those years ago. You used to bark it at me and I resented it."

"It's a compliment."

"Nothing is a compliment when it's being yelled at you in front of thirty other people while you're in a ridiculous ballerina costume, believe me."

"I seem to remember you giving it back pretty easily. Didn't you threaten me with a broken-off piece of the set?"

"I don't recall that."

"I do. I thought you would really beat me with the thing."

"You were snapping at one of the other dancers, I felt it my duty to step in! Would you like it if a stage manager was yelling at Grace?"

"Of course not, but I was not yelling. I think I just asked her to stop sticking her used-up chewing gum on the props. It's not my fault that my manner comes off as gruff to some people."

"Okay, I didn't know about the gum thing, that's gross."

"There, you see. I don't shout at ballerinas without a good reason."

They reached the path in the wood, leading off to the Lakehouse. They had walked it a few times together and this was their most sluggish pace yet.

"Careful," Arthur said suddenly. "There's ice."

As if jinxing her, Jasper slipped on the uphill climb and Arthur bolted forward to steady her. Unfortunately, in his eagerness to stop her from falling, he tripped and skidded on the ice himself. He landed as gracefully as he could and let out a resounding curse of pain.

Jasper clapped a hand over her mouth, trying to stop her laughter from bubbling up. "Are you okay?"

He winced and Jasper hunkered down next to him. "I'm fine," he mumbled.

"Yeah, I don't believe you. What hurts?"

"This is humiliating."

"No, getting all toxic and pretending that getting hurt is for weaklings, *that's* humiliating. Now tell."

The corners of his lips twitched into an almost smile. "Left ankle."

"Can you walk?"

"Yep," he said assuredly, letting her haul him to his feet. He bit back another curse and attempted the hill once more. "Ah, fu—"

"Yeah, no, you shouldn't walk on it," Jasper said gravely. "Lean on me."

"As if," he scoffed. "You're a foot shorter than me and you're in heels."

"I'm not the one who got hurt. Lean."

Jasper attached herself to him, wrapping an arm around his torso and gently escorting him up the remainder of the path, helping him fight the ice and keep his balance without further injuring his ankle.

"Dad!" she bellowed, as they neared the entrance of the Lakehouse. "We have a damsel in distress here."

"This is grim," snorted Arthur.

"You're deeply wounded and I'm getting you to safety. Aren't I gallant?"

The front door popped open and Jasper's father poked his head out into the winter cold. "What's happened?"

"We have an injured visitor," Jasper called back.

Her father gamely vaulted down the front steps of the house and took Arthur's other arm.

"This really isn't nece—"

Arthur's words were cut off by the two Montgomerys shepherding him into the house.

"I'll get him some ice!" volunteered her father, before dashing from the room.

"Your dad is certainly a man of action," Arthur murmured, as Jasper gently lifted his ankle, so she could shove a cushion underneath it.

"He sure is," she said distractedly. "Does that hurt?"

Arthur shook his head but his right eye was twitching in pain. Jasper merely sighed.

"It obviously does," she muttered. "Dad! Bring some Tylenol, as well, please!"

"I'm fine," insisted Arthur, as her father returned with a basin of ice and some pills.

"That path is a terror," her father said sympathetically. "I've landed nose up on it a few times. I didn't know it was icy tonight, or I'd have salted it. You managed in those terrible shoes, though, Jazz. Good girl."

Arthur opened his mouth in outrage, but Jasper clapped a hand over his lips. She was laughing while he glared at her.

"I tripped first, Arthur caught me. That's why he fell."

Arthur's eyes softened and she slowly withdrew her hand.

"Well," her father glanced between the two of them and brusquely cleared his throat. "I'll boil the kettle then, shall I?"

Jasper reached into the basin and took out some blocks of ice, which she wrapped in the flannel her father had laid over the top of the bowl. She pressed it against Arthur's now swollen ankle.

"You wanted to walk," he pointed out crustily.

"Oh, yes," she said. "It's all my fault."

"It is," he mumbled, flexing his foot and shuddering.

Jasper sat neatly on the floor by the sofa, still pressing the ice to his injury. "Ice now, heat later on."

"Yes, doctor."

They sat in silence for a moment before Arthur said, "You must have had a lot of injuries, as a dancer?"

"Oh," Jasper said, bemused. No one was ever interested in a dancer's pains and aches. "Yes, I suppose. A couple of bad ones."

"Didn't you break both arms?"

"Both wrists," she corrected. "Yes. *Peter Pan* rehearsals went a bit wrong, landed badly."

"If I'd been managing that rehearsal or performance, it would never have happened."

"No, probably not."

"I remember seeing you that Christmas with casts on your arms."

"Yes," Jasper said, frowning. "I don't remember seeing you."

"Well, you never really saw me. We moved in completely different circles. A cat can look at a queen, and all that."

"You really have been keeping tabs on me."

"It's just a tiny town."

"Whatever I did to make you dislike me so much, I'm sorry," Jasper said quietly, adding a little more ice. "You've always had it in for me. We had loads of fun the other day, but it did make me think a doppelganger had taken your place."

She said it teasingly, but when he did not respond, she glanced up at him. He was looking at her with something she was too nervous to name. Something serious and unbreaking.

"I don't dislike you," was all he said, when she could no longer hold his gaze. "And I really approve of the dress."

She blinked rapidly and then clumsily reached for the Tylenol. "One or two?"

"Jasper."

"I think the instructions always say to take no more than two, but doctors always prescribe—"

Her words cut off as he reached over and gently removed the packet of pills from her hand. He placed them on the wooden floorboards and then took her outstretched palm. He smoothly pulled her closer to him, until their faces were inches away. Jasper felt as if she were about to dance. It was that same racing anticipation, something she had not felt in years. It was the excitement mixed with shivering nerves and all of the things that could go wrong paled against the elation of what could go right.

His hand slipped up into her hair and he gently ran the tips of his fingers along the top of her ear. She moved closer and the guard dropped for a moment.

"Never," he spoke, brokenly, "disliked you."

The front door crashed open and Christine's voice called, "Hello?" which made Jasper leap back, almost knocking over the bowl of leftover ice.

"In here," she said.

She regretted speaking immediately as Christine marched into the room. She took in the sight of Arthur Lancaster on the couch with a propped-up ankle.

"You finally pushed him down some stairs," she said loftily.

Jasper made a high-pitched sound and avoided looking at either of them. "Not exactly." She silently begged for Christine to leave.

"I'll call Henry to come and get you," Christine told Arthur with deadpan courtesy.

Jasper cast a quick glance at the invalid. He was looking right back at her, clearly wanting them to be alone.

Christine, if she could see this voiceless communication, ignored them both. She took out her phone and asked Arthur for his brother's number.

"I don't remember it and my phone is dead," Arthur said.

"Fine, I'll call the Arthouse," Christine said, fixing him with an unyielding look.

She dialed the number.

"Henry," she said, her voice full of importance and small-town royalty. "Come and get your brother, he's thrown himself onto our driveway and snapped his ankle."

She did not wait to hear what Arthur's brother had to say, the phone call was already ended.

"Christine," Jasper said softly. "I—"

"Jasper, go and fill up a flagon for them," Christine ordered, her eyes never leaving Arthur. "I have teenage memories of how freezing-cold Henry's car is."

Jasper sighed, but Christine was not to be disobeyed, she could tell. She moved to the back of the house, to the kitchen, and started filling up a flask of hot tea. She was still feeling the effects of the moment she had just shared with Arthur.

"Everything okay, Jazzie?" her father asked, as he emptied the kettle.

"All good," Jasper said breathlessly. "Fine."

Christine waited for her sister to enter the kitchen and then closed the living room door.

Arthur exhaled wearily. "What's the problem, Christine?"

Her eyes shone in the firelight as she glared at him. "What are you doing?"

Arthur pointed to his tender ankle. "Literally nothing, this is agony."

"With my sister. What are you doing with my sister, Arthur?"

He met her gaze, defiantly. "We're friends."

"Rubbish," she sneered. "We've had this conversation before, you and I."

Arthur remembered it well. His father had told him to help out with some backstage work at the annual *Nutcracker* performance. Mr. Lancaster had disappeared to help with the lighting and Andrea Montgomery had thrown a clipboard at Arthur and made him stage manager. He had busied himself in the wings, bantering with the male dancers and occasionally bringing water to the orchestra pit.

The nursery dancers had arrived to rehearse their one number in the show. Four-year-olds who were excited to be on a real stage. They had huddled together and gazed around them in awe. Christine had clapped loudly and barked at them, ruling the little group with fear. Arthur had rolled his eyes and went back to checking cues. He'd called places into the microphone at his desk, knowing it would feed into the dressing rooms and alert the company.

When he had next looked out at the stage, his life was changed.

At fourteen, he was easily swayed by pretty girls, but the prettiest girl he had ever seen was now crossing the stage from the opposite wing, dark brown hair was pulled into a bun, her legs long and her smile bright. She was not smiling at him, though—of course not. She was holding her arms out to the gaggle of little girls. They shrieked and squeaked in delight at the sight of the prima ballerina. She hugged each one of them, with the affection of an older sister.

She had looked like a princess.

"What are you staring at?"

The words had been barked at him by the princess's older sister. Christine had scowled at him then.

She wore the same scowl now.

"Do you really think it's not obvious?" she asked.

They both stared at one another in the Lakehouse living room with years of distrust lingering between them.

"Do you think I don't see how you look at her? Do you think the whole town isn't aware? Saff says all you ever did when you were with her is talk about my sister."

Arthur shifted his position on their sofa, grimacing as he forced himself to sit up straight. He did not want to take on Christine Montgomery in a showdown, with a wounded ankle, but he would if he had to. "I don't know what you see."

"Jasper's too nice to tell you, but she's not interested."

It was like someone carefully snipping off little chunks of his heart. "Okay."

"She's not interested in boyfriends or girlfriends, period. Or dating. She's going back to university. She's getting out of this town. She probably won't come back. I told her to stay in the city, but she came back because she missed home and her best friend. But I know she's going to see what I saw at her age. That this town swallows girls like her up. She's not made for it. If your dream is to get married and raise a family, it's great. That's what I want. It's what I'm getting. My college days were to have fun and meet someone, hers are to actually get qualifications. But she'll never find a career here and *that's* what Jasper wants. She's going to get out. So don't think for a second you're going to keep her here. You won't."

Arthur was shocked to hear panic and fear in Christine's voice. "Why was she sent away?"

It was the question he had always wanted answered.

"What?"

"Why was Jasper sent away to some fancy university, miles away? In the city? There are other colleges, closer colleges."

"She wanted to go," whispered Christine.

"I don't believe you. She loves this town, she adores Odette. She may not show it as enthusiastically as other people, but it's there."

"She went because my parents are paying for her education. That course. That university. They wanted her to get her undergraduate and then go to law school and follow in our father's footsteps."

Pieces of the story were suddenly written out in full for Arthur. Her parents had selected the university, the course, all of it. He felt defensive on Jasper's behalf. A student could work until they dropped, they still wouldn't be able to pay for college tuition alone. Her parents had leveraged that against her. Money in exchange for obedience.

"She doesn't want that," snapped Arthur. "She's creative. She's artistic."

"They wouldn't pay for anywhere else, so she caved. It was too late for her to apply for finance anywhere else. Our parents have always been good at ultimatums."

Christine moved away from the door, casting a worried glance toward it—as if fearful that Jasper would hear or walk in.

"You know, I went out with Henry for a summer?"

Arthur's eyes shot open. This was brand-new information. "When?"

"The summer before we went to university. It was a fine few months. Young love is nice and all, but not in a freezing-cold car that barely runs, with a guy who will never leave the junky old cinema his family own."

Arthur gritted his teeth, against the pain and against her words. "Henry is getting out as soon as I take over."

"Tell yourself that. Both of you. But Jasper deserves the world and you can't give it to her. Now, why can't you just have what Henry and I did? I'll tell you why. Henry never looked at me the way you look at her. You're too serious about her and I don't like it."

Arthur was about to rebut, when a car horn sounded outside. He watched Christine mask a small flicker of vulnerability with ease and move swiftly to open the front door.

"Hey," came Henry's low voice and Arthur was suddenly able to recognize a whole host of memories inside of it.

"He's in here," Christine said flatly.

They both appeared in the room and Henry's face broke into a grin. "Hey, walking wounded. Happy birthday, indeed."

Arthur did not even try to hide what he was feeling. "Let's go," he told his brother fiercely.

"Well, hold on," Henry said, his rarely used big brother tone creeping in. "Don't rush up, let me help."

Arthur just wanted to get home. "No. We're leaving." He hurtled up from the sofa, cringing at the pain, and he limped out of the Montgomery Lakehouse without once looking back. He was feeling raw and he hated that Christine could see.

He had always written her off as someone who was completely self-obsessed. Now, knowing that she had been reading his face and understanding his feelings, before he had even understood them himself, he had no wish to remain in the Lakehouse at all.

Act Two, Scene VI:
The Documentary Part One

Jasper was sleepwalking through her shift at Pete's cafe.

She wanted to tell Odette all about what had happened after Arthur Lancaster's party, but the air was too frosty between them. Neither of them had reached out to the other. It was uncharted territory.

She completed her work orders on autopilot, casting a glamor about herself, one that told people not to speak to her.

"But that's so soon!" Sophie's voice came suddenly, as she, Danny and Arthur Lancaster entered the cafe mid-conversation.

Jasper ignored the groaning, grinding feeling of envy as her mind wandered and wondered if they were arranging a date. First the girl had poisoned Odette against Jasper, and now she was moving for Arthur.

She stopped herself, appalled that she had even had the thought. It was not her business, she reminded herself. He could take her to Pete's cafe, just like he took Saffron. He clearly asked girls out if he was interested in them. Actions spoke louder than words, if he wanted to he would—a million mantras flashed through her mind, beating down any soft feelings and memories of ice under starlight.

"I've said from the start," Arthur's voice rumbled as he spoke the words, sliding into a booth with Danny and Sophie, "there won't be much of a story yet. Just a collage of town things. We have a ton of interviews and clips that he will pull together. It'll be cute. Nothing more."

They were discussing the documentary. Jasper exhaled.

"Will I get the best seat in the house?" Sophie asked silkily.

Arthur looked visibly confused by this and it almost made Jasper smile.

"By the way," Sophie went on, " Marcus asked me to Christine's wedding. I know who I really want to go with, but he's taking too long to ask me so I thought . . ."

She deliberately let her words trail off and Jasper felt a flash of sympathy for Arthur. Learning to read between the words that other people used, trying to find their actual meaning, had taken Jasper years. She still struggled on occasion to register what they actually wanted, when they were making small talk. She was well-versed enough to know that Sophie was fishing for Arthur to be her date to the wedding.

"You'll have a good time?" Arthur eventually said, making it sound like a question rather than a statement.

Jasper did not need to glance across at them to know that this was not what Sophie wanted to hear.

"Maybe you could ask me?" she said bluntly and Jasper almost whistled in respect at the girl's forthrightness.

She had more courage than Jasper, it would seem. Though Jasper inwardly noted the long, drawn-out silence from Arthur following Sophie's abrupt words.

"What about Marc, does he think you're going together?" he finally said.

"I'll get him another date," Sophie said breezily. "Jasper! Hey, Jasper?"

She called Jasper's name loudly enough for most of the cafe to fall silent.

Jasper could feel Arthur's eyes on her, but she stared at Sophie warily. "Yes?"

"Would you go to your sister's wedding with Marcus? I know no one else will have asked you. I'm sure he'd love to take you. In fact, I know he would."

"Hey," growled Arthur. "What the hell."

"I'm good," Jasper said quietly.

"Oh, has someone else already asked you then? That's not what I heard!" Sophie asked needlessly. Her face bore a friendly smile, but there was something sharp in her eyes.

"No, no one," Jasper answered honestly. It was perhaps a vulnerable admission to make in front of them, but she did not care. Preparations for a wedding, rehearsing the girls for the ballet and potentially losing a dear friend had all seemed far more important than a date.

"Really, Jasper?" Danny piped up. His eyes were wide and his nice face was open with surprise. "I'll take you! No problem at all."

Jasper had to smile at his earnestness. "Thanks, Danny. I—"

"Excellent!" crowed Sophie before anyone else could speak. "You have two choices now—Marc or Danny, Jasper. It's all good."

"You're quite the matchmaker, Sophie," Arthur said stonily, fixing her with a calculating stare.

"Nah," Sophie gushed, missing the undertones. "I'm just a girl's girl."

"Don't let Marcus down yet," Arthur interjected roughly. "I'm not going."

Sophie's entire demeanor switched in an instant. Her cheerful, gleeful disposition transfigured into disbelief with a tiny, delicate touch of rage. "Excuse me?"

"I'm not going," he repeated, getting to his feet. "If people are free on Thursday, the Arthouse is screening the early cut of the documentary on Lake Pristine. Starts at eight, hope you can make it."

Then he stormed out, leaving most of the cafe to sit in awkward silence while Sophie visibly seethed and Jasper wished she could just dematerialize.

Lake Pristine was abuzz as the premiere of the rough cut grew closer.

Marcus seemed a little taken aback by the excitement, Arthur noted. His cousin came to the Arthouse the day before the event and expressed surprise and nauseousness at the town's enthusiasm. Marcus had been locked away editing for the last few nights. While Arthur enjoyed the directing and filming, Marcus was happier in a darkroom, cutting it all together. He had emailed Arthur the cut, and the latter was very happy with it.

"People are really excited," Henry said, as the three of them surveyed the larger of the two screens.

"We're just shy of selling out the whole house," confirmed Arthur. "It's going to be an impressive turnout."

He was somewhat fascinated by the anxiety Marcus was starting to show. Arthur was keen to see their project on the big screen, still hopeful that it would provide him with the clarity he needed for his final cut. He was not convinced they had the finished story yet, this was just a preliminary screening—sweet cuts of small-town life. He was hoping the audience would steer him with their reactions.

"See you at the premiere," Marcus mumbled, before rushing to his car.

The two Lancaster brothers watched him drive off.

"Do you think . . . it's going to be bad?" asked Henry.

"No," Arthur replied, though he sounded more confident than he felt. "It'll be fine. I've seen it. He's just being Marcus."

Their eyes met and they both burst into snorts of laughter.

When Thursday night, and the debut of the film's rough cut arrived, the Montgomery family were dressed to the nines at the Lakehouse and preparing to leave for the cinema.

"How's my fit?" Andrea asked her husband, while checking her hair in the hallway mirror.

"Grand," Howard said, kissing her cheek quickly. "You'll be the prettiest one there."

Jasper smiled at her parents. She herself was wearing a black dress and a choker. No heels on this occasion, just a pair of her old ballet flats. Christine was all in white and Kevin was in his engagement party suit.

"Ready to promenade?" Christine's fiancé asked, grinning at his soon-to-be in-laws.

"I hope none of you embarrassed yourselves with those boys while they were filming," Christine said as they made their way into Lake Pristine.

"They've filmed some pretty intense stuff," Jasper said quietly, sitting back in the car and stimming lightly.

"Don't do that with your hands," her mother said quickly, but Jasper hardly heard her.

"Oh, my God," she breathed, as her father pulled into Main Street. Her mother was in the passenger seat, Jasper in the back, while Kevin and Christine were following behind in Kevin's Mercedes. "Dad, you're not going to find a parking space."

The whole town had come out to see the documentary screening. Cars were lined up and down the pavements outside of the Arthouse and a crowd had gathered. There was even local press.

Jasper was suddenly hit with a devastating sense of foreboding.

She was about to tell her family that they should turn the car around and go home, but her parents were already getting out. Her mother looked glamorous and her father looked proud. Kevin and Christine joined them, every bit the golden couple, and Jasper knew it was too late to back out, no matter how strong the instinct to run away was.

She followed meekly behind her family as they joined the line of townsfolk waiting to get into the screen.

"There's a waiting list for returned tickets, apparently," Mrs. Heywood said elatedly. "This is more exciting than when we had that beauty pageant."

The beauty pageant she spoke of had been for dogs. Still, Jasper couldn't help but feel that a dog beauty pageant would end in far less anguish than this documentary.

Henry scanned their tickets at the doors.

"Have you seen it?" she murmured, as her family found their seats.

He looked at her with an expression that was impossible for her to read. "Some of it. Rolled the first five minutes to check it would run. I wouldn't look so worried, Jasper."

"Is it all good?"

"It's pretty sweet, I wonder if there's going to be a big twist!"

He was teasing her, but Jasper winced. "Oh, Henry, don't, I've got a bad feeling about all of this."

Henry tried to respond, but there were overzealous community members waving tickets in his face. He threw Jasper an apologetic look and got back to work.

Jasper was breathing rapidly as she joined her family. She sat next to Kevin, with her father on her right, and spotted Odette, Sophie and Craig a few rows down from them. She wanted to scream over to her best friend, regardless of their current status. Odette could be angry, and Jasper was, too. She was hurt. But that would not put a dent in her loyalty. She hated to see Sophie and Craig there together, while Odette was being lied to and gaslit.

Marcus and Danny were near the front and Grace was sitting with Arthur by the aisle, in the row right in front of Jasper and her family. Grace glanced back and waved happily at Jasper. Arthur turned to see who his sister was addressing and they stared at each other for a moment.

Jasper was starting to feel terrified. Christine had been counting on this documentary as some beautiful, pre-wedding video that would capture her and Kevin in a romantic light and paint Lake Pristine as the dream town to live in. A place where Christine was queen.

Her heart had started to race, her blood felt chill and her head tight.

"Christine," she said, in a small and frightened voice. "I don't—"

The lights dimmed in the cinema, while Henry, Arthur and Marcus took to the front of the auditorium, all holding microphones. Marcus was looking an odd color, while Henry was putting on a brave face, and smiling out at what now appeared to be the entire town of Lake Pristine.

"Good evening, everyone," Henry spoke into his microphone with a knowing look and a voice filled with anticipation. It lit a spark of exhilaration in the room, and people started to cheer and applaud.

Jasper dug her fingers into her thighs and squeezed, her hands desperate to move and stim, but she had to keep a lid on herself whenever she was with the family. Her whole body must have been humming with anxiety because Kevin leaned in to ask if she was all right.

"Fine," she said on a breath, still staring at Marcus and Arthur. "I'm fine."

"So, this is the day we've been waiting for since my brother picked up Dad's old camera," Henry said, and there was friendly laughter throughout the room. "He's got a cut of the film to share with us all today. As I'm sure you're aware—this is not the finished piece. Marcus has impressed that upon me and told me to remind you all, so here I am, reminding you. This is not the final edit. But it's pretty complete. Over to the filmmakers!"

The room erupted into applause, but it only made Marcus grimace. Arthur looked unreadable as ever, but he did cast his cousin a questioning look. This made Jasper even more afraid. She was having trouble reading his cues, understanding his expression. His emotional state was a mystery to her as he stood upon the small raised platform before the massive screen, his hands shaking slightly as he held his microphone.

"Thank you, everyone," Arthur said, causing the clapping to settle. "Thank you. Wow. I really did not expect this turnout, or this reaction. I thought we would run a rough cut of the film to a few faces and then I would be run out of town."

He laughed a little too loudly and sharply.

"Anyway, thank you all for coming. Great to see so many of you. And thank you for giving up your time for interviews and constant filming. I know some of you found it far more annoying than others, but I do appreciate it."

He paused and someone coughed at the back of the room, everyone waiting for him to hurry and introduce the film so that they could see just what he had been documenting.

"This cut won't be the final one, like we've said, but we're glad to share it with you." He glanced at his friend once more. "Marc?"

"I hope . . ." Marcus looked down at his shoes and squinted slightly against the cinema lights, "I hope some of you will forgive me. I just really wanted it to be seen."

He shoved the microphone into Arthur's hands and took off for the back of the theater. People watched him leave in astonishment, while the Lancaster brothers stared after him. Arthur was alarmed and fully prepared to pause everything, but—

"Well," Henry looked bewildered, but he sprang into action. "Roll the film, Agnes! The Lake Pristine Arthouse is proud to present *Love in Lake Pristine: a Documentary*. Enjoy!"

Arthur stared at the back of the theater and had to be manhandled by Henry off the stage. He moved with a dazed expression and Jasper wondered if she should pull the fire alarm.

The room exploded into more cheers and the lights fully dimmed. The red curtains parted to reveal the screen and a countdown from five was projected onto it. Jasper held her breath and did not share in the eagerly impatient murmurings that were sparking all around her.

The film began.

The camera faded in, opening on a wide shot of the actual Lake Pristine. The shot held for a few seconds, the only sound heard was the gentle hum of water and birdsong. The audience began to cheer, everyone thrilled by the sight of their hometown on the big screen.

The titles bled into the shot, just the words "Lake Pristine."

Jasper let out a shuddering breath, waiting for what was to come. She was shocked when a voiceover began, and the voice was instantly recognizable.

"Lake Pristine is possibly the greatest town you could ever find," her father's disembodied voice said over the peaceful sight of the lake. "I grew up here. My wife grew up here. And when I worked in the city, it was never a question for us. We weren't going to leave. We'll probably die here."

Appreciative laughter followed this statement and even Jasper's lips twitched into a smile.

The next shot was of Main Street, everyone buzzing around in a gentle fall of snow. The different small business fronts were featured as soft piano music played. It was a beautiful montage of the town, capturing individuals that Jasper had known her entire life. They were smiling and going about their day, some deliberately waving into the camera lens. It was decidedly pleasant.

"Well, Lake Pristine is filled with the same old families, but we love newcomers," Mrs. Heywood said, perched on a bench in town and smiling at someone off-screen—Arthur, presumably—while the camera was zooming in on her face. "I've lived here most of my life. And we do love a wedding."

The film cut to show numerous people from the town discussing the wedding, in short, sharp clips.

"Oh, yes, Christine and Kevin's wedding is going to be the event of the season."

"A New Year's Eve wedding, I think that's quite lovely."

"Kevin's such a lovely boy. And a fearsome attorney!"

"Weddings are such a great way to bring everyone together."

"And so good for business."

Jasper took another deep breath, attempting to calm herself.

The film cut to a bunch of happy Lake Pristine residents sitting outside Pete's cafe in the sun. Marcus's voice off-screen asked them, "So, what about the bride?"

Their faces all froze for a moment and they hesitated, pondering the question. Jasper stared up at their faces on the screen and her heart sank.

The film cut immediately to a montage of Christine. It showed her slamming doors, snapping at people to get out of her way and barking orders in the town square. Jasper could only stare in horror, while cautious laughter started to filter throughout the room. Laughter that held lots of understanding and familiarity, but was laughter nonetheless.

The next scene showed Christine sitting beautifully on a stool in the Lakehouse, smiling at the camera and the crew. "Are we rolling?" she asked sweetly.

The deliberate contrast made more people in the cinema start laughing and Jasper could feel Kevin turning to his fiancée, her sister, while she stared at the unfolding disaster.

Henry Lancaster was suddenly on the enormous screen. His interview had clearly been filmed in the cinema foyer and it was a little surreal to see.

"Christine is a lot of work," on-screen Henry said with a clipped laugh. He spoke with personal experience laced into his words, but no bitterness. "She likes things exactly how she likes them."

The footage cut to a shot of Christine measuring the bandstand for her wedding, grabbing the tape out of someone else's hand.

Henry's interview continued, his voice overlaying the shots of Christine. "She's a bit of a perfectionist."

The film jumped to Christine in the florist's: "I don't understand why you keep saying 'not in season,' as if I'm not giving you notice to get them in time for it being 'the season.' With a little advanced prep, you can have them in season, correct? So, I don't see the issue."

Jasper felt sick. Christine in context was sometimes a little tricky to deal with but out of context, she looked utterly monstrous.

"I first met Christine Montgomery when she was in pigtails," Pete said, speaking to the filmmakers as he leaned on his counter at the cafe. "My father drove the ice-cream van and Christine would always cut the queue. If someone said they wanted the last strawberry cone, Christine would change her order from vanilla to strawberry, just to spite them."

Pete said it with humor, but the words did not have a light-hearted effect when paired with footage of Christine shooing children away from the edge of the lake so that she could have the little beach to herself.

Odette's mother, Mrs. Cunningham, was next on the screen.

"I first met Christine Montgomery while I was waiting in line at the market," she said, sorting through a basket of ribbons as she spoke. Her interview was being filmed inside of Trimmings, with the bridesmaids' dresses hanging in the back of the shot. "She's a fiery young woman, which I like. She was arguing with someone about the price of the lemons. Well, whatever was said, Christine did not approve. She emptied the entire bag of lemons onto the floor and stormed out. Now, would I ever allow my daughter to behave like that? Not in a million years. But it was entertaining."

Jasper was afraid to look at her sister, but she forced herself to. Christine was completely still, her eyes fixed to the screen and her face unreadable. It was a kind of calmness that completely terrified Jasper.

Odette was on screen next and Jasper felt the overwhelming urge to plug her ears.

"What is there to say about Christine Montgomery that has not already been said?" Odette mused, as the camera followed her through Lake Pristine. "Well. Personally I've always found her to be a bore and a bully, but don't put that in. She's emotionally immature. Always has been. She doesn't realize her behavior is as terrible as it is, she's like a perpetual child. Don't put that in either, though. Off the record."

Eight hundred people all stared up at the screen, at the clip that had absolutely, without a shadow of a doubt, been on the record.

"She once deflated a bouncy castle at my birthday party," Odette added. "Guess she wasn't getting enough attention."

"My daughter is an extraordinary person."

Andrea Montgomery appeared on the screen and Jasper could see her mother visibly react to her own image. She looked displeased. Her hands went to her hair as she looked up at the enlarged version of herself.

"Christine was my first baby and she was perfect. She slept beautifully, she played well with others."

The film cut to a blink-or-miss-it shot of Christine shoving a dress sketch into her maid of honor's hands while snapping, "Ew."

An oblivious Andrea kept talking. "She had a rebellious streak, just like me. A little mini version of me."

A shot of Christine and Andrea striding through Main Street, both wearing wide-brimmed hats and looking every bit mother and daughter was up on the screen.

Jasper briefly covered her eyes and made a tiny noise of pain. It was all so much worse than she had imagined. The rest of the audience seemed amused by the film, but Jasper knew what this would be doing to her family. Her painfully proud family.

"She wears her heart on her sleeve," on-screen Andrea concluded. "Not like Jasper."

Jasper winced and shivered in her seat. She could not look at the massive screen, knowing what she would see.

It was her turn now.

Act Two, Scene VII:
The Documentary Part Two

Arthur had to be honest with himself. He had spent the last month wondering if Christine should be shown up on camera a little, with some of her behavior exposed or commented upon. However, now that he was staring up at the documentary, knowing that everyone in it was real and someone he knew, that feeling was leaving him rather quickly. The realization hit Arthur like a hammer to the temple: Marcus had edited a second, secret version. This was not the sweet and short cut he had been shown.

The film, thus far, was mean. There was no denying that Christine had given them an ample amount of material, but the editing was deliberate. Arthur had never intended for any of this to happen. This had never been the story he wanted to be told. He had never truly worked out what he did want, but it was decidedly easy to know what he didn't when it was up on the screen in front of him.

Then Jasper walked into the frame.

The shot was intentionally flattering. Jasper was walking about ten feet behind her mother and sister while they surveyed the town bandstand. The camera was filming a wide shot and Jasper seemed unaware. The film was slowed down and Jasper looked beautiful. Her long hair was down and wavy from drying in the cold winter air. She was wearing her large dark sunglasses and a baby pink coat with icy white faux-fur cuffs. Her face was a serene mask. It made Arthur's chest tighten just to look at her.

Now the audience were seeing her as he did.

The next scene was a quick montage of Lake Pristine's residents talking about Jasper. Their faces all lit up at the off-camera questions and they spoke with love and reverence.

"Jasper is the biggest sweetheart."

"I love that girl; she is always so polite. She once drove me to my hospital appointment when she saw me waiting for the bus, in the rain. She's an angel. She waited in the car park for me to be done, as well."

"Jasper Montgomery is the only person my grumpy little dog actually likes in this town."

"Jasper went away to university and the town isn't the same without her. I miss seeing her around, you know. She's just got a calming presence about her."

Arthur turned to look back at Jasper. Her hands were covering her nose and mouth, but her eyes were not watching the screen with overwhelmed emotion or delight. They were watching with horror. Arthur could tell that Jasper was internalizing every compliment and watching it morph into an insult against Christine.

Which was clearly what Marcus had intended.

Arthur felt a cold, cramping rage inside of him and he wondered if it would draw too much attention if he got up to strangle his cousin. He kept bracing to head over to the projector, ready to put a stop to the whole thing, but he couldn't move. He felt pinned down, rubbernecking his own creation with horror.

Clips showing Jasper's subservience to Christine and her wedding plans began to play. The whole room watched as Jasper bowed and scraped to her older sister. It was something Arthur had seen in person many times, he had captured the footage after all, but there was just something different about seeing it on a big screen with piano music playing softly underneath.

There was a section on the ballet school and its rehearsals for *The Nutcracker*, which offered the Montgomerys a slight respite. The dancers were interviewed and old archived footage of previous performances was played. Arthur had requested the old film, but had not watched it yet, let alone consented for it to be added to the documentary. This was not what he had signed off on. Marcus had betrayed him, and he was not afraid to use that word. This was an act of complete mutiny.

Arthur caught a glimpse of his father crewing one of the older shows and his heart almost stopped. A ghost, alive once more on the screen. He felt Grace squeezing his hand in the darkness, as they both stared up at the glow of their dad, captured for one ephemeral moment.

There were more quaint little scenes, documenting town life. It painted Lake Pristine as a sweet but eccentric place, full of colorful people. Arthur felt uncomfortable. It was like watching a horror film; he was bracing himself for the return of the monster. He did not allow the sweet detour into town niceties to lull him into a false sense of security.

Lake Pristine *was* going to be in a documentary someday. A true crime one, where Arthur was on trial for killing his cousin, former best friend and film editor.

The camera faded out of a picturesque scene by the lake to an interview with Sophie, who looked very pleased with herself.

"I don't get the fuss around Jasper Montgomery," she said confidently. "I think it's all an act to get people to like her. Bet she's really nasty underneath it all."

"How do you know that?" asked Marcus off-screen.

Arthur stared up in horror. He had not signed off or even seen these interviews. They had not been on his schedule.

This was not his film.

Back on the screen, Sophie looked befuddled for a moment, but then shrugged aggressively. "You can just tell. It's, like, an aura thing. She just radiates disapproval. Like, you can't pinpoint an exact thing that she's said or done, but she just makes you feel bad."

The film consciously cut to a shot of Odette and Jasper. They were laughing together in Trimmings, their genuine affection for each other seeping out of every inch of the frame.

"Jasper has been the love of my life since we were kids and she helped me escape the world of ballet," Odette's voice said as the footage rolled. "She's actually super shy. I think that her quietness sometimes reads as indifference or something. But she's the sweetest person. Super loyal. I'd take a bullet for her and she would for me."

Arthur cast another glance back at Jasper and felt protectiveness well up inside as he noticed she was tearful, staring up at her friend and looking openly mournful. He was about to get up when another scene began to unfold on-screen.

Jasper was standing outside of the maze, the camera filming her profile, and she was staring at something with an expression of disbelief and dismay. The lens panned to capture Craig and Sophie leaving the maze. The camera caught the intimate looks they shared, the forbidden and private moment on the cinema screen for all to see.

Arthur heard a gasp and looked across the auditorium. Odette Cunningham had risen to her feet and was glaring up at the large projection of her boyfriend and good friend, as the whole room was able to tell from a few shots what was going on between them.

Odette yelled something indecipherable and kicked Craig's knees so she could get by him before fleeing from the theater, clearly very distressed. Mrs. Cunningham hurried after her, with Craig and Sophie following shortly behind. Arthur could see Jasper watching both scenes unfurl with empathy on her face. She remained in her seat, but her eyes followed Odette until she was gone from the room.

He looked at Christine Montgomery and what he saw shocked him. It was eerie, especially in contrast to the rather justified rage displayed by Odette. He thought Christine would swear, curse and rail at the sight of the film. Instead, she looked young. For the first time in his life, she looked vulnerable. She was unmoving, her eyes hypnotized by the screen. It was disconcerting and it put real fear inside of Arthur.

He forced his eyes back to the screen.

"Can you tell us about our friend and director Arthur Lancaster?" Marcus asked.

A few oohs echoed throughout the cinema as the documentary turned its lens to Arthur. A roughly cut montage of his comings and goings in town was suddenly playing. He wore his signature scowl in every shot; they even included a scene of him yelling at Marcus to leave, while he was sorting some deliveries for the Arthouse.

Wasps stung Arthur's senses. He couldn't understand why Marcus had done this.

"My brother is the best," Grace said, suddenly appearing on screen, and her words earned some smatterings of applause from the room. "The townspeople love him really, even if he is super grumpy with all of us."

"My son is very driven," Arthur's mother was next, speaking at his birthday party with a drink in her hand and Brian beside her. "He's like his father but without the softness. But there's one thing he wants but won't go after."

The film cut to a tearful Saffron, sitting on the town bandstand.

"I didn't get it until I saw them at that cafe," she snarled, and Arthur realized that this interview was right after their supposed break-up. "It makes a stupid, sick sort of sense, if you think about it. He talked about her way more than is normal. And he always sort of . . . reacts when she's near. Like he's tuned into her."

The wasps vanished. Suddenly Arthur knew what was about to happen.

Henry was back on the cinema screen, talking freely. "I love my brother. God knows, I love him more than anything. But he's such a martyr. He won't let himself think about him and her. Almost like he's mad he even feels that way. I reckon that's why he's so gruff with her. He's never unkind, don't get me wrong, but he's always this grumpy version of himself around her. Like he's trying to warn her off. But he can't resist her. He came to me a few weeks ago, saying we needed to show more classic movies. Old black-and-white pictures, you know? I had no idea why, but he's the real genius about film, so I said fine. Anyway, she came and saw almost every single one he put on the program. Then it clicked for me! That was the reason. He was hoping she would walk in one night and she did. She was the only person who ever came to see any of those films. He did it for her."

Arthur flexed his hands and shifted in his seat. But nothing could prepare him for what came next.

"I can tell you a big secret about my brother," Henry went on. The interview was clearly from the night of Arthur's surprise party and Arthur could tell that his brother was unaware of the phone filming him. It was in an oddly fixed spot for a shot and Henry was sitting in a position that was too relaxed. He did not know he was on camera and that made Arthur extremely nervous.

"What secret?" asked Marcus off-camera, his voice more muffled than normal.

Arthur suddenly knew what was about to happen. The secret he had been keeping in his ribs, every single day for the last few years, was about to be broadcast on a cinema screen in front of his entire town. In a film he had made. This was Arthur's creation. He had unknowingly orchestrated his own downfall, his own exposure.

He looked up and waited. Henry's double on the screen leaned in conspiratorially and laughed, not unkindly. Arthur inwardly allowed his brother some grace, knowing that he would never have revealed what he was about to reveal had he known that the camera was on him.

Say it, willed Arthur silently. *Then maybe I will be free of it.*

Maybe if everyone knew, he could learn to bear it better.

"Arthur's in love with Jasper."

Arthur closed his eyes. There it was. The truth. The truth he had been unable to admit for years. The truth he felt he was never allowed to say aloud.

He turned at last to look at her, only to spot her leaving the auditorium. She walked quickly and determinedly, never looking back. Before he even knew what he was doing, he was out of his seat as well. Striding toward the rear of the cinema with purpose.

Many people watched him go. The revelation had not brought on gasps, or any kind of audible reaction.

They knew. They all knew.

Henry leaped out at him as he entered the lobby.

"Art, I'm so sorry. I had no idea—"

"Later," bit out Arthur. He could see Jasper pushing out of the front doors and heading into the town square.

"Arthur, come on. I'm sorry."

"*Later*, Henry."

His brother reluctantly let him go and Arthur jogged out of the cinema and glanced around to see where Jasper had gone. The square was deserted, everyone either at home cosied up and away from the winter cold, or inside the cinema watching his personal life being shredded on camera.

He finally spotted her, on the bandstand. She was deep in thought, but, at the sound of his feet crunching in the light fall of snow, she looked up.

They stared at one another.

"So," she finally said. "Are you happy?"

Act Two, Scene VIII:
The Documentary After-Party

Jasper watched Arthur step up onto the bandstand. She could see her breath and feel how rushed and tight it was. She could not fully comprehend what she had just watched. She did not want to imagine what people were currently seeing at that moment, back in the cinema.

All she could see was Arthur Lancaster. Every person was an enigma to Jasper, but none more than him.

"The two of you," she said quietly, "have utterly humiliated my sister. You've ruined her."

It was an old-fashioned term, but it was the only thing Jasper could think of to say, the only thing that accurately described how Christine would feel after that devastating portrayal. It was close to what she was feeling, too, though she couldn't find a word to describe everything pulsing through her either. The despair she felt over Odette, the worry for Christine, the embarrassment, the anxiety about a falling out with her family and then Arthur Lancaster's revelation, the explanation for his behavior. It was all enough to push her over her threshold.

"I don't want to talk about Christine," Arthur said softly. "And I had no idea it was edited that way."

"That's crap!" yelled Jasper, and the sound of her raised voice shocked her. It echoed within the bandstand. She was breathless.

"Bullshit, Arthur Lancaster. He may have stitched it all together, but you made the fabric."

"I know. But I didn't mean for this to happen. I didn't want this."

"I don't believe you, you've had it in for us for years. You can't blame this all on your cousin, you should have stopped this!"

"I don't want to discuss Marcus or your sister, Jasper."

His voice was quiet but steady.

"Tough," growled Jasper. She was unable to keep her emotions bottled and, for once, she was unwilling. "You saw what he did to her. That edit."

"Still her words. Still her."

"Arthur!"

"It's true! I'm sorry that happened in there, but Christine deserves some humbling. She treats you like crap, Jasper. The whole town is sick of seeing it. And I'm sick of seeing you let her."

"You had no right," Jasper said, the words choking her. "No one in my family has ever asked for your approval or your opinion, Arthur Lancaster. I don't even want to look at you right now!"

"So, what else is new?"

"Oh, what would you know?" Jasper barked, laughing bitterly. "Just shut up, Arthur. Shut up. I always had you down as grumpy and gruff, but never cruel."

"Jasper. I did not do this. I saw another cut. I approved another cut. One that was way less harsh. One that didn't expose me either. Want to talk about that part? No, of course you don't."

She ignored that, determined to stay on her train of thought, her fear for Christine.

"My sister has to stand up in front of all these people again soon, and you've stolen that moment from her. You've sullied it. You've embarrassed her!"

"Marcus did, not me. I didn't know he—"

"But are you happy, Arthur?" Jasper asked, her voice full of poison—a completely foreign sound. "It's exactly what you've always wanted. Everyone was laughing at her. You really showed us, Lancaster. You and your cousin finally got one over on the two of us. You must be delighted."

"I never wanted that."

"Everyone has been so supportive of your film," she said, pain creeping into her voice. "I sat for you. I let you interview me."

Arthur's face was red with the cold but also with shame. "I never would have chosen to do this to you."

"Well, it was done to my sister. It was a huge, public display of nasty, sneering bullying and it was aimed at Christine. You both owe her a retraction."

"For once, Jasper, don't hide behind Christine. He humiliated you, too. Made you look like the perfect princess you like people to think that you are. Didn't capture any of what actually makes you great. Because, believe me, I captured a lot of you just being fucking great."

"Then why have you done this to me?" Jasper forced out, and her voice made him wince. "Why, Arthur? I thought, stupidly, maybe you liked me a little, I thought we were on the road to becoming friends. With the bowling, and Grace, and the movie talk—I thought you had at least stopped hating me—"

"Hating you?!"

"But then you and Marcus do this, and I—"

"*Marcus* did this. Not me. Him! I don't care if Christine is embarrassed, but I care if you are, Jasper. I didn't mean for this to hurt you."

"Well, it has," she said. Eighteen months, perhaps even eighteen years, of supressed feelings were starting to fill Jasper up. "This really has hurt, Arthur. In fact, not just tonight. This whole sullen, hateful routine for the last few years, it has hurt! I never did anything to you. I was only ever nice to you. And you would treat me like some kind of . . . there isn't even a name for it. What did I ever do to you?"

"Jasper," Arthur said, his teeth gritted together and his voice quiet. "You heard what my brother said on that screen. You know why. The whole town does. Everyone has been politely letting me pine in peace. Why can't you?"

"You don't know me," she breathed. She pressed her back against one of the bandstand pillars and glared at him, hating how good he looked. "No one does." The last statement was a barely audible admission.

"I know enough," Arthur told her, moving closer. "I know you will put literally every other person before yourself, even if it ends up with you curled up on a nightclub floor. I know you help girls by brandishing a golf club at the guys making them uncomfortable. I know you check on the elderly and the vulnerable. And you make sure the camera is nowhere near you when you do it. What I don't know is why you hide some really fucking awesome parts of yourself from everyone. That I do not get, Jasper. Why the perfect girl act? Why not let them have it sometimes?"

Jasper exhaled a heavy, visible breath and looked out at the town. Lake Pristine, which she loved so much. "Do you know about mimicking?"

Arthur looked, quite rightly, perturbed at the switch in conversation subject. "What?"

"Mimicking—in nature. Some animals, if they want to avoid being attacked by another member of their species, will mimic them. In order to prove that they're not a threat. They make sure to make themselves smaller, if need be. They mirror. They match."

She could feel him staring at her in confusion, but something had been unwound in her. Released. She could imagine lifting the mask from her face and casting it down into the snow. There seemed little point in wearing one now. People being unable to see through it never felt like a reward. It felt safe, for certain, but it made everything harder.

"You can't imagine," she told him, staring down at the floorboards of the bandstand, "how aggressive people can be if you don't mimic their cues. We think humans are so advanced, so different from animals, but sometimes they're not. If a thousand nonverbal cues aren't adhered to, if they aren't mirrored in the right way, a human can become a predator." She finally raised her eyes to look into his. "So. If you don't naturally mimic those cues. If you're a person who cannot instinctively move the way the rest of the herd does, what do you do?"

He reached out a hand and then forced himself to pull back. "You learn to mask."

She regarded him with defiance. "Exactly. You become a tabula rasa. People project whatever, or whomever, they want onto you. It's safer that way. So, whatever you think you know about me, it's probably not real."

He was right in front of her and she had to bend her neck to look up at him.

"The whole town just saw what was real to me," he told her. "They all saw it. On a huge cinema screen, in high definition. So, don't you stand there and tell me that it's all in my head."

Jasper swallowed, suddenly aware of how close they actually were. "I'm in your head?"

"You're everywhere," he said.

The words were terrifying to Jasper. She shook her head hurriedly. "It's just an idea of me."

"No," he said remorsefully. "It's you. It's been you since you told me how you felt about Omar Sharif. Since you were nice to my sister. Since you made my dad laugh. Since I first saw you onstage. Since the moment I met you. This feeling is real. It's not about seeing through you, it's seeing *you*. And I see you. And I think you're fucking incredible."

Jasper let out a watery laugh, unable to process what was happening. "Arthur, don't."

"Can't help it," he said. "I've tried your masking thing. Doesn't work for me. Clear as day, watching that stupid film, it doesn't work. Everyone can see how I feel about you, it's written all over me."

"You think you can see me?" Jasper challenged, raising her chin. "All right then, how do I feel about you, Arthur Lancaster?"

It was not only a question for him, it was the one she was finally daring to ask herself. She thought about his shoulders and his face and his hands more than she cared to admit. She wore lipstick if she was going to the Arthouse, knowing that he would be there. She wondered if he had a special interest, something he was deeply passionate about. She had thought about him multiple times a day since arriving back in town and, since the night at the bowling alley, he had taken over every moment in her mind.

He did not directly answer her question. "If you want me to leave you alone, say. Say it, Jasper, and I'm gone. Want to be friends, we can be friends. I'll take whatever I can get and I'll respect it. But tell me. Straight."

Jasper was feeling more defenseless than ever before, in her entire life. However, that last little strand of armor was impossible to let go. "You drive me out of my mind."

It was not untrue.

"Well," he said, shrugging. "I'm all about you. All of the time. So. Whatever."

Before she could get out another word, he was kissing her.

She kissed him back without hesitation and it was nothing like the awkward, humdrum exchanges she had experienced at college parties in the city. He was nothing like those boys. This caused sensation to spread everywhere, until she was dizzy with it.

She slipped her arms around his neck and his hands kneaded her hips. He maneuvered them over to the wooden bench in the middle of the bandstand, pulling away from her for only a moment while he sat down. He pulled her into his lap and they were back to it, the kiss becoming lazy, slow.

Jasper would have quite happily stayed there kissing Arthur Lancaster all night, but the sound of sudden shouting and running interrupted them. She glanced over at the cinema and tried to refocus.

"What's going on?" she murmured.

"Don't really care, right at this moment," Arthur said, trying to recapture her mouth.

Jasper let him, releasing a small sigh. However, the distinct sound of someone being shoved into the snow while screaming alerted her back into reality and the two of them leaped up.

Kevin and Marcus were rolling around in the snow, fighting. It was certainly not the most impressive battle Jasper had ever witnessed, and it soon became obvious that the high-pitched screams had been coming from Marcus.

Christine stood with the rest of Jasper's family, and Henry Lancaster, by the pavement.

"Knock his teeth out, babe!" bawled Christine, through messy tears.

"Don't," Howard Montgomery instructed fiercely. "Kevin, that's quite enough. Get in your car, we'll deal with him properly."

"Jasper Montgomery!" Andrea yelled, spotting her younger daughter on the other side of Main Street. "Come here at once! We're going home."

Jasper wanted nothing more than to stay on the bandstand with Arthur. She did not move, even though her mother looked ready to fight herself. Christine was being ushered to the Mercedes by her fiancé, while Marcus lay in the snow, dazed. Andrea marched to her husband's car, while Howard called over to Jasper.

"Jazz," he said, his voice firm. He gave Arthur a cold stare. "Let's go."

Jasper started to move, but Arthur was still holding her hand. He gently let go, as she turned to whisper to him.

"There's a shed beneath one of my windows," she said, her voice hushed and low. "The one on the east side."

"Jasper, say goodbye to the boy and let's go," her father ordered, his voice harsher and colder than she had ever heard it.

Arthur nodded to her, almost imperceptibly, and they shared a tiny smile. Then Jasper jumped down the stairs and jogged over to her father. She maintained an air of innocence with him as they walked to the car, and only when she was safely in the back seat did she look over at the bandstand once more.

Arthur was leaning against one of the pillars, watching the car drive away. Jasper scratched one finger against the glass of the window, a tiny little wave. He mimicked the gesture.

Lake Pristine felt different, all of a sudden. More possible. Changed.

Act Two, Scene IX:
Home Truths

The family were completely silent as they switched on the lights inside the Lakehouse. There was an unspoken agreement to gather in the living room, so Jasper sat on the floor by the fireplace and watched the rest of them file in. Her mother in the armchair by the window, Christine and Kevin on the sofa and her father on the small love seat against the north wall.

"That was . . . horrendous," her mother finally said.

"Yes," her father agreed. "I'm going to cut everyone some bits of watermelon and then I think we should go to bed."

"Nah, I'd rather talk about it," Christine said, her tears drying up as she found her fury. "Jasper?"

Jasper glanced up at her older sister. She could sense that Christine, and her mother for that matter, were itching for a fight. Whenever they needed to get vulnerable, whenever they needed to talk about how hurt or upset they were, they would always pick a fight first. They would scream and yell and get the other person to scream and yell, too. Then, once they had reduced the other person to tears, they would finally feel powerful enough to allow their guard to come down. Her mother was locked into the pattern and she had passed it down to Christine like an ornament from an ancestor.

Jasper had spent her entire life wishing that they would just learn to talk about their feelings. She had prayed for them to acquire the ability to regulate their own emotions and manage their bad tempers. However, it was clear that they were past the point of learning.

"You spent all of that time with him at the studio," her mother snapped at Jasper, her tone and words accusatory. "You knew about this."

Jasper's instincts were to defend herself against this ridiculous allegation, even though she knew it would do no good. She knew her mother was aware that she was being unreasonable. It was never about making sense, only ever about starting an argument. So Jasper kept her expression blank and got to her feet.

"I had no idea that they were going to do any of that," she said curtly.

"She's right," Kevin said firmly. Rubbing Christine's arm, attempting to soothe her. "This was all Marcus. I could see Arthur, he looked horrified. It's clear that his cousin thought it would be funny to screw with the edit."

Christine relented, her expression softening slightly, but Andrea Montgomery was still seething, the indignity and injustice of the evening clearly making her feel backed into a corner. Jasper had watched her mother get into arguments with hospitality workers and flight attendants, and when Andrea started, she did not back down. No proof or evidence would act as a balm for her temper, only groveling.

Jasper was not going to grovel. Not this time.

"I haven't done anything wrong," she said, her voice dangerously quiet.

"What did you say?" her mother replied, her tone also softly menacing.

Jasper loved her family. She chose to. She woke up each day and forgave her sister's icy words, her father's appeasement and her mother's emotional unavailability. She had learned to control and compartmentalize her feelings, to the point where she sometimes thought she would make an excellent spy.

She was like the lake outside of their house. Calm and serene, while life teemed and abounded beneath. As her mother raged about the documentary, Jasper felt her lake freezing over. Ice and coldness covering her until she was numb.

"I said," Jasper spoke again, a little louder this time, "I haven't done anything wrong."

It wasn't Lake Pristine that was the problem. It never had been. It was her family.

"Let me get us the fruit," her father said hurriedly. "It's been a difficult evening."

Jasper stared down her mother, unafraid of the woman who was now quivering with wrath. Andrea knew Jasper's sore spots, she knew exactly where to press. She was the one who had placed them there. It was for this reason alone that Jasper had learned to become a vessel of silence whenever her mother was in a temper. She had learned to predict the signs by watching how much gin would go in the glass, or how quickly the wine was brought up from the cellar. When she had been in the ballet company as a dancer, she could tell by the way her mother's cane hit the floor whether it would be a peaceful rehearsal or not.

"Your sister has just been humiliated," her mother railed. "The whole town has seen it. In glorious technicolor. Meanwhile, you came out looking like a perfect little angel. So, no one is going anywhere, young madam, until you explain how that came to be."

"You think the twisted little dynamics of this house are reality, but they're not," Jasper said, her voice coarse and raw. Her sense of loyalty was gone—momentarily lost and replaced with a desperate need to make their sky fall, even if just for a second. "You've always given Christine an easier ride. You've always held me to impossible standards. You've always treated me like a person who needs to be apologized for. I'm never allowed to be home with a cold, I'm never allowed to miss rehearsal or, God forbid, be in a low mood. Christine can rip through town like a tornado and leave chaos in her wake, but I have to be 'on' all of the time."

"This is not about you," Christine said weakly. "I'm the one who's been targeted here."

"You're absolutely right, Christine," Jasper said softly, turning to examine her older sister. "It's not about me. It's never been about me. You are the main character in this family and I'm a background extra."

"Jasper—"

"No, Dad," Jasper said fiercely, and she could tell that her rare show of passion was unsettling all of them. "If you stand in the middle of the road, you get run down. So, pick a side."

"I can't pick sides," her father said, almost laughing out of pure nervousness. He glanced at his wife and then tried to seem stern. "I'm the peacekeeper in this family."

Jasper stared at him, disappointed. "You're not a peacekeeper if one side knows no peace, Dad. And I have had no peace. All this family has ever done is teach me how to bury things. Well, I'm digging them back up again and I'll do it with my own bare hands. You all made me think the world would hold me at a distance because you did. Because of—"

"Jasper," her father said, before she was able to finish her thought. "That's not true."

"This town doesn't hold me at a distance," Jasper said, realizing the words to be true as soon as she said them. "And he doesn't."

No one needed her to clarify that she meant Arthur Lancaster.

"Sweetheart," her father said, his eyes begging her to let it be. "Let's just—"

"Want to hear something fun that wasn't in that little documentary?" Jasper interjected. "This whole time I've been at college? I barely went to class. It's like all of those years at school made me burn out of pretending juice. Can't do it anymore. I'm sick of trying to be like everyone else when I usually end up failing anyway. I'd rather fail at being who I am than fail or succeed in a mask. So, I cut class to watch old movies."

"Jasper!" her mother exploded, horror etched all over her face. "Stop this!"

"Why, Mum? No camera now. Don't worry, who's going to see? And, by the by, I have no intention of going back to university. I'm going to save you a ton of money. I'm not going back to that place. I have other plans. I've been keeping that from you, too, but I could have probably written it all over my walls and you still wouldn't have cared."

"You've been lying to us?" Christine breathed. She looked small to Jasper, for the very first time. Her sister always loomed so large, but at that moment, she seemed fragile.

"Christine, I love you," Jasper said sadly. "But I've been gone. Haven't you noticed? I've been a ghost since I came home. Since I left. And the only person, in this entire town who actually gives a shit is the guy I just left on that bandstand!"

"That's enough!" her mother shouted. "What a thing to say to your family, especially after what Christine has just been through.

You've had every privilege given to you, young lady. You don't get to stand there and act hard done by when your sister is hurting."

"Why did you always push me so hard?" Jasper demanded, rounding on her mother. Her voice was breaking and her eyes were quickly dampening. "Why? Why was Christine always allowed to be imperfect but not me?"

She never spoke to them like this. Not ever. Something about that dreadful film, and the way Arthur Lancaster had looked at her, it was fueling her. She still felt him on her. He had looked at her as though she was allowed to exist exactly as she was. There were no conditions or consequences to her real self in his eyes, and something about that both terrified and electrified her.

He accepted all of her.

"Was it because of what I am?" Jasper asked, speaking to her mother with a trembling voice. "Is that it? Was one little diagnosis so bad to talk about with your book club and your lunch friends, you had to push me to breaking point? Because that's what you did."

She could hear her father's rapid breathing, his obvious distress, but she did not look away from her mother.

"I never cared about what the world thought," she added brokenly. "I still don't. I cared about what *you* thought. You guys, and this weird little town—I cared about being perfect for all of you. And every time you made me repeat a step until my feet were bleeding or dance until my body was broken the next day, I heard you loud and clear. Don't worry. The message was well and truly received."

"So, what are you going to do with yourself without our money?" her mother asked, sounding desperate. "Become an artist? I thought we'd knocked that little notion out of you. Well, not him.

Your father was always too soft with you. There's no future in those jobs, Jasper."

"There's no future for me anywhere if I don't try," whispered Jasper.

The room fell into a stunned silence. Kevin was too afraid to look at her, Christine was covering her mouth with both hands and her father looked tearful. Her mother merely stared, regarding Jasper as if it was the first time she had ever laid eyes on her second child.

"You made me think that just because you don't accept everything I am that the rest of the world would be the same," Jasper said quietly. "But he accepts me. This town would accept me. Maybe even the wider world. Me, Jasper. Just me. Neurodivergent, creative, quiet and no longer studying psychology or going on to law school. I'm done. I'm out. And now, I'm going to bed."

Up in her bedroom, Jasper shut the door and smiled at Chum, who was stretched out on her pillow. She scratched his chin and grinned through tears as he purred deeply. She wriggled out of her evening dress and dumped it into her laundry hamper. Once she had slipped into a silk crop top and matching pajama bottoms, she drank from her water bottle. Her eyes kept darting to the east window. She pulled the curtains and slid the windowpane up, granting easy access to any midnight visitors. She put on some soft music and positioned her dressing-table stool against her bedroom door, providing a small barricade against her family.

When she returned to the window, someone stood below.

Arthur Lancaster looked up at her and she smiled down at him.

"Think you can manage to climb up?" she whispered and they both had to fight to contain laughter at the absurdity of it.

He did manage to nimbly mount the shed and, with her help,

he hoisted himself up and crawled through her window. When he landed on her rug, they both had to cover their mouths to stifle the sounds that they were making.

Jasper closed the window and pulled the curtains closed. When she sat back down on the rug, next to him, the laughter faded and they were back in that strange hypnotic trance from the bandstand.

"I, um . . ." Jasper suddenly felt shy and self-conscious. "I didn't invite you up here to . . . you know . . ."

"I know," he said gently. "I wasn't expecting . . . that."

"Not that I don't want to," Jasper added quickly. "But . . . maybe not—"

"With Christine and your parents within earshot. Understood."

Jasper smirked. "Exactly."

She could feel Arthur studying her face. His fingers stroked her cheek and she was finding it hard to look him in the eye.

"You've been crying," he said quietly.

"Yes."

"I hate seeing you upset."

Jasper ran her knuckles across the faux-fur rug they were sitting on. "When have you seen me upset?"

"Most of tonight. The night Christine made you go to that club."

"Yeah, that was a grim night."

"Saw you crying at my dad's funeral."

Jasper finally looked up at him. "Of course."

"We didn't think you would come. No, don't look like that, I didn't mean it in a bad way. We didn't have any expectations."

She could see him recalling the painful day as he spoke and it made her reach out to hold his wrist.

"There was so much more to do than I realized," he said. "Mum did most of it, Henry, too. I looked after Grace. Then, when everyone was arriving at the church, all I could think was, 'I wish Jasper was here.'"

Jasper felt fresh tears brim as he said the words with such raw honesty.

"Then when we were burying him, there you were. Black umbrella, black gloves and black heels. And you were crying for him."

"Crying for all of you," Jasper corrected, running her hands up and down his arms. "It must have been so awful."

"It . . . was," Arthur said, and Jasper could tell that he was rarely given the opportunity to talk about his father.

"I really wanted to hug you that day, but I was convinced that you hated me," she told him.

He stared at her. "I have never hated you."

She nodded.

Perhaps it was giving herself permission to look directly at what she had been feeling, or perhaps it was her need for comfort about confronting her family, but whatever the reason, Jasper hugged him tightly. She crawled into his lap and hugged him, the way she had wanted to when his father had passed on. She relaxed against him as his arms tightened around her and they just sat there, fused together. She could feel his face in her hair and the horrible parts of the evening became less important and she let herself be touched by someone who genuinely cared.

When Jasper finally sat back, she was feeling drowsy. "I think I should sleep and stop touching you, because it's making me want things." She detached herself and he rose to his feet.

"Want me to go?"

"No," she said. "Stay. Stay as long as you want."

They faced each other on her bed, Jasper beneath the covers and Arthur on top of them.

"Can I ask about something?" Arthur said delicately.

"Yes."

"Did you think we were complete losers in high school?"

"Who's 'we?'" Jasper asked.

"Me, Marcus, Danny . . ."

"I've never thought of anyone as a loser. Except the two people who have just betrayed my best friend. Other than them, no one."

She watched him wince.

"Arthur?"

"I just think tonight happened as part of some sad, bitter revenge mission."

"Marcus?"

"Yeah."

Jasper exhaled. "I know Craig and the other guys weren't nice to people. I'm sorry if Marcus was at the end of that. I should have said something."

"You did any time it happened in front of you. And I snapped at you for it."

Jasper couldn't believe she was lying in bed with Arthur Lancaster. She couldn't adjust to how many things had changed since coming back to Lake Pristine. If she were being honest, everything had altered dramatically after he had pulled her out of Stone. She had seen a completely different human being. As she stared into his face, wondering how she could have misread him so badly, a memory came to her. He must have seen it flash through her eyes because his focus sharpened.

"What is it?"

"Just remembered something."

"What?"

"Did you ever have Miss Rooney?"

Arthur looked surprised by the question, but he nodded. "For maths."

"Well. The first Valentine's Day after my diagnosis, I got this love note in my locker. It was handwritten, shoved inside and had lots of little rose petals inside."

"Show-off."

She laughed. "It was obviously anonymous. I asked Odette, she didn't know. It wasn't one of the guys in our group, the writing was too good. So I took it to Miss Rooney, who was our tutor. I showed it to her . . ."

Arthur's smile slipped as he realized that this was actually a sad memory for Jasper. She watched him study her with concern. "What happened?"

"She sat me down and told me that someone had done it as a joke," Jasper reported softly, remembering the scene as if she were back there again. She noted Arthur's horror at her words. "Yes. She said, because of my . . . my diagnosis, I didn't understand that it was a prank. That no one would actually want me like that."

"That's despicable—"

"That's not the part I really want to talk about though," Jasper said quickly. She had never found much pleasure in wallowing or feeling badly done by. She had let Miss Rooney's words haunt her for too long, during her schooldays. "The best part, the important part, is this: I went home and told Christine what happened. And do you know what she did?"

Arthur shook his head.

"She got so angry. Not with me, though. She said, 'Who told you that?' I said, 'Who told me what, Chris?' 'Who told you that you weren't beautiful? That you weren't loveable? That you were a joke?' So, I told her. And she, in true Christine fashion, had a word with Miss Rooney's department head. The woman never bothered me again after that."

She watched Arthur allow a begrudging expression of respect to show. "Wow."

"It's really hard being a girl in this world. Autistic or not. You're bombarded with what you should be, what you shouldn't be, what will get you killed, or get your reputation killed. You'll be blamed for every bad thing, ignored for every good. Plus all of the people you inevitably compare yourself to are splashed across social media, which you need to be on if you want to find a community or keep up with your friends. You have to be your own best friend, and develop a voice inside of you that will keep you strong and healthy. But that voice gets drowned out at every turn. And so when Miss Rooney said that, I believed her. It was so easy. So natural."

The truth came out of her like wine knocked over on a table. The words spilled and he listened to every syllable.

"So, when a beautiful boy looks at you from the wings of your mother's ballet theater, and you can see something in his face— something new, something raw—you know what you *want* it to mean," Jasper told him. "But you can't believe it. You stamp out the thought right away because you don't want to be an arrogant kind of girl. Or a hopeful kind of girl. Or a soft kind of girl. Or a hard kind of girl. Or the kind of girl who only thinks about love and boys. Or the kind of girl who never can. You go through this projector in your mind, trying to work out who to be. And I was never sure, Arthur. I was never sure around you. I didn't know what kind of girl to be."

"I want you to be my girl," he said, his hand slipping into her hair. "I want you to be you. Not just the polite version you let the old folks have. All of you. The shouty parts as well as the quiet parts. I have always wanted *you*."

Jasper was not sure who moved first, but she was kissing him again. He groaned against her and the covers were somehow gone in the space of a few seconds. He was careful not to put his whole weight onto her, but she pulled him closer, sighing when he moved her legs so they were wrapped around his hips.

A sharp, sudden knock jolted both of them out of the moment.

"Jasper?" Christine's demanding voice sounded from the other side of her bedroom door. "What are you doing?"

"Maybe she'll go away?" breathed Arthur, pressing his face into her neck.

"No way," Jasper whispered. "She'll break down the door."

"I can hear you, Jasper, open this door right now!"

Jasper muttered a curse and slipped out of bed. Their voices had been hushed, but clearly they had not been quiet enough for Christine's insanely astute ears. "I'm on the phone to Odette."

"Liar! You've got that boy in there!"

Arthur leaped to his feet as well, but Christine had already barreled her way into the room, knocking the stool placed in front of the door to the ground. Her eyes landed on the two of them, and then the rumpled bedding.

"Daddy!" she screamed at the top of her lungs. "Jasper's got a boy in her room!"

"Christine, you nightmare," snapped Jasper. "What the hell?"

Howard Montgomery appeared in the doorway and his face transformed from a worried father to a prison warden in mere seconds.

"All right, son," he said resolutely, gesturing to Arthur. "With me."

Arthur stepped in front of Jasper but did not move to leave the room.

"We were literally just talking," Jasper said firmly. "He's fully clothed."

"I can see that," her father allowed, still holding open the door for Arthur. "But Mr. Lancaster and I need to have a few words in the car. I'll drive you back to the cinema, son. Come on."

Arthur took one long look at Jasper and then made to leave the room. Jasper watched in despair. Arthur threw her a look of reassurance as he was walked onto the landing and down the stairs, leaving Jasper alone with her sister.

They glared at each other before Jasper finally spoke first.

"Christine," she said, trying to sound calmer than she felt. "I'm sorry about the documentary. None of us knew that was what Marcus was planning. Arthur didn't either."

"Oh, really?" Christine replied. "You had no idea he was putting together this lovely romantic film about two people in love? Only, instead of Kevin and me, it was you and *him*!"

Her voice was a crescendo of utter rage and Jasper raised her hands defensively.

"Christine. I had no idea."

"Oh, come on, Jasper. You had no idea of what? How he felt about you? Please don't say stupid shit like that to me, please."

"I didn't! I've only just worked out how I feel about him!"

"Well, you're the last person to know."

"Then why have you never said anything?"

"Because I don't want you to end up trapped here and I don't want you to be like me!"

The words exploded out of Christine and the outburst seemed to surprise both sisters.

Jasper's mouth hung open and she was certain that she must have looked a state. She stepped closer to Christine and attempted to find her voice, but the words were awkward and garbled. "What . . . what does that mean?"

Christine sighed and some of the anger seeped out of her body. "Jasper. Listen. I went out with his older brother. I know how the Lancasters can be. It's fun and he's charming and you like how you feel. But soon you'll love how you feel. Then you'll love him, if you don't already. Then you'll love him so much, you stop loving how you feel and start worrying about losing him. So, you'll make sacrifices."

Jasper shook her head slowly. "I'm not you, Christine, and Arthur isn't Henry."

"No, you're right," she said blankly. "You and Arthur are way more intense than Henry and I ever were. And I do not want you staying in this town. Slumming it at the cafe for barely any money because you're afraid of losing a guy."

"That's not going to happen."

"Isn't it?" she asked sadly. Then, she gestured to herself and let out a strangled sound of frustration.

Jasper frowned. "Christine, you love Kevin."

"Of course I do," Christine conceded. "Kevin is the person who made me realize that everything is going to be okay. He'd come with me wherever I ask, he's never wanted to ground me. I love him. But before Kevin, there were so many guys I stayed in town for. I can't, Jasper . . . I cannot see that happen to you. I won't let it. All I wanted was to marry a rich guy and settle in this town, I never wanted a job and I never wanted to be poor. I don't care if that's old-fashioned, that's what I wanted. But you want a career. You need one! And if you stay here for a guy, no matter how much he loves you, if you stay, you'll start putting the career off. And that guy looks at you like you're his whole world. He's not going to let you go."

"Christine," Jasper spoke with gentle reproach, taking her sister by the hand and sitting her down on the ottoman. She patted their interlocked fingers. "Please don't take this the wrong way. But . . . a career is non-negotiable for me. I'm not letting anyone stop that from happening."

She reached under the bed and drew out her lockbox. She opened it up and let Christine see all of the money saved up inside of it.

"I'm getting out of here, but it's not because of Lake Pristine. I love Lake Pristine, I do. You know Mum and Dad want what they want for me, and they want it enough to cast me out, I feel," Jasper said quietly. "So, if it's between a career and this town, I have to get out. With or without love or a guy or anyone else's approval. I've applied to a school. It's going to happen."

They both stared at the money for a moment before Jasper locked the box back up and slid it beneath the bed once more.

A tear slipped down Christine's face and she ferociously wiped it away. "Good. Well . . . that's good."

"You can't tell anyone," Jasper said softly.

"That's why you do what everyone wants all of the time," Christine said, pensively. "Because, deep down, you know you're leaving. You've always been planning to go."

Jasper shrugged. "It sounds kind of heartless when you say it like that, but yeah. And by the way, Christine? You are twenty-three, you goose. You can have a career whenever you want. If you end up changing your mind."

Christine smiled faintly. "Mum says marriage is a full-time job."

"Mum had a career, Chris. She worked all while having us and being married to Dad. Don't let her run your life."

"Don't make me say the real thing, Jazz. I hate hard work, okay!"

Jasper laughed. "You could rule the world, if you really wanted to."

Christine nodded and sniffed, wiping another tear away and glancing about the room. She took in all of the posters and even reached out to stroke Chum, though the cat did flinch and wriggle away.

"I'm so ashamed, Jazz," Christine finally whispered. "Watching that film tonight, I've never been more embarrassed in my entire life."

"Oh, Christine," Jasper said wearily. "You've been under a lot of wedding stress."

"No, Jazz. Don't defend me. I've been horrendous. I've been a monster."

Jasper smiled and wiped one final tear away from her sister's beautiful face. Christine had cried her make-up away and there was no one watching them now. She was raw. Jasper could see the truth in her sister, she could hear the pain in her apology. "Well. You're here now. Don't look like a monster to me."

Act Two, Scene X:
Closure

Jasper stayed indoors the following day, taking time to catch up on sleep and think about how she was going to face an entire town who had witnessed her family exposed on the big screen. Her father had been very secretive about his conversation with Arthur Lancaster and her mother was still refusing to see people because of the premiere. Christine and Kevin went for a drive together, away from Lake Pristine.

But there was one person that Jasper desperately needed to see.

She threw on a warm coat and set off for Trimmings. The shop was closed upon her arrival, but after a couple of tries at the bell, Mrs. Cunningham appeared.

"Hi, baby," she said soothingly, kissing Jasper's cheeks and smiling fondly at her. "You doing okay?"

"I'm fine," Jasper said meekly. "Is she . . . ?"

"Upstairs."

"Can I?"

"Absolutely. You'll be like medicine."

Jasper smiled and headed for the stairs at the back of the shop. She ascended quietly and entered the flat Odette and her mother shared. She headed to Odette's room, the inside of their little apartment as familiar to Jasper as her own home. She knocked.

"I'm still not hungry," Odette's voice said drearily.

"It's me," Jasper said.

There was a beat of silence and then the door was wrenched open. Odette stood in the frame, her hair braided and her eyes red from crying.

Jasper did not ask any questions or wait for any words to be spoken. She wrapped her arms around Odette and squeezed, with as much gentle might as she could manage. She tried to convey all of the love and forgiveness she had for her best friend and made soothing sounds as Odette began to cry.

Odette never cried. This was serious.

"You were telling the truth," Odette finally rasped. "I knew that. Deep down. I'm so sorry, Jasper."

"You're good," Jasper said. "I was telling you about a vibe. I don't blame you for being skeptical."

"But I gaslit you," Odette said, her face crumpling in despair. "I told you that you had misunderstood. That's unforgivable, Jasper."

"It hurt," Jasper granted. "But you were hurting."

"Craig chased me down after I left the cinema," Odette said, moving to her bed and blowing her nose. "Said I was misreading it. Even though that film confirmed everything you said you saw, which he said you were lying about. And then, Sophie showed up. She came clean. But only because she was angry about Craig denying their relationship. Apparently he's been saying he was going to leave me."

"Bet she wasn't thrilled when he was begging you to stay."

"She was not."

"Craig is despicable," Jasper sighed. "Please tell me you're finally done with him."

"I'm done. I just don't feel any closure."

Jasper felt a mischievous sense of newness come over her. She was listening to an impulse that, up until recently, she would have completely ignored. "You know . . . it's a rainy night. They're probably all in town somewhere. The arcade? He always hangs out there."

"Mmph."

"And there will be witnesses."

Odette's eyes lit up and she met her friend's gaze. "Closure?"

Jasper grabbed her friend by the hand and grinned, a little wickedly. "Closure. Put on your best outfit and I'll drive!"

"Tell me what you're going to say!"

Odette swallowed and considered Jasper's words. "I . . . I want to say something cool, Jasper."

"This is just like in the movies, when the heroine finally sees through the bad person."

"I'm the heroine?"

"Yes!"

"Then what are you?"

"I'm the best friend, who is played by a charming, winsome, up-and-coming newbie actor or comedian."

Odette laughed. Then, as the car whipped down toward the middle of town, she quietened. Something thoughtful entered her face. "You definitely looked like the heroine in that documentary."

Jasper focused on the road ahead of her and said nothing.

"I mean," Odette watched her old friend carefully, "it was . . . pretty eye-opening."

"Was it?" Jasper said lightly. "I thought it was pretty mean."

"Oh, sure," Odette allowed, still regarding Jasper. "Christine got a rough go of it. So did I. But you . . ."

"You need closure," Jasper repeated firmly, refusing to be diverted. "Closure is a huge part in the movies. You say what you need to and what the audience and secondary characters need to hear as well."

"So what do I say?"

"Tell him what he's done to you. It's not even the cheating. It's the way he's made you into this less colorful version of you."

"Right."

"All his broken promises," Jasper continued, letting years of anger and frustration about Craig and his grip over Odette spill out. "Love isn't supposed to feel like a test. It isn't supposed to feel like an audition."

She paused, as she tried to think of what to hand Odette that could end it all, once and forever. Everyone in the movies could find the right words, the screenwriter always gave them that privilege. Jasper was not going to let her closest friend go in there unarmed.

"He's made a diamond necklace feel like a chain."

"Oh, I like that," Odette said softly, as Jasper pulled into the small car park outside of the bowling alley.

The girls entered the arcade in Lake Pristine and followed the loud, pulsing music toward the pool tables and air hockey. Jasper had taken a couple of painkillers in the car, to counterbalance the potential headache she would get from the overstimulating environment. They squeezed each other's hands before they made their way over. The night was already well underway and while their entrance did not cause the music to scratch to a stop, many people noticed them and grew still.

"So," Jasper muttered, "if they haven't seen the doc, they've definitely heard about it."

"Oh, no, they all saw it," Odette murmured back.

Jasper grimaced but said nothing.

"Craig!" Odette yelled, and her voice was loud enough for the girl deejaying to jump and lower the volume of her setlist. People gathered around the perimeter of the room, all desperate to see what was about to happen.

Jasper glanced around until her eyes settled on a figure moving toward the two of them, crossing the arcade.

Craig was wearing a suit jacket that was a little too tight on him and he was staring at Odette, as if seeing someone he had been thirsting for. She did look great. Jasper had made sure of that. She had dressed her in pinstripes and a black trilby. Sophie stood a little behind Craig, wearing an outfit that, rather tragically, appeared to be a poor attempt at recreating Odette's inimitable style.

"Hey, babe," Craig said, clearly trying to sound wounded. To Jasper, it just sounded pathetic. "I've been trying to call you."

"Yeah," Odette said coldly. "I thought you might want to know what it feels like to be left on read for a while."

People reacted audibly to her tone, delighted by the drama unfolding in front of them, this time in flesh and bone rather than on a cinema screen. Jasper stood alongside Odette, a proud and supportive sentinel, while her friend aired the feelings she had been denying for too long.

"We should talk outside," Craig said.

"No, we're going to talk here, Craig," Odette said. She took a deep breath, her hands on her ribs, and then fixed Craig with a look that was both judgmental and resigned. "You have been like a chain around my neck. Except I'm the idiot who let myself think it was a diamond necklace."

Jasper's line earned appropriate gasps from the onlookers.

"What?" he said, scowling. He never had been one for poetry.

"You have never treated me well. You have gaslit me. You have emotionally abused me. You have tried to turn me against my best friend. You have pushed me to the verge of breaking up with you, only to swoop in when I start getting free to make me think that I'm crazy and that you actually care about me."

"I do care about—"

"Whether you think you do or do not is irrelevant. Love should not feel like this, Craig. Hell, casual dating should not feel like this. You don't get to treat people the way you have treated me."

"You and your friend"—Craig cast a glare toward Jasper, who merely glowered right back at him—"have misunderstood everything. I don't like Sophie like that."

This was enough to make Sophie storm from the room, muttering something nasty toward Odette as she did. Jasper watched her go, but Odette's gaze remained fixed to Craig.

"You cheated and you lied," Odette said softly. "Then, when I asked you to explain, you made me think I was imagining it. *Enough*. You will never get to treat me like this again. We are done. We are done over text. We are done on social media. We are done if you see me in the street or in here. We. Are. Done. After too many stupid years, I am finally finished with you. You are a disease, which I have had and now got over. I'm immune."

She turned to leave and Jasper followed. However, as they reached the food bar by the door, Odette turned around for one final word.

"You know, I never appreciated you insinuating that I always needed to lose weight," she said loftily. "But I guess I just did lose some. One hundred and sixty useless, stinking pounds. Gone!" She grabbed a cupcake from the table and took a large, happy bite. "Delicious!" she yelled, slamming a bill down on the bar and holding the cake up.

She sauntered out of the room, a swagger in her walk which gave her lovely figure a jaunty arrogance that Jasper adored. She followed her friend and slipped her arm around her waist.

"Love you," Jasper whispered.

"Love you back," Odette replied. "Let's get gone."

"Sure thing," Jasper said, her eyes landing on the female bathroom. "Just let me powder my nose."

She entered the bathroom and found exactly who she was looking for inside. Sophie had been bending over the sink but straightened up at the sight of Jasper, her face scrunching into a deep scowl.

"Just wanted a quick word with you," Jasper said serenely, leaning against the bathroom door. "Girl to girl."

"I have nothing to say to you," snarled Sophie, washing her hands and avoiding the other girl's gaze. "Get out."

"Craig is the worst person alive," Jasper said in a conversational tone. "Don't get me wrong. There is a special circle in hell reserved for him and the sooner he gets there the better. But I haven't forgotten about you."

She took a step closer, blocking Sophie from her only way out.

"I know what it's like when Odette treats you as a friend, it's the best feeling in the world. How could you take that and do this to her? How could you violate girl code this badly?"

"Maybe Odette needed humbling," Sophie said shortly. "Maybe you do, too."

"You can say what you want about me, Soph," Jasper said under her breath. "But not my best friend. She was good to you, she was kind to you, and you did this to her. You're despicable."

Jasper turned to leave, but Sophie spat some final words at her back.

"Nice, sweet Jasper Montgomery. Everyone always talks about how you're so good to people. I sure don't see it."

"That's because you and Craig aren't people," Jasper said pleasantly. "You both cheated on Odette. You both hurt my oldest friend, which means one word from me and neither of you can show your faces in this town again. You and Craig are not people. You're detritus."

She turned off the bathroom light as she left, leaving Sophie in darkness.

Jasper loved the Lakehouse at night. Her family was having dinner in the back of the house and the lights from their meal spilled out of the tall windows onto the glassy lake. Jasper headed for the water instead of the house, reaching the edge of the lake. It was completely covered in ice and she knew what she was going to do.

She took out her list and looked at the very first item: *Skate on Lake Pristine.*

She slipped Odette's borrowed ice skates out of her bag and placed the list on the pebbled beach. She secured it safely with one of the larger stones. As she pulled on the skates, she ignored the sensible part of her—the part reminding her of the dangers of skating on nature. Alone. At night.

"It's on the list, so I'm doing it," she told herself. "Running out of time."

Her application to design school was complete. She had done the interview, sent her essays and coursework. Her references had been submitted. She had applied for financial aid, hoping to secure it before next September, when she would hopefully be enrolled.

Her administrator from her former course had emailed to let her know that her place had been formally interrupted. Jasper had calmly replied to confirm that she would never return. She would work and scrape and save to pay for the design course. She just wanted to get in. She would do anything, she just needed to get in.

As she started to glide upon the ice, she told herself that the decision was now out of her hands. Her future was in someone else's inbox. There was nothing she could do except wait.

She flew across the ice. It was true peace. She closed her eyes, adoring the cold against her cheeks as she soared. Her body was pure adrenaline, partly from the danger and also from the skating itself. Parts of her soul which had been crumpled up and cramped in corners of her spine were allowed to stretch and elongate. She was taller than ever, soaring across Lake Pristine, and as at one with the water as the mermaid they all said was hidden in the depths.

Act Two, Scene XI:
Some Like It Cold

"Jasper Montgomery!"

Arthur stared in horror at the figure on the frozen water. She knew how to skate, she moved with fluid grace and barely any hesitation—but the moon was now the only light shining on the lake and there was no way to predict the darkened ice she was skating on.

"Hey," she called over to him, sliding into a stop. "Come in, the ice is lovely."

"Absolutely not," he said, his heart hammering in his chest like it was trying to break free. "You know that's super unsafe?"

"Sure do."

"I'm scared for you," he said, forcing a laugh out of his lungs, pretending that he wasn't as afraid as he felt.

He watched her sit down upon the ice to remove her skates. She tossed them toward the small beach and walked on the lake in her bare feet, wincing only once at the contact.

"Come and feel the lake," she told him, holding out her hands. "The cold of the ice, it feels incredible."

Arthur shook his head, but he was already kicking off his large boots. He stripped off his black socks and made his way toward the ethereal girl who was clearly on another plane. She could probably have told him to break the ice and dive down to the bottom of the lake, and he would have considered it. He hissed and swore at the cold under his feet, but he kept his gaze fixed on her.

When he reached her, he took her frozen trembling hands and waited for her to come back down to earth. He could feel the electricity in her and it was more enticing than ever before.

"How are you not hypothermic?" he asked after a moment of stillness.

"Not sure," she said breathily. "Autistics regulate temperature differently. Maybe it's not so bad for me. Some like it cold, I know I do. I like being warmed up."

He took this as his cue to lead her onto dry land and wrap his large lumberjack coat around her. They sat on the stones and she leaned her back against his front.

"Skate on the ice all you want, just wait for me to spot you," he finally said. "I . . . I don't want you to . . ."

He didn't need to finish his sentence, she knew what he meant. She blew out a puff of air.

"I had to do it, it's on my list."

He felt her whole body instantly tense as soon as the words were out of her mouth.

"Your list?" he asked lightly. "What list?"

"Nothing."

His eyes suddenly landed on a small scrap of paper beneath a pebble. "That? Is that it?"

He scooped it up before she could. She turned around in his arms and there was something in her face that alarmed him. His smile slowly dissolved and he raised the list to his eyes, squinting to make out the writing in the dark.

"What is this, Jasper?" he asked.

She wouldn't meet his eyes, so he repeated the question.

"It's just a silly to-do list," she finally said. "I'm crossing things off."

Arthur read the collected items on the list, the things she wanted to do. "What . . ."

"I can put COMPLETED next to number one now," she said contemplatively. She snapped a pen out of her bag and did just that.

1. Skate on Lake Pristine—COMPLETED
2. Find Odette a better boyfriend/girlfriend/partner—anybody but vile Craig—SORT OF COMPLETED.
3. Make Mum proud with an amazing *Nutcracker* performance
4. Eat cupcakes at Vivi's—COMPLETED
5. Visit the Christmas Maze—COMPLETED
6. Buy an ornament from the Heywoods at the Winter Market—COMPLETED
7. Tell family I'm leaving Lake Pristine (and college) for design school—COMPLETED (almost!)
8. Get into design school
9. Help Christine have the most beautiful wedding
10. Catch the late-night shows at the Arthouse—COMPLETED
11. ~~Try to be civil with Arthur Lancaster~~
12. ~~Enjoy Christine's bachelorette party~~
13. Do something brave

Arthur blinked down at the seventh and eighth items on the to-do list. "Design school?"

Her somewhat breezy smile faded. "Yeah."

"So, this isn't just any list?"

"No," she allowed. "It's . . . it's a list of things to do before leaving Lake Pristine."

"That day in the library, you were telling the truth?"

"I was. I'm leaving."

He stared at her. "For good?"

"Yeah," she breathed. "This December . . . it's my last one here. I don't think Lake Pristine is my home anymore."

Arthur felt panic beating against his sternum. He stared at Jasper in disbelief and she looked back with sad resignation. "No!"

"Arthur," she chastised softly. "Come on."

"No, I won't come on! You're going? You're never coming back."

"It's not my home. It can't be, as long as my parents control my life. As long as they get to call the shots."

"You're not going back to keep studying psychology," Arthur said, putting the pieces together while staring down at the little goodbye list.

"No. I've applied for a design school. It's forty minutes from here."

"So live at home!"

"My parents will never let me, as soon as they realize I'm not going back to the life they've planned out for me, they'll cut me out. Not off, *out*. I will be banished. The Montgomerys don't do well with people making their own choices. It's not how I would want things. But I can't stay here. I won't be able to afford Lake Pristine rent."

Arthur felt as though he couldn't breathe. People who were not from Lake Pristine would never understand. People did leave, of course, but they always came back. Christine and Kevin left to study, but they had moved home after graduation and were now about to start their marriage in a three-bedroom near the town boundaries. That was what people did. Everyone had accepted Jasper leaving, purely on the promise that she would return.

Now she was sitting by Lake Pristine and telling him she would not come back.

"It's not about Lake Pristine. I love this place," Jasper said quietly. "But I need to be in control of my life. I'd love to study and live at home, but I can't let my parents decide my future anymore. They don't want design school, they want me to become a lawyer and they won't accept anything less. So, I'm making my own way. And I can't wait!"

"Live at the Arthouse," Arthur blurted out, his brain desperately scrambling for another solution. One that did not involve her driving away and never coming back. A solution that allowed Jasper to live her own life while still calling Lake Pristine home. "I'll turn the ballroom into a whole apartment for you. I'll do whatever you need."

Jasper stared at him. "You would do that?"

"Absolutely."

"Arthur, I can't."

"Yes, you can," he said bluntly.

"You could move out of town."

"No," he said hoarsely. "The Arthouse, Dad's cinema, and Grace . . . I can't go."

"Then we are where we are."

"I can't believe you!" he said, more harshly than he meant to. "These last few weeks, the whole time, you've been carrying around this little list, ready to leave all of us. Would you have even said goodbye?"

"Of course I would," Jasper said, her voice catching in her throat. "Arthur, don't be like this."

"Nothing has changed your mind? That night, on the bandstand, in your room? You still . . . Even after us?"

She carefully took the list back into her own hands. "I never knew there would be an 'us.' I thought you didn't like me."

"You know that isn't true," he said. "This is just . . ."

"Arthur," Jasper pressed against him, running a thumb over the stubble on his face. "We're teenagers. There will be other girls."

He let out an embittered puff of air. "Not for me."

"Arthur—"

"No. I know what I know, I knew it years ago. I've not expressed it well, that's fair, you can lay that one on me. But I know how I feel. I know what's permanent. This isn't fleeting, Jasper. Not like it was with any of the other girls I've known."

Images of his father's devastated face after his mother left passed through his memory. He could choke on them. They suffocated him in his darker moments. His father's love had not been enough to stop a cab at eleven o'clock at night and separate Christmases.

"You say you can't rely on your own family to be there for you and support your dreams?" he said shakily. "You can rely on me."

"I need to rely on *me*," Jasper pleaded. "My parents want a perfect trainee lawyer, this town wants the masked version of me, and I need to break free from all of that. I don't want to fight with you, Arthur."

"Were you going to tell me you were leaving?"

"Eventually, yes. After the wedding."

"After the wedding? Jasper, you're killing me."

"I did not expect any of this," Jasper said fiercely. "I didn't factor you into any of this when I made this list, I had no idea that this was going to happen."

Arthur kissed her then and it was not the explorative kiss from the night in her bedroom. It was hard and greedy and a fight for control.

Jasper loved kissing Arthur. She loved the scrape of his five o'clock shadow and the smell of the fireside that always seemed to linger on his skin. She loved how strong he was, how vulnerable he allowed himself to be with her.

"Arthur," she pressed her mouth to his ear, "don't be angry with me."

She could feel the argument still lingering in his body language—the hurt he had felt still tense and present in his hold of her. His hands were gripping her hips, pulling her to him, but he was still rigid with betrayal.

"Seeing you once a term or even less than that," he said, his breathing uneven, "it's not enough."

"You've just had eighteen months without seeing me."

"And it sucked. Besides, that was before . . . this. It's hard to quit something when it's out of sight. It's impossible when you have it."

Jasper still struggled to process how quickly things had changed. Maybe pride and insecurity and poor communication skills had wrecked the both of them on the rocks when it could have been easy sailing. Maybe while the ego had been threatening to bolt the door, the heart had just been waiting to come home.

"I'm not giving you an ultimatum, that's what your parents did and it's toxic," Arthur said quietly, his chin resting on top of Jasper's head. "I'm not going to beg you to stay with me or ask you to choose. But I need you in my life."

Jasper kissed him and it was hungry. She slipped her hands under his shirt and pressed them against his back. His fingers were stroking her hair when a light flashed onto both of them and they pulled apart to see what it was.

A torch was being shone in their eyes, causing both of them to flinch. Her father was on the path to the Lakehouse and he looked incensed.

"Jasper. Extract your hands from the boy and step away. Both of you, in my office. Now!"

Act Two, Scene XII:
The Judge

Howard Montgomery sat behind his large mahogany desk in his expensive dressing gown and surveyed his youngest daughter and her sullen beau with considered curiosity.

"Why were you . . . by the lake, at this late hour?" he asked

Jasper cast a sideways look at Arthur. He was clenching his jaw, refusing to out her despite everything. She could see him trying to keep a lid on the hurt he was feeling.

"Dad," she spoke slowly, "remember when I said I wasn't going to class?"

"I've tried to forget, Jazz."

"I'm not going back at all. I meant what I said. I've applied for a design school."

Her father was regarding her with disbelief. "Which one?"

"The Davenport."

"That's closer to here than the university!"

"I know. I told you that in my senior year. You and Mum said it would be a waste of time and money."

"Jazzie," her father's voice was exhausted. "The arts . . . it's such a risk, petal."

"But it would be my risk. And I'm going to make my own way."

"You should let her go and you should let her live at home," Arthur said suddenly.

"I'll get to you in a moment, son," Howard replied sharply,

pointing a finger at the tall boy who stood in front of him. "And don't tell me what to do with my own family."

"I'm not your son, I'm my father's son. And he never called me into a study like an employee. He never tried to reroute my life, he never tried to control any of us. There were no conditions with him, he was the most unconditional man in this town."

Howard stared at the young man chastising him in his own home. "How long has this been going on between the two of you?"

Jasper clasped Arthur's hand. "Not long."

"Don't lie to me, Jazzie, I saw that film the same as everyone else."

"She's not lying," snapped Arthur.

"Dad, I want to study interior design," Jasper pleaded. "It's not painting or singing or figure skating. Or ballet. It's applied art. There are plenty of employment opportunities."

"Everything feels so important when you're young," her father said softly, reaching out to take Jasper's other hand. "Everything seems so urgent and life or death. Every boy might seem like the great love of your life. But it's not. You can take your time, sweet girl. You can try for design school after getting your undergraduate degree."

Jasper gently extracted her hand from her father's. "No, Dad. I do have time. But it's mine."

"Jasper—"

"Dad." A single tear dropped from Jasper's eye to the carpet she had picked out for her father, his favorite thing about the study. "You shouldn't have let me dance. If you didn't want me to be creative, you should never have let me dance."

His resolve fractured at the look on Jasper's face and he exhaled heavily.

"Arthur," he addressed the boy with resignation. "It's late, you should be at home."

Arthur looked to Jasper. His body language told the two Montgomerys in the room that it was Jasper, and Jasper alone, who would dismiss him. She gave him the smallest of nods and he turned to go. They locked eyes as he closed the door and she turned back to her father with a desolate expression.

"Jasper," he spoke soothingly. "There will be other boys. You're not doing all this for him, are you?"

"No, Dad."

"Because I expect that of Christine, but not you. You were always the level-headed one."

"He's not put me up to anything, I applied for design school long before this . . . started."

"Your mother and I just want structure for you."

"A gold cage is still a cage."

"Jasper!"

"I'm sorry, Dad," she said, looking down at the crumpled list in her shaking hands. "I love you. I love Mum. I love Christine. I love this town, I've lived for it. I don't want to go. But I can't teach Mum's dance classes and get married and never achieve what I really want to. I can't work at Pete's and walk home alone every night. I can't study psychology. They can't teach me anything, I've studied neurotypicals my whole life, I know every move."

Her father smiled wanly at that.

"I can't go to the university that you want or to law school. And you said that was the choice. So, I need to go. I don't want to, but freedom and my own path, I won't give that up."

She placed her list on his desk and marked off number twelve: *Do something brave.*

"I understand if you can't support me," she told her father, pocketing the list before he could ask her about it. "So, I'll go. I'll support myself. I know what you both want for me. But I don't want it. I'm sorry."

She left her father alone in his study.

Howard Montgomery stared at the wallpaper, the delicate lights on the walls and the curtains that Jasper had chosen because they had reminded him of his grandmother's house. The sofa she had sourced after he had given up on trying to find the exact one he had pictured.

Her talent was draped across the whole room and it caused him to bury his head in his hands.

Jasper was finishing off her final shift at Pete's cafe before they closed up for the holidays. While *The Nutcracker* was firmly on her brain, she still found herself searching every corner of the town for Arthur.

Hera and Odette were sitting in the cafe, drinking hot chocolate—the two of them decidedly close now that Craig was out of the picture. Jasper made a little small talk with them, but her gaze kept darting to the cafe door.

"All right, I'll bite, who are you looking for?" Hera asked.

"Arthur Lancaster," Odette said in a singsong voice. "She's looking for Arthur Lancaster."

"Mind your manners," Jasper said with a smirk.

She had not seen Arthur since her father had ordered him out of the house. She did not have his phone number, and did not feel brave enough to call the cinema. He was one of those rare cases who didn't have social media, something she grudgingly respected him for. She wondered if he regretted everything that they had shared, but then, just as quickly, she would force herself to remember that this was her anxious thoughts speaking and not logical truth. She relived their shared moment on the bandstand whenever she could.

"The documentary really exposed the two of you," Hera said to Jasper, as the latter took a quick second to scroll through her phone. "Not that it was hard to miss. You were both pretty nauseating at the bowling alley that day."

"Oh, really?" Odette asked, glancing at Hera. "Everything really does go down at the arcade these days, huh?"

"Yep," Hera said, eyeing the other girl. "Although my favorite thing so far has been you breaking up with that monumental loser. That was . . . yeah."

Odette smiled at Hera, and the other girl mirrored the expression. There was a loaded pause, where unsaid things clicked like sonar.

Jasper did not hear them. She suddenly could not hear anything.

An email had landed in her inbox and, while she had not even opened it yet, the opening lines were visible on the screen and they made her heart start to gallop.

Dear Miss Montgomery. Thank you for your recent application to The Davenport School of Design. We are pleased to inform you—

"They're pleased to inform me," Jasper gasped. She slid in between Hera and Odette and she dropped her phone into her lap, grabbing hold of the both of them. "THEY'RE PLEASED TO INFORM ME!"

Odette stared at her friend and then snatched the phone. She opened the email and read the entire thing, her eyes scanning the screen with the speed of a hacker.

"Unconditional offer," Odette panted. "A fucking unconditional offer! Jasper, you did it!"

The three girls screamed with complete abandon, ignoring the customers who tried to shush them. Jasper would have been mortified at a customer telling her off a few weeks ago, now she could not bring herself to care. She smiled unrepentantly and burst out laughing, the joy and elation too much to contain.

"I did it," she breathed.

She wanted to tell Arthur. In the moments following her elation, it was all she wanted. Before anything else, she wanted to see his face.

Henry found his brother at an almost empty Arthouse.

"Hey," Henry said carefully. "You all right?"

"Not really," Arthur replied. "Howard Montgomery kicked me out of the Lakehouse and basically told Jasper she would find someone better."

"Yikes," Henry said. "This whole town is too melodramatic, but he might be the worst culprit."

"I'm not giving up, he can warn her off as much as he likes. Although . . ."

"Although what?"

"We sort of had an argument."

"All you two do is argue."

"This one was different."

Henry slid him a bottle of water and Arthur drank from it gratefully. The lobby was suddenly full of people as Agnes let the final showing out. A lot of people greeted Arthur with sympathetic nods, as if acknowledging that he had been through a few tumultuous days. He nodded back and drank more water. Then, the cinema doors opened with a crash and Arthur turned to see who had made the commotion.

The room fell silent when Marcus walked further inside. It was the first time Marcus had been seen in public since the event. He had clearly been hiding from the whole town. Everyone's judgment and distaste could be sensed in the atmosphere and it was almost powerful enough to make Arthur feel sorry for his cousin.

Then he remembered the night of the screening and that feeling quickly dissipated.

Marcus looked around at everyone and sighed bitterly. "I just wanted to show the truth for once."

A few people pushed by him and Henry made a noise of disbelief.

Marcus's eyes landed on Arthur. "Art—"

"Don't look at me," Arthur growled. "You almost ruined everything."

There was a flickering of triumph in the other boy's face. "So, you admit it."

"You're a shit friend to me right now," Arthur replied, refusing to let him control the flow of the conversation. "You could have told me, warned me."

"You wouldn't have screened it."

"Yeah, go figure," snapped Arthur. "You humiliated a whole bunch of us. It was meant to be a slice of life, small-town doc with some wedding stuff. Not . . . whatever that was."

"Do they want you in their little family now?" Marcus asked, neither he nor Arthur concerned with the other town members now watching their exchange. "Remember when you used to try to talk to her, Art? In high school? Her friends would all laugh, her sister would scoff."

"But Jasper didn't," Arthur said quietly, realizing for the first time that it was the truth. "She never did." He stared at his cousin. "And you know it."

Marcus wavered slightly but pressed ahead. "She was never going to look at guys like us, Art."

"*Us*. Did you say 'guys like us?'" Arthur did not look away from Marcus. "You liked her."

His friend's face paled slightly and he shifted uncomfortably, seemingly aware of all the eyes now on the two of them. "I . . . No. Maybe. Like, a long time ago. Once."

"That's what all this was? You wanted to screw me over in front of the whole town because she likes me back."

Marcus made a snorting sound. "Who says she likes—"

"She does!" Arthur interjected. "She told me. She told me after that stupid screening of yours, and a thousand other times since. And I hope that kills you."

Marcus shook his head softly. "It doesn't mean anything. And she's not going to stay for you. She's going to up and leave, just like she did last time. She's—"

"Marcus. That's enough."

Arthur, Henry and Marcus turned, along with most of the room, to see Christine at the entryway. Kevin stood stoically behind her. The elder Montgomery sister wore a calm and measured expression, and her voice was soft but firm. She had never looked so mature. The petulant child was gone and replaced with an unruffled woman.

"I think it's time you drop this and get going."

Christine said the words so casually. None of her usual ferocity. As she moved gracefully into the room, her eyes never left Marcus. The crowd who were gathered to watch the little scene were utterly silent.

"I think you've done enough damage to my sister," she said quietly. "Maybe I deserved some of that film. Maybe I am a bit of a tyrant."

Arthur watched in fascination as the young woman's eyes shone and her jaw stiffened.

"But not Jasper," she went on. "Jasper didn't deserve any of that. She's not anyone's business in this town, she's done enough. Given enough. She did not deserve to be treated that way."

"Yeah," someone at the back of the room said, their voice loud and full of concurrence. A few other murmurs of agreement rippled through the throng.

"If Jasper takes off from Lake Pristine and never comes back, it would be perfectly understandable," Kevin said and his voice was full of rebuke. "She breaks her back for everyone in this town and look at what you did to her."

His chastising words were for the whole room of people, not just Marcus.

"Jasper wants to study design at the Davenport," Christine said, also addressing the crowd. "I think everyone should be in a position to help her make that a reality."

Arthur felt removed from the scene as people made noises of approval and Christine started delivering orders and formulating a plan with her soon-to-be husband. He moved away from Marcus and Henry to look up at the picture of his father. He stared at the man's laughter lines and his one gold tooth. His father would never have done what Arthur had. He would never have been ashamed of loving someone, ashamed of being found out. Arthur had fallen in love with Jasper from the first moment she had walked out onto a stage. The feeling had been so overpowering, he had decided to hide it. No one would suspect him of wanting her if he was gruff and unfriendly and unapproachable. The disguise had worked far too well and now there was nothing tempting her to stay in Lake Pristine. His father would have risked rejection and possible humiliation. He would not have been afraid.

Seeing Marcus, a good person who had allowed bitterness and his own narrative to twist his behavior into something ugly, it made Arthur feel a sense of panic. He didn't want to be like that. He didn't want to be so afraid and nervous of strong feelings, and the people who inspired them, that he shut everything out. He didn't want to turn off the lights in his own heart out of fear that strangers would see it all aglow.

He pushed his way through the crowd, ignoring Marcus who called after him.

He set off for the Lakehouse.

Act Two, Scene XIII:
Grand Gesture

When Jasper reached the Lakehouse, she found Grace Lancaster waiting by the front door.

"I've come from town," Grace said breathlessly. "You've been nominated for Snow Queen!"

The young girl was winded with her excitement.

Jasper smiled. "Who else is nominated?"

"Christine, of course," Grace reported. She listed off three other names Jasper recognized—all girls from old Lake Pristine families like the Montgomerys. "Then you! I voted for you!"

Jasper gave her a thankful look, an indulgent one. "Thanks, kid. It's appreciated. I look forward to being soundly beaten by Christine, but it's just an honor to be nominated, as they say." She had once found the Winter Carnival more thrilling than anything, but she was no longer sad about constantly losing to her elder sister.

"I'd die to win it," Grace said, her hands fizzing and her eyes wide. "I hope that you get crowned."

"I'll live if I don't, but you have my vote. You should be nominated."

They sat in comfortable silence for a moment before Grace spoke with amicable pointedness.

"You know, my brother's had a picture of you in his room for a few years now."

Jasper could feel her cheeks heating, but she did not move or react in any visible way. "I doubt that."

"Oh, no, he does. He cut it out of the town newsletter when he was sixteen."

"Try not to completely embarrass me, bean."

The gentle reprimand, spoken in a deep voice and accompanied by a crunch of snow caused Jasper to spin around. Arthur Lancaster stood on the bottom of the path, at the edge of the woods and the border of the Lakehouse. He looked up at her with a soft expression and she suddenly wished his younger sister was safely somewhere else.

She knew he was still guarded, still bruised from the discovery of the list. She could sense that he had things to say.

"Arthur!" Grace cried out. "Jasper's been nominated for Snow Queen!"

Arthur offered Jasper the smallest and most sardonic of bows, making her laugh. "Congratulations."

"And who did you vote for?" she asked him teasingly.

His eyes sparkled as he shrugged. "Haven't cast my ballot yet."

"Anything I can do to win your support?"

"Nothing I can say in front of a minor."

"Ew." Grace hurried down the path and smacked her older brother, causing him and Jasper to laugh.

The three of them made their way to Lake Pristine. The actual lake. They sat right by its edge, beneath stars that were so bright, it seemed to stun Jasper. Arthur watched her face as she stared up at the piercingly clear night sky. The mist that had obscured the sky when he had found the list was now gone and everything was strikingly clear. For Jasper, everything had dramatically transformed and settled all at once. A blizzard had become a gentle fall of snow inside of her and she no longer felt outside of the glass.

She had stood beneath the stars by the lake so many times, almost always feeling torn and twisted and wrong. Now she felt serene. For the first time in a long time.

"There are no stars in the city," she told Arthur, noticing his stare. "I'd forgotten."

The lake was still completely frozen over, but Arthur shot down Grace's suggestion of ice skating with such vehement ferocity, it made the other two laugh. Jasper caught his gaze and nodded, taking the unspoken scolding. No one was allowed to endanger themselves for fun in Arthur Lancaster's presence.

"So," Grace said conversationally. "Are you two . . . you know?"

Arthur could see Jasper fighting a smile and he found himself feeling a little melancholy. He did not know what they were. He knew what he wanted them to become, he knew what he felt about her, but she had been through so much of late and with the wedding and the ballet performance on the horizon, he did not want to push her. She was pushed by too many people. He was not going to become one of them. He wanted to tell her so, but Grace was an accidental chaperone for the two of them, making him less able to speak freely.

"Never mind us, you need to rest before your debut," he told his little sister. "It's practically here."

"Don't remind me, I'm a bag of nerves," muttered Grace.

"You'll be great," Jasper said quietly.

Both Arthur and Grace looked at her and Jasper smiled a sad smile that Arthur could not quite understand.

"No one ever told me I'd be great," she said, casually. "I was pushed and prodded and criticized. Then, when I was too afraid to be mediocre, Mum would just sort of nod. And I had to take that as a sign that I had done a good job. But who really knows?"

"You were a wonderful dancer," Arthur said, his tone a little more exacting than he meant it to be. His feelings were stronger than his ability to contain them, it would seem. He was desperate for her to see herself the way he did. Though, he did note, there was something changed about her. He had seen it when she had spoken back to her father in his study. Arthur was about to ask her when they heard the disturbance of the stones behind them.

They turned to see Henry, Odette and Hera. The latter pair were standing very close to one another.

"Can we join you?" Henry asked.

"Sure," Grace said cheerfully. "Just don't say anything too serious."

"Me?" Henry replied. "Never."

The six of them sat by the lake and perhaps Arthur was imagining it, but he had the distinct feeling that this was the end of a chapter. Something irrevocable was at play and he could not pinpoint what it was.

"We should be celebrating," Hera said, breaking his reverie. "Jasper got into design school!"

Arthur felt as though someone had just shoved him into the middle of a road. Glaring lights before him, no one to pull him back. He was aware of Grace exclaiming in excitement and his brother obnoxiously whistling in approval. He could see Jasper blushing.

"You got in," he eventually uttered.

She finally turned to meet his gaze and she smiled. "Yeah."

He forced himself to say the right thing. "I'm so proud of you."

It came out sounding every bit as intimate as it felt and the rest of the group raised eyebrows and started to scoot away from the two of them. When Jasper and Arthur had relative privacy, she pushed her hair out of her face and offered him another small smile.

"Found out tonight," she explained.

"That's amazing. You're doing it. Living the dream."

"Well, attempting to," she said.

He hated that he wanted to beg her to stay. He felt his defenses creeping in, wondering if he was not enough.

"What's wrong?"

She spoke the words without judgment or reproach, but Arthur still bristled slightly, knowing that he had no right to feel the way that he did.

"It will always be hard," he said, shrugging. "Watching you drive away. But I've done it before."

She glanced away. "Arthur . . ."

"You can cross that off your list," he said, not unkindly. "And I know your ballet is going to be a smash, so you can tick that off, too."

He looked out at the lake, the beautiful and sometimes formidable body of water that the whole town was named after. Frozen in ice and almost a mile to the other side, it was a stunning sight.

Arthur's love for Jasper was like the lake, he realized. It would always be here, it would wait as long as it had to. It would shift and alter slightly with the seasons, but ultimately it would never change. A fixed and perpetual thing that could always be relied upon.

"Want to come in to the Lakehouse?" Jasper asked him solemnly. "It's cold."

He looked back at the imposing house a few yards away. "Sure. As long as we don't get hauled into your dad's office again."

Henry made a proper show of announcing that he would take Grace home, while Odette hugged Jasper and said goodnight.

"You going home?" Jasper asked, her eyes flitting between the two girls.

"Uh," Odette glanced at Hera and Arthur noticed a flush of color on Jasper's best friend's neck. "We'll take a walk around the town for a bit, I think."

Hera smiled a secret smile and they walked off in the direction of the path to town, their hands slipping together when they thought they were out of sight. Jasper made a small, contented noise and Arthur silently thought about how much more of a positive pair the two of them made compared to Odette and Craig.

"There's only your old Jeep in the drive," Arthur said, as they headed up the driveway to the Lakehouse. He closed the front door while Jasper checked her phone for messages.

"They're all out for a bit," she said slowly, her eyes scanning the screen. "They've just ordered drinks in town."

Arthur understood her subtext: they would be some time before they made their way back. They were alone.

Arthur coughed and was about to ask if she wanted him to leave when she slipped her arms around his neck and pressed her lips to his. It was like an electric shock for him and he instinctively pulled her into him. She was more forward this time and he soon found himself backed into a corner of her hallway. She had to stand on her toes in order to kiss him properly, but she was an ex-ballerina, so it was no problem for her.

"Jasper," he said, forcing himself to pull away, even while every inch of him protested. "Are you going away for good?"

She wiped a bit of lipstick away from the corner of his mouth and her eyes looked a little pained. "I don't know."

"Then what are we going to do?" he asked, his voice mildly breathless and his hands aching to grab her and not let go. "Because I don't want to influence your decision."

"I won't let anyone influence my decision," she said gently. "But I'm definitely going to go, Art. I want to go to design school. I've been saving. I've been waiting."

"Then you've got to go," he said, trying to push as much enthusiasm for her as he could muster into his words. He was thrilled for her, she deserved the career that she wanted. However, the selfish part of him could not bear it. The part that was in love. The part that was growing greater with every passing day.

"Right now, I just really want to fool around with you," Jasper said bluntly and it made him laugh.

A week ago he would have chopped his right arm off for just fooling around, but now he was already pining for more. He did not want to be some guy Jasper Montgomery fooled around with before leaving Lake Pristine for a fancy design school, with no plans of ever coming back.

But she was irresistible to him so they did fool around.

On the sofa in the snug, and Arthur was too into it to worry about whether or not he was just a distraction for Jasper. He made sure to alternate from slow, lazy kisses to the hard and overwhelming kind. He felt like he was getting drunk on her. She was ambrosia to him. As he had always suspected she would be.

He wanted to say something impressive, something inspired. Something that she would talk excitedly about to her friends when they were apart. But all he could manage was—

"You're so pretty, Jasper."

He could see a flash of doubt in her eyes. He hated whoever had put it there.

She fixed him with a contemplative look.

"What is it?" he asked, still catching his breath.

"Did you never want to go to college? Or leave this place?"

"I want to run the Arthouse by myself someday," he said.

"Is that your dream?"

"My dream? No. My dream would be to renovate it beyond all imagining and make it like Radio City."

"Why don't you?"

Arthur hesitated, running his hand up and down her thigh as if to soothe himself. "Henry likes it exactly as it is. He doesn't want an inch of it changed."

"Why?" Jasper asked and then realization dawned in her eyes. "Because of your dad?"

"Yeah. I don't know, I never want to push. Henry's the eldest, he had him the longest. And when Mum took off to move in with Brian, to escape this town and all of the memories, I think the cinema sort of became this weird shrine."

"Can you talk to him about it?"

Arthur shrugged. "None of us like talking about it."

"You're the smartest guy in town, Arthur. You should be able to do what you want to do, career wise."

He gently pushed her long hair out of her face. "It's nice hearing you say pleasant things to me for a change."

She laughed in disbelief. "Well, wait a minute. I have notes."

"Notes?"

"For the cinema."

"Thank God. For a moment there, I thought you were going to give me romantic feedback."

"You need better snacks at the Arthouse. It's not the prices that has people sneaking their own food in."

"I don't know why people try to hide that they're doing that," Arthur said loftily. "It's not illegal, we can't stop them."

"Right, but the choices at your place? Not great."

"Well, that's part of my plan. I would love for there to be an actual kitchen making real food on site."

"That's a great idea!"

"And fresh popcorn, not the heated-up stale kind."

"Exactly!"

"Plus a better stocked bar."

"See!" Jasper cried, leaning back against the arm of the sofa they were lounging on and stretching her legs out over his lap. "You've got ideas, you've got a vision. You should one hundred percent take over and redo the place."

Arthur's smile dropped away. "I just . . . we've all been through a lot of change."

"Bad change," Jasper acknowledged softly. "This would be good change."

"Yeah, maybe."

"I really hope when I come back to town from school, the Arthouse will be more under your control."

"I hope so, too."

They looked at one another for a moment and Arthur knew that Jasper was doing the same thing he was. She was wondering if the attraction, the heady connection, was something that could be permanent. Arthur knew it was for him. He had tried in vain to move on from his feelings for Jasper Montgomery. May and Saffron had been unfortunate casualties of his denial. He regretted that more than anything.

"I'm a sure thing," he told her guardedly. Then, he forced himself to pull open the gate and let everything he felt for her show on his face. "I really am, Jasper."

Her eyes shone in the cool and artificial light. He could see that she wanted to believe him. "Arthur," she said quietly. "I really like you. More than I realized. I'm sorry to say, I'm clearly the kind of girl who needs something spelled out on a giant cinema screen before she will believe it to be true."

"Big gestures," Arthur said, contemplatively. "Got it."

Jasper stood alone in her mother's dance studio. It was hours until *The Nutcracker* and she was full of nervous energy with nowhere to go. She swept her leg into a fan kick and practiced some chaînés. She stood en pointe and closed her eyes, letting go of every negative thought she had ever allowed. She let her feet drop slowly back to the floor and started with fright as she heard some applause.

Her mother stood in the doorway, smiling with pride.

"No one ever could dance like you," she said.

Jasper released a noise of derision. "Christine was—"

"Never as good as you," her mother interrupted softly. "Didn't have the discipline. Or the fortitude."

Jasper's eyebrows shot up, as she was astounded by this compliment. "You've never told me that."

They had barely spoken since the argument.

Jasper could not remember every word she had said, but she remembered how she'd felt. She remembered voicing frustrations that had been held inside for too long. Now, as she and her mother looked at one another, she wondered if those words had acted as a lesson or would be used against her as a weapon.

Andrea walked to stand behind her, going into ballet mistress mode. Jasper understood the non-verbal cue and moved into position. She performed her pirouette and, to an outsider, it would have appeared flawless.

"Spotting needs to remain consistent," her mother said. "Keep that focus until after the movement, not just the end of it."

Jasper did it again.

"Better," her mother murmured.

They both stared at themselves in the mirror on the wall and did not speak for a few moments.

"There is no point in correcting a dancer who will never be great," her mother finally whispered, her voice suddenly fragile. "It's a waste of effort. A good teacher must be hardest on the dancers who they know can be magnificent. The ones who will be superlative. Those are the ones you are fiercest with, those are the ones whose feet will bleed. They will cry and they will curse you. They may even hate you. But they will also be great. They will soar the highest."

Jasper chose peace in that moment, accepting the olive branch with understanding silence. She did not say that the love of dancing had been worn away by the pain. That she no longer called herself a dancer because it hurt too much. That her mother's harsher treatment of her, next to a softer hand when it came to Christine, had made her give up the fight.

"That Lancaster boy really is crazy about you," her mother remarked.

Jasper could feel her face flushing. "Nothing happened in my room, Mum."

"Don't be silly, of course something happened. You fell in love with him."

Jasper was not sure if she could speak about matters like this with her mother. The room suddenly felt like a sauna.

"And while your father probably tried to frighten the life out of him, I doubt it worked. He seemed determined."

Jasper remembered the look on Arthur's face when they had been alone at the Lakehouse and she was suddenly smiling to herself. "I'm concentrating on Christine's wedding and *The Nutcracker*."

"Tush, tush," her mother said sharply. "You've given everything to both of those things, they're well-oiled machines. You deserve something for yourself."

"I got into design school, Mum," Jasper said, her voice so unsure and quiet. "I'm going to accept."

"Of course you are," her mother said briskly, avoiding her eyes. "You've got incredible potential, you cannot waste it."

Jasper jerked her body around to stare at her mother. "You're not angry?"

"No."

"I won't be able to teach here anymore. I'll have classes. And I'm walking away . . . from everything you and Dad gave me. The other degree."

"I've discussed all that with your father," Andrea said, choosing her words cautiously for the first time in their history. "We were perhaps a little too overzealous with all that business. And we shouldn't have used tuition money as an ultimatum."

Jasper was staggered by this admission. "I—"

"We'll help pay for your course still. If that's what you want."

Jasper felt her whole soul fill up for the first time with her mother. "I appreciate it so much. But I've applied for aid. I want to do it myself."

"Well, what about accommodation?"

"Sorry?"

"We also think asking for rent is a little old-fashioned. Parents shouldn't be their children's landlords. If you wanted to keep your room at the Lakehouse while studying at the Davenport, that would . . . that would be all right."

Jasper's eyes filled with water and she had to close them for a whole minute before her vision cleared. "Are you serious?"

"Perfectly," her mother said, as if she had not just handed Jasper the words she needed to feel better, to make everyone—including herself—happy. "Christine will be in her new home, the place will be so quiet. Your father and I will drive each other mad. We need a third party in the house. Not that you'll be there for anything but sleep—I imagine your studies and that boy will keep you busy."

"Mum," Jasper's voice was fragile and small. "Thank you. That would be . . . you have no idea . . . I want to go to this school so much, but this makes everything so much easier. I wouldn't have to—"

It had never been about Lake Pristine. The mask her parents had, perhaps unknowingly, demanded that she wear had grown too tight, too suffocating and too tolerated by others. She had convinced herself that there was no acceptance waiting for her in Lake Pristine without the mask.

But that wasn't true.

Arthur had started that realization. Now, as she stood in the old ballet studio, she felt it all. The possibility. The future.

A future in Lake Pristine as herself.

Her true self.

"I wouldn't have to leave everything behind," was all she managed to say.

"Hush your mouth," her mother said faintly and Jasper felt six years old again. When her mother had told her to work with Odette and teach the other little girl to love dancing as much as she did. "Whatever you do, you'll be great."

They stood in silence as the light dimmed outside of the ballet studio, the sounds of winter surrounding the small shrine to dance like a fist closing around snow for a split second and then letting it go.

It was Nutcracker Eve and Grace was hours away from her debut. Arthur and Henry had been snapped at all day, as her nerves got the better of her. They had been walking on eggshells, too afraid to even wish her good luck as she packed her things and left for the final rehearsal before the show.

"Break a leg," Arthur murmured, as she stalked away. "We'll be in the audience."

She ignored him and Henry waited until she was gone before spluttering out a laugh.

"God, she is scary."

"It's not funny," Arthur replied, rubbing his face with both hands and releasing a shiver. "I thought she was going to behead me at lunch."

"Should we even go tonight?"

"Of course! She'll kill us if we don't."

"She might kill us if we do."

They returned to the cinema, preparing to close up so that they could make the performance. As the last few customers were ushered out, Henry caught Arthur staring up at the black-and-white classics that were advertised on the wall.

"Have you seen her?" Henry asked nonchalantly.

"Yes," said Arthur, not even pretending to misunderstand who Henry meant. "No more run-ins with her father, at least."

"Yeah. Let me guess. Did he tell you his daughter is a precious pearl who needs an oyster you can't afford?"

"No," Arthur said, frowning. "He said Jasper would find other boys."

Henry's smile vanished. "He did?"

"Yeah. He clearly thinks she can do better. Probably telling her right now that I'm not a good fit and that—"

"Well, hey, look," Henry said gently. "You don't know what will happen. You might go out until summer and get sick of each other."

"I'm never getting sick of her, Henry," Arthur said with resolve. "So, I don't know. I guess the ball is in her court."

"Super romantic of you."

"I don't know how to be romantic, you saw that documentary. Hell, you apparently saw everything."

"She loves those romantic old movies. Do something from one of them."

"She likes them through a critical, self-aware lens, Henry," Arthur said, with a small smile. "There's romance in the movies and then there's real life. The two should not really cross over. There's a thin line between romantic and creepy."

"Cheers to that. We all had to sit through that film and never was that made clearer."

Arthur faked a punch in his brother's direction. Henry dodged it with a laugh.

"What about you?" Arthur asked, as they both sat in the cinema lobby and regarded one another. "Feeling any pangs at Christine getting married?"

"You mean am I going to pull a 'speak now or forever hold your whatever?' No. I'm good."

"I still can't quite believe the two of you went out."

"We were never a good fit," Henry said with mild amusement. "I was also a stepping stone for her, in order to find out what she wanted. Or who she wanted."

"Jasper's not like that," Arthur maintained.

"No, she's not."

Arthur sat in thought for a few minutes. He thought about Jasper. He thought about how he had never been able to stop thinking about her, not since he saw her on that stage all of those years before. He thought about his father. He thought about Grace. He thought about how much happier their mother was now. He thought about Brian and how much he loved his mother. He thought about Christine and Kevin and the documentary. He thought about how Marcus had been almost run out of town.

He thought about his father. His father, who had loved life so much. Most people were too afraid to love as hard as he had; they were afraid of the pain. If the love was too much, so the loss would be, too.

Arthur had let himself become unattached. But he didn't want that anymore. Now he wanted to be more like his father. To honor his father's legacy in countless ways, in the town that Tayo had loved so much.

And so he thought about Jasper's special interest. The films she loved. The arthouse she had loved seeing them in. The romantic worlds she liked to escape to.

And the idea arrived like fresh snow.

"Meet me at the ballet," he said, jumping to his feet and exiting the cinema.

It was starting to snow again in Lake Pristine. Arthur jogged to the winter market, letting out a noise of relief when he caught sight of Mrs. Heywood and her stall. As he made his way to her, he took a moment to really take in the town. For the first time in a lifetime, he understood its beauty. The lights covering each stall and each wall, like stars brought down to the ground. People smiled at one another as snowflakes landed on cheeks and the whole place was abuzz with goodwill. Arthur felt shame at how he had treated it. People crossed oceans and searched the world to find homes like this.

His father had loved this town. He was still alive in this town. Arthur knew, as he looked at the vendors and the couples darting toward the maze, that he had allowed his grief to turn to bitterness. If one looked for bad faith in the world, they would always find it. And Arthur had spent the last eighteen months looking for little else.

Now something had changed. Lake Pristine had stealthily become home again. Somehow in the snow, something had grown again.

"Afternoon, Arthur," Mrs. Heywood said, beaming brightly at him as he stopped in front of her. "Merry Christmas Eve. Can I help you?"

"Yes," Arthur said, exhaling and pointing to her wares. "I kind of need all of them, please."

Finale

Jasper stood in the wings while the auditorium filled with people. It was their busiest *Nutcracker* yet, with standing-room-only tickets sold out and a waiting list for any returns.

Grace Lancaster appeared by her side.

"You okay?" Jasper whispered.

"Terrified," Grace replied.

Jasper regarded her. "You don't look scared."

Grace blushed and smiled up at her. "I'm not. It's just . . . what we're supposed to say, isn't it?"

Jasper laughed. "I don't think either of us should be worried about what we're 'supposed' to do or be. You're excited? You should be. You get to go out there and do the thing you love most."

"I know," Grace breathed, elation coming off her like sparks. "I can't believe it's happening. Arthur and Henry are out there, so's Mum. I was nervous earlier, tetchy. Now, I just want to go."

When the music quieted for a brief moment and the crowd fell into a hush, Jasper stepped back. She watched the dancers hurry to their marks as the lights went down. When they came up again, Grace was center stage. She was so alive. So delighted to be there. So deserving of it all. The crowd applauded without invitation and Jasper felt her eyes dampen.

"You show them all, girl," she said, too quietly for even the stage manager to hear. "You're the best of them all."

* * *

When the performance was over, Jasper was dragged onstage by one of the male dancers. As she moved to accept the applause, she realized what a long time it had been since she had last stood in front of a crowd. Her time in a tutu was long gone. But she accepted the rapturous reception with ease and relief.

There was only one person she was really hoping to see.

She spotted him in the audience—but the lights went down before she could read his expression.

Christmas Day at the Lakehouse was calm. As Jasper's family didn't really celebrate the holiday, Odette and her mother came over for Chinese food. The Montgomerys would return the favor on Lunar New Year, as was also tradition. Kevin cooked for everyone, with Mrs. Cunningham supervising from over his shoulder.

There was no fighting or arguing about wedding decisions.

Jasper felt at home.

Two days later, at her sister's rehearsal dinner, right in the middle of the difficult days that bridged Christmas and New Year's Eve, Jasper sat among her friends and family and smiled dutifully when required. She raised her glass and laughed when expected. She made small talk. Jasper accepted congratulations for the ballet performance and answered people's questions about planning the wedding.

"I've got something for you," Christine said to her, as drinks turned to dancing and mingling.

"For me?" Jasper looked her up and down. "Is this a gimmick?"

"Shut up and follow me."

Jasper traipsed after her older sister, who was heading for the powder room. Once they were inside, Christine handed her a package

wrapped with soft tissue paper. Jasper stared at it for a moment before tearing it open. She binned the wrapping and held up a long,
chiffon dress.

Salmon.

"I don't . . ." she stared at the strapless gown, as the pieces fit
together in her head.

"For my new maid of honor," Christine said.

Jasper felt emotion well up inside of her and she ignored her
usual instinct to suppress it. She let the feelings bubble over and
reached over to embrace her sister. They held each other for three
minutes straight, silently sobbing. Jasper finally drew back.

"Don't want to crease it," she said, holding out the dress with
veneration.

"You'll look great in it," Christine said decidedly. "Really beautiful."

Jasper looked at her sister through wet eyelashes. "Not too busty?"

"Never."

"Thank you, Chris."

"Oh, and there's one more thing."

"Not sure I can take much more right now," Jasper murmured,
checking her mascara in the mirror. When Christine did not respond, Jasper turned to look at her sister. The bride-to-be was
holding out an envelope. Jasper took it, hesitantly.

It was a check. For a substantial amount of money, enough to
make Jasper's stomach drop a few inches, her other hand grasping
the sink for balance.

"Chris, what is this?"

"It's a collective donation from Lake Pristine. We all felt you
deserved a bit of help with your new degree. Gas money for your
new commute."

"Everyone did this? Christine, you got everyone to do this?"

"This town loves you. Almost as much as I do."

"I'm not accepting it."

"Yeah, we thought you'd say that."

"Make it scholarship money. For someone else. Someone who's family don't own the lake, maybe."

Christine laughed at the reproachful gratitude in Jasper's voice. "Fine. Typical."

She left and Jasper could only stare at the slip of paper in her palm.

She tried to compose herself. She looked at herself in the mirror and felt a sharp pinch of gratitude. Since her acceptance letter, everything had started to balance out in her life. They had all been a little more mellow with each other. Odette was finally free of Craig . . . and then there was Arthur.

Arthur Lancaster.

Now she could acknowledge that she had always found Arthur to be intimidating because she was discombobulated by her reaction to him. She had created a narrative around their vibe because it had scared her. She liked him so much. More than she had ever really liked anyone.

She splashed a little water on her face, mentally instructing herself to calm down and return to the party as if everything was perfectly normal and she wasn't considering running off to be with the local cinema manager.

However, there was a large group of people gathered at the door of the restaurant as she made her way back to the group.

"What's going on?" her mother asked, irritated.

"Don't know," Charlotte said, moving over to the doorway. Anna and Rebecca followed and then Charlotte let out a little cry.

"Oh, my God," Christine said. "Jasper! Come look!"

Jasper frowned and moved to join the other young women at the door. It was still snowing outside and the town was lit up in bright holiday colors, people milling about and enjoying the maze, the market stalls and the new little ice rink for children.

"What is it?" asked Jasper.

"Come out and see," Anna said, throwing open the door and pulling Jasper with her.

They walked into town and Odette was suddenly jogging toward them.

"I actually cannot believe it," she told Jasper, greeting her friend with a fast hug and a jubilant laugh.

"Believe what?" Jasper asked.

"Look!" Odette barked, grabbing her friend's shoulders and turning her so that she was looking at the town square, the bandstand and the arthouse. "Look closely."

Jasper let out an exasperated noise but did as she was told. Then she blinked. "Are those . . . ?"

The whole town seemed to be covered in hanging ornaments. There were hundreds of them all over the place, hanging from branches, street signs and lamp posts. Many on the woodland trees that were on the edge of Main Street. One hanging from the ballet studio sign. Some on the maze entrance. A handful around the bandstand.

"There must be thousands," Christine said.

Jasper moved toward one, catching it in her hand. It was a pine cone. Just like the one she had bought from Mrs. Heywood, where you could write your favorite person's name.

"They all have the same name painted on them," Odette said sincerely, watching Jasper with shining eyes, waiting for her friend to comprehend.

Jasper slowly turned the pine cone over. Her own name looked back at her. She grabbed another. Then another. Then one more.

They all said "Jasper."

"I've checked every single one I could find," Odette said, as they moved further into town. "They all have your name on."

Townsfolk smiled knowingly at Jasper as she passed them. Mr. Heywood, Mrs. Heywood's husband who lived and breathed for the Lake Pristine Winter Carnival and very little else, was standing at the bandstand with a microphone.

"Ah, good, they're here!" he called, his voice echoing around the small town and the surrounding woodland. "Congratulations, Jasper Montgomery. This year's Snow Queen. A close race! Though if we were to count all of these tokens, I think you'd win by a few thousand."

Jasper stared in awe at all the little ornaments wearing her name. "I . . . I don't—"

"Happy to relinquish my ten-year reign," Christine said softly, applauding with the rest of the crowd while Odette pulled at Jasper.

"Come on, make a speech," her friend said.

Jasper was still gazing at her name, written a thousand times. "Who . . . ?" she asked, her breath short and her chest tight.

"Oh, come on," Odette said affectionately. "You know exactly who, Jasper Montgomery."

Jasper was forced onto the bandstand steps and Mr. Heywood

handed her the microphone before sprinting to get the twinkling, ice-like tiara he made every year.

"This is an honor," Jasper said, trying to sound serious. "I thought my sister would take this crown with her to the grave."

She spotted Grace and Henry Lancaster in the crowd, both beaming up at her, but not the face that she really wanted to see— the face who was responsible for all of the glittering votes.

"I feel that one person and one person alone has swung me a victory," she said into the microphone. "So, as a good sport, I must abdicate. I choose a Snow Queen regent in my place."

She took the tiara from Mr. Heywood's hands and held it out to Grace. The young ballerina's eyes widened, but as the crowd cheered approvingly, she staggered forward and allowed Jasper to crown her.

"I can't." The young girl, still glowing from her performance as Clara, stared up at Jasper. "You . . . Jasper—"

"Crown looks great on you, kid," Jasper said, hugging her briefly. "Soak it in. You're the new queen of Lake Pristine."

She leaped down from the bandstand while Grace waved to an adoring crowd. Christine stood at the very back of the enthusiastic onlookers, wearing a small, barely-there smile as she watched her successor. People tried to grab Jasper for conversation as she pushed her way through the mass of people. Ordinarily, she would have stayed, but she had somewhere important to be.

"Merry Christmas, old movie house!" she said as she jogged down Main Street.

Jasper reached the Arthouse while Grace and the rest of the town celebrated, everything else around her melting away. Arthur Lancaster was sitting on the steps of the cinema, waiting for her.

He smiled at her and Jasper let out a short laugh. She could feel everyone else stepping back, giving them space.

"This was you," she said, feeling silly for voicing what was so obvious.

It felt difficult at first, wearing her heart on her sleeve But when she looked at Arthur, all of the fragments Jasper thought would break apart seemed to just be. They floated. At ease in their separateness and all forming a better whole.

"The films," she said, nodding toward the old cinema. A piece of the past in their small town, standing tall among the cameras and the gossip. "You knew I would come and see the films."

He nodded. Watching her carefully.

Her special interest. He knew.

No one else had ever tried to know. No one had ever wanted to get to that part of her story.

She had wasted years watching people fall at the first hurdle. Learning to make herself appreciate that and never expect anything else from others.

She had been waiting all her life.

"Princess," he said quietly.

"Why did you do it?"

His hands were on either side of her face. The tips of his fingers against the corners of her mouth.

"Because, Jasper, *you're* my special interest."

He kissed her then. She did not care about who was watching them, she did not care about the two of them becoming tittle-tattle or the next day's gossip.

"If you need a big gesture to know I'm a sure thing, this is as big as I can afford right now," he said and she laughed against his mouth.

"It's pretty good."

She kissed him again. Then again. Then did not stop, despite a few howls from the far-off group of onlookers. Finally they didn't care what any of them thought.

At long last.

"Got a date to your sister's wedding?" he asked, when they drew breath.

"No. Might go stag."

"I repeat. Do you have a date to the wedding?"

"Yes. You."

He grinned. "Correct."

She laughed. Then grew serious. "Listen. I need to tell you. I—"

He smiled sadly at her. "You're going to study design. I know. I haven't forgotten and I want you to go. I'm so proud of you. You're going to be amazing."

"I'm going to be living at home."

Hope and relief entered his face all at once as he pulled back to stare at her. "What?"

"You heard."

He glanced down at their hands, which were now clasped together. "You're . . . you're not doing that for me, are you?"

"No. I'm doing it because dorms can be horrible and I don't do well with strangers for roommates."

He released a shaky laugh. "Well, all right."

"Why?" she teased, gazing up at him. "Do you want me to stay?"

He shrugged. "I'll love you wherever you are. Always have."

"If I do leave someday?"

"I'll be there with you."

"Well," Jasper beamed at him. "That's not a grumbly thing to say at all."

His smile softened into a look of real tenderness and Jasper pressed closer, sighing as his fingers stroked her hair. She raised her face and kissed him again, smiling against his mouth as he groaned. She put all of what she was feeling into the embrace.

Since she was a little, neurodivergent child, she had been told girls should rescue themselves. It was part of a strong pushback against centuries of damsels in distress and female oppression. You need no one, little girl, go forth and be fabulous and independent and never let anyone carry your bags or listen to your problems when they've become sewn into your skin and too overwhelming to manage.

Jasper intended to be a voracious feminist for the rest of her life. She was going to have an amazing career. She was going to buy her own home. But she knew, as she was pressed up against Arthur and feeling safe and seen for the first time in years, that letting people try to climb the tower she had locked herself in was not weakness. The garden of thorns was to keep people out and it did not matter if the princess raised them up herself. She was alone either way. Jasper did not want to be alone any longer. She wanted to be with Arthur.

Choosing yourself did not mean you could not also choose other people.

"And listen," she said, when they came up for air again, "when I graduate, we can give this old place a makeover. I'm thinking art deco."

She jokingly gestured to the arthouse.

Arthur nodded and grinned. "Yeah, I wouldn't mind my new office getting redone, to be fair. In my favorite color."

"Which is what," ribbed Jasper. "Black? Brown? Grumble gray?"

"Green."

"Emerald green? Bottle green?"

"No." He kissed her and then leaned down and whispered in her ear, "Jasper green."

The Credits

Christine and Kevin were married on New Year's Eve in a beautiful white marquee with most of Lake Pristine watching on.

Both Howard and Andrea Montgomery cried and Kevin's best man gave a speech that was both entertaining and moving. As Jasper Montgomery watched, she smiled at the happy reactions from the wedding party. She had gone over the speech with a fine-tooth comb so it was vindicating to see it going down well. When he had begged to keep some of his riskier jokes, Jasper had gently told him that his freedom of speech was important to her, but so was his life. She had explained the specifics of what Christine would do to him, should his intended speech go ahead. She was thrilled to hear that he had seen reason.

She smiled warmly at the catering staff as they came to clear the dinner plates and looked out at the room full of people. Her mother and father were mingling and Christine was dancing with the rest of her bridesmaids. Kevin and his brother were encouraging their mother to do a shot at the bar. Saffron was scowling in a corner while a groomsman slid into the seat next to her, holding out a slice of wedding cake. Odette was dancing with Hera, her last-minute wedding date, and the two of them looked as though they were having the most fun of all.

Jasper looked down at her thigh, where her hand was settled inside someone else's.

She looked up at Arthur Lancaster's face. He was wearing a royal blue suit and he looked incredible.

"You're so pretty," she said to him, quietly.

He glanced down at her and his face broke into a wide smile. There were no guards or walls or masks between them now. He pressed a firm kiss against her temple and squeezed her hand.

"I'm glad Christine finally saw sense and made you maid of honor," he said.

"Joke's on me," Jasper replied. "I've had to hold her dress up twice while she's been peeing."

Arthur barked out a laugh and Jasper loved the sight and sound of it. She leaned against him as they watched people on the dance floor.

"It's a beautiful wedding," Arthur eventually said. "You did amazingly."

"Well, thanks," she said wryly. "Almost caused a family rift and a few mental breakdowns, but the swans look lovely."

"I'm so proud of you."

The words were spoken softly and seriously, making Jasper glance up at him once more. She leaned in and pressed a kiss to the corner of his mouth. The full meaning of his words was unspoken. He saw, when no one else really did, that she had found herself again since coming home. Her authentic self had become the trinket hidden inside of the music box, while everyone else had stared at the spinning ballerina. She had told herself lies about what the world needed to see.

When the polite, meek and mild Jasper Montgomery had come into the spotlight, she had been encouraged and saddened by how happy that made so many people.

Not Arthur Lancaster.

He had always wanted her as she was. The backstage parts of her soul, not the onstage performance.

She had realized, as the first cut of the film had played before her, that heartbreak was a hidden thing. It stayed buried inside of you. Whether it was heartbreak from grief, loss or losing love. It could not stand to be seen by anyone.

Since that day, Arthur had decided to reshoot everything. Not for the contest, but for the town. He wanted to capture every love story from Lake Pristine. From elders who had lived there for sixty years, to newly-weds and young families. Marcus had been banned from the redo, which was a relief to everyone. Arthur was in his element around town, asking people to share their beginnings. Jasper could not wait to see the final result. She knew it would be beautiful.

Falling in love was transparent. Jasper had thought of herself as such an unreadable slate, but love is never that easy to hide. Everything Jasper and Arthur had felt had been obvious.

"Want to know something terrible?" she said to him.

"Always."

"I'm really glad Marcus made that horrible edit of your film."

Arthur's eyes widened at her words and he released a gruff laugh. "Oh, yeah?"

"Yeah."

"Can I ask why?"

Jasper kicked up her legs so that they were stretched across his knees. She leaned her head against his shoulder and he ran his hand up and down her thigh.

"I was watching it, horrified. For sure. It was a complete train wreck. But then suddenly Henry was onscreen saying you were in love with me."

"Yeah," Arthur said, flushing red. "He was."

"And then it cut to the two of us. And . . . I could see it. Somehow, the camera made me see things clearly. You know how you see a photograph of yourself or hear yourself on tape, and you don't recognize it? I suppose I was misreading you from the start. Deliberately misreading you, perhaps. But the camera laid everything bare."

Arthur's hand stilled and he squeezed her leg, silently encouraging her to go on.

"It was like when I'm watching a movie. I could see how it was supposed to end."

"And how is it supposed to end?"

As an answer to his question, she kissed him.

The storytellers of the past had made Jasper feel that girls like her were not made to be loved. That they were there to serve some other purpose, one less poetic, less universal. Or sometimes, that they did not even exist at all.

Arthur loved her. She felt it in him. When he accepted her private moments of overstimulation, her shortness of breath after an unexpected social interaction or her stimming, dancing hands after a wonderful adventure, when he loved and appreciated them, she felt defiant: as if she had won. To be loved so well for exactly who you are, after being told you are unlovable: it was a beautiful, golden act of revolution.

"You know what's funny," Arthur said, his voice gravelly. "I think you might be the love of my life."

He said it so matter-of-factly, it made Jasper's eyes water and her hands tremble.

"Love you, too, Grumble."

The wedding photographer caught a shot of the two of them, but neither Arthur nor Jasper noticed. The picture would come out at a later date, slightly blurry but completely full of adoration, obvious for anyone looking at the snapshot to see.

It was not pristine.

But it was love.

Acknowledgments

Fiction has always been the lens I've used to understand the world. I consumed stories to map my way through life. As a neurodivergent teen, everyone had an opinion on what I was and what I was going to be. Reality, I'm not so adept at. But the people who helped make this book a fact, rather than a dream, are all too real to me.

Thank you to my agent, Lauren Gardner. We sat in a Brixton cafe when I had four pounds in my bank account and I told you, "One day, I'll need to write love stories," and you were in support, and have been ever since.

To Annabelle, even though you abandoned me.

Thank you to Eishar and everyone at Knights Of. Having wings doesn't mean much at all if they're never used. You helped a flightless bird to soar.

Thank you to everyone at First Ink Books at Macmillan and Eileen and her US team.

To every editor who put their money where their mouth was for an autistic romance. Your faith meant so much.

To Emma Jones, most of all. I said I would know by instinct when the perfect editor would pitch for the book. When you spoke about Arthur and Jasper, I thought, *Oh, there you are.*

To Charlie, Beth, Rory, and everyone at Macmillan who has championed the book in its infancy. I'm writing this not knowing its future. Thank you, regardless.

To my parents.

To Tom Waits.

To Nora Ephron. Thank you for showing the world that love should be taken seriously.

To all of my peers in the book world, amazing booksellers like Molly, Joanna, Rhiannon, Tess, Matthew, Fiona, Amoy, Natasha. Incredible authors like Jennifer Bell, Alwyn Hamilton, Hux, Richard Pickard, and every sensational person who offered to blurb this book.

To every single individual involved in *A Kind of Spark: The Adaptation*. Lola, Caitlin, Georgia, Ella, Eve, Zach, Anna, Kim, Graine, Ally, Wendy, Luke, Amy, and every other person who has touched the project. We showed the world new ways to dream, we really did. I love you all and I'm so proud of you.

To my cinema manager and our bratty dog.

To the readers. Especially neurodivergent readers. We deserve more than just an invite to the party. We should get to throw the party. Thanks for coming to mine.

About the Author

Elle McNicoll is a bestselling and award-winning children's novelist. Her debut, *A Kind of Spark,* won the Blue Peter Book Award and the Overall Waterstones Children's Book Prize, as well as Blackwell's Book of 2020. She is four-time Carnegie nominated, and was shortlisted for the Books Are My Bag Awards 2020, the Branford Boase Award, and The Little Rebels Award. Her novels have been published in the U.S. and translated into multiple languages. The TV adaptation of *A Kind of Spark* was created in partnership with 9 Story Media Group and BBC Children's and is now Emmy-nominated. Elle is an advocate for better representation of neurodiversity in publishing, and currently lives in North London.